TH
MADNESS
LOCKER

THE MADNESS LOCKER

E. J. RUSSELL

Copyright © 2019 E.J. Russell
Original cover design by Murilo Manzini

The moral right of the author has been asserted.

Apart from any fair dealing for the purposes of research or private study, or criticism or review, as permitted under the Copyright, Designs and Patents Act 1988, this publication may only be reproduced, stored or transmitted, in any form or by any means, with the prior permission in writing of the publishers, or in the case of reprographic reproduction in accordance with the terms of licences issued by the Copyright Licensing Agency. Enquiries concerning reproduction outside those terms should be sent to the publishers.

This is a work of fiction. Names, characters, businesses, places, events and incidents are either the products of the author's imagination or used in a fictitious manner. Any resemblance to actual persons, living or dead, or actual events is purely coincidental.

Matador
9 Priory Business Park,
Wistow Road, Kibworth Beauchamp,
Leicestershire. LE8 0RX
Tel: 0116 279 2299
Email: books@troubador.co.uk
Web: www.troubador.co.uk/matador
Twitter: @matadorbooks

ISBN 978 1789018 509

British Library Cataloguing in Publication Data.
A catalogue record for this book is available from the British Library.

Printed and bound in Great Britain by 4edge Limited
Typeset in 11pt Adobe Garamond Pro by Troubador Publishing Ltd, Leicester, UK

Matador is an imprint of Troubador Publishing Ltd

To Louise, my partner, guide, support and inspiration & Pema (our beloved cat) who has kept me company in the small hours of the morning as I toliled to get this novel to the finish line.

INSPIRED BY A TRUE CRIME...

On Christmas Day, 1986, a seventy-year-old widow's body was discovered inside a wheelie bin in the Eastern Suburbs of Sydney, Australia. Despite a long and intensive investigation, the police fail to unearth a motive or identify a suspect. Lacking any clues, the police file it as a cold case. This fictional story, inspired by the true event of her murder, proposes a plausible motive.

BERLIN

Winter 1941

I would have died when I was ten. But I didn't, and you would think that that was my good fortune. Except other people that I hold dear died and another paid dearly in my stead for that stroke of luck. And, well, it is a strange and bewildering memory to behold, but back then, as I think of it, and I do think of it often, the shards of a shattered past that reflect on my life today are a constant reminder of how an orderly, ordinary life unravelled violently. It did so with such ferocity, and that may be the salve that quiets my troubled conscience; that no one, least of all me, had time to prepare or plan. The irony is that had my life not imploded I would not be here and the events that unfolded would have never happened.

It started well before I was even born. I was ten when I became keenly aware of the troubles. That's how I often heard my parents, Heinrich and Alana Lipschutz, refer to the upheavals in Germany. I would be in bed, listening intently, late at night, to their hushed conversation in the dining alcove that was adjacent to my room. I could tell that they were upset and worried. But most of what they said I didn't understand. They talked about evacuation, deportation, Palestine, *Nationalsozialisten*, Hitler.

On one particular occasion other couples came by, without their children, which I thought odd, and they all huddled around the dining-room table, drinking tea or wine, and the same words came up. Except a word that I had not heard before had them all in a state of panic: Kristallnacht.

I am Ruth. And it took a little while longer for the troubles to trouble me. I had just turned ten when I was called into the school principal's office. Herr Baumgartner, a dour man with a permanent frown, asked me to sit down as soon as I came in. My parents were there too, seated with their backs to the door. As soon as I saw them I knew I was in trouble. My heart sank, and in a state of panic I thought back to every little misdeed that I had committed to prepare a defence for what might have come to light.

"Mr and Mrs Lipschutz," Herr Baumgartner began in a hoarse voice, "Ruth is a wonderful pupil: well behaved, excellent marks, impeccable attendance. And for our part this school has tried to keep our pupils protected from all the troubles that are going on out there. As such I have been avoiding this. But…" Here he faltered and placed a piece of paper on the desk, right side up, facing my parents.

My father reached across and took the piece of paper and held it between him and my mother. They both read silently.

I could see Father's face turn grave, like when he learned that Grandpapa had died, and Mother started sobbing.

"I am now forced to comply or I will be fired from this post and put in jail. Or even worse," Herr Baumgartner resumed, seeing my mother's distress.

My father was overcome with sadness and didn't say anything. He just nodded and reached for my mother's hand. Silently they stood up and both shook Herr Baumgartner's hand, taking the paper with them. For the only time I can remember, Herr Baumgartner displayed a smattering of emotion. His hand quivered and, in a voice edged with pain, he said, "I am very sorry. I will go and collect Ruth's things from the classroom. If you can just wait in the outer office."

My parents did not speak until we got home. We each carried some of my school belongings: books, notebooks, drawings, old assignments, stationery and even a commendation that I had received from one of the teachers. A sad parade of departure from what had hitherto been my daily life.

At home, Father didn't say anything other than that he had to go back to the shop. Mother made me a lunch of a marmalade sandwich, milk and chocolate biscuits: my favourite. But I couldn't eat. I didn't understand what had happened other than that I had been expelled from school for no reason, which had caused my parents to become very sad rather than angry with me. Finally, my mother sat down with a cup of tea and explained.

"Liebchen, you cannot go back to school for now. It is not your fault. It is all the troubles that we are having. It is for your own safety. Until then your father and I will arrange for you to be tutored at home."

Up until this moment I had not realised my fate. In a matter of a few hours I had lost my friends, my daily activities and classes. I was no longer wanted. The suddenness of it filled me with a loneliness that I had never experienced before, and I burst out crying. I felt my mother's arms embrace me and she started rocking back and forth, all the while making soothing sounds.

"Can I still go over to Anna's?"

I would dearly miss my school friends, the classes, the activities, but most important was my dear friend Anna Jodl. We walked to school together, sat next to each other in class and walked back to Nürnberger Straße where we lived. We even stopped by my father's shop on the way where we always got candy, a piece of chocolate or even a pastry.

My mother hesitated for a moment and then nodded with a tight smile.

I didn't want to ask about the troubles. I had been hearing about them for a while now, and whatever they were, I couldn't understand anyway.

A week later a large woman with tight black curls, a wide, pasty face and a loud voice arrived early in the morning after Father had gone to work. She introduced herself as Frau Sundmacher, my tutor. She told us that the school had given her the curriculum and that she could teach me as if I were in class.

Winter had come early and it was already freezing outside. I missed not walking in the snow with Anna; however, being tutored at home, even though I didn't like Frau Sundmacher, made me feel like I still belonged. The weeks passed without the troubles getting any more troublesome.

In the afternoon, after I finished my homework, I would visit Anna or she would come over and we would play together. Other times, my other friends from school would come over. Curiously, when they did, we would have to play at Anna's. The troubles prevented them from playing in our home.

But then in February the worries grew; the troubles became incidents, and Helga arrived.

During one of those late nights of hushed conversations my mother started to sob. The radio was on, but it was turned down low. Despite that, I could hear a man speaking angrily, threateningly. Every so often he would stop and the crowd would roar, "*Seig Heil*" or "*Heil Hitler*". I had heard Hitler before. *Is this the troubles? Why is Heil Hitler preventing me from going to school or having friends over other than Anna?* That night after the radio broadcast my parents added new words to the string that I had heard before: *Juden*, Gestapo, SS, vandals.

In the morning Father left for the shop, and when I was seated with Mother I asked her if she was feeling well.

She nodded and, with heaviness in her voice, added, "There was an incident at the shop."

I wasn't aware of anything different because I had not been by my father's shop: I had not walked by since I was expelled from school. I waited for her to say more but she proceeded to quietly put the dishes away and clear the table so that Frau Sundmacher could have her cup of tea and start my lessons.

I couldn't wait for the afternoon so that I could ask Anna what the incident was; I knew that she would tell me. After all, she still walked past the shop every day from school.

In the afternoon, as Frau Sundmacher's considerable backside waddled down the stoop, I listened intently for Anna's voice. She soon rounded the corner and bounded up the steps. This time she had another girl in tow, short and plump with dark wavy hair and brown eyes. Her face was freckled and her eyes had a malicious glint to them. Unlike Anna's cheery smile, her friend's mouth was turned down in a snarl, like a stray dog's. Anna and I looked very similar, like sisters: me with blonde hair and green eyes, Anna with blue eyes.

"Ruth, Helga is staying with us. She is from Munich. Helga, say hello to Ruth. She is my dearest friend."

The girl hesitated for a second, then reached out her hand to shake mine. Her hand had a cold, clammy feel, like a dead fish.

"Is she sitting next to you at school?" I asked.

"No. She is just visiting for a few weeks."

I was relieved and my heart swelled with love for Anna.

"Why aren't you in school? Are you sick?" Helga stood resolutely on the landing and stared at me reproachfully.

I shrugged. "It is all these troubles we are having."

Helga pointed at my chest. "In that case, why aren't you wearing a yellow star?"

My mother appeared at the doorway to our building, greeted Anna and Helga warmly and invited us in. As soon as we were seated around the dining-room table Helga started looking suspiciously around the room.

"Why don't you have a picture of Adolf Hitler on the wall?"

"We don't have a picture of Hitler on the wall either. Papa says he is a mad fool who should go back to selling postcards," Anna answered for me gleefully.

As soon as my mother placed biscuits and drinks on the table, Helga scowled in disgust.

"We shouldn't eat Jewish food; it is poison to German children."

"Well, in that case my whole family should be dead. We have been buying food from Herr Lipschutz for as long as I can remember." Anna dove eagerly for the biscuits and drank to the bottom of her glass, smacking her lips in satisfaction. "See?" She looked triumphantly at Helga.

In the end they left. I sorely missed not having Anna to myself for the whole afternoon, but I was glad to be rid of the horrible Helga.

Notwithstanding Anna's friendship, I was left with a feeling of disquietude. I was being shielded from troubles that now affected girls my own age. Not just the expulsion from school: I was no longer separated, but segregated – I wasn't allowed to stray too far from our house; I couldn't have any friends over other than Anna; I was asked why I didn't wear a yellow star, why we didn't have a picture of Hitler on our wall; and Helga would not eat our food because we poisoned German children.

I am *a German child.*

This growing sense of isolation and silence that engulfed my life became claustrophobic. I wanted to lash out and protest at my unjust fate, but did not want to upset my parents any more than they were already.

But silence had its own deadly clamour that shattered our world soon after Helga's visit.

BELLEVUE HILL, EASTERN SUBURBS, SYDNEY

Autumn 1986

Ernie Weissman died this year. He didn't die well, as they say, somewhat paradoxically, as death is never good; suffering through a long and protracted illness which led him in stages from a graceful retirement in reasonable health at home to confinement in an old-age home battling a blood disorder, and then to a private hospital where he deteriorated into dementia and finally death.

When he finally succumbed, his wife of fifty years, Ruth, was relieved. Despite her unwavering love and devotion to Ernie through all the years, and bearing him one son, it had become impossible for her to see any pleasure in his life in the latter years; it had turned into one prolonged routine of ministering to an ever-increasing state of disorientation and debilitating illness, such that, by the end, it was impossible to identify the Ernie she loved in the hollow and frightened mask that stared at her, unrecognising, from the pillow in his hospital bed. It was more of a wraith that clung to the last pulse in an emaciated body refusing to give up the ghost.

In the first few months following his death Ruth found her widowed state impossible to fathom. For as long as she could remember her life had been occupied together with Ernie; whether it was the weekly trip to the Northern Beaches to spend the Sunday with their son's family, the daily domestics, movies, theatre, concerts, overseas and local holidays, or attending *Schule* during the high holidays. Ernie was not just her partner of half a century but also her closest confidant and friend.

Even as his life deteriorated, withdrawing from those activities that described their lives, her routines nonetheless focused on maintaining a semblance of a life with Ernie by developing new routines that encompassed his existence: cooking meals that she knew he loved and taking them up every morning to the old-age home, and then to the hospital. Sitting silently by his bedside, as he lay there, unconscious to the world, holding his withering hand firmly, believing that he knew it was she, even though his eyes betrayed no recognition. Reading him the Saturday paper that they used to enjoy together; shaving him and changing his pyjamas when she thought he appeared bedraggled. In the last days, when death was all but inevitable, she never left his side, except to use the bathroom or grab a quick meal in one of the nearby cafés.

On the 14th April, an overcast Tuesday, she returned from the hospital café to find the nurse pulling up the sheet over what remained of the person who had been Ruth's inseparable companion. At first she was disbelieving, even though at a deeper level she knew this to be inevitable, her knees wobbling as she grasped for the nearest chair and fell into it, unable to look up at the bed that now contained no more than a sheathed corpse.

With a slight shudder she started to weep silently, more out of a sense of relief that Ernie no longer had to endure the illness that had robbed him of his dignity and rendered him helpless. He could rest and be no more the curse of all those humiliating whispers of well-meaning acquaintances and friends.

After a while, left alone in the grey, grim room, she rose up, lifted the sheet off his head, kissed warmly his shuttered face, replaced the sheet and left.

Back at home, her life was suddenly empty. It had been a life with Ernie. It had been a life lived in the care of Ernie. And now it was just her.

After the service, the funeral and kind words dissipated she was left alone, as she had been the last few years. Except her life now had no purpose. She continually turned down invitations to go out, to play bridge, to go to the movies, to the theatre, to stay with friends. She even refused to travel with her son to his home and spend time with his family.

She felt totally empty. Staring blankly at the TV at night. Eating tastelessly through her meals. Changing into her going-out clothes, even though she could have remained in her housedress; she never left the front door. The groceries were delivered courtesy of her daughter-in-law; the bills attended to by her son.

Somehow life sailed along with her presence in it: the days changing, the nights coming even though she did not participate in them. Strange, she thought. In the past she always believed that you created motion by being in motion. She would get up, get dressed, go to the market, cook meals, take them up to Ernie, look after his well-being as best she could, come home, sleep, and another day came. Now, nothing happened, and the days came and went. Motion exempt her involvement.

It was in this state of emotional coma, when one evening she turned on the TV and, while watching an old movie, a phrase jumped out at her: 'dead man walking'. She was a dead person walking. She was breathing, eating, moving, but not actually living. She was essentially a dead person. And with that realisation came a deeper one: that had she been the one to die first, the last thing she would want was for Ernie to remain on earth and be a dead man walking.

She stared at the TV some more. Then slowly the realisation deepened that life had not ended for her; a state that hitherto she had not contemplated. There were things to live for yet, albeit without Ernie. And with that realisation she began trying to imagine a life without her lifelong companion. What would she do? What would her life be like? She had her son, Jacob, and her daughter-in-law and the two grandchildren that brought so much joy to her and Ernie. She had her friends and their mutual friends. And there were the things that, even when Ernie was alive and present, she had done by herself: charities, community work, bridge nights.

Despite this realisation she still felt paralysed by her loneliness; it was as though, by getting off the couch and actively resuming her life, she would be severing her life from his. Somehow by being a dead person walking she remained linked to his passing: he was dead and she was dead. And with that bond their life together remained intact, even though he was no longer here.

She let her eyes wander around the room with its many mementos scattered throughout. A lifetime of accumulated memories. There was not a single thing that belonged solely to her: everything they had bought and owned together. Even those few times when they disagreed about the acquisition, in the end either she or Ernie compromised and the item became their shared possession.

How could she bring herself to collect all his clothes and belongings and donate them to charity as Jacob had suggested? How could she celebrate her life with Ernie and continue to live? She couldn't see past that point, even though the realisation had come to her that she was alive, but dead to the world around her.

She was alive. But if she started to live, the bond with Ernie, ethereal though it may be, would cease to be. If she remained in this comatose state she might as well be dead. It was a question of preference; what did she want more: to live with the memory of Ernie forever, or to resume her life without him?

The predicament took her back to another time in her life, before such impossible choices had to be made. When she realised that her parents had been taken from her forever. Her last remaining memory after they both put her to bed and kissed her warmly to sleep. In the early hours of the morning her world was upended and within hours she needed to make a choice between following her parents to a terrifying future or setting out on a path that would take her from the madness that engulfed her homeland.

The friends who rescued her from the tentacles of the Gestapo made the choice for her. Many times throughout her journey that eventually brought her to Australia and her new life with Ernie, she had contemplated that choice. Whether, left alone, she would have followed her parents, or fled.

The will to live is certainly more prevalent than the desire to die, except when the choice to die is made easier by realisation that living is more painful. She hadn't realised until this moment that it wasn't so much her loneliness that was paralysing her but the pain of her loss, exacerbated by the loneliness. As long as Ernie had been alive, even in a vegetative state, she had not been alone, except at night. But in the morning, she would return to his little room, clean and feed him, talk to him, read to him. He was there, even if he didn't respond. Somewhat akin to her life now: she was here, even if she didn't participate.

But his death had left a gaping hole that she could not fill. A painful daily reminder that she could only assuage either by following Ernie to his grave, or by starting a new life and letting Ernie drift into the ventricles of memory.

The 'dead man walking' realisation wasn't so much about her being alive but emotionally dead to the world, but more that she was as dead as the actor in the movie, with only the final deed separating her from the fact. Unless she chose a new life for herself. Long ago, in another time, she had been rescued. Now there was no such hand to lift her from her dilemma. She was alone. She was an adult. And she had shut the door to her world as it was before Ernie died. No one was going to walk in through that door at the last moment and rescue her. No one thought that she needed rescuing, just time to be left alone to heal.

She stared blankly at the TV, the pictures swirling past as if in a haze, the early-morning light streaming through the open blinds. It would be easy, very, very easy to exit the pain, quickly and painlessly. Yet, like a runner in a relay race, she would be leaving another kind of pain behind, with her son and grandchildren and close friends of many years. They would be left to wonder at their complacence in not doing enough, not seeing the signs.

Yet one can never measure the pain in another person's body. But how was she going to leave that message behind so that her pain would end here and now and not infect others?

A soft knocking on the door stirred her from her reverie. She became frightened. Who would be knocking this early in the morning? It wasn't even five. She almost laughed at herself. Here she was contemplating taking her life but worrying about it being taken by a stranger. Wasn't the latter the better way? At least no one would feel guilty about her death.

The knocking resumed. She moved her aching feet from under her onto the floor and padded to the door, listening intently, frightened to make a sound. Maybe the intruder would walk away. Then she realised that the TV was on and that whoever was outside the door could probably hear the muffled sound.

Her voice, rather cracked and dry from lack of use, reverberated in the small vestibule. "Who is it?"

"It's Sammy. Sam Steimatzky from next door."

She relaxed. Relief washed over her that danger was not lurking behind the door. "Is there a problem?" Her voice was gaining in confidence now.

"No. No problem. I just heard the TV and thought you were awake; maybe you wanted some company?"

Ruth hesitated a moment, thinking on whether she was keeping him awake, or whether the sound of the TV had betrayed her wakefulness. She finally decided on the former.

"I am very sorry. I will turn it off." She turned to go back into the living room.

"No need. I just thought that maybe you were not able to sleep. That's why I was asking."

Now what? Was this the same hand that had reached out all those years ago; rescued her from death? Then it was a dear neighbour; now, a friend – more Ernie's friend than hers, but a friend nonetheless – appearing at her time of loneliness and loss. If she turned him away, she could continue with her decision or deliberation. If she let him in then she would be turning away from solitude and letting someone into her moment of indecision.

He was Ernie's friend. Ernie had sent him, sensing her pain and fearing her decision. She reached for the latch and drew the chain back. She unlocked the door and looked out into the hallway. Sam stood there, erect as ever; his face handsome even in old age, his light blue eyes glimmering behind sandy lashes. His fine blond hair, streaked with grey, was carefully combed back over his full head.

Certainly he appeared more Aryan than Jewish, as she had repeatedly told Ernie, who'd just as frequently dismissed her suspicions. She'd even pointed out that his initials were SS, which Ernie pooh-poohed by reminding her that the husband of one of her best friends was called Adolf and another friend's last name was Reich. Clearly the separation of German Jew and Gentile went beyond the notion that because

Sam Steimatzky appeared more German than Jewish and his initials were SS, that automatically made him an impostor.

But now he was standing here, a warm smile on his face, ready to march in if she stepped back. Well, if she was right, he might proceed to harm her, which was fine and according to plan, and if she was wrong, then history was repeating itself. Either way, she stepped back and let him walk in.

UNIVERSITÄT LEIPZIG

Autumn 1934

Times are different now. Germany is on a rebound. Four years ago, just as I started pre-med at Universität Leipzig, the country was slipping into anarchy for the second time in fifteen years. I was one of the fortunate ones. My father still had a job at the Benz factory in Bremen. Millions of others did not; six million to be exact. His pay was halved but we had an asset that couldn't be rendered worthless by inflation: my grandmother's house, which she willed to my father. It was rented out and made up a little of the pay he had lost. It is ironic that one of the songs that typified the era was *We're Drinking Away Grandma's House*.

Back then in 1930 as I arrived as a first-year student, the situation was precarious and remained that way all throughout my pre-med. At any moment my father could have lost his job and I would have had to drop out and come back home to Bremen. I don't know what I would have done if that had happened, other than loiter around the welfare office collecting my forty marks per month, then like a discarded newspaper drift from the pavement to the gutter. Looking for work would have been an idle pursuit: emotionally grinding without any prospect.

But like I said, I was one of the lucky ones. My father kept his job, and I continued to study. There were others like me, and four of us shared a house within walking distance of the university: Franz Heidegger from Dortmund; Martin Keller from Hanover; myself, Friedrich Becker, from Bremen; and Johann Ziegler, a local from Leipzig.

Today we are graduating. There is a sense of relief, both for having survived the four years and for passing our exams. We are seated at Café Krüger, our favourite daytime hangout, halfway between the university and our house, enjoying coffee and pastries before we pick up our bags and part ways.

"So, Becker, where to next year? Back here?" Martin Keller, the son of a grain merchant, is resplendent in a starched white shirt, bow tie, light blue blazer and dark trousers. His face is oval and jovial, his blond hair cut short and parted on the right. His eyes are brimming with confidence.

"I am not sure. Certainly back to Bremen to see my parents, then maybe a trip to Holland to look at this teaching hospital in Utrecht."

"Utrecht? What's wrong with here, or even WWU at Münster?" Johann is leaning towards the table to pick up his cup, looking at me with stark bewilderment.

"Yeah, Becker, what's wrong with here? Johann's father teaches here. Isn't that right, Zeigler?" Franz, whose father is a senior banker, jabs me playfully in the side. "Maybe it's not just the university. Maybe there's more, huh, Becker?" He continues his ribbing, not getting an answer from me. His unfashionably long hair falls over his brow, and he absently flicks it back. He is dressed similarly to Martin, except not as dapper: his shirt is creased, his tie exhibiting memories of past meals, his trousers slightly rumpled, his shoes scuffed, hungry for polish. Ironically he is expected to be fastidious in his attire, yet he looks more like a grain merchant scion, whereas Martin looks more like the banker.

"Yeah, he's always the secretive one. A Dutch maiden in clogs, is that it, Becker?" Martin joshes me from the other side.

"I have never even been to Holland. But it would make a good change from Germany." I look around the table. "Don't you guys agree?"

"I don't know. Things are starting to look better. Weimar is gone, thank God. I don't think Germany could have withstood another election." Martin, mulling the prospects, munches on his muffin.

"Are they?" I look around the table again.

"Well, like Martin is saying, Weimar is gone. That is already a step forward. The Nazis appear to have the Reichstag reined in, better than Von Papen and that other idiot that was booted out – what was his name?"

"Brüning. Germany was doing very well until the stock market crash in the US." Johann answers Franz's question.

"Well, that tells me that our Weimar prosperity was propped up by American dollars. For how long? Sooner or later the gravy train would have ended. Germany needs to stand on its own, not with the help of outsiders, Americans or anyone else." Martin rattles the coffee cups and plates by jabbing his point on the table.

"I agree. But is Hitler the answer? He has, after all, some rather bizarre ideas, not to mention that the National Socialist Party is a workers' party."

"Come, Becker, what is wrong with that? Workers are the backbone of the economy. We manufacture things and then export them; that's how the country makes money. Your father works at Benz?" Martin dusts the last of his muffin from his fingers.

"Yes, my father works at Benz. And it is doing reasonably well. But I don't know: the burning of the Reichstag and blaming it on the communists; the Enabling Act; blaming all of Germany's problems on the Bolsheviks, the stab-in-the-back thing, the treaty, then the French annexing the Ruhr in reprisal for non-payment, and then suggesting that the whole mess is orchestrated by an international Jewish conspiracy. Does that sound to anyone like Hitler has a rational policy?"

"It's good policy if it gets the German economy going. Besides, since when does political policy make sense?" Franz breaks out in guffaws, and we all join in.

"It may get the economy going, but giving anyone, never mind Hitler, total control, like Hindenburg has, with his peculiar ideas, is not a good start. Weimar before the crash was great. That tells me that if we can get the economy going without the Americans and keep our democracy, it is better for Germany long term."

"That's a big if, Becker." Franz looks dubiously at me.

"Maybe Herr Hitler is right; maybe it is a Jewish conspiracy," Martin pipes up, only half joking.

"I doubt it," Johann answers quietly.

"Why, Ziegler?"

"I am Jewish. My father is a professor here. He fought in World War I. Matter of fact, Hitler just awarded him a medal, as he did all of the front-line soldiers who fought in World War I. Where is the conspiracy in that?" Johann replies guardedly.

"Ouch. I didn't know you were Jewish, Ziegler." Franz looks across mockingly at him.

"That's the point, isn't it? It shouldn't make a difference."

"Anyway, to return to the main point of this discussion, why is Becker off to Holland? This is more interesting gossip than cuckoo Hitler." Franz is prodding me again.

"Yes. Becker. You cunningly evaded the question by stirring up a political debate. That is the conspiracy." Johann perks up.

"Why don't you come to Bologna with me? Italian women are much prettier than the chunky Dutch, very voluptuous. The food is great. No more bratwurst." Martin is looking eagerly at me.

"I didn't know you were off to Bologna."

"I just found out yesterday that I have been accepted to Collegio Superiore." Martin doffs an imaginary hat in the air.

"OK, Keller, my turn to ask you: why Bologna? What is wrong with here or WWU?"

"It is a chance to travel and study at a great school."

"Good enough; same answer to all of you. It is a chance to travel and study."

They all chuckle at my deft rejoinder, and with that we rise up from the table, taking our individual rucksacks, and head out of the café.

On the pavement, despite our exultation at coming to a successful end of our studies at Leipzig, we are sad to depart. We have formed strong friendships, and take away happy memories despite the grim four years overshadowed by the bleak events in Germany.

We exchange our addresses and promise to stay in touch. I can't help but notice that to a man we all shake Johann's hand more firmly, with generous wishes of good luck. If Hitler sticks to his fanatical belief that the Jews are the root of Germany's woes then the Zieglers could be in for a rough ride.

I catch a taxi to Leipzig Hauptbahnhof to take the train to Bremen. Johann is heading back to his family home in Leipzig, which he shared with his parents and two sisters before we lived together. Martin Keller catches a separate cab to the regional airport to fly to Milan and from there go by train to Bologna. Franz Heidegger is staying on at Leipzig to do his medical degree and move into the dormitory on campus by himself. He promises to stay in close touch with Johann; however, now that Jews are accused of being the grand conspirators behind Germany's downfall, I doubt that Franz will be knocking on Johann's front door any time soon.

It's a good thing that I have traversed Leipzig Hauptbahnhof previously, otherwise it would be very easy to get lost and miss my train in this colossal, cavernous hall. It makes Bremen's train station look like a country stop. I board the 10.15am.

As I recline into the cracked leather seat, or what passes for leather, I glance around me at the other passengers. Many are students like me, going back home. Others painfully remind me of how far we have fallen since 1929: families huddled together, clutching their meagre belongings, shuttling from town to town in the desperate hope of finding work, food, lodging. They all look the same: numb with hunger and fatigue.

A short four years ago this was not Germany. We were living the high life: jobs were aplenty; the money was good; people were well fed; the arts, music and theatre were flourishing; and it looked like we had finally walked back from the abyss of 1923.

Yet here we are again. But this time the drop has been far more precipitous. We started at a higher point than post World War I. Nevertheless, it never ceases to amaze me how fast and far a family can fall.

It pains me because it could have been us. The Beckers. We are a middle-class family living securely in a respectable neighbourhood. Regardless, we could have just as easily tumbled to the gutter. The post-war years wiped out our savings. My parents had scrimped and saved a small nest egg for my sister and me, and their golden years. But the value of the currency got swept away under the deluge of inflation.

I remember as a youngster running with my mother to the Benz factory gates to await my father's pay packet and then hurrying to the shops before the money diminished to half its value. It was like carrying water in a leaking pail. What kept our heads above water was my father not losing his job and Grandma's house. Take away either or both and it could be us on the street.

The carriage is swaying gently from side to side as we pull out from Leipzig on the way to Bremen. The thoughts swirl in my head as I stare out the window. I wonder at my decision to leave Germany. Am I abandoning my country because it is failing? Have I lost hope of a resurrection? Or is it my sense of unease about Hitler and the Nazis? I know I want to go somewhere where my remaining years of study will not be racked by worry as my last four years at Leipzig have been.

BELLEVUE HILL, EASTERN SUBURBS, SYDNEY

Autumn 1986

"So you can't sleep?" Sam watched as Ruth went about setting out cups and saucers in the kitchen and turning the kettle on. When Ernie was alive he would unhesitatingly walk into the kitchen and stand close by Ruth, chatting. But now he knew that the proximity would make her feel uncomfortable and him awkward.

With the clatter and the noise from the electric kettle she couldn't hear him. He didn't mind. He rose from the couch and started wandering around the comfortable living room. Except that now, with Ernie's death, it seemed different: suggestive of possibilities. He could easily see himself in these familiar surroundings. And why not? he thought to himself. After all, he still felt virile. And Ruth, well, Ruth was what Ruth had always been: very attractive. In fact, he would go so far as to say sexy. It didn't matter that she was just shy of sixty. It was all relative.

When he was in his thirties, a woman of early to mid twenties was attractive and desirable. Now he was in his mid seventies, so a very trim, healthy woman with pearl-white skin, green eyes and a head of full, flowing hair was very desirable. Naturally he wondered about the even colour of her hair. But then what did it matter – women needed more cosmetics to safeguard their vanity than men. And besides which, he wouldn't be lusting after a woman who appeared frumpy in a housecoat with straggly grey hair. At any age, one needed to look after oneself.

Appearance. Yes, that. Appearance and intimacy. Such odd bedfellows. And here, well, if there were possibilities, the two would remain irreconcilable. Nevertheless, there was always the foolishness of the phrase 'Love conquers all', but Sam was too level-headed to fall for such prattle.

"Sam!" Ruth was standing by the coffee table with the cups laid out, and about to pour the coffee. He didn't hear her come back into the living room.

"I am sorry, I was looking at the photos and remembering what a wonderful friendship I had with Ernie." Sam moved away from the mantelpiece and sat down opposite where Ruth was standing.

She knew he meant that kindly, but somehow, like everything else about Sam Steimatzky, it sounded false. Like he was expressing a sentiment that was rehearsed or scripted and expected of him. Always correct, always infinitely polite. German. Very German.

She ignored his remark and proceeded to pour steaming coffee into the two cups. Without asking, she placed two sugar cubes in his and added a dash of milk. She had prepared his coffee enough times.

Reaching for the edge of the saucer, he placed it next to him on the side table and settled back into the settee. He waited for Ruth to get comfortable before he resumed the conversation.

"I was saying before when you were in the kitchen – you have trouble sleeping?" he enquired diligently.

"Sam, I know that you told us before," she said, as though Ernie was in the room, "but where were you during the war?" If she was going to befriend this man that Ernie had sent along, then she needed to stop feeling awkward and suspicious around him. Either that, or Ernie would need to send another emissary to keep her company and stay her hand from death.

If Sam was rattled by the question and the obvious change in the conversation, he didn't appear so. Pausing as if to collect his thoughts, he sipped at the warm coffee, set it down, and looked up directly at Ruth. "Well, that would depend what part of the war."

"Well, let's say 1943 to 1945, the final years. When it became obvious that Germany was starting to lose. Where were you during that time?" Her face remained intent and resolute, as though whatever answer he gave would require further scrutiny.

"Well, I have to say that I am rather ashamed to admit I was not doing anything heroic. I had managed to escape to Switzerland. I arrived in Zurich in the middle of 1943 and looked up an aunt on my mother's side. She was extremely pleased to see me, so I stayed with her." A cleanly bandaged answer. Nothing messy and disorderly, like an archetypal

Jewish refugee story. Mayhem; capture; escape; betrayal; another capture; another escape, this time from certain execution; nights sleeping in woods, subsisting on scraps; and then by some miracle crossing over to the Russian side. Parents? Dead. Relatives? Mostly dead, or scattered beyond reach. Siblings? Dead.

Ruth had to admit that Sam's sterile answer spoke of someone who was uncomfortable with the war, got into a Benz sports car, drove across to Zurich and whiled away the time between cafés and trips to the Alps. She certainly did not know anyone Jewish who had had such a comfortable and carefree exit from Germany across to Zurich and then waited out the war in a relative's apartment.

"How did you manage to get out of Germany?" Her eyes narrowed, watching for any discomfort on Sam's face. If Ernie were alive he would steer the conversation away from a topic that he knew Sam found awkward at best and difficult at worst.

"Ah, that would take a long time to tell, and involved quite a bit of subterfuge. Maybe we can defer that story to another time, when you are not feeling tired. And we are just having a pleasant cup of coffee." As always, the neat answer swaddled in comfortable and plausible excuses.

"Yes, I would be very curious to hear how you managed to get out." Ruth reached for the plate in the middle of the coffee table and slid it over to where Sam was sitting, offering him bagels with various toppings as if to suggest that time was not rushing and she was not tired.

"Ah, bagels. Emma used to get them with salmon and herring from Glickstein's. Do you shop there too?"

Ruth didn't doubt that Sam's deceased wife had in fact shopped there – but it was the emphasis he placed on the Jewish deli and slathering on the salmon and herring that felt like he was trying too hard. Then again, maybe seeing the bagels *had* reminded him of his wife. Either way it failed to narrow the gap between them, which in times past Ernie had bridged. Her doubts notwithstanding, it didn't necessarily make Sam a Nazi impostor, as she had always suggested to Ernie. There were many shades of grey in between.

The obvious question was why would he masquerade as a German Jewish refugee? She wouldn't care if he were a German Gentile, as long as he had no past links to the atrocities of World War II. After all, she knew better than anyone that not all Germans were Nazis; otherwise she would not be here.

Again Ruth chose to ignore his question and, without appearing to press him on his actual escape from Germany, decided to get at least a feeling of the truth from a different angle. "Did Ernie ever discuss with you how he escaped from Germany?"

Now Sam seemed to be willing to return and participate in the conversation. "No, actually he did not. Not in so many words. I wouldn't mind hearing that."

Anything to digress from your own history, Ruth thought cynically to herself.

"Well, you know that he was taken by a transport from Bremen to a camp?" She deliberately let her eyes narrow, laser like, to see if the mention of a camp would rattle him.

Sam, at least for a second, appeared to lose his composure. He narrowly avoided spilling coffee on himself as his hand jerked the cup back into the saucer. "Yes. Yes, he did mention that." All of a sudden his voice took on a raspy undertone, as if he were speaking out of fear or guilt.

"Well, he had trained as a doctor, so that was a very valuable skill both for the Germans and the Jewish and other prisoners in the camp. So his life was spared. He also had easier access to move around. Because he was German and a doctor, as the war got worse for the Nazis, he was relocated from the camp, I guess they figured that the prisoners could be spared medical treatment, and was moved to the Eastern Front. I believe he ended up close to St Petersburg. As luck would have it, the Russians captured him. He was at first treated as a prisoner of war, but when they realised he was a doctor and a Jew they released him and put him into service. With the fall of Germany he returned to Bremen. But there was nothing there to return to. The family home was rubble, bombed by the Allies. All his immediate family were either dead or lost, God only knows where. So he left."

"Did he come straight to Sydney?"

"Oh no. He took up the cause of medicine as a way to heal himself and went off to become a doctor in Africa. He ended up in Uganda, of all places."

"Yes, that part he mentioned. But I wasn't sure if he travelled there before or after he came to Australia."

They were digressing, as uplifting as it was to recollect Ernie's life. But Ernie was dead, and that line of conversation wasn't leading anywhere useful. The fact was that Sam was alive, but he was also cloaked in a potentially questionable past. At some visceral level Ruth wanted to let her emotions bypass that uncomfortable suspicion; to dive in and figure out how to navigate the currents later. But that was just it: that sort of strategy could either set you on an adventure or get you drowned. In another time, at the prime of life, she would have let herself go. But now, with life on the wane, risk was not the course to steer her through; caution was. But how much caution, and to what level? At some point you need to let yourself trust someone or not. She was never going to get all her questions answered to perfection. Some things remained murky, cloaked in the mishaps of youth. Forgive and forget, as it were. And perhaps that was it: she was prepared to reach that crossroads, to forgive and forget, except she did not want to do it blindly. In effect, forgive and forget, knowing what she was forgiving.

With a brazenness that she would later recall with some misgiving, she lunged forward. But she was tired from a harrowing night of dark thoughts and hopeless choices. And maybe just a little too old to be playing these games that were more the province of teenagers than people their age.

"Listen, Sam, I would like to be perfectly candid with you if I may? I am enjoying this conversation that we are having, and I am also grateful that you came to enquire as to my well-being. But you are not here just to check on my health. There is a more – how shall I put it? – a more personal motive. No, no, that's OK" – Sam edged forward in his seat, about to protest his innocence at this assault on his intentions – "you are a man, a very attractive man. You were a friend of my husband's. Ernie is dead, and you figure you can strike up a friendship with me. See where it leads. And that's fine. But men, they tend to be less suspicious, generally, than women. Ernie liked you and he chose to ignore a few inconsistencies, for want of a better word, in your life story. But if you want to come into my life and become my friend, then that is a risk I am willing to take –

to a point. Friendship is like that. But there are some things that I must know, and unless I get some comforting answers I will have to risk not having your friendship, if that makes sense."

For a stark moment her voice and the words that she had spoken reverberated in the room. And then the room fell into an awkward silence. She didn't know whether it was what she said that shocked him or her level of candour. Either way, he sat there, frozen in the chair, cup and saucer suspended in mid-air. Gradually, he thawed. His skin grew taut, either in anger or in offence at her suspicions. The few lines that marked his face grew deeper until they formed clear ridges on either side. Slowly, ever so cautiously, he edged the cup and saucer over to the table; patted both sides of his ash blond hair that seemed to glisten with perspiration.

His voice, when he spoke, was a mix of indignation and hurt. "Well. I came to see if you were – how shall I put it? – sleepless. For a number of nights – at least since Ernie's funeral – I have heard the TV or radio the whole night and into the early morning. I did not want to intrude. You and I have always been polite to each other. Never friends. Just polite. Hello. Goodbye. So I figure I won't intrude. Then I think, well, maybe I should have a look, because you are not leaving the house. It is time that, for my friend's sake, I check on your well-being, as you say. You have reason to be sleepless. Maybe you find yourself lost. I don't know. I came to see if I can help." Sam rose from the couch and stepped over to the window. Drawing the blind back, he looked out to the valley, which was now glistening with the early-dawn drizzle.

Speaking more pensively now than in indignation, he looked back at Ruth, who appeared to be rapt with attention, perhaps hoping to hear that what he was about to say would allay her suspicions.

"You think you are so clever. Trying to quiz me on what happened in the war. Where was I? How did I escape? Where did I serve? Maybe I'll make a mistake and slip up, as they say, reveal something incriminating. And then you can jump up and say, 'There – I knew it. You are a Nazi!' You think I don't know this? Ernie did not choose to ignore, he just chose to accept that maybe friendship is at times not knowing everything. Men are better at that. Less gossip. Huh? If you are so clever, why didn't you think to ask the obvious question?"

"What? What question did I not ask?"

"If you are not sleeping, how do I know that you are not sleeping?"

With that he walked over to the door, and at the last moment turned back. "Ruth, you should think to yourself that maybe you are not the only one that cannot sleep at night. I have not slept a full night since, well, for as long as I can remember. Even when Emma was alive."

With that he drew the door back, walked out into the grey morning light and slowly closed it behind him.

RACKELSWEG, BREMEN

Autumn 1934

The train pulled in at Bremen at just past noon. No one is waiting. I didn't tell anyone I was coming.

Our house is on Rackelsweg. A quaint little street surrounded by ordinary trees and shrubbery, a short distance from where I disembark. I decide to walk a little way now that the weather is not inclement. If there is abject poverty and irredeemable desperation I see it less than in the cities I passed on the way. Unemployment is regionally high and young people, particularly graduate students, represent most of the unemployed: sixty per cent of the total as opposed to thirty-four per cent for white and blue collars.

No one bothers me as I walk. If there is begging it is probably confined to the higher-density areas: more people to feed the multitude of hungry hands.

After nearly an hour of walking unhurriedly I finally turn into our street. It is quiet and empty, as I always remember it. The gardens appear well tended and the elm trees provide shelter for the homes lingering in the noonday sun. There is no sign of the misery that has been racking Germany for the last three years. If people are unemployed and on the verge of losing their homes, no one is saying, but there was a suicide a year ago: a sales manager who lost his job and could no longer support his family.

Standing on the corner, I can see our home. It stands as it always has, no different than when I left and the few times that I came back on holidays. It is my childhood home. I want to remember it always as a happy place, despite the desperation of 1923 and the turmoil of now. In Holland I will be shielded; I will be protected. At least that is what I believe. And maybe when I get there I will learn something new about my own psyche: that I cannot be a German in exile. It is like the maudlin maxim, 'Home is where the heart is.'

But that's just it – where is home, when you lose it?

Above the gardenias I see my mother's head bobbing as she clips a wayward branch here, a wilting flower there. She thinks she sees a figure in the distance, pauses for a minute, squints, doesn't recognise me, then continues pruning. The garden is her passion. The home is her love.

I take a few more tentative steps and walk along the hedge. My mother's head bobs up again.

"*Juhu*, Freddie!" she cries from behind the bushes. She drops the secateurs and rushes to the gate. It swings open and she is out on the pavement, embracing me. "Why didn't you tell us that you were coming back? Father would have borrowed a car and picked you up." She is already reaching for my rucksack.

"I wanted to surprise you."

"Well, you certainly have. Father and Brigitte will be delighted to see you."

We are walking along the flagstone path to the front door. I am following Mother, lugging my bag while she fumbles with my unwieldy rucksack. Soon we are indoors, the familiar smells and sights of home replenishing my soul beset by uncertainty. I feel a sense of hope again, but I know that it is transient. You can only be a child at home at one time in your life. You can always feel like a child at home, but at present I am an adult with my future swinging precariously between wanting to stay and needing to leave.

I know that once I tell my family about my plans to leave Germany they will be greatly saddened and dismayed. The long-term plan was for me to complete my medical studies and become a doctor in Bremen. They would probably even be willing to accept that I might practise in another town or city so long as it is in Germany. But to go abroad is not something that they have even contemplated. Neither did I until Hitler came to power.

To explain my disenchantment with Hitler would reveal nothing more than the general portent of fear and terror that is sweeping across Germany like a toxic cloud. We lived with the anxiety and fear of economic chaos and civil anarchy under the Weimar; now we are being ushered into an era of terror and brutality under Hitler. We have traded one horrible state of affairs for another.

But although my parents are well-educated, middle-class people they choose to remain politically blind, abiding by the law and order of the day regardless of its colour and creed. Somehow I need to reduce my misgivings and unease into a simple construct that they can assimilate and understand, not begrudging me my desire to leave. But how? This perplexes me, and I will cogitate on it until I find the compelling narrative and present my case. It is not that I have to persuade them of the justification of my aims, but that I need to silence my guilt over leaving them behind.

My mother is pottering around the kitchen, putting on pastries and a hot drink so that we can sit and talk about Leipzig – similar to when I was home last year.

"So you have graduated?" She pats my hand proudly.

"Yes."

"So can we call you Herr Doktor now?"

I am aiming to strike a fair balance: not wanting to utterly shutter their illusion, but at the same time not set unrealistic expectations.

"I still have to complete my thesis," I explain calmly, sensing that the process of earning the title is likely seen by her as mere academic bureaucracy. But at this moment I see an opportunity for me to explain why I have to go abroad.

Her face sours slightly. I believe that the burden of incurring loans for my education over four years has been more than enough hardship for my parents. Added to the upheavals of the Weimar Republic and the crash, which lost them their savings.

"I will be able to work and pay my own way, though, so you and Father need not worry."

She is not easily placated, she averts her gaze sideways towards the window, pausing to let the light of reality seep in.

"What is the matter? Is there something wrong with Father?"

"No. It is not that. But you know, he has been working very hard, taking extra hours and shifts where he can to help support you. I was hoping you could open up a clinic and work as a doctor right away so that he can cut back."

The guilt knife has plunged into my conscience already, and I haven't even brought up the subject of my leaving Germany. I am beginning to wonder if she means cutting back to normal hours or semi-retiring, which he can do at fifty-five. But I don't push the question; instead I try a different tack.

"I understand. And I would be willing to help, but I am not fully qualified to practise yet. But if Father does not need to support me any longer, won't he be able to cut back anyway?"

"Have a slice of strudel, I know it's your favourite."

To placate my mother I pick up a piece and munch without too much gusto. I stay silent to get the full measure of where she is headed.

"Good, huh?"

I nod my head.

"Part of the reason that your father is working hard is also to rebuild our savings. With Hitler in charge the currency is stabilising and the economy is improving. We may be able to accumulate enough to retire."

I was half right. It is not just semi, but full retirement. Not an uncharitable thought under the circumstances. The Weimar Republic and the crash of 1929 have plunged them into a financial hole and they are desperately trying to dig themselves out with whatever shovel they can get:

Father working extra shifts; the expectation that I will work as a doctor to help pay off the loans; supplementing their income; maybe even Brigitte marrying someone wealthy. Had the prosperity of 1923–1929 continued uninterrupted, being the parsimonious type, they would have had a sizeable nest egg by now in addition to Grandma's house. In their mid fifties they would have been able to retire comfortably. As things stand at the moment, Father will have to work at least another five years until he is sixty, on top of which they need to start recalling favours and getting assistance from the only source they are not embarrassed to ask, both of which point to me.

I refrain from totally disillusioning my mother, but explain my predicament – "I won't be able to get my licence to practise without specialisation" – implying that their four years' investment in Leipzig will be wasted. If there is anything my parents abhor it is waste.

She nods her head, beginning to understand my situation. "Why don't we wait until your father comes home and then we can discuss this tomorrow when we are all fresh? He does not work on Fridays – he works the Saturday shift, gets better money."

I agree. I tell my mother that I need to rest a little after my trip and go to my room.

In Leipzig I imagined that all was well at home. I never asked and they never complained. They suffered the burden of my board and tuition quietly, stretching their endurance to the limit. The limit is now. They never expected to hear that I will be taking longer to start practising. That's beyond what they can endure.

If I leave to go to Holland they will see it not only as a betrayal but as a desertion. The only way that I can see to persuade them that it is a good move is to not discuss Hitler or the Nazis and my misgivings, but the shorter path to my practising.

I am lying back on my bed, the same one that I lay on as a teenager dreaming of leaving home to study. I left with the sense that home was the bulwark of my being. It took just four years away for me to realise that the foundation on which I was relying is fragile and cracking at the seams. I don't begrudge my parents their vulnerabilities, I just never anticipated the role reversal to arrive so early in my adulthood. I expected them to grow old and be grandparents before they came to rely on me for help.

But the devastation of the 1929 crash and the Weimar's incompetence brought the clock forward. What if Hitler can revitalise the economy and stabilise the currency; might that slow things down again? My father could work normal hours; his pay packet restored to what it was before it was sheared in half. Maybe then I will not need to shoulder the responsibility of repaying my parents the debt before I have even become a doctor. I need to be the child just a little longer. In some tangential way Hitler is a saviour to us too. It doesn't ease my conscience regarding his aims and ambitions, and certainly not regarding his methods, but it does allow me to find benefit even in a flawed messiah. It is the bedrock of compromises: we accept certain things half-heartedly because they serve our purpose too. The Weimar and the crash brought us Hitler.

I feel better about being back. Sitting in the dining room being plied with chocolate cake I felt like I was choking on a bribe.

I look at my watch. It's getting late in the afternoon. I wonder where Brigitte is? I never thought to ask. She is my younger sister and we have always had a strong bond. I would like to air my thoughts with her before discussing them with the whole family. Mother is prejudiced, after all. Not that she loves Brigitte or me any less, but she and Father are getting old and they need their security. That is as plain as it gets; we are still young and time is on our side.

I am awake. I must have dozed off. I study my watch; the afternoon light from the window has turned to dusk. I turn on the night lamp: it's six o'clock. The short nap on the train from Leipzig relaxed me. That and being in my old room and having graduated pre-med drained my body of any lingering anxiety. But just as soon as I relish the relief it is replaced by a sinking feeling in my stomach: I still have to confront my parents about my upcoming plans. Sooner rather than later we are going to have that conversation, and despite the sound rationale behind my reasons for leaving it will not be an easy discussion.

Father will most likely mirror my mother's disappointment yet their stoic Teutonic attitude and ultimate desire to see me succeed will prevail and they will sit there and smile benignly and assure me that everything will be fine. But in another four years' time when I return home from Holland I might discover that their life has deteriorated further: my father aged faster than his years; the house fallen into disrepair and the only asset to sustain them in their old age, Grandma's house, sold off so they can survive.

That is the lateral view, I remind myself, to alleviate my growing sense of anxiety. The wild card is Hitler. If he can restore Germany to the prosperity of the pre-crash years then things will look up. I remember seeing him parading around in a Benz; that's a good thing for Father's plant. But then again, Hitler can afford a Benz – how many of us can afford one, is the key.

I hear voices downstairs: Father's, then Brigitte's and then Mother's. All the family is home. I swing my feet over the side and then on second thought roll back onto the bed. Knowing the predicament that I face now, I shouldn't have come back. I ought to have gone straight from Leipzig to Holland. They would have found out sooner or later and I would have made up some story as to why I was completing my medical training overseas. Now I am trapped by my guilt.

Footsteps come towards my room. They are soft and tentative. Then a quiet whisper, Brigitte's: "Freddie, are you awake?"

Her head is in the door and the night lamp is on; I can hardly pretend that I am not. She rushes in and hugs me.

"Oh, it's so good to see you."

"Sorry. I fell asleep. I didn't think I was that tired."

She sits on the edge of the bed. "Don't worry, you were tired; who cares why? You are home now. Are you home for good? Father thinks that you are."

I point to the door. She nods her head, walks over and shuts it.

"What's going on? Did something happen in Leipzig?"

"No, no. Everything is fine. It's just that they want me to start working as a doctor right away, even open up a medical clinic. But I am not there yet. I have a way to go."

"Ouch."

"Ouch, what?"

"Well, Father has been running around telling everyone that Dr Becker is coming home. He has even been making enquiries locally for your clinic."

"Ouch!"

"Well, he will have to go back and tell everyone that he spoke too soon." Brigitte shrugs nonchalantly.

I shake my head in bewilderment.

"So, there *is* something wrong."

"Not quite wrong, but disappointing."

"You'd better tell me so that I can soften the blow for them."

"I am thinking of going overseas to complete my studies."

"That is going to be a blow. May I ask the reason?"

"*Reasons*. I need to get away to get some perspective on what's happening here."

Brigitte points outside the door.

"No. Not home. Germany in general."

"What? You are not persuaded by Dr Goebbels' promises of a new era for Germany?" She smiles sardonically.

I shake my head and smirk but don't say anything.

"Look, I got a teller's job in Domshof. Deutsche Bank. Eight, nine months ago I wouldn't have bothered trying."

"Are you saying that things are improving?"

"The mood of the people is certainly improving."

"Well, that is something for some people. Others are going to fare worse."

"That's always the way, regardless of who is in power. A lot of people did well under Weimar, before the crash, and others still lived in barns. We were fortunate. Father kept his job."

"But they lost their savings."

"They lost their savings. What can you do?" Brigitte says it more as an unavoidable consequence than as a question, shrugging her shoulders. "You said *reasons*, before."

"Reasons?"

"You know, for leaving Germany."

I nod my head. "And to get away from this." This time I point towards the door.

"I know what you mean. Before I got a job they would set me up every week with horrible dates. Remember Ulrich Koertig, the one that used to work at the school with Mother?"

"The caretaker?" I am dumbfounded. Brigitte can do better both socially and physically. Though I would describe her as more pleasant looking in a traditional sort of way, her fleshy features taking after Mother's, with light-blonde hair, green eyes and standing above average in height, I concur that Ulrich falls short in every way. I don't say it and neither do I express the view that our parents must have been panicking with Brigitte still not spoken for and the economy floundering in even suggesting the caretaker.

"Yes, the one and the same. I don't think that we could fit on the same bed together." Brigitte and I burst out laughing. "I would be in the kitchen preparing meals all day, every day just to feed him. Anyway, now that I am working, they ask me about men at the bank. They are worried that I will become an old maid, like Auntie Agnethe."

"I didn't even think of that."

"What, that I will become an old maid?" She slaps me playfully on the shoulder.

"No; that they will put the same kind of pressure on me. You know, to meet someone, settle down."

"Maybe we should marry each other. We get along."

We laugh again.

"Listen, why don't you rest some more? If you want me to, I will tell them that you are tired and will sleep through to tomorrow. Don't worry about them. All parents have expectations and children end up disappointing them."

I start to feel better. Some of the load is easing off my shoulders.

"Tell them I will be out in a little while. I will have a shower, freshen up and then come out."

"Good idea." She kisses me in a sisterly manner and eases out the door.

Mother has prepared what would be a traditional holiday meal for this occasion. She is a wizard in the kitchen; I don't even know how she got it all done in just the afternoon. By the time we get to the *butterkuchen* I can hardly fit in a single slice without loosening my belt a notch.

We have talked about Leipzig, Father's work, Brigitte's prospects socially and at work, Mother going back to working part time. The only thing we haven't talked about is the subject on everyone's mind: my future. But nobody wants to be the first one to raise it for fear of spoiling the mood.

Finally Brigitte broaches the subject in an ingenious subterfuge, taking the heat out of the topic. "Freddie has to go another year; specialisation. Overseas. To complete his degree."

Father looks, flabbergasted, from Brigitte to me. "Is that so?"

I pause to collect my thoughts, trying to sound as convincing as possible. "All doctors are required to put in a year of internship abroad."

"Africa?" Mother is looking worried.

I nod my head sagely. "Could be. But I chose something closer to home and safer: Holland."

"Very good." Father slaps his thigh.

Brigitte has saved me from having to disappoint them and turned a potentially unhappy reunion into a happy farewell.

"Where are you going in Holland?" Father turns to me with a beaming smile. He can now proudly tell people that his son the doctor is specialising overseas.

Fortunately I already have the name. "Universiteit Utrecht."

"Utrecht! Your mother and I have been there. It's a very beautiful old city and quite the university town. The good news is it's only four hours by car from here. We can come visit you."

They are both excited and ecstatic now. Strange thing is that Leipzig wasn't that much further and they nary came the once. They probably see going to Utrecht as an overseas holiday; Leipzig is just another town in Germany.

The rest of the evening is spent making plans to visit me. They decide that they will do so over the Christmas break when Father and Brigitte can take time off from work.

By nightfall I sneak into Brigitte's room and kiss her on the forehead. "I owe you."

She chuckles, tucked in under her blanket. "That's right, Herr Doktor, and don't you forget it."

I spend a month in Bremen. Father parades me around to his friends and colleagues as Herr Doktor and they all, to a person, bestow me the honour. I am extremely uncomfortable with this travesty, but the alternative would be devastating for my parents and their fragile middle-class egos. I sincerely hope that nobody asks me to do a house call. After four years of arduous study I am knowledgeable enough about human biology to understand the physiology, but taking an instrument to a live person or prescribing medicine would unravel the lie and make a mockery of my parents. They would never live down the shame.

Happily, fate conspires with my half-lie and I am not asked to perform any parlour tricks. I am a half-doctor, if anyone cared to check.

At the beginning of autumn I repack my duffel bag and rucksack and make my way to the bus station. There are no trains to take me to the border with the Netherlands. Instead I take a bus to Nijmegen and then board a train from the border town to Utrecht.

UTRECHT

Autumn 1934

I disembark at Utrecht Centraal just before noon, a short two-hour trip from Nijmegen on the all-stations trains. Given my eventual impecunious station, and that I'll need to find accommodation immediately and employment within a matter of weeks, I plan to do both at the university.

The attendant at the train station points me in the general direction and assures me that my destination is an easy thirty-minute stroll. But if I don't feel like a brisk jaunt, I can walk to Steenweg, five minutes away, and from there any number of buses will take me right up to the university. I don't mind walking all the way but am not certain of my whereabouts, and getting lost would leave me without student lodgings so I walk just as far as Steenweg.

On the train I tried to imagine what Utrecht would look like, drawing comparisons with Leipzig and even Bonn, which I have visited. But nothing prepares me for this medieval city with its maze of canals and split-level houses and warehouses. Whenever I think of canals Venice comes to mind, but Utrecht's waterways are just as quaint and romantic as the Italian city's, and though I've never visited Venice I imagine that it is culturally rich with museums, cathedrals, magnificent plazas and sculptures arrayed throughout the city. Utrecht is not dissimilar in many ways. It is known as a university town but not in the way that Leipzig is: overrun with students, clubs, bars and student housing; more like Oxford or Cambridge, criss-crossed with canals and beautiful architecture.

When I first thought of Utrecht, the fact that it had a prestigious teaching hospital and its proximity to Bremen were what first attracted me to it, notwithstanding its foreignness. But now I feel quite at home with the genteel nature of the town; the unhurried pace of the passers-by, the air of learning imbued in the historical richness of the place. I slow down and draw my breath in deeply; I have made the right choice.

On the way I am struck by the most obvious question that I am likely to be asked: *Why are you not continuing your medical degree in Leipzig?* There is little doubt in my mind that if a place is available at the faculty of medicine at Universiteit Utrecht, based on my pre-med grades, I will be admitted. But Utrecht is a foreign city and speaks a foreign language. It will take some effort on my part to acclimatise to the Dutch language so that I can follow the lectures and read the books. What academic reason do I have for undertaking such a venture? I can't argue pedagogy or the course curriculum; I don't know enough to draw a favourable comparison.

I arrive at Steenweg and board the bus. The trip only lasts a few minutes but, preoccupied as I am, I almost fail to notice the university campus looming up ahead of me and am alerted by the bus driver who announces the stop. I disembark, not having as yet formulated a plausible explanation as to my choice of Utrecht. It doesn't have to be surreptitious or suspicious, but the cultural change and linguistic challenge invite curiosity and a persuasive answer will smooth the enrolment process.

I disembark at Servestraat with the university gate just ahead of me. As I start to make my way into the campus, I find my reason, walking past me: two obviously Jewish men dressed in black cassocks and hats, sporting scraggly beards. They resemble those vulgar caricatures that denigrate and accuse the Jews of being vile and devious moneylenders plotting to destroy Germany, courtesy of *Der Stürmer* – a virulent anti-Semitic tabloid – and Joseph Goebbels, Hitler's propaganda minister. I rebrand my mother, Marlis Becker (née Wolfssohn – the only other Jewish person I know besides Zeigler), as Jewish, so I am perforce half Jewish. I can't make my father, Herman, Jewish with a surname like Becker. I am counting on the fact that Holland is traditionally racially tolerant as a rule, and in particular to Jewish people, who have a long and prosperous history in Amsterdam. The reason for my leaving Germany and wanting to study in Utrecht is now ironclad, easily justified.

I enter through the massive wrought-iron gates adorned with a crest inscribed in Latin and entwined with creeping vines through the bars. They are drawn back for another day of learning as students and faculty stream through. Just within the courtyard, a short distance from the gate, is the most famous landmark in the city, the Dom Tower. An inscription at the bottom identifies it as the highest church tower in the Netherlands, and that it was built between 1321 and 1382 as part of the Cathedral of St Martin.

I am impressed with the antiquity and architectural grandeur, but I am rather indifferent towards its religious significance. If I was devout anything I would be leaning towards the irreverence of Lutheranism, the religion of my birth, and not the obsequious reverence of Catholicism, of which this church is clearly part.

Aside that, and the other myriad reminders of Catholicism scattered throughout the city, which do not feel oppressive, I shrug it off, maintaining my initial impression of Utrecht, and continue towards the centre of the courtyard. A signpost is planted right in the middle with labelled arrows. I try to decipher in them 'admissions' or 'new students', but nothing close to German jumps out at me.

A young woman pushing a bicycle stops next to me. She asks me something in Dutch. I shrug my shoulders and shake my head. She then reverts to English. I answer hesitantly, "Sorry, I am German. My English is better than my Dutch, but not fluent either."

To my surprise she answers back fluently in German: "That's all right. I am quite comfortable speaking German. You looked lost, looking at the signpost."

I can't believe my good fortune. "Are you German?"

"Oh, not me, my mother. She is from Leipzig."

"Leipzig? Really?"

"Why? Don't tell me you come from Leipzig. That would be too much of a coincidence."

I find myself too instantly captivated by her easy-going manner and the sparkle in her light green eyes to mind her forthrightness. "No, no. I am from Bremen. But I just finished four years of pre-med in Leipzig."

"And?"

"And? And what?"

"Now you are in Utrecht to do your medical?"

"That's right."

"May I ask why Utrecht and not Leipzig, or even Münster? They are just as good if not better."

I am furiously debating whether I should test out the lie that I just invented. I am inclined to do so given that, if it does not convince, there will be no penalty. But it is too soon in the conversation. "You are right, Leipzig and WWU are very good. It is personal."

That whets her curiosity. I am flattered that she is interested.

"Personal? How personal? A girl? Or something other, confidential, none of my business?"

I smile bashfully. "No, not a girl. Who has time in pre-med?"

"Then...?"

I clam up.

"Sorry, here I am prying into your life and I don't even know your name."

I reach out my hand. "Friedrich Becker."

"I am Emma. Emma van Bergen."

Her hand feels warm and small in mine. I like the tenderness and vulnerability of her touch.

"So, Herr Becker, now that we know each other, why Utrecht?"

"Herr Becker is my father. I am Friedrich, and I will happily tell you except I need to get to admissions, enrol and find a place to live."

"Well, young Becker, walk with me; I work in admissions and I can help you with accommodation. So this is your lucky day. So, why Utrecht?"

We walk away from the Dom Tower and head past a series of similar old-looking buildings with the words 'faculty' and 'institute' forming part of their names, but other than recognising that I can't make out the actual disciplines. Medical school is going to be hard going here in Dutch Land.

"Utrecht is the nearest place I could find outside Germany where I think I can fit in and complete my degree."

"Really? You can't even read a signpost; how do you propose to get through medical school reading all those dense textbooks, never mind the lectures?"

"Well, OK. I need to enrol, find accommodation and brush up on my Dutch."

"I think you need to do more than that. Regardless, why put yourself through all of that?"

"You are a curious type, aren't you?"

"Curious and direct, but only when I like someone."

I am flattered even more by her indirect compliment. I instantly know why I like this young woman: her directness and natural curiosity aside, which don't sound crass or obtrusive coming from her, she is the exact opposite of what I dislike about German women; she is sprightly and easy-going. I catch myself jealously wondering if she already has a boyfriend, and yet I only met her a few minutes ago.

I am glad that I declined the invitation to go with Martin Keller to Bologna. It was tempting to have a friend in a foreign city facing nearly the same challenges as I am here: oppressive Catholicism, foreign language and culture. Yet intuitively Holland felt right just as Italy felt wrong.

We walk quietly for a minute or so and then Emma stops. "Would you like to have a drink before filling out forms?" She is pointing to a squat building to our left. It is more industrial and modern-looking than the surrounding stately institutions of learning.

I hesitate.

"I am here. So you can't fill out forms and enrol without me." She pulls her bicycle into a rack and leads me gently by the arm into the interior.

It is nearly lunchtime and the large hall is crowded with people. She points me to a table by the window that is not nearly as full, and we gravitate towards it.

"What can I get you?"

I am trying to come up with what I would eat if I were in Leipzig. I hadn't thought of food yet, so I haven't noticed what they eat in Utrecht. "Can you get a beer and a pretzel?" I smile sheepishly.

"Beer, yes. I am not sure about the pretzel."

Emma wends her way dextrously through the crowd and I am left alone at the table with a group of noisy Dutch students: two males and two females. They eye me curiously and one of them leans over, rattling something in Dutch.

"*Nein* Dutch," I attempt politely.

Another of the group stands up and salutes – "*Heil Hitler!*" – mimicking *Der Führer* by substituting two fingers in place of a toothbrush moustache. They all burst out laughing.

I ought to have expected this, but not on my first day and not in this casual setting. I turn away and look for Emma in the crowd. I can see her head at the counter.

The Dutch student who spoke to me first leans over and taps me on the shoulder. He attempts, in broken English, "Why you here in Utrecht?"

I turn to face him with a sullen stare. "Study."

He stands up and mimics a chopping motion over his penis. "I am Jew."

I get it. Circumcised. This is getting ugly. I fully expect it to end up in a brawl on account of their antipathy to Germany. Ironically I am here for exactly the same reason, but being taunted in this manner I can't make that point. I smile benignly. What else can I do? I turn again to look in the direction of the counter. Thankfully Emma is heading back with two beers and, amazingly, two pretzel lookalikes.

She arrives at the table just as the second student, the one who imitated a Hitler salute, walks up to her and speaks aggressively in Dutch. She sets down the beers and pretzels and assumes a belligerent pose, firing back at him. An argument ensues, with the other three students at the table joining in. I am tempted to get up and stand by Emma but fear that my intervention will escalate this argument into a fist fight. So I remain seated, hoping that they do not get violent. I can't see them attacking Emma; she is, after all, one of them. Thankfully the other students around us take cursory notice of the scene, engrossed in their noisy conversations.

Eventually the heated discussion loses steam and Emma sidles into the seat opposite me, shaking her head with dismay.

"Thank you for the beer and pretzel; how much do I owe you?" I can't think of what else to say.

"My treat."

We remain quiet.

"I am sorry to cause you this much trouble."

"No. *I* apologise. Normally, people here are very friendly. I am not sure what happened."

"Please do not feel that you have to apologise. I can understand their hostile feelings."

"Can you? Because I can't. They don't even know you and are blaming you for what the Nazis are saying and doing."

We drink our beers and eat the quasi-pretzels quietly, ignoring the hostile stares and muttering to our left. The alcohol helps to settle my nerves somewhat. As soon as we finish we don't linger, but take our trash and leave the table. More taunts flare up behind us as we make our way out. Some of the words are deliberately uttered in English for my benefit.

But there's nothing I can do about who I am or how I look: I stand close to two metres tall with a muscular build, thick blond hair, and what passes for a handsome Nordic-like face with light blue eyes and peach-coloured skin. I speak with a distinctly northern Germanic accent. I am the model Aryan, if one chooses to espouse the idiotic posters that the Nazis are putting up.

Ironically none of the party members that spout this drivel match their own embodiment of the perfect German. They are either mousy-looking, squat with dark hair, brown eyes and a scrawny body, or obese and ungainly, or half crippled and mentally feeble. So they laughably fail to live up to their own standards and resemble more the caricatures that they vilify.

But by creating this mythical German Zeus they indirectly place me in the line of fire, as though I am the ambassador for their crackpot politics. Which I am anything but – yet, now I have crossed the border to the Netherlands it lands me in hostile situations such as this one. I need to present myself in a better light and distance myself from Nazi Germany as much as I can.

"You are OK?" Emma is by my side, pushing her bicycle towards the administration building.

"Yes. Thank you for standing up for me. I don't know what I would have done had I been alone."

"Forget it."

We reach an older but pedestrian-looking building on campus, not of the same standard as the stately cathedral and faculties that we passed previously. Emma parks her bicycle and leads me inside. She points me to a counter at the end of a large room, then goes through a door and comes out the other side facing me and picks up a stack of forms. There are several clerical people working at desks behind her.

"First you have to fill out this form. It is for foreign nationals such as yourself. For address, you can put down mine."

I look at her hesitantly.

"I share a house not far from here with a couple. There's a room for one more person. That could be yours if you want it?"

My sense of alienation has swung back to feeling at home. I nod eagerly and take the form. It's in English, the lingua franca the world over. I fill in my particulars, leaving the address in Utrecht blank, and hand it back, together with my passport as proof of identification. I then fill out the enrolment for the medical degree that I will be undertaking and attach my certificate and transcript from Leipzig. There's a question about my level of proficiency in Dutch. I leave that blank and hand it back to Emma too.

She fills out her address on the first form and, on the second, writes *Passing* for reading and writing comprehension in Dutch. I refrain from commenting due to the other people in the office behind her, but raise my eyebrows in surprise at that blatant fabrication. She stares back – "Trust me, you will be" – then clips the forms together along with my enrolment processing fee and passport.

She then pulls over a map of the campus and places it in front of me. "Why don't you go over to the library and spend the afternoon there? Strangely, they have newspapers and magazines from Germany. I will collect you when I am done here. Where are your things?"

"At the train station."

"OK. The library is here." She points to a building two lanes over from where we are. "Try and stay out of trouble."

"I will try." I smile back.

"We will collect your things on the way home. Welcome to Utrecht."

I am tempted to lean across the counter and give her a peck on the cheek, but doing so, even innocently, may cause problems for both of us given her position. Instead I nod gratefully and head towards the library.

I recognise the library by the wide portico with three columns arrayed on either side of the entrance. Between the columns are statues of classical scholars: Aristotle, Plato, Socrates, Pythagoras and Archimedes. Rising above them on the pediment is a large cross with a cursive Latin inscription that I don't recognise.

Just as I start to mount the steps, the same group of students from the lunch hall accost me, blocking my ingress into the building. My first thought is that they are spoiling for a fight and now that Emma is not with me they have no reason to hold back. I come abreast of them, betraying no fear.

"So, Mr Aryan, where is friend?" It is the same student that gave me the Hitler salute.

I ignore the question and proceed to push my way to the wooden doorway. They shove me back.

I raise my hands. "Don't push!"

"Or what?" This is the student that airily chopped his penis.

But there is no time to get into a fracas, for two campus officials rush up. They grab the two male students and push them up against the wall. A terse and loud dialogue ensues between them. There is some head-nodding, a cocky smile from the students and they are released to continue on their way.

The salute student turns to me as he is leaving. "Next time you no so lucky!"

I flick the backs of my fingers under my chin and proceed to walk into the library. The one girl from the earlier lunchroom encounter softens her hostile glare and actually gives me a mischievous smile. I can't tell whether she is spiting me or in some bizarre way admiring me. I haven't displayed any great courage other than being foolishly stubborn.

I am followed into the library by one of the campus officials. "Sorry for that."

I nod. "Not to worry. Thank you."

The library is a massive semicircular building rising up four storeys. Each storey is lined with books right the way around, stacked ten shelves high. The bottom level has rows of study carrels with a goose-necked lamp attached to each one.

I make my way to a wall rack lined with German magazines, select a few and find an empty carrel. Regardless of their underlying political or religious affiliation, they all contain articles on the Nazis and Adolf Hitler, with one particular magazine featuring him on the cover – a dark, brooding likeness, rather than the more common menacing look – with the caption *Germany's Saviour?* I am relieved that the editor or publisher had the sense to add the question mark.

Among his followers, Hitler has assumed messianic status, the sort of fanatical fealty that suffocates those who do not support him. My parents are avowed law-abiding neutralists and, if Hitler's machinations do not threaten my father's livelihood or their money, they will remain safe. So the weight of my guilt lessens. I do not feel that I have abandoned them to a precarious state. I don't know any people from the disenfranchised group, other than Johann Ziegler. I salve my conscience in the hope that the senior Ziegler's academic status will protect his son and family from any misfortune.

I don't bother with my magazine-reading any more; it just makes me feel more nauseous. My last full meal was mid morning when I stopped at Nijmegen to catch the train to Utrecht. The pretzel and beer helped tide me over, but I am looking forward to my first dinner with Emma.

It's 3.45 and I would like to step outside and tour the grounds rather than sit here and wait, but Emma might stop by at any minute. So I replace the magazines on the rack, grab a book off the shelf to look busy and think through my first day in Holland. Emma has taken me under her wing. Is it because she is half German and facing the same harassment as me? Perhaps. Or maybe she can just empathise because her mother faces the same scorn? Even so, she has gone beyond empathy to trust me and invite me to rent a room in her house. But that can also be construed as a financial decision: more housemates, less rent for each to pay. That's how the four of us – Martin, Johann, Franz and I – ended up together in Leipzig sharing a house.

If I think back to Emma's earlier curiosity, which I attributed to romantic interest, I see it now as her sussing me out as a potential housemate, not mate. In that light, her hastily processing my enrolment falls under the same rubric. My ego deflates slightly; yet even if her interest in me is driven by finances it still fulfils my need too: a place to live and being enrolled. I got lucky in that, and in that Emma is half German, otherwise I would be at the mercy of the university dormitory and enrolment bureaucracy.

A tap on my shoulder. "I expected you to be deeply immersed in a book, not your thoughts." She points to her watch and then the door.

It's 4.30. I stand up and replace the book on the shelf and follow Emma to the lane bordering the library.

"You know, the welcoming committee from lunch greeted me at the library," I tell her facetiously as we step outside – my eyes are already scanning the perimeter.

"What?! They followed you here?" Emma stops and stares incredulously at me.

"No, I don't think they followed me. They just happened to be here when I got here."

"So what happened?"

"The same as before, plus some shoving and pushing. But some campus officials stopped it from getting too ugly."

"Phew. What's this about? I have never experienced such antipathy – well, no, there was an incident last week with a German academic. But he provoked it."

That statement has just altered my view on why Emma chose to empathise with me. I wrongly assumed that it was because of her mother being German and copping the same abuse as me. But Emma just told me that she has never experienced such antipathy towards Germans before, so that would preclude her and certainly her mother. So why? I am tempted to ask, but I'll save it for a more personal setting, maybe over dinner.

We collect my duffel and rucksack from the train station and then hail a taxi, mounting Emma's bicycle on the back rack and stowing my luggage in the boot. We take a short ten-minute trip from the train station to a street called Kromme Nieuwegracht. As we disembark from the taxi in the fading light I can see that the street is not asphalt, but brick-lined. On either side the houses are also made of red brick, with the front windows facing onto a narrow canal. I immediately like the old-world feeling of the street and houses. I would like to revert to thinking that Emma took a personal interest in me for reasons other than financial ones; this street evokes romance.

We pay the driver and enter the foyer. The house is dark and silent.

"Lijsbeth and Jacob are away in Rotterdam. They are visiting his parents. They will be back next week. You will like them. They are very friendly." She flicks on the light in the living room: spacious, long and narrow. Rugs are strewn about randomly but with tastefully matching colours. There are a few unframed posters on the wall and a large Van Gogh reproduction: the bridge at Arles, I seem to recall. Immediately to my right is a fireplace, with logs bundled next to it and a set of bellows, tongs and a poker. Against the wall opposite is a brownish three-seater leather sofa partially covered by a quilted throw and an assortment of cushions. On either side is a maroon armchair with an antimacassar flung over the headrest. It is a very homely place with a quaint Dutch feel to it, without being overwhelming in its decor or furnishings. A set of stairs ascends directly opposite the fireplace leading to a second storey, which I assume is where the bedrooms are.

"Let's leave your things down here for now. I am famished. We will make some dinner, relax, and then I will show you to your room."

"All sounds good. How can I help?"

"Take the vegetables from the basket over there; make up a salad. I will prepare a quick *pannenkoeken* with cheese and meat."

"What is that?"

"Pancakes. Very easy, very good."

Soon we are working side by side like an old married couple; Emma breaking eggs, kneading a flour mix, sprinkling spices, then adding slices of cheese and sausage. I place the salad on the table, add plates and cutlery, then poke around the fridge for beer or white wine. I find both and place them on the table.

The pancakes smell like home. Except we don't have them there; but we do have the sausage and spices and we add eggs and have it for breakfast.

In less than half an hour we are seated at the table and eating ravenously. We stop when the plates are empty and reach for the drinks: Emma for the wine, me for the beer.

"That was nice; thank you."

Emma toasts me. "It's nice to have someone here. Jac and Beth often go out or away and I am left here all alone."

"Is it their place?"

"No. It's mine."

"Yours?"

"Well, actually it was my grandparents' house, but my parents own it now."

"So why did you take in a couple?"

"I didn't. Beth is a family friend, so I asked her to move in. She met Jac later and asked if he could move in. I agreed. Before I realised the awkwardness of living with a madly-in-love couple."

I don't say anything. But inwardly I am hoping that I can counterbalance – even if it's just as a companion. Sitting opposite her at the dining table, watching her in the soft light – her tousled golden-brown hair curled at her shoulders, her glinting green-hazel eyes, her luscious full lips and beautiful oval-shaped face – she's almost irresistible. But I can't be drawn to act on my emotions so soon. Not without some mutual sign from her. The few things she said earlier today could be construed either way.

I have been lucky; no sense in acting recklessly and being asked to leave. But I feel that I have been subtly led into a liaison that has kindled my romantic feelings. The street;

the welcoming house; preparing dinner together; being told about Jac and Beth as a couple; feeling relaxed and comfortable in each other's presence. It only feels natural to reach my hand across and place it on top of hers. But if I am wrong, well, it will make living together even more awkward for her and impossible for me.

"So, Herr Becker, what's your story?"

I am tempted to elaborate some fanciful image of myself, other than the dull middle-class boy from Bremen who has just completed pre-med. I feel that I need to be heroic; have some outstanding attributes: wealth, aristocratic lineage. I don't ordinarily think of myself as someone who'll spin tales to impress anyone, let alone women. It hasn't been my focus hitherto. Yet all of a sudden I feel I need to impress Emma.

Come to think of it, I have never thought of myself as a romantic person either, not even after reading the de rigueur poets of that era: Goethe, Byron, Keats and Shelley. Any feelings that I have, have been dormant and unexplored, largely because I find German women unromantic and sexually unattractive: Rubenesque in proportion, but lacking the voluptuousness of the Flemish painter's models and the charm and seductiveness of the French.

It is also my first foray outside of Germany, other than a family trip to Tyrol in Austria. I was still a gangling, awkward teenager then, and any women that I considered attractive felt unattainable. So I caution myself to remain prudent and not be drawn in by Emma's beauty and allure; it just may be that I am unfamiliar with her type of woman, intoxicated by my first seductive temptress.

Yet if it is a trap, I am willing to submit to it.

"You must mean my father?" I reply cheekily. "If you'd like to hear his story you will need to wait for him to visit."

"Does he intend to visit?"

"Yes, the family is coming over for Christmas."

"To celebrate it here?"

"Only the tradition, not the religion. What about yours?"

"My mother is Jewish. So we celebrate like you: the tradition without the religious overtones, out of respect for my father."

The lie is drawn out of my mouth, involuntarily: "We are the same." As soon as I hear myself say it, I regret it. It is my animalistic desire to be attractive to this woman, so I carve out a path of deception to her heart, knowing that it will resonate.

I get a curious and puzzled look. "You are the same?"

"My mother is Jewish." It sounds hollow. I am glad that I am an unconvincing liar.

Her look transforms into one of bewilderment, followed by incredulous surprise. "You, Jewish? Really?"

"Half." I stress it to dampen the lie.

Emma is silent while she studies me. "I must say, I am very surprised; there's absolutely nothing Jewish-looking or -sounding about you."

It was a stupid miscalculation which may have the opposite effect to what I intended. Now she is suspicious. If there was any intimacy lingering from the dinner and the ambience it has now been dispelled by the fallout from my obvious lie.

To break the awkward silence I get up and start clearing the table. Emma remains seated, but grabs my hand.

"I hope you didn't say that just to please me."

I set the plates down. "In the morning, when we were walking to the lunch hall, you asked me, 'Why Utrecht?' I couldn't give a simple answer. But now you know, you can understand why."

Emma's look of bewilderment softens and she stands up and starts clearing the table with me. We wash up and wipe the kitchen clean. The weather is still balmy outside so a warm fire, despite its potential to set the mood, would be superfluous. Tucked in the alcove of the living room is a piano that I failed to notice before. It is covered with a dark purplish paisley cloth and an array of photographs on top: Emma and her parents, and a young man that I presume must be her brother; Emma with her couple friends, Jac and Beth; Emma on holiday in London and Paris – Buckingham Palace and the Eiffel Tower in the background; a pair of elderly people who are most probably the grandparents whose house this was. Scattered between the photographs are little ceramic figurines from the places she has visited. I try to think what I collect. Nothing. My family's life to this point has been a yo-yo and a struggle to stay afloat. We never lacked for the essentials, but there was never the time and money for life's little trinkets and luxuries, other than the one trip to Austria, by borrowed car.

If I think of a luxury, it was art classes for Brigitte and piano lessons for me. I can play, but I don't play the turgid Germanic music that people expect of me: Schubert, Schumann and Mozart. Although on occasion I will condescend to a sprightly Bach arrangement, but not the *Variations* or *The Well-Tempered Clavier*, both of which bore me to death. A disappointment to my parents, especially my mother, who paid for our lessons by toiling at a large clothing factory until her arthritis forced her to quit and take up a clerical position at the school. To their displeasure I have gravitated towards what they call 'monkey music': jazz. Ellington, Monk, Peterson, Tatum – they are my heroes. And that's another thing about the country I have left behind: all the jazz greats are for the most part black, whom the Aryans consider subhuman – Untermensch. So in Leipzig whenever the opportunity came up to play, I lied and said I didn't play an instrument.

Here I have a chance to redeem myself. I peek under the paisley cloth and anticipate the inevitable question.

"Do you play?" Emma is standing close behind me. Intimately close. She is giving me the benefit of the doubt on my supposed Jewishness.

"So-so. I am a bit rusty." I am trying to impress by understating.

Emma moves around me and removes the photographs and figurines, placing them on top of the mantelpiece. She then peels back the cloth, revealing a gleaming Steinway. I have only had a few opportunities to play a piano this elite. Usually it is a poor copy.

"Please, maestro." She takes a step back, leaning on the lid.

I am almost tempted to make some raucous sounds, but I have been trained too well to pretend otherwise. I get comfortable on the bench and with a flourish belt out an opening to a famous Peterson piece, *C Jam Blues*. I haven't played in a while so it takes me a little time to build up the rhythmic tempo and get into the improvisation groove. As my confidence swells I stray far from the Peterson motif, artfully crafting my own notes. I am getting carried away, enjoying the music I am making, when I am reminded of Emma's presence. I quickly glance up and notice the same bewilderment that I witnessed before, only this time it is laced with wonderment at my musical ingenuity, not incredulousness at my Jewish invention. I bring the music back to the Peterson theme and gradually wind down the composition. The notes reverberate around the room for a little longer, then the room settles to a stunned silence.

"So-so? Becker, you are a phenomenal pianist!"

I smile sheepishly. "I wouldn't go so far. Largely self-taught."

"I don't care if you are self-taught; I know any number of places in Utrecht that would love to have you on stage. We have jazz clubs here, but their performers don't sound half as good as you." She is gushing. I am glad. I need to remediate my earlier gaffe.

I remain seated. She leans closer. "You have to play something else."

I slow down the fervent pace and set in motion *Night Train*, also a Peterson piece, swing-like, still jazz-flavoured but more the head-nodding and less foot-tapping variety. This time I play longer. I take the piece out from the core motif, adding my own classical inventiveness to the underlying theme, weaving in and out with flowing dexterity.

This time when I rest my hands, Emma is beaming. "I don't think you are self-taught. You have a classical bent. Listen, I am so excited that tomorrow night we are going to visit Club Hot, our best club, and I am sure that Stefan will give you a job."

"We shall see. I may sound all right here, but in a club, with an audience and a professional combo, I'll probably come off as amateurish."

"Nonsense. They might be the ones sounding amateurish."

I gently close the lid on the keyboard and rise up out of the seat. Emma doesn't replace the cloth, probably in anticipation of more playing.

It's not late but it has been a long day and I feel like settling in; unpacking, showering and getting some sleep. I am glad that it is the weekend tomorrow.

"Come. Let's take your bags up. I will show you the room." Emma takes the cue.

The stairs creak on the way up, as do our steps on the landing. There are two rooms on the right and a bathroom at the end of the hall. Veering left from the bathroom there appears to be a narrow hallway leading to what I suspect is another room. I presume that it is the smallest of the three and mine, but to my surprise Emma leads me into the first room to my right.

"This is yours, next to mine. The one around from the bathroom is bigger and more private; that one belongs to Jac and Beth."

The switch is next to my head. I flick it and am greeted by a very cosy-looking, cream-coloured room: a free-standing double-door wardrobe, a small couch, a single bed, a desk with drawers and a lamp, and an ornamental rug in the middle. There's a window next to the desk looking out over the street, obscured by closed shutters. I hear some muffled voices outside and a car go by.

"You like?"

"Very much. You didn't tell me how much?"

We place my duffel and rucksack on the floor next to the wardrobe. Emma pushes her hair back and looks up at me.

"Well, what are you comfortable paying?"

I recline on the couch. "Well, if there are four of us, then a quarter of all expenses, plus rent. Otherwise half and rent."

"It sounds fair. We can work this out after the weekend. I shop at the market on Saturday; you can come along and pick what you like."

She stands there momentarily and then turns to go. "Why don't you settle in? You know where the shower is. I will see you in the morning."

She is nearly out the door when I call her name. She turns instantly, blushing. "Yes, Friedrich?"

"Thank you for everything."

"I am glad you are here." She waves me a goodnight and shuts the door behind her.

I remain on the couch, relaxed and in no hurry to unpack or shower before bed. The way Utrecht has turned out for me is the closest I've come to a spiritual experience. I don't believe in the piffle that the Bible spouts: miracles, prayers, and lighting candles to ask God for blessings. My take on my life being charmed is that when I follow my heart, I am on the right track. I didn't want any part of the German way of life: politics, people, music, culture or education. So I left and chose Utrecht. From the moment I set foot in this town I knew that I made the right decision, and everything that flowed from that came easily, like it was meant to be.

Obviously there are contrasting elements of my make-up that don't seem natural, but so what? It is expected of me to play classical music, but it doesn't thrill me; I am moved to my core when I play jazz. To look at me you wouldn't see it, but that is a hidden attribute. Certainly, severing that part of me that is indisputably German cannot be achieved without losing something of myself, and perhaps it is a part of me that I am prepared to let go. Yet, I would like to straddle Utrecht and Bremen to keep my parents and sister within me.

But I have reservations about them coming to Utrecht this soon after I have settled here. There are characteristics that they embody which I don't want on display in Utrecht; parts of me that I would like to shed. Yet, if they come here it will be like the skin I have shed has been forcibly re-grafted.

I love my parents and sister. I pause at that thought. *Do I? Or did I when I lived in Bremen, in Leipzig?* I fear that the parts of me that I want to shed include my ties to them. I inwardly gasp at the realisation that their memory has faded like they have been gone years from my life, yet it has only been twenty-four hours. It is part of the human psyche that I don't comprehend. We change and the person that we become does not leave room for certain feelings and the people tied to them. We can continue, remembering, but the feelings have evaporated and cannot be reinstated.

When I crossed the border and arrived in Utrecht it wasn't just the time or geographical distance; a wider gulf opened, and I became someone that I'd wanted to be all along, rising out from under Germany's and my parents' shadows.

All of a sudden I am struck by a realisation that pains me: I have become uncomfortable with my family. Their middle-class values; Mother a seamstress; Father a mechanical engineer; my plain sister still living at home, working a clerical job at a bank. They are an unsophisticated family despite their attempts to rehabilitate by classically training me and teaching Brigitte painting. If they believed that by doing so they would vicariously rise up and become cultured, well-bred people, it doesn't work that way.

Fine breeding doesn't trickle backwards. My parents sit around reading tabloid newspapers; listening to silly programmes on the radio; playing canasta with their friends; going to the *bierstube* for meals and drinks. I can't ever recall them going to the opera or a play or a concert. We did visit the Belvedere Museum on our trip to Austria. Our home life is humdrum. Merely looking at this house and its trappings as an extension of her parents' home, it is clear to me that Emma comes from a well-to-do family with a strong cultural heritage and professional public standing. What are her parents and mine going to talk about? Father walking up and down the assembly line, checking on quality control, or Mother sewing buttons and stitching seams? That's hardly conversation that the Van Bergens would be interested in. Of course, they will listen politely and then behind closed doors mutter at the inequality between us.

I need to find a way to stall this, at least until I have established myself here. But how? The thought vexes me. It is easy to let go of a thought or a feeling, they are ephemeral; but a biological part is blood, skin and bone. We can't simply sever that which we are physically and regenerate a new part. It is that which binds us to this earth.

I am afraid that if I cut them off I will lose myself, I will become untethered, drifting on the ocean like flotsam and jetsam. Alas, the things that matter deeply to me – my jazz-playing, the easy-going persona that I am cultivating, unfettering my thoughts from race and religion – come at a price. And maybe it is that, mutual exclusivity: I can be German with all the traits that I dislike about myself following me around like a shackled ghost, or a stateless person espousing the music, culture and persona that I want.

Can I not bridge the two? This I don't know, until I try it. This is the magic and mystery of life: there are things you cannot experience unless you take the risk. What is certain is that until I know, I can't have my family to visit over Christmas.

The room feels stuffy. I rise up off the couch and open the window over the desk, then unlatch and push the shutter outwards. The lamp posts flicker over the canal directly across the narrow street. I watch and wonder what it would be like to hold Emma. I have dreamt of this life even before I knew what it looked like. At heart, I realise all of a sudden that I may not really be an aspiring doctor, but a jazz musician.

It never occurred to me because I never thought to follow my heart, until now, when I followed it to Utrecht. If I don't go on to become a doctor I owe my parents the tuition money at the very least for the wasted four years of pre-med. And that's just the financial obligation. The extra hours and days that my father put in to pay my way, I can't repay. Maybe subconsciously I have chosen to disown them so that I don't feel the guilt and pain of owing them.

I pull the shutter to. I get undressed. My thoughts are stretching too far, too fast. It is four years of my life too. I need to become a doctor. Is it the rational, strait-laced German in me? Ought I negate that and throw everything to the wind and start down a new path?

I open my duffel bag, take out fresh underwear, a pair of loose cotton slacks, a singlet, a towel and my toiletries, and listen at the door to make sure that Emma is not using the bathroom. It's quiet. The door opens with a creaking sound. I pause and listen again. All quiet. The hallway is dark and there is no light under her bedroom door. She must have dropped off as soon as she hit the bed.

I tiptoe along the dark hallway, pausing at every creak to make sure I haven't woken her up. Under her door is still dark. I take another step, and then pause. It takes me another three steps to make it to the bathroom door. My hand reaches the handle and just as I am about to turn it, I notice a faint light peeping under the threshold. It must be a night light left on to avoid tripping when entering the bathroom.

Despite the warm weather, at night the temperature drops precipitously and my teeth start chattering. I push the door and enter confidently, closing the door behind me to stay the cold. I swiftly fling the towel over the shower rod and remove my underwear, letting them fall to the floor. To my surprise the bathroom is warm and the chattering stops. The light I saw earlier is poised directly above my head over the sink and mirror. I can't see myself, though; the glass is covered with condensation. Emma must have used the shower before me. With the edge of my palm I wipe away some of the vapour so that I can see my face. I have some stubble; my eyes look tired and my face drawn. I tousle my hair over my forehead. I am pleased with the look: away with the dapper and strait-laced, in with the bohemian, hard-living artist look.

Without warning the door opens on my stark nakedness. Emma, dressed scantily, is about to enter the bathroom. I quickly stammer an apology and reach for my towel.

"Sorry, I should have knocked. I thought you were asleep." Her hand rises to her mouth to suppress an impetuous grin underscoring her customary cheerfulness, which does not desert her despite the awkwardness of the moment. "Obviously not."

I am still fumbling to find my words as I struggle to wrap the bunched-up towel around me. I am finally able to get it tucked in around my waist.

"Do you need to come in? I can wait." I attempt to edge out the door.

She blocks my egress by slowly pulling the door to. "No, that's all right, I will use Lijsbeth's bathroom."

As I hear her padding away I let the towel drop and this time secure the latch on the door. I am suffused with embarrassment. Yet, Emma did not seem all that fazed by the experience; yet another facet of my German reserve as opposed to the carefree attitude here in Holland, at least in my limited experience.

After a few minutes of resting on the edge of the bath I regain my composure and resume my ablutions. As I shower I can't deny that, despite my innate embarrassment, I was excited by the encounter. Still, propriety trumps my inward desire and I resolve to stop by her bedroom and apologise for my forgetfulness in failing to latch the door.

As I enter the hallway I find that her door is now ajar and her light is on. I knock softly. At her invitation to enter, I slip my head demurely through and notice that she is lying on top of the duvet, calmly reading a magazine. She is smiling at my discomfiture.

"I just wanted to apologise for not latching the door. I should have been more careful. I thought you were asleep."

"That's all right."

I am uncertain of what other conversation could ensue from this limited encounter; nevertheless I remain straddling between the hallway and her bedroom, feeling that I need to say more, searching for the final note before heading to bed.

"Would you like to come in? I am not that sleepy after all that exciting jazz."

I smile. I am hardly dressed demurely: cotton slacks, underwear, singlet and the damp towel flung over my shoulders. "I don't want to disturb."

She pats the right side of her wide double bed. I enter hesitantly and sit tentatively on the end of the bed, barely resting myself comfortably on the mattress's edge.

"So now that we are on more familiar terms, care to tell me a little more about yourself?"

"Like what?"

"Why did you decide to leave Germany?"

I sigh at the implication of the question. My rationale is so entwined in the events of the last few years: how I feel about Germany in general, my cultural and social disconnectedness, the current political status quo, my parents and their expectations. It's not really one reason but a multitude converging into a single emotion: disenchantment. But how do I crystallise it all into a conversation between incipient friends?

"I... I wouldn't know where... it's complicated. I haven't even discussed it with my sister... and she is the closest person to me. I am afraid that I would take up too much of your time."

Emma sets her magazine on the night table and turns on her side to fully face me. "I am not working tomorrow. The night is young." Her inviting smile sets me at my ease. I don't feel that she is intruding or asking merely out of curiosity or boredom, but that she genuinely wants to know.

I am not wearing any footwear, so I push myself up on top of the duvet and sit cross-legged, remaining at the edge of the bed. "I think that I have always had these thoughts, feelings of not really belonging. At first I put it down to the rebellion of youth, but as I started to get older, I noticed that my desire to take on another culture, another way of being, became ingrained and I couldn't pretend that it was merely a coming-of-age thing. It was like inwardly I was a person of the New World, America, and I was stuck in the Old World. Jazz was my first foray into the New World and then I followed it up by reading about the carefree, uninhibited culture of that world, and here I was stuck in some ancient world surrounded by prudish values and narrow attitudes, cultural strictures that belong in the Dark Ages, and just generally a world of darkness as opposed to a world of light." I pause and study her face. "I am probably boring you."

"On the contrary – after the jazz from earlier tonight, this is the second most interesting thing that I have heard in a long time. Please go on."

I must have talked for a long while, because at some point, it started to get cold and we both got under the duvet. At first at opposite ends, our feet at each other's heads, and as I grew progressively tired, my inhibition relaxed and I lay next to her.

It is early dawn. I find that I am lying under the duvet with my clothes on the floor. I instantly turn to my right: Emma is lying next to me, seemingly sound asleep – I needn't peek to discover her state of undress: I can feel her nakedness next to mine.

If it were possible for a body to be physically smiling, my state would describe it. I am shorn of anxiety and my future is bright. I arrived here twenty-four hours ago straddling a bleak past, worn with uncertainty and disenchantment, and a future full of hope and promise. Now I am standing fully in the latter. The past is gone. I am so enchanted with my future that I am thinking of adding 'van' to the middle of my name to Dutch-ify it. Friedrich van Becker. I like the sound of it. But Friedrich still sounds cumbersome, Germanic. Maybe Rich van Becker. That's it. That's my stage name. If I can get the job in the jazz club that Emma feels is certain.

The only sound in the room is the rain pattering on the shutters. I feel like getting up and playing. Strangely, the sounds swirling in my head are from Schubert's *Piano Sonata D. 958*. I would have expected Bach's *Sonata No. 17* if anything. That is morning music: sunny, brilliant with a cloudless blue sky and lush green valleys stretching out as far as the eyes can see. The *D. 958* is more introspective, evening, romantic. I let it play on in my head unopposed.

I gently clutch Emma's hand as we both remain lying on our backs. I am totally contented. Slowly we snuggle under the blanket and embrace each other in the warmth of the bed. We don't say anything; words are superfluous. Our sexual appetites fully quenched, we let our drained bodies succumb to fatigue and fall back to sleep.

The next time I awake it is morning. For the first time I notice the interior of her room. It is roughly the same size as mine, but with a three-door wardrobe and a chest of drawers instead of a desk. There is also a small dressing table with an oval mirror and a number of bottles and jars arrayed on top.

The walls, from what I can tell in the dull light, are painted a dark shade of pink or violet, and there are a number of framed prints of women dancing or frolicking near a lake or a pool. They seem to be oriental. I recall that Holland had historical ties with Indonesia dating back to colonial times. These prints could be related to that connection.

The shutters are wide open but the window is closed. I rise up on my elbows and glance around me. An adjoining door that I failed to notice in my room is now fully open. It must have been behind the wardrobe. I can smell breakfast downstairs and hear the clanging of dishes and plates.

I stagger naked to the bathroom and study my face in the mirror. There is a jauntiness about my being and I feel light-headed. I sit on the edge of the bath to steady myself. Fragments crowd my brain: the jazz; Emma inadvertently entering the bathroom and catching me in my total nakedness; me talking late into the night in her room; the awkward first moments of intimacy; the passionate lovemaking; waking up in an adjoining room. They appear like distorted images from a feverish brain. But I did wake up in her bed, and the adjoining door to my room is wide open.

In some uncanny way my desire to counterbalance Jac and Beth as the other 'madly-in-love' couple has come to pass. So I am elated in that, but the hastiness with which events have unfolded unbalances me. I feel like I have lost control of my destiny. Emotionally it feels like another lifetime ago, but it was just last night that I wondered if I could straddle Bremen and Utrecht. Now I have awakened in a status quo that makes me consider remoulding my identity to fit my new reality.

It is jarring, moreover (while I am loath to look a gift horse in the mouth), the swiftness with which the pieces have fallen into place and erected a wall between my past and future without allowing me to intellectually and emotionally assimilate the change. I am gliding on an emotional high. I need to slow down and reassess. I came here to complete my medical degree. That was my goal and my destiny. The jazz-playing was a spur-of-the-moment gesture to show off and I got carried away. I felt a need to be admired for the oldest reason in the world: the desire to impress and possess a beautiful woman; it is in our male genes. I recognise and accept that. But other than that I play for pleasure, not for gain. If I can translate that talent to pay my way it will be another lucky break to add to my current streak. But I am not about to turn pro. I just don't have that in my genes.

It is obvious to me that I let the pendulum swing too far in one direction, to the point of losing myself in the ecstasy of the moment. But I need to bring the pendulum back to centre and maintain the balance between my past and present. Otherwise I will lose myself, and I can't afford to do that. Not here, in a foreign country, after all.

There is a soft knock on the door. "Friedrich, Liebchen?"

"I am just going to be a few minutes."

"That's fine. I am downstairs. Breakfast is ready. We need to get to the open market before noon."

"Ah. What time is it?"

"Just past ten."

"OK."

I hear the creaks in the wooden floorboards as Emma steps away.

The pendulum slowly returns to centre. I start to feel more grounded. I attempt to stand up, wobble slightly, but I steady myself by clutching the side of the sink.

Rather than veer one way or the other, I need to find a way to forge a path to Bremen, treasuring that which is dear to me and fusing that which I have already gained here, albeit in a very short time.

I shower hastily and dress out of my duffel, the shirt and trousers creased but clean and smart nonetheless. I hang up the rest of my clothes and put away my belongings. I place a framed picture of my parents and Brigitte on the desk by the window. Instinctively I touch the glass and kiss my fingers.

I bound down the steps, and at the sight of Emma my heart leaps. I bask in her love. From the blush in her cream-coloured cheeks I can see that it is mutual. I continue down the steps until I reach her and we embrace passionately, letting a long kiss linger between us.

We separate and Emma points to the door. "I have made you a sandwich. No time for a sit-down breakfast."

We dash out the door and head out for our day as a couple.

The new semester begins in six weeks. During the past three months we have developed a routine where Emma teaches me Dutch every morning in a quasi-classroom setting. While we were at the market we procured an easel and a board and set them up in the opposite corner from the piano. Her fluency in both languages smooths my way in overcoming the syntactical and grammatical hurdles, thereby easing my learning curve. Nevertheless, during the first weeks Dutch sounded foreign, harsh and guttural, but that was the unfamiliarity and pronunciation. Once I got my head around the grammar and syntax the words became clearer.

We break for lunch, and in the afternoon we focus on medical studies. Emma is in her second semester of pre-med, aiming to specialise as a medical researcher working either for a pharmaceutical company or an academic institution. Having recently graduated pre-med, I help her navigate through the dense medical texts, some of which are also available in German.

By the time Christmas comes around I feel sufficiently confident that when the semester begins in February I will be able to follow the lectures. Exams and rounds may prove challenging, but the latter is not likely to happen till the second year, by which time I aim to be sufficiently conversant to participate.

When evening rolls around we break. Our relationship has evolved beyond the sexual ardour, embracing our studies, our mutual interest in art and music, and seeing eye to eye on many issues, amongst them political and social. We even talk about our bright future, after we both graduate.

The only dark cloud hanging over our lives is Emma's failure to question my Jewish fabrication. Odd that I should expect her to question my dishonesty when I could just as easily confess the truth. It was my lie after all. And there has been no shortage of sexually intimate moments for either of us to raise it in context.

But neither of us did. Instead I chose to carry the burden as a punishment for my sin – turning my back on my family and country – letting the unexpiated guilt spread like a virus, poisoning everything. Paradoxically I began to resent Emma for it, believing that she took perverse pleasure at my squirming whenever we were naked. At other times when my gloom lifted I reminded myself that neither is her father Jewish, so I am not that much of a contradiction after all.

But the levity didn't last. I began to curse myself for the German I detested: mirthless and morose. Truth be told, I told a convenient lie. Given Emma's light-hearted nature she probably passed it off as a silly one.

Nonetheless, once doubt sets in, life becomes complicated.

Jac and Beth returned from Rotterdam a month later than expected. Jac's father's health, routinely poor due to a lifetime of heavy smoking, had taken a turn for the worse, and he was now permanently confined to a hospital bed with no prognosis for a discharge. Beth confided to Emma one evening that he wasn't expected to live long as there was nothing that the doctors could do for him. That being the case, they decided to relocate from Utrecht to Rotterdam and resume their studies there. They stayed with us for two weeks before packing up and departing.

I was curious to see how I'd get along with Emma's close friends, before I became aware of their plans to leave. Beth was bubbly and easy to befriend, telling Emma that she had landed a catch in me: smart, talented and handsome to boot. Jac proved to be a more introverted character. I don't know if it was his father's condition or whether he just took an instant dislike to me – as had the group from the lunch hall – owing to my nationality, but whenever we were left alone we couldn't get beyond a few awkward words before the conversation dried up. One evening he got up to play the piano. He attempted an étude by Chopin to complement the mood: rain outside, fire crackling inside.

By the time he had trodden through the piece with heavy and blundering hands it was soaking inside and the piano looked good for firewood.

Both Emma and Beth applauded enthusiastically once he finished, despite wincing throughout while he was playing, and then hastily volunteered that I played the piano too.

"I am not very good. A bit rusty," I demurred, hoping to avoid alienating Jac any further.

Emma cackled loudly. "Nonsense, that's what you said the first time you played for me. Plus you have a steady engagement at Café Django."

Jac immediately blanched and turned to me with a surly look. "You play at Django's?"

I waved it off. "Background noise; dinner crowd. Nobody pays any attention."

Jac nonetheless remained seated at the piano, unwilling to surrender the bench. Finally Beth spoke up. "Come on, Jac, let him play jazz. He is not classical like you."

That haughty distinction got him off the piano. I stood up diffidently and sat down, appearing nervous and apprehensive. I decided to dissipate the tension that had unintentionally risen, settling on Tatum's *All the Things You Are*; a wonderfully complex piece of piano composition, melodic and melancholy – perfect for an evening like this.

I played for almost twenty minutes, stretching the piece out, dextrously weaving in elements of Chopin without losing the jazz flavour. I wound it down softly, letting the final notes permeate the room and disappear behind the crackling fire.

Beth spoke first. "You are phe-no-me-nal. Emma said you were great. Why don't you play professionally?"

Emma piped up. "Good, you ask him. Because I haven't been able to persuade him to go beyond playing the piano at a café, which in my opinion is wasting his talent."

I glanced over at Jac, hunched next to Beth, looking morose. "Playing music professionally is not the same as playing background: it requires constant rehearsing and coming up with new arrangements and material."

"OK. Same question: why don't you play professionally?"

"Maybe he is just not good enough. Stop nagging him," Jac muttered peevishly, downing the last of his wine. "Anyway, I am off to bed."

Two days later they were gone.

Emma apologised for his moodiness. I shrugged it off – whatever the reason, I didn't care. I will probably never see him again.

I was more interested in meeting Emma's parents, but did not push the subject other than casually asking if we ought to invite them over.

"I would rather they dropped in impromptu and I introduced you as a housemate, than bring you to their house. It would have a different connotation, if you take my meaning."

Maybe my suspicions were right.

A week later her parents did drop by on an unexpected visit. Edgar van Bergen stood taller than me with a mane of grey hair, a pointed chin, a narrow face, a slender physique and piercing grey eyes. He bore an air of seriousness and dourness about him that was intimidating. Emma's mother, Tessa, on the other hand, stood considerably shorter with sandy-blonde hair and a strikingly beautiful face and blue eyes. Her demeanour also contrasted with that of her husband. She had a buoyant personality, reminiscent of Beth's, and a nervous disposition that I found annoying and amusing at the same time: she would constantly interrupt during conversation or jump up and walk around the house, checking on cleanliness, crockery and groceries. Edgar, I found out, was a solicitor in a partnership with three other lawyers in Utrecht. He was quick to point out it was the leading civil litigation firm in the city. Tessa worked for a publisher translating German novels into Dutch, and occasionally worked on educational textbooks.

Initially they appeared comfortable in my presence, particularly as I graduated pre-med in Tessa's home town, Leipzig. The atmosphere cooled once they found out that Emma and I were living alone together.

Tessa, who was in the kitchen inspecting the cupboards, hastily returned to the living room. "What? What happened to Jac and Beth? I thought they were happy here." She had barely sat down before she began breathlessly firing off questions.

"Yes, Mum, they were. But Jac's father is in hospital, dying. So they decided to spend time in Rotterdam with his family."

"Have you advertised for someone else?" Edgar enquired in a gravelly voice.

"No need. Friedrich and I are managing very well." Emma gave me a loving look.

They could not fail to notice.

I excused myself, saying that I had to go to the bathroom, to give them time to assimilate to the change in their daughter's status. I was barely halfway up the stairs when the conversation reverted to Dutch – unbeknown to the Van Bergens, I was already fairly conversant in the language, thanks to Emma.

"You are living here alone with him?" Tessa exclaimed in an alarmed tone.

"Yes."

"Since when?" Edgar asked.

"Since some time ago," Emma replied warily.

"And you didn't think to tell us? What do you know about this boy? What do his parents do? Where are they from?" The barrage of questions continued unabated from Tessa, not giving her daughter a chance to respond.

Emma remained unfazed, though. "Why don't you ask him when he comes back down?"

I had only gone as far as the landing, but pretended to use the bathroom, then casually made my way downstairs.

As soon as Tessa saw me reappear she cleared her throat. Edgar leaned back and Tessa crossed her legs, trying to appear casual, but their stony-faced expressions revealed their concern and disapproval.

"Emma tells me that you are managing alone by yourselves. May I ask what you do?" Edgar questioned me rather sternly.

I sat down next to Emma on the couch and looked over at both parents, who were sitting in armchairs on either side of us. "I am studying to be a doctor and I work two nights a week at Café Django."

"What? As a waiter?" Edgar practically scoffed at the idea.

"No. I play the piano."

The atmosphere went up a notch.

"Well, then, play something for us."

No sense in repeating the rusty routine; these people were concerned about their daughter being taken advantage of by an unscrupulous student, and a German to boot. Time to ease the tension with Bach. I had never played anything classical in this house, so this was a first for both Emma and her parents.

I approached the piano confidently, raised and propped the lid, pushed the bench back slightly, adjusted my posture, pumped the pedals and launched into a profoundly intimate piece, perfect for a late afternoon. I played the first two movements of the *French Suite No. 1*: *Allemande* and *Courante*.

As the final notes faded in the room, the patter of the rain on the windows returned. I stood up and joined Emma on the couch. She was beaming with pride.

For the first time since he'd walked in, Edgar had a rictus of a smile on his face. He removed his black-framed glasses, pretended to clean them with his tie, then turned to me. "Don't tell me you are playing Bach at Café Django?"

"No. That would put the patrons to sleep."

We all managed a polite laugh, which quickly subsided.

"So, Friedrich, what does your father do?" Tessa was now relaxed in my presence again.

"He works for Benz in Bremen. Engineer."

"Mother?"

"Hausfrau."

"Very good." Edgar looked at his watch, then addressed us: "Why don't we take you both out to dinner? A proper restaurant."

I never thought that I would have much use for my years of practising the piano. I certainly never considered myself all that talented. Regardless, that gift had paved the way for me on a number of occasions since I had arrived in Utrecht.

Emma and I went upstairs to change. From the top of the landing I could hear Edgar tell his wife that I was a very talented pianist, obviously from a very good family.

We were barely inside our combined room when Emma pulled me to her and gave me a deep and passionate kiss. "They love you."

"I am relieved. When they first found out about our living arrangement, I thought I would be asked to leave."

I took out the clothes I wear to Django's – a pressed dark blue shirt and a pair of cream-coloured pants. I have an elegant camel-hair blazer that I purchased to match, and pulled on a pair of black half-boots and added a dash of cologne. Smart turnout. Emma put on an elegant black dress adorned with a string of pearls, draped a coat over her arm and gave me an approving nod.

When we returned downstairs her parents sized us up and, by their silence, gave their approval.

They took us to a restaurant that, judging by the menu prices, would blow our combined weekly budget. If not monthly, if I include the wine list. My family never dined this expensively, so I felt slightly uneasy in the company of these wealthy and prominent people. From the moment we walked in a number of patrons greeted Edgar and Tessa on the way to our table as we were ushered obsequiously by the maître d'.

No sooner were we seated than a group of smartly dressed men and women to our right waved to Emma's parents. They excused themselves and walked over to talk to them.

"That's the Vice Chancellor and his wife; and the guy next to him is the Mayor, with his current girlfriend," Emma leaned over to whisper to me while stealthily sliding her hand alongside my crotch.

I playfully pushed her hand away. "They might notice."

"Relax. I don't care about this place or those people. I find them boring."

The dinner went pleasantly, particularly as other diners constantly interrupted, so the focus was not on us. Towards the end I was curious to see what the bill would be for this outing. But the maître d' never brought a bill over. Edgar merely motioned with a wave of his hand and the maître d' nodded acquiescently. No doubt the firm had an account here.

Back in Bremen we don't even run a tab with the local grocer. Partly because of inflation – the morning's tab doubles by the afternoon – but also due to the high rate of bankruptcy; no business can afford to run a debt ledger: they would go broke.

Very little was said on the way back; we were all sated and pleasantly tired. As I disembarked from the car, Edgar leaned over to me from the driver's side. "Look after Emma. She is very dear to us."

Mildly tipsy, I took the liberty of placing my hand over his arm. "She is very dear to me too."

He merely nodded his head, but before pulling up the window added, "If you have any problems at the university, let me know."

I immediately wondered whether he meant administratively, or whether Emma mentioned the incidents in the lunch hall and library.

We stood for a moment by the front door and watched their gleaming black car glide away into the dark and wet night. I couldn't help but notice the tri-pointed star on the grille's apex: Mercedes-Benz.

That night we made love with total abandon. I sensed that her parents' approval of me was a tacit factor in blessing our relationship. Needless to say, I felt relieved and pleased, but at the same time wary of what my fate would have been if they had disapproved. Sometimes the line that separates our fortune from our failure is thin and cuts both ways.

Since meeting Emma's parents and witnessing their social status I have been fretting about the imminent meeting between them and my parents over Christmas. Ironically a fortnight before mine are due to arrive I receive a letter from them. My heart starts pounding as I slit open the envelope. Happily Emma isn't around to witness my trepidation. As I hurriedly read the first paragraph my heart rate drops to normal and I fall back with relief on the kitchen chair. They aren't coming after all. Due to the increased production at the plant my father isn't able to get the time off. Despite my immediate sense of relief at this visit being forestalled, I am also dismayed: the cloud surrounding this issue will continue to hover over me till the summer, when they might be able to come.

Throughout the year my studies progress well. I follow the lectures in Dutch but take notes in German. Although my Dutch speech is halting in some instances I nonetheless make myself clearly understood. Other than the initial hostile encounters in the lunchroom and library, I have not met with any further display of animosity. My fellow students, who comprise other nationalities besides Dutch, befriend me openly and I have even made two close friends: a Frenchman and a Belgian; Jean-Paul and Bruno. To my delight when we study together they defer constantly to my notes and interpretations; they don't have the benefit of an Emma in their court.

We are now regularly invited to visit her parents on Friday night for dinner. It is inherently a Jewish tradition, but none of the ritual is performed: the blessing of the wine and bread, lighting the candles or saying a prayer. It is mutually agreed between Edgar and Tessa that they will not bring religious rites into their lives other than the perfunctory Friday-night meal and the celebration of Christmas with the tree, gifts and lunch. Christ is never mentioned.

I complete the year with excellent grades in all subjects. I am thinking of suggesting to Emma that we travel to Bremen to meet my parents. But I am conscious of the increasingly strident anti-Semitic rhetoric and, more alarmingly, the sporadic acts of harassment and violence against Jews in Germany. I don't for a moment believe that there is any threat to Emma. She is Dutch and half Jewish. But her awareness of her ancestry will make her presence in Germany very uncomfortable for her. I don't even know what my parents' reaction will be to her being half Jewish. We don't know anyone Jewish in Bremen, half or otherwise.

With the coming of the New Year, 1936, Germany is sweeping all this darkness away. As a precursor to the hosting of the Olympic Games the country is putting on a new and resplendent face to the world. The virulent rhetoric is wound down; the vituperative posters are stripped off the walls and the welcome mat is laid out for all peoples.

This I learn from Johann Ziegler, whom I have written to in order to test the waters. His latest letter, which arrived just at the close of the first semester of my second year, radiated with hope. His family, who felt threatened, denigrated and harassed, are now treated as equals. The pace of persecution has abated. But despite their relief at this turn of events, Johann's father believes that the hiatus is temporary. Once the Olympic participants and public have left Berlin, the persecution will resume with greater gusto.

In anticipation of this return of anti-Semitism, Johann's father has applied for a teaching post in Canada and been accepted to a university in Montreal. They are leaving, while they are still allowed to leave and take their possessions and assets. Other Jewish families are opting to stay, believing that Hitler and his minions have only exploited the anti-Semitism frenzy for as long as it served their political ends. Now that Hitler is firmly in power, Germany is resurgent and the Olympics are being held in Berlin, there is a very real chance that the future will be free of any harassment of non-Aryans or those opposed to the political creed – communists, socialists and such – or those thought of as morally degenerate (homosexuals) or socially inferior (Jews and Gypsies). In short, the Nazi vernacular basket is 'Untermensch', or 'subhuman'.

I don't share my correspondence with Emma. I read it and write back to Johann in secret. When I finish reading his last letter I mull it over. I agree with Johann's father. Hitler is an opportunist. He is keen to present a clean and vibrant Germany to the world, not a nation that torments ethnicities that the Nazi Party targets as 'enemies of the people'. He also basks in pageantry and thrives on idolatry, and once the

Olympic torch leaves Berlin he will need a new momentum to stir the masses. Anti-Semitism is a popular rabble-rouser, and so is flexing Germany's muscles to annex territories for resources to power the country's military might. Plus there is the ever-rankling humiliation of Germany by the British and French in World War I that needs to be avenged. Hitler the opportunist is certain to exploit this in order to galvanise the masses to war. This I have suspected from the outset and now, more than ever, I believe that it is his ultimate goal. Whatever fire he is able to ignite to achieve that aim, he will: anti-Semitism, revenge, annexation of territories lost in World War I.

I personally believe that Hitler is not such a patriot as he makes himself out to be; his taste for vengeance is a personal vendetta that harkens back to some injustice long lost in the vestiges of his youth. Given that propensity it is only a matter of time before those in the upper echelons realise that his goals are personal and not public and the tide turns against him. The problem is time. How long? The longer it takes for that realisation to sink in, the harder and costlier it will be to get rid of him. He is already surrounding himself with a gallant core of fanatics, the SS. Any honourable Wehrmacht officer of the old school will find himself dead if he chooses to oppose the almighty Führer.

I write back to Johann telling him my thoughts and make him promise to stay in touch once his family get to Montreal.

Semester two is more gruelling than the last one. There are rounds at the teaching hospital, on top of the lectures and the heavy study load. Emma and I don't find time for each other until the weekend. During one visit to her parents' I doze off after dinner. Emma apologises for my tiredness and explains that doing my rounds, attending lectures and studying is taking its toll. She also explains that I am playing three nights at Django's now to supplement my income. When I come to, Edgar pours me a brandy snifter and asks whether I would prefer playing at a posh restaurant.

"They don't have a pianist over at La Scala. I know the owner; if you like I can mention you to him. It is a very elegant establishment, with a wealthy clientele. I am sure that they would be interested, and that they would be willing to pay better." His eyebrows shoot up enticingly.

I think on it for a moment. I like the proposal, but I am uncertain as to whether I want to be in Edgar's debt. So I don't reply immediately. When he steps away to light his cigar I mention my reservation to Emma.

"My father is not like that. He will do you a favour, but he won't hold it over you; either he likes you and wants to help you, or he just ignores you," she reassures me.

As we are leaving, I peck Tessa on the cheek and thank her for dinner. I look over at Edgar, who is standing by the door. "If it's no trouble, I would like to play at La Scala."

Edgar nods sombrely. "No trouble."

Partway through the year my parents write to say that they won't be coming over in the summer; with the Olympics about to take place in August they are keen to stay in Germany. I don't press the issue. I write back to say that if they don't come for Christmas, I will be coming to visit with my friend. I don't reveal too many details in case Emma decides against coming.

Emma is off to work half-days in admissions. I am alone at home. I wait for the post to see if there is a letter from Johann. There is, and the stamp is Canadian and the address on the back flap is in Montreal. I am overjoyed that the Zieglers are safe but sad to lose my contact in Germany. I can't have this kind of dialogue with my parents or even Brigitte. They would wonder why I am curious about the fate of the Jews.

As I read through Johann's letter I learn of a new contact in Germany: Johann's sister, Margret Huber. Her husband is Catholic and they have a son. The Hubers believe they are safe from Hitler's sword.

I write to both: Johann and Margret. I remember her vaguely from when she came by the house that I shared with her brother, Martin and Franz. She was rather frail-looking, with a roundish face, black wavy hair and a grating, nasal voice. I didn't take to her on first impression, but I am grateful for the contact. I explain to Margret my predicament and ask whether she thinks it would be safe to travel in Germany post the Olympics.

I despaired of hearing from her and feared that my letter had either gone awry or fallen into the wrong hands. But a response arrives almost four months later. The fate of the Jews, as rightly anticipated by the elder Ziegler, has deteriorated after the Olympics. Laws are now being enacted that forbid Jewish doctors to treat non-Jews and Jewish lawyers to appear before the court, unless they are accompanied by Aryan lawyers. Margret, absent the sound of her voice, is quite pleasant in her writing, and warns Emma and me against travelling in Germany as two single people. If we were to marry, then Emma would be classified as a non-Jew in her travel documents. But that too could change. Either way, caution is in order.

Whatever hope I had for Germany evolving into an openly welcoming and friendly nation in the aftermath of the Olympics fades with the letter from Margret. I want to visit my family, it's coming up on two years since I last saw them, but I want them to meet Emma too, whom I consider, despite my reservations, to be my future wife and hopefully the mother of my children.

Summer comes and goes without a letter from home. They have already written to say that they are staying put over the summer, but I am increasingly concerned about the silence – I know my parents' predilection for clamming up in times of anger, but I am still hoping that they will make the trip out to Utrecht for Christmas. This longing is despite my lingering misgivings about them meeting the Van Bergens.

Inwardly I have found a way to straddle my new home and my love for my family, despite disliking where they live. In the first months I struggled to separate the two, but I have since discovered within myself a way to reconcile my Germanic self as distinct from the abhorrent new regime under Hitler's tutelage by sassily crafting a fusion style of playing, that is at once jazz-like but not grounded in blues, as is the case of the American Negro, whose roots are African, but classical. I see myself in the vein of classicists like Carl Maria von Weber, or Schubert's lieder, where folk music elements are subtly interwoven into their compositions.

Sadly for Germans like me, Hitler has come to symbolise the resurgent Germany, more so for appending the 'National' to his party nomenclature. But I don't see it that way – certainly from the safety of Utrecht I can make that statement boldly. Does it make me a coward? No. It simply makes Hitler a bully and a villain. I am certain that within the Germany that I knew pre-Hitler, there are many like me who find his rule of tyranny abhorrent and untenable and not fitting within the identity that we have come to represent: a nation of culture, philosophy, science and music. These attributes are in total conflict and contrast with the alienation and persecution of those differing from the mainstream, the elevation of Aryan to a national status to the exclusion of all others, and the nascent hostility and aggression towards our neighbours.

To my way of thinking, Hitler is not the face of the new Germany. His is a face of rage and hatred that is festering on our misfortune post World War I, not unlike an opportunistic disease. Preying on those that are manifestly vulnerable: the impoverished, the unemployed and those who have lost hope. He has exploited those vulnerabilities to his own end by appealing to the basest element that is within all of us: self-preservation. And fear. And greed. Not just Germans, but humans in general.

So I am exiled. Despite that state I have found a way to retain my love of home and country and exclude the darkness that is engulfing it, treating it as a pestilence that one day will be eradicated. But how many will die before that happens, I don't know.

My reason for disquietude despite my reconciling my own dilemma is the question of whether the Hitler epidemic has infected my parents and Brigitte. They are uncritical and law-abiding to a fault, and can be easily manipulated despite their inherent decency.

But them not visiting me for two years, despite their initial excitement at the prospect of coming to Utrecht, and the fact that they have not written in a while, has me worried. Do they believe now that by choosing to study and live in Utrecht I have become unpatriotic? I would be loath to think so. But Hitler is charismatic and mesmerising, and if he has managed to save Germany from the abyss, some, if not most, will see him as a saviour, not as a virus.

I decide to sit down and write a short but candid letter to my sister.

Dear Brigitte,

How are you, my dear sister? I have not set eyes on you since I left Bremen in 1934, so it is now almost two years since we have had a chance to talk and laugh like we used to.

My studies are going well, and next year, I will be two years away from becoming a doctor – Father's wish at last!

But I am not sure that I will be coming home to Bremen and opening a medical practice, or working at Benz as the plant medic.

I am now living with a wonderful and beautiful Dutchwoman, whose mother is German, from Leipzig. Her name is Emma.

I wanted you all to meet her and become friendly as I am certain that once I graduate and start to practise, we will get married – so she will become family too.

Emma is half Jewish, and I am concerned about coming to Bremen. What is the situation in Germany now that the 'friendliness' of the Olympics is over?

I understand from Father's last letters that he is working good hours and that his pay is up. Also, the mark has stabilised and their retirement account should be looking healthier.

Write to me as soon as you can. I would like to visit before I start my final year in 1938.

Your loving brother,
Friedrich

Brigitte's reply is swift to arrive. Emma brings it in and wants me to read it out loud to her. I have no choice. I slit open the flap and read the letter with increasing consternation.

Dear Friedrich,

So wonderful to hear from you – Mother and Father never tell me anything, other than "Find a boyfriend and get married or you will end up old and lonely!"

If they are annoyed with me, they are very angry and disappointed with you. Mother has been stirring the pot by telling Father that you deliberately misled them about your specialisation in Holland. They made some enquiries and found out about the extra four years that you have to take in order to become a doctor.

You never know with them – tight-lipped and grumpy, as you know – but I am fairly certain that they feel betrayed, and that you relied on their financial and moral support and then decided to study and live overseas.

The situation in Germany is much better now: people are hopeful, there are many more jobs, and pride in Germany as a nation is back. Other than the fanatical Nazis nobody pays much attention to Hitler's bombastic speeches. They are long, repetitive and boring. But they put up with him because nobody wants to be hungry and homeless again. And if it means that the Jews take the blame, so be it.

I wouldn't dream of coming home with a Jew; Mother used to work for one and she and Father both blame his meanness for her arthritis. He was one of those bearded Jews with a black hat who run sweatshops.

It is best if you stay in Utrecht with your friend and only come home by yourself. If you stay for a few years Mother and Father will forgive you for your lies and the money you owe them; you are still their son and they love you, they are just upset and hurt. I am sure that you understand.

Bringing a Jewess home would not be welcome.

With love,
Brigitte

I sit, stunned and numb. I daren't raise my eyes to Emma, who has been sitting next to me on the couch, lovingly stroking my hair, longing to hear warm and inviting words from home. Instead an icy cold descends on us. I feel her hand gradually withdraw, in tune with the letter, until she is seated as far back from me as the couch will allow. I steal a sideways glance at her: her expression is the same as mine, shocked and numb, but also deeply hurt. She is on the verge of crying.

I place the letter on the table, holding it by a corner as though it's tainted, and wordlessly lean back on the couch. After a minute or so, Emma gets up and slips on her warm coat by the door and leaves the house. Not a word or a look has been exchanged between us.

I feel that I need to get up and stop her; say something. But I don't know how to respond to these injurious and hurtful statements. I know that Brigitte is not malicious, which makes it all the more difficult for me to comprehend the insensitivity that is apparent in her letter. Is it impulsivity? Plain churlishness? Or just stupidity?

Even if she believes in what she is writing, it is not like Brigitte to be mean to anyone. She must see her comments as no more than offhanded and flippant. Like the one about the caretaker at school – "We couldn't fit on the same bed together" – an oblique way to refer to his obesity. Brigitte is honest and direct. I can't believe that she has fallen under Hitler's spell; she is not that gullible. I instantly take heart from that realisation, reinforced by her reference to Hitler's speeches: *long, repetitive and boring*. Similarly, she is merely being forthright about the status of the Jews in Germany.

I try to view this damaging episode in a different light: it is far better that it came in a letter and can be assimilated as such, than for Emma and me to be in Bremen and be assaulted verbally or physically, or even worse; sticks and stones and all that nonsense.

Of course, I am glossing over the lie that I told over two years ago: that I am half Jewish. Brigitte's letter makes it abundantly clear that the only Jewish person my family know is the owner of the sweatshop where our mother worked. So that is something I must answer for – if I ever get the chance.

I look over anxiously at the dining table stacked with books: I need to review a medical text and take notes on cardiopulmonary disease, but in my current state of mind I can't even focus on ingrowing toenails. So I get up and sit at the piano. I need a reflective and healing piece, and I dredge my mind for a composition. I come up with Monk's *'Round Midnight*.

I extend the piece by improvising for around thirty minutes, not realising that Emma has returned in the interim and sat down on the couch behind me. I am about to launch into another Monk composition when I hear her fidget.

I turn around slowly, not daring to face her: I am too ashamed and embarrassed. But I feel that I have to take the cue.

"Look, Emma, Brigitte makes flippant comments about everyone; there is nothing malicious in what she says."

When I dare to look up, Emma is red in the face and her eyes are puffed. She has been crying.

"It is just her way of expression. We are very different in that way. What she says is true, about the situation in Germany; she is certainly not responsible for that."

Silence.

"I will give you an example: at home, when I started to play jazz instead of classical music, I found a monkey mask on my pillow."

I finally break the ice. Emma giggles at that.

"I mean, how childish and silly is that?"

The mood has altered, but Emma turns serious again. "Tell me about the obvious fabrication: you being half Jewish."

I shake my head. I can't explain such an unnecessary lie. All I can think to say is, "I wanted a simple and straightforward answer for being here. That came to mind as an obvious one."

"Really? What, you thought you would be rejected by the university if you just said that you were a conscientious objector to Nazism? On the contrary, you would have been welcomed with open arms. We have many Germans, Jews and non, who are teaching and studying here because of the politics in Germany. You are not unique in that."

"You are right. It was stupid."

"Stupid is right. Good thing I never pushed it with my parents."

I merely nod my head.

"I hope you didn't think that telling me you were half Jewish would have made a difference with me. I liked you the instant I saw you lost by the signpost. And my family couldn't care less: my father is not Jewish. We don't care about those things."

I remain silent for a moment, absorbing the obvious truth in what she is saying. "I can't think of what to say, other than that I felt insecure."

"Felt insecure?" Emma sits up, looking bewildered.

"I had never been out of Germany, other than for a short holiday to Austria. I wanted to fit in. I wanted you to like me."

"So you lied to me?"

"Emma. This may come as a surprise to you, but before you I had never even had a steady girlfriend. I left home at nineteen to study. Now I am going on twenty-six. That sums up my life, pretty much. I was trying to impress, I guess."

Emma appears to reflect on my candid confession; then, "What was that piece you just played?"

I turn to look at the piano as though the answer is there. "*'Round Midnight.*"

She nods her head in appreciation. After a minute of silence, she says, "Friedrich, I am going to have to think about all this. We are a couple, yet your family can't be part of our lives. It is something that I never considered."

"I understand. But I also believe that Germany will change. My parents are not bad people. I have never heard them say anything malicious about anybody, let alone Jews, other than the snide remark about my mother's boss. But I also heard my father call his factory manager a penny-pinching Bavarian slave driver, when they increased his hours and halved his pay. So I believe that the comment about Jews was made in the same vein."

"Not the same."

"Well, that's because of the political backdrop. But if you ignore that, it's just a comment that they—"

"But Friedrich, Liebchen, we can't ignore the politics. It's clear from your sister's letter."

"For now."

"For now. That's something that I have to come to grips with."

I am back to being called Liebchen again. I take a deep breath and move from the piano to the dining room and delve into the textbooks.

"You are not just going to sweep all this under the carpet and get on with your studies, are you?"

I turn around apprehensively. "What more is there for me to say?"

"Well, I would like you to take a stand. Write your sister and family a letter. Tell them about us: our life together, our reactions to your sister's insensitive and hurtful comments. How we are planning to have a future together. And I want to see the reply, when it comes."

The battle lines are drawn.

I pull a sheet from the pad in front of me and start writing.

Dear Brigitte,

I was pleased to get your letter, but less so once I started to read it.
Emma was sitting next to me and I read it out loud.
I know that the comments you make are not made with malice, but with a certain flippancy that nevertheless can cause offence. This was a case in point. Emma and I have been living together as a couple for two years. Once I graduate we intend to build a life together. I know that is something that you want for yourself, and I hope that you will find it one day. I know that, as my dear sister, you mean the best for us and will love and accept Emma as my wife.

Our parents are old-fashioned and their ideas are sometimes antiquated, and they don't understand the things that we do and think. But I know that you understand me and we have always had a strong bond as brother and sister.

One day the political climate in Germany will change. And I intend to come and visit with Emma and hopefully as a couple.
I expect you to welcome us as one.
Before I left you cleverly explained my decision to study in Utrecht to our parents and helped us avoid a squabble.
Please exercise your diplomatic gift again.

Love from Emma and Friedrich.

We both sign it.

I don't get any studies done that afternoon or evening. Instead we go out to dinner and come home late, lie in the bath together and then make passionate love. The next morning I wake up early, shower and go out to mail the letter.

Except I never do. I tear it up and place it in a rubbish bin a block away from where we live.

I just do not have the heart to force the issue, with the political climate in Germany being what it is. I am counting on Hitler and the Nazis being dispatched from power and history soon and Germany restored to sanity. And when that happens Emma and I will simply travel to Bremen together as a couple.

I don't return home right away. I stroll around for a while, pondering my actions. Here I am, besmirching Hitler as nothing more than a crass opportunist. Am I any better? Granted, I am not advocating disenfranchisement or persecution. But is that only because there is no angle to them that benefits me? I came here to escape the upheavals in Germany, the poisonous and appalling political climate, the lack of opportunity and jobs. I have been welcomed into a loving and caring family. But I won't fight for the woman I love. Why?

I had presumed to bridge Bremen and Utrecht, but as this last encounter proves, I haven't. First I did not want my parents to visit, owing to their pedestrian, middle-class views; now, I don't want to rankle my family because of the Jewish issue. I am a coward, that's basically it. There's no better way to characterise my action in not mailing the letter. What is my next step? Abandon Utrecht and return to Bremen now that Germany is on the rise? What if Germany experiences another downfall? Return to Utrecht?

I head back home to find Emma preparing an early dinner.

"How did it go?"

"Fine."

"You were gone for a while."

"I mailed the letter outside the post office, rather than from a box. Safer and quicker."

I get a reassuring smile.

I hope that we don't have an intimate evening; my demeanour would crack under my lies and cowardly behaviour. After dinner I insist that I have to have certain texts read by Monday, which only leaves me with tonight. Emma doesn't object and reclines on the sofa with a book.

I stack up a number of medical textbooks as a shield and start writing a letter to Martin Keller in Bologna. He wrote to me while I was still in Bremen, and I kept his address. Of my three former housemates, he is the one I would consider to be a close friend. Perhaps it's because his family are of the same station as my own, while Franz's and Johann's are of the upper crust: banking and academic. The Kellers have done well, though, and own a large granary, as a result of which they are independently wealthy.

I describe my situation as candidly as I can without ascribing any judgement to my behaviour. I go on to explain my predicament and being pushed to make a choice, and ask his advice.

Two weeks later a reply arrives. Fortunately I get the mail before Emma comes home from her job at the university, otherwise she would want to know what Martin has to say; she knows about him from my stories about Leipzig.

Dear Freddie,

It was quite a thrill to get your letter – almost made me forgo my evening capers, but not quite!

I nearly gave up on ever hearing from you, it's been so long. But surprise, surprise, there you were, and writing from Utrecht, no less. Not that I was too surprised about that; I knew that that was where you were headed, but I thought that you would have had enough of Holland and gone on to Münster, and maybe, even better, decided to come to Bologna.

I had to read your letter twice in order to grasp the essence of what advice you were seeking from me.

Look, I am not one to beat about the bush; you have got yourself into a tight spot. You and Emma in Bremen is not a good idea. But you need to return at some point to make peace with your parents and sister. You only have the one family, like them or hate them!

The problem with going home is that Mr Adolf is thirsting for war. People our age will be drafted and thrown into some crazy war with the Bolsheviks. It is Der Führer's *obsession, not mine or yours. And quite frankly I am enjoying life too much to end up crippled or dead on some battlefront for the cuckoo corporal.*

But here is the thing: if you graduate in Utrecht and return to Germany, you can get yourself assigned to an elite unit, like the SS, as a medic. You will see no action and stay in Germany. A relative of mine told me that they will even pay your debts if you have any, plus you get a top salary to start. They are plainly desperate for qualified anything – the majority of them are just street thugs.

I am not in the same boat as you, so I am staying put in Bologna. Mr Adolf can keep his money; I have got plenty of my own.

Advice? If I were you, I would take that offer. There is nothing to stop you from leaving after a year or two of service, after which you return to Utrecht debt free, and you've made peace with the folks in Bremen. Everyone is happy.

If you decide to go home and then return to Utrecht, do make a side trip to Bologna. I would love to see you. And I have got some bellisime *Italian women who are keen to* amore *you.*

Incidentally, I forgot to ask, how are your studies in Dutch coming along? If you are still there and in your third year, you must be doing all right. Italian is not that hard; I learned a lot from pillow talk.

Your friend always,
Martin

I feel better already for reading Martin's letter. Some part of me wishes I had gone with him to Bologna. I miss him. For one thing, he makes me laugh. He is irreverent, while I am overly serious; while I tend to worry, he takes life one day at a time; where I treat relationships as serious affairs, he sees them as one-night stands. In a way Bologna is perfect for him; he has the Italian joie de vivre and penchant for taking life easy. Martin can afford to slack off and end up back home in the family business, without ever becoming a doctor. I can't. If I don't graduate I'll end up being a male nurse and supplementing my income playing jazz. Hardly better off than my father.

It's not that I begrudge Martin his good fortune, though in some ways I envy him for not having had to run after his mother with his father's pay packet to buy groceries before inflation ate up the currency. It's just that I can't afford to be him.

The year progresses uneventfully with no news from home. I don't expect any, but I am constantly on the lookout for a letter nonetheless, in the event that Brigitte or my parents decide to write. But my parents are angry and disappointed and Brigitte has had her say; there is nothing more to add, save for the fact that I have never replied to her letter.

If a wayward letter does arrive and Emma notices it, and it mentions not hearing from me since the last letter from Brigitte, I could always lie and say that my letter must have been intercepted or lost. Once you get on the path of lying it gets easier to find your way. I see my prevarication as none too wicked, more an act of self-preservation. I have a little over a year to graduate, and I don't need to rock the boat. I am thinking more seriously about discharging my tuition, both Leipzig and Utrecht, courtesy of the SS. It is an incentive to return and make peace with my parents. Paying them back for four years of Leipzig will go a long way towards achieving that goal. Plus, if I take a job in Germany, that will help heal any feelings of betrayal and disappointment.

The idea of working for the SS makes me feel wretched in every way: it is a stab in the back to my adopted family, the Van Bergens; it is the ultimate betrayal of Emma; it flies in the face of every value I have ever espoused. It is, after all, the reason I am in Utrecht.

So it is a grave dilemma. I need to make amends back home and I need to keep a path to Utrecht open. So whom do I betray? That is not a question that I can pose to anyone, not even Martin. It is my own inner battle between my sense of self-preservation and appeasing both the Van Bergens and the Beckers. Except the two are irreconcilable. But if I were to write down the advantages and disadvantages of each, returning to Germany would stack up more favourably. And, like Martin says, I don't need to serve but the two years – if I can stand it that long – and then return to Utrecht. If war breaks out in the interim, well, as they say, my goose is cooked. I will need to desert and flee to Utrecht.

I almost chuckle at the absurdity of it all. Arriving in Utrecht dressed in an SS uniform. The confrontation in the lunchroom would be mild in comparison.

Edgar, good to his word, arranged for me to play at La Scala. The schedule is less gruelling; I play two noontime sets and one dinner. As promised, the pay is far better and the crowd more appreciative, judging by the tips that will help me disburse some of my Utrecht tuition. The noon sessions are over the weekend. In a bizarre sort of way I am grateful to get away from Emma. I feel like I reek of lies and it's best that we don't spend too much intimate time together. I apologise for leaving the house at eleven and returning at six on both days.

As I wrestle with my dilemma, I decide that the smoothest path for me is not to betray either. I don't need to tell Emma that I am joining the SS. I merely have to say that I am going home to visit. I know she won't want to come. By the time I leave Utrecht I will have been gone from Bremen for four years. If I spend just two years away from Emma and the Van Bergens it will countervail the time I spent away from Bremen. I will write and stay in touch – if I can.

So my mind is made up. In the autumn of 1938 I will make the excuse that I need to visit Bremen for Christmas.

Emma has asked once or twice about a reply from Brigitte. But then she forgot about it. She appears to have reconciled herself to the fact that until attitudes change in Germany she may never get to meet my family.

We spend Christmas 1937 with the Van Bergens. Edgar and Tessa treat us to a holiday in Amsterdam and I get to meet Emma's brother, who is married and lives in London. Jan van Bergen does not bear the same striking looks as his sister. He stands as tall as his father, with intense, dark eyes and a chubby, pasty face. His light brown hair is already receding at the relatively young age of thirty-one. His wife Romy is pretty in a homely sort of way, with a cheerful manner and a tendency, like her mother-in-law, to persistently ask questions until she gets the answer she wants. But that is not her least attractive quality; rather, it is her bluntness that makes Tessa appear discreet by comparison.

Jan is the commercial attaché at the Dutch Embassy in London, while Romy manages an art gallery just off Piccadilly Circus, on Shaftesbury Avenue. Emma reveals to me confidentially that Romy's family is originally Dutch Afrikaner, and extremely wealthy, something to do with diamonds and South African mines. I suspect that running an art gallery in London is a way for her to keep busy whilst Jan manages trade relations between Amsterdam and London, rather than a means to keep a roof over their heads.

We meet at a fashionable hotel for lunch.

As soon as we sit down, Romy turns to me. "So Emma tells me that you are from Bremen. German, right?"

I nod politely. What else can I say?

"I hope you are not like those crazy people that we hear about on the news?"

Even Tessa is embarrassed. "Romy! Please. We want to have a nice, quiet lunch."

Romy is astounded. "What? I asked him a reasonable question. What is your name, Friedrich? Listen, Friedrich, you know that Tessa is Jewish, right?"

Immediately I see Edgar and Jan cringe at the implication. If Jan is an experienced diplomat, it would appear that none of his skills have washed off on his wife.

I don't answer the last question. I notice, though, that Emma, seated diagonally from me, is giggling, and twirling her index finger to indicate to me that Romy is nuts.

I remain quiet. But that doesn't faze Romy in the least.

"So, Friedrich, how do you propose to introduce Emma to your family?"

I surreptitiously glance over at Emma. She shakes her head vigorously. I am assuming that the answer will be embarrassing for everyone at the table. We – that is, Emma's parents and I – have been keeping a lid on this topic to avoid having to discuss a subject that is fraught with difficulty. Obviously her parents are firmly opposed to Emma travelling to Germany, her marital status notwithstanding. I don't perceive a problem. Despite the letter from Brigitte and the oblique warning from Martin, I still remember Germany, and more specifically Bremen, as I left it in 1934. I refuse to believe that anyone, least of all my family, will act inimically towards Emma.

"Well, I have suggested that we visit. But they" – I sweep my hand around the table to take in Emma and her parents – "feel that now would not be a prudent time to go."

Romy is jeering, realising she has opened up a painful subject. "Prudent time to go? I would say not! Emma will be arrested. And so will you for consorting with a Jewess. Don't you see that?"

I have foolishly fallen into the trap that this wily woman has set for me. I stare at the ground. Not unexpectedly, I have lost my appetite. Thankfully a waiter approaches, and we all turn our attention to him, to divert the conversation to something ordinary.

As soon as he leaves the table with our orders the focus is back on me. I feel like a blowtorch has been turned on me.

"May I ask, what is your last name?" Romy is back on the warpath.

"Becker," Emma replies for me.

"Becker? Hmm. Do you have any Jews in your family?"

I shake my head meekly.

"Do you know any Jews in Germany?"

I shake my head again.

No one is throwing me a lifeline. I start to feel like Romy is asking the awkward questions that Emma's parents meant to ask, but out of deference to Emma and me, refrained from doing so. The difference is that Edgar and Tessa want answers out of concern for their daughter, whereas Romy is interrogating me out of sadistic pleasure.

"So, Herr Becker, what is your stance on this issue, the Nazi Party going after the Jews in Germany?"

I clear my throat and look up humbly. "The reason I came to Utrecht in the first place is that I am opposed to the Nazis. Does that answer your question?"

"Maybe, maybe. But that doesn't quite answer it. Who knows why you came to Utrecht? But the reality is that you are here now and living with a Jewess. That is officially a crime where you come from. Would you have made the same choice in Germany is what I am asking?"

Romy is eyeing me sternly. But so are Edgar and Tessa. Emma's face is averted from me. No succour there.

I have no answer for that.

"So, Friedrich, if that is a crime in Germany, how do you propose to introduce Emma to your parents?"

I have no answer for that either. I remain quiet. Romy looks over at Emma and reverts to Dutch. I can understand fully what she is saying. Halfway through their discussion, Tessa alerts Romy to the fact that I am conversant in Dutch.

"Well, I haven't said anything rude or untrue. I am telling Emma that she needs to think of her future. There is no place for her in Germany, or with your family. So the truth is, if you decide to leave tomorrow – nostalgia, whatever – Emma is stuck."

The waiter has since brought our entrées. I haven't touched mine. I feel totally humiliated.

Romy is not done yet. "Have you made plans? Marriage? Children?" She is looking from me to Emma for an answer.

My self-esteem is battered, but I feel that I need to answer. "Yes, we have made plans once I graduate," I reply weakly.

"And when will that be?"

"This coming year."

"Well, congratulations. So you become a doctor. And then?"

Finally someone puts a stop to my humiliation, but it is not Emma's parents, nor Emma herself, but Romy's husband, Jan. "Romy, I think you have said enough. Can't you see that you have totally disgraced the man?"

Romy bares her teeth and stares over at me. "Oh, come on, Germans are tough, look at how they are bullying everyone. Isn't that right, Friedrich?"

My sense of propriety is forcing me to stay and take the battering, but my self-respect is telling me that I ought to stand up, thank Emma's parents for lunch and leave the table. I am not going to eat, anyway. I look across at Emma to get a sign, an inkling of whether she feels the same. To my devastation her eyes are fixed on me, but the warmth and love that are normally there have been replaced by a look of hardness and suspicion.

I deserve that. Despite Romy's gruelling questions, I should have stood up better for us.

I reach for my glass of beer and take a sip. The others recover from the onslaught and start eating their meals. The conversation turns to mundane topics. I notice that Emma is nibbling at her entrée. I leave mine untouched.

The waiter clears the entrées and asks whether I would like something else. I merely shake my head. The same routine is repeated for the mains and dessert. No one seems to be disturbed by the fact that I am not eating.

About mid afternoon we leave the restaurant. Romy and Jan decide to take a taxi to their hotel.

"Well, Friedrich, it was nice meeting you. I hope that you look after Emma." Romy shakes my hand warmly, but I detect a glint of animosity in her eyes. This is a subtler reaction than that I encountered in the group at the lunch hall and library all those years ago, but in meanness it is equal. Then it was strangers, this time it is family.

Jan merely nods in my direction and they both turn to chat briefly with Edgar, Tessa and Emma. Eventually they hug and kiss, deftly avoiding me, and then flag down a taxi. As the taxi speeds away they wave warmly without actually looking in my direction, disappearing into the afternoon traffic.

I feel gutted.

Inside Edgar's Mercedes-Benz the silence is deafening. Finally Tessa turns around to me. "Friedrich, I noticed that you didn't eat anything. Weren't you hungry?"

"Sorry, no. I am feeling a bit queasy."

"You should have said something. You could have ordered soup, instead of meat or chicken. Or even grilled fish."

"That's all right. Really. I will eat at home tonight."

Back home, we enter the house and Emma heads straight up to bed without saying a word to me. I don't feel that I can mend this with some piano-playing. We are past that.

I follow her upstairs. The door to her room is closed. I enter mine. The adjoining door has been firmly closed too.

For the first time since I left Bremen I feel alone, frightened and lost. Then I had no emotional connection to anyone. I was grounded in my own sense of self; my own being; my identity and my home. Since then I have gone through a radical transformation. I am no longer a middle-class undergraduate from Bremen. I am a year away from becoming a doctor. I have made a life for myself with someone who has become near and dear to me; I am now firmly part of her family.

Except, the confrontation this afternoon has brought to the surface all that we have been avoiding since the troubles began in Germany. Ironically, Hitler was meant to quell the turmoil, revive the economy, reinvigorate the nation and by doing so restore Germany to pride and prosperity. He has done all that, but also by the victimisation of the Jews, the annexation of territories and his hostile speeches directed towards Germany's neighbours, he is alienating those of us who merely want to exist in a world that is not just Aryan.

I am just a person. I never thought of myself other than in terms of my societal status, my ambitions, my family and my dreams. Nowhere in that is there anything reflecting the path that Hitler is carving for Germany. Yet he has forced me, by his hostility, intransigence and persecution, to make a choice. I ran away because I was uncomfortable; now I am unwelcome. Paradoxically, he is driving me back to Germany.

I am confused. A few hours ago, I had a plan. I was going to become a doctor, return to Bremen for a year or two, have my loans discharged, come back to Utrecht and resume my life. Simple. But nothing is ever that simple.

Underneath that surface of naivety were bubbling unresolved issues that Romy has stoked into a fire to burn down my life. The bedroom door closing signifies an end to what has been the most wonderful relationship that I will perhaps ever know. But I can't blame everything on Hitler. I lied. I can't deny that. I never mailed that letter to Brigitte. I conducted a correspondence in secret with Johann and later with Martin. I learnt things that in a trusting relationship I ought to have shared with Emma.

But I didn't. Self-preservation? Cowardice? Shying away from facing problems in the hope that they would just go away? But they never do. They just crowd around the periphery of my life as so many ghosts that eventually take on a life of their own and ambush me. As happened today.

I have no one to blame but myself.

It is the flaw in my character. Bremen. Utrecht. I am still the same person; I really haven't learnt anything, even though I'm now a year away from graduating. Now my plans have been brought forward by a year. Looks like I will be graduating at my old alma mater, Leipzig.

I look up at the top of my wardrobe. There's the duffel and rucksack that I haven't laid eyes on since I unpacked my belongings and started my life in Utrecht; the life that has now been abruptly ended.

I take them both down and shake the dust off. I rest them on the bed and commence packing. I am not going to have room for everything; I have accumulated a great deal more than what I arrived with. So I walk back downstairs and look for a carton or another bag.

I re-enter my room with a box and a canvas bag. Emma is sitting on the bed. Her face is red, her eyes are puffed, and the little mascara that she put on for lunch is smeared down her cheeks.

"So, Becker, just pack your things and sneak out?"

I drop the box and bag on the floor and sit next to her on the bed. I am utterly devastated.

"You know, when I set eyes on you for the first time, I knew instinctively that I wanted to spend the rest of my life with you. I believed that you were the perfect man for me. Until now."

I remain speechless.

"Aren't you going to say something?"

"Nobody is perfect, Emma."

"I am listening."

"I am weak."

"So, things get tough or uncomfortable for you, you just run away, is that it?"

"No. That's not it. But I don't know how to fix this."

"Meaning what?"

"Emma, I have a family. I love them. And I don't know how to bridge the gap between my home and family here, and my family in Germany."

We remain silent for a while and then Emma asks the question that I had been hoping she never would.

"You know, Friedrich, the afternoon you went out to mail the letter to your sister. When you were gone for a while. Did you ever mail the letter?"

I don't answer.

"I thought so. May I ask why?"

I stay silent. Hearing myself tell the truth would hurt me more than hearing Emma do it. I just can't bear the pain of my weakness.

"Let me ask this in a different way: supposing we get married next year, become a family; you know, like we planned. Would you fight for your children, for me?"

I shake my head in desperation.

"Is that a no?"

"No. It is not. It's just that I never imagined myself in that predicament."

"I see. Tell me something else: if I had not come out just now to face you, would you have just left?"

No answer.

"I just refuse to believe that I misread you this badly. But apparently, I have. So what is the plan?"

"Well, I was going to visit my family in Bremen before starting next term. It's been three years. I'll tell them about us face to face, then come back and finish my final year." I am addicted to my lies; it's like an opiate that sates my weakness.

"Really? And you couldn't tell me this before leaving?"

"I was going to write a note."

"A note?!"

"I will only be gone for a few weeks over the New Year and then return."

Emma casts her eyes around the room. "From what I can see here you were packing your whole life to take with you."

"In a way."

"So you *were* leaving?"

"I was going to take a room at the dormitory, let things settle between us, and then, if you still want me back, return here."

"I don't understand."

I let my exasperation sink into my tone. "Emma, I sat through an entire lunch being humiliated by your sister-in-law. No one, *no one* spoke up for me. So what am I supposed to think?"

"Has anyone asked you to leave?"

I silently stand up and pick up the box and bag and take them back downstairs. I return upstairs to find Emma packing just the rucksack for me. I thought for a moment that I had an easy exit from my dilemma, but now I am back to being undecided.

I pick up the rucksack and head downstairs. I call the Van Bergens and let them know that I am going home for the New Year. No, Emma is not coming with me.

We walk silently to the bus stop. The bond of trust between us has been broken, as has the intimacy that we shared hitherto. It is up to me to restore both by returning in a few weeks.

We hug closely, but without the warmth and depth that have marked our relationship from the outset.

"Don't forget me. Us."

I nod my head to reassure her, and embrace her once again.

As the bus pulls away from the station I look back to see Emma standing under the awning: a small, solitary figure, waving weakly. I try to wave back confidently, but I can't find the strength.

Within hours I am back in Nijmegen and then, with a short delay, cross into Germany. This is not the country that I left in 1934. There is vibrancy in the air, but also a sense of intimidating tension.

I am excited to be back, but perturbed that a life that I lived for three years has evaporated with nigh an iota of regret in a course of a few hours. I don't understand how I can be that ephemeral. And maybe that is the factor that defines my weakness: that I can't hold on to anything for any length of time.

In a few hours I will be in Rackelsweg, my home street in Bremen. Whether I stay or return to Utrecht will depend not on me, but on whether my family and Nazi Germany welcome me back or make me feel unwelcome.

GRÜNEWALD S-BAHN STATION, BERLIN

Winter 1942

Friedrich Becker stood on the platform, watching the train being loaded. People shoved in through the doors like cattle: young, old, women, children, the frail and the sick. They arrived every half-hour or so in trucks that pulled up next to the empty carriages. The trucks barely stopped before the tarp was pulled back and the occupants were literally thrown out and herded to the waiting carriages.

This was his third assignment since he voluntarily enlisted in the Schutzstaffel in November 1939, to forestall conscription to the Wehrmacht. The latter was inevitable when, in June of that same year, Hitler invaded Poland, forcing the British to declare war on Germany. Two years later, also in June, Hitler shredded the Non-Aggression

Pact with Stalin and launched a war against the Soviets. It was a foregone conclusion that, as a Wehrmacht conscript, Friedrich would end up either on the Western Front fighting against the British or, worse yet, on the Eastern Front against the Bolsheviks. In either circumstance he would be deployed in a combat unit as an active soldier or in an auxiliary capacity as a medic. Regardless, he wasn't interested in dying for the Third Reich.

From the outset the Nazis' vitriolic diatribes and violent methods repulsed him. He had heard them often enough on the radio and seen them in print and posters – Hitler, Goebbels and Streicher – and frequently witnessed their acolytes on the streets bullying homosexuals, socialists and Jews. This was not the Germany that he grew up in; neither was this the country that he wanted to devote his life to as a doctor. He understood and sympathised with the plight of the masses, the unemployment, the worthless mark and the demise of Germany post World War I, but the medicine that he would prescribe for its healing was not fascism and unchecked aggression against its citizens and neighbours.

Just the same, he was not prepared to flee; he preferred to wait and hope for an outcome that would see Hitler and his cronies swept into the dustbins of history and Germany restored to its former pride and glory. But with each passing year from the rise of the National Socialists, the situation deteriorated. Six years after Hitler assumed the role of Führer, Germany was at war with the world, and many of its former citizens were being alienated, forced from their homes and now subjected to deportation. How could the price of restoring Germany's prosperity come at the cost of such depravity?

Friedrich dared not confide his deep misgivings to his parents and sister. They would deem it unpatriotic to criticise the National Socialists and Hitler – after all, they were the ruling party in the Reichstag, regardless of their politics and polemics. That only left him with the option of sharing his misgivings with his university colleagues and erstwhile friends from Bremen, but in this climate fraught with fear and suspicion that could be downright perilous.

With his doctor's degree commenced in Utrecht and completed in Germany he felt that the safest and most prudent course to steer would be a quasi-medical administrative role within the current regime, a position that would also shield him from active duty. However, he soon learned that enrolling in this regime meant taking on a party hue.

He was assigned the non-commissioned rank of *Unterscharführer*, sergeant, in the SS and appointed to work in a recruitment centre in Berlin. After a year at the centre, providing medicals for potential SS recruits, including the moronic testing for racial purity, he was transferred to a more august medical facility that catered exclusively to the Reich's elite: commanding officers of the Wehrmacht and the SS, high party officials, their wives and children.

At first he was relieved, albeit equally sickened by having to spend his working days cheek by jowl with the very people he abhorred, that he didn't have to unctuously exhibit the requisite enthusiasm for the young bloods who so zealously joined the SS on the Nazis' mission of eradicating undesirables from the Reich. But if the mood was less exuberant here, it was also much darker, the solemnity cast by the ominous presence of so many Nazi officials at the highest levels of military and government. There was no reckless bantering here of 'bullying Untermenschen', 'vandalising Jewish property', 'terrorising communists and Marxists' and such taunts. Instead there was the ever-watchful eye of Gestapo agents lurking in the corners, eavesdropping on conversations, reading private notes and files, interrogating staff and doctors about their patients. Forever looking for the tiniest smidgen of disloyalty, a single morsel of casual conversation that might uncover a conspiracy, the least inadvertent remark made in total jest that might lead to immediate demotion or expulsion.

Friedrich didn't care about that. No one ever told him anything incriminating, and even if they did, he wouldn't pass it on. Besides, he couldn't care less about what happened to these people, or about their motives. Nevertheless he gradually got used to the work, the wives and children lightening the sombre mood.

But then the new decrees came in curtailing the activities of Jewish doctors and medical and nursing staff, and everything changed for the worse.

Esteemed colleagues that he worked alongside were summarily denigrated and demoted to lab technicians collecting and processing samples. One particular professor, who had lectured Friedrich at Leipzig and was the facility's erstwhile director, was demoted to a staff doctor and then again to work under supervision in the lab. Competent medical staff were demoted to janitorial services: cleaning rooms; making beds; emptying chamber pots.

If the humiliation of demotion was not enough, erstwhile Jewish doctors and staff were subjected to daily denigrations and degradations. Singing Nazi anthems in the morning and at night. Saluting Nazi officials with anti-Jewish proclamations. And to top it all their pay was reduced to a pittance.

Becker had witnessed this before in other walks of life, but these people were close to his heart and home; it affected him directly. As did the invasion of the Netherlands in May 1940, casting a shadow over the lives of people that he personally knew in Utrecht. What gnawed at him the most was his inability to speak out and vent his frustration. He wore the uniform; he was beholden to the creed and committed to the allegiance.

He could, however, do his job lackadaisically. Blame the inefficiency and delays on the lack of competent doctors to render qualified opinions and accurate diagnosis, and experienced staff to deliver prompt results. The inference was clear: *You got rid of the good doctors and medical staff; now we are stuck with subpar.* His sudden poor performance and insouciance came to the attention of his commanding officer, SS-Hauptsturmführer (Captain) Nieland. He decided to "rub Becker's nose in it" and transferred him to work at the train station. On issuing the order, he smirked to his *Leutnant*: "See how that softie likes this posting. This will toughen him up."

And now Friedrich was here, standing on the platform watching the deportees huddling together as they clambered into the train carriages, their faces terrified, confused; carrying their meagre possessions, yearning for the nightmare that had begun in the small hours of the morning to eventually end. They were told that the resettlement was for their protection.

He stood impassively erect, careful not to betray his displeasure again, as they were packed onto the carriages, oftentimes overflowing when the giant wooden doors were finally sealed and the next carriage was starting to fill up. No food or water, and one bucket for waste to last them on a harrowing journey that could last several days.

He knew that his superior, the station commander, SS-Standartenführer Wolff, was looking for the slightest excuse to pack him off to the Eastern Front. Wolff knew of Becker's previous record. On more than one occasion he'd spat out at him his suspicion that Becker had links to trade unions, socialists and other subversives. He'd even hinted that Becker might have homosexual tendencies that could account for his squeamishness. All false. But in this current climate, one of terror and betrayal, Becker knew that a mere rumour could derail his stationing in Berlin.

If he could ride out this assignment, Hitler the madman was bound to fail and Germany would be restored to sanity. Then he could go home and resume his career, which is where he wanted to be. The question in his mind was not whether he could, but whether he would be allowed to do so. When this madness ended, would Germans of conscience be excused from complicity and allowed to resume their lives?

He could stand here and watch passively, ostensibly keeping the order, but as his beloved Milton wrote, *They also serve who only stand and wait*. In another context, he would be complicit.

He could write something down. But how would that exonerate him? After all, he was wearing the uniform that was part of this mass evacuation and deportation. If by some miracle he managed to survive this assignment, there would be nothing left for him to do but escape to another place and start a new life.

"Becker!"

"Yes, *Standartenführer*?"

"You know the assignment is not to stand around and dream all day about your idyllic life back home. Your job here is to keep the herds moving. Moving. You understand? I have ten transports to get out today. Ten!"

"Yes, *Standartenführer*!"

Becker quickly moved into the fray and started issuing orders to the soldiers unloading the trucks and shoving the people onto the train. An older gentleman fell to the ground and blocked the flow of people. Without hesitation, Becker immediately raced up to the fallen individual and kicked him until two other people knelt down and picked him up and carried him into the carriage.

He continued in this manner until the *Standartenführer* was back in the depot, and then receded into the background under the eaves. He knew that the Gestapo weasel standing by the truck would report him again. But he had proved his mettle. The most they could accuse him of was being lazy and a daydreamer.

What a joke; the *Standartenführer*, an uncouth butcher's son from Hamburg, giving him orders. But then, in a hierarchy where the supreme leader was a crazy corporal from Braunau am Inn, it made sense that someone as educated as himself ended up at the bottom, while the boors rose to the top.

He looked at his watch. Nine more transports; nearly five thousand people. And this was just one train station, in one day. Staggering numbers.

Where were these transports heading?

From his corner he could see the Gestapo re-entering the station. He immediately emerged from the shadows and marched over to where a new truck was unloading its cargo. He started barking orders at the soldiers in the truck to not wait until the truck stopped, but to start shoving out the occupants on approach.

Out of the corner of his eye he saw the *Standartenführer* re-emerge from the depot. He looked over at Becker barking orders and shoving and kicking people, nodded his approval and walked back into the station.

It was either this farce or the dispatch to the front, at least until his conscience buckled and he could no longer pretend, and then it was neither. He would end up at Prinz-Albrecht-Straße-8, Gestapo Headquarters. And from there it was rumoured that no one emerged. Or if they did, they emerged insane. But by then it would not matter.

DEPORTATION, BERLIN

Winter 1942

It was being in this twilight state that bothered her the most: unable to stay truly asleep or alert. Prior to all that she recalled Anna's father, Helmut, and Herr Lipschutz grabbing and dragging her into the bedroom and forcing some kind of bitter potion down her throat. She resisted bravely. But in the end she succumbed. The one man (did he resemble Helmut?) pinioned her arms back and crossed his powerful legs over her weaker ones. Gradually she receded into this state: between awareness and semi-consciousness.

In the latter state she was being carried between two people down the steps, across a hallway; the next minute she was cold, rushed through the night, bundled in a thin blanket and her pyjamas; and then she was indoors, warm again. She sensed she had been here before. She felt her head lolling back and struggled to keep her eyes open, the images fleeting through the slits: across a narrow hallway and up a staircase and onto a landing and into a room. And then the rushing stopped. She dozed off. At the edge of her consciousness she heard voices speaking softly, but with an urgent undertone. The firmer of the speakers fumbling with a blanket and resting her pliant body on a bed, then the other voice pulling a blanket over her, then silence.

The light went out, and she receded into a dream state. Munich. Her grandmother's house; her soft, watery eyes and brittle voice; the *Eintopf* cooking on the stove; the warm fire replacing the cold outside. She longed to stay warm: warm and embraced; warm and wanted, and to finally come to a place where she could feel at home.

Otto Dreschler never came home. So Grandma explained. Bad men killed him. Why did she want to know? She couldn't explain now, she was too young to understand. But Grandma's son loved her dearly. He was a good son, a loving father, a decent man who did an honourable job. He was a policeman who bravely stopped a band of criminals who wanted to destroy their safety, their security, and create a state of anarchy. Leutnant Dreschler did that. And then he was killed for it.

Were the criminals who killed her father put in jail? Yes. What else could Elsa Dreschler say? They were jailed and served a mere fraction of their sentence and then released. If anything their incarceration served to highlight their cause – it made them heroes to a certain segment of the population. It was a myth invented to solidify their struggle for power.

Her daughter-in-law, Ann-Marie, was livid that they executed her husband. She took it as a personal affront when neither Police Chief von Seisser nor President von Kahr would speak up for her husband, when it was they who ordered him to suppress the coup. But by then they had secured plum jobs within the Nazi hierarchy and let Leutnant Dreschler and others – the low-hanging fruit – take the blame and pay the price. They were always cowards. The three of them: Minister President Gustav Ritter von Kahr, Armed Forces General Otto von Lossow and State Police Chief Hans Ritter von Seisser. The so-called triumvirate. They secretly despised the Weimar Republic and supported an overthrow but, fearful that it might fail, stood back to see which side would win and backed the winning horse. In 1923, the Weimar Republic won and the coup was suppressed. A decade later, in 1934, a year after Hitler became Chancellor, the Nazis were the winners and they came seeking vengeance. But by then the triumvirate flew the winning colours: the swastika. But Hitler and his henchmen were not to be dissuaded from baying for blood. Otto Dreschler was thrown to the dogs.

Ann-Marie championed her cause forcefully and vocally through whatever channels were available to her. She couldn't bring Otto back, but she sought to rehabilitate his reputation by letting all know that Otto Dreschler did support the Nazis. But he supported law and order first and foremost, political affiliation second. If nothing else she sought to shame the triumvirate, to show them up as the spineless cowards they were, who refused to stand up for Leutnant Dreschler.

Gustav Kahr did relent to speak with her. He asked that she not attract attention to the situation of 1923. Germany was in chaos and mistakes were made. He even admitted that she might have a just grievance. But this was not the time to raise it and the Nazis were not the regime to satisfy it.

But she was not to be dissuaded. Either they came forward and declared Otto Dreschler an upstanding citizen and an honourable policeman and grant him the posthumous recognition he deserved, rather than being tarnished as a communist and a Jew lover, or she would take her crusade all the way to Berlin.

She was invited to Berlin to 'discuss her case', but on the way she was assassinated. The triumvirate and Berlin blamed the communists and the Jews. A comfortable attribution that pleased them both, trading in a currency that was easily transacted and accounted for any ill that befell the Nazi regime. Neither could the accused dispute the accusation: they were powerless and voiceless.

One morning a policeman appeared at Elsa's doorway with Helga in tow to say that the child was an orphan. Elsa was too old and frail to take up the fight. The Nazis had claimed her son and now her daughter-in-law. Let the Jews and communists take the blame.

That's what she told Helga. That Hitler was a good man and the Nationalist Socialists patriots. The lie did not quite erase the opprobrium that besmirched Elsa's son but it protected Helga from seeking vengeance and dying to right a hopeless wrong. She sang Nazi songs, listened fervently to Hitler's and Goebbels' diatribes on the radio, and loyally adhered to the party by wearing the *Hitlerjugend* uniform.

With time Elsa grew infirm and could no longer be the surrogate mother to a growing child. Helga was now twelve. Elsa asked Otto's brother, Wolfgang, to look after her, at least until she turned eighteen. He refused, saying that he had enlisted in the Wehrmacht and would not be around to look after a teenager. The truth was that he did not want the ignominy surrounding Otto and Ann-Marie's daughter to cloud his future. The Nazis did not brook even a hint of dissension.

Elsa unwillingly sold her modest house, took up residence in a nursing home and packed Helga off to her niece Magda Jodl in Berlin. There simply wasn't anyone else. She explained in a brief letter the tragic fate of the Dreschlers and Helga's circumstances, and included a sum of money secured from Helga's parents and from her own savings. Elsa had never set eyes on her sister's daughter, Magda. She threw the seed into the wind and hoped that it would take root.

Six months later, Elsa expired, heartbroken, in the home.

Helga is twirling in the small kitchen, watching her grandmother hunched over the stove preparing supper. Their little schnauzer, Arlo, is yelping happily: dinner for them, means dinner for him. German military songs are playing on the small radio resting on the counter; the prelude to a Hitler speech. Suddenly Arlo is barking loudly, in German, nuzzling her zealously to wake her up.

She can't find the strength to move, let alone wake up. Once more she is lifted by two people and bundled in a blanket. Dragged across a landing and down the staircase into the open doorway and the cold, cold street. She has been here before. When? How long ago?

The thoughts fade, drowned in a sea of voices, noises, shouting, people barking orders. What is happening? She struggles to rouse herself from the dream, the stupor, to force her eyes open and look around. It is night, the street lights casting yellow haloes on the pavements. A man is holding her to his chest. He is moving quickly through a crowd. She is placed on a cold metal surface, and the man clambers on behind her, picks her up and places her on his lap. She is safe again. She lets her eyelids droop, and dozes to dream.

"Why is it you can't resume a dream?" she asks Elsa.

Her *Oma* turned from the stove and looked at her with pride. *You are a bright girl*, the glint in her eyes said silently to her granddaughter.

"I don't know, Liebchen. I believe that dreams are like little gemstones. Each one unique and radiant, and strung together they make a beautiful necklace. So you can thread dreams together like gemstones."

"Will I ever have a beautiful necklace?"

"Oh, I am sure that you will have many beautiful necklaces. Not just one."

The radio blared. Rudolf Hess introduced *Der Führer*. The spell of the moment was overwhelmed by harsh words, cast adrift on a roaring, angry sea.

"Do we need another war?" Oma muttered to herself.

"What was that, Oma?" Helga spoke above the din.

Wiping a tear from her eyes, Elsa turned to her granddaughter. "I miss your father. As I am sure you do."

"He died a German patriot. For Hitler."

Oma pursed her lips as tightly as she could and turned back to complete the meal. Sometimes the lie you tell shields the painful truth.

The rumble of the engine and the rocking of the truck stopped. Once again Helga was rattled from her dream.

The back gate was swung open with a sharp metallic clang. Orders were barked into the interior and people were starting to move. She was handed across to another person who held her under her arms and set her down on the ground.

Gemstones strung together. Another gemstone to thread to the last one; soon there will be a necklace. One of many, Oma promised.

Once again I am cold. I can feel myself swaying with the movement of the truck. But I am standing on the ground. Two sets of hands grab me from either side and I am led, wobbling, across the ground and up to the steps. They haul me up and I am standing on a platform. We all stand still.

The twilight is starting to even – it is early dawn. My eyelids flutter open and I can see hordes of people on a train platform. Am I going back to Munich? Back to Oma? But Oma went away and I was sent to Berlin. I don't understand. I look up and stare at the faces: the Lipschutzes. Why are the Lipschutzes taking me back to Munich?

We are in motion again. This time, moving towards the train boxcars, Heinrich stumbles on the metal rungs and falls to the ground. A man dressed in a uniform rushes up to help him. The conductor? No! He is kicking Heinrich in the groin and hitting him with a club. Other people help Heinrich up; he is tottering, and I stagger back.

Dreams can also be nightmares. Oma always told me if I woke up scared from a bad dream to remember if I saw blood. If I did, it didn't happen. Heinrich has blood oozing from a cut above his forehead. This is not happening.

I am pulled into the boxcar after Heinrich and in front of Alana. It is dark and musty inside. Nearly all the people are taller than me; I feel small and suffocated. More people are entering the boxcar. Everyone is standing. A woman with a baby clutched to her breast is standing close by me. Two young boys enter the boxcar and stand up against the side opposite me. I can hardly breathe. I can't even move to get more air.

I wait. When they all sit I will get some air.

Alana hands Heinrich a handkerchief. His hand is shaking as he holds it to the gash on his forehead. He is no longer bleeding. Now I panic. This *is* happening. I am going to suffocate to death in this boxcar with all these people around me. And the baby is starting to cry. We are squashed in to standing room only. The large door is rolled shut. It is now pitch dark and airless.

"Is this the train to Munich?" I ask in a faint and frightened voice.

Heinrich looks down at me, then at Alana. "Could be." I am not sure who answered.

We stand like this in the airless, dank and dark boxcar and wait. No one says anything. The sounds from outside are mixed with the heavy breathing inside the boxcar: people too terrified to speak their thoughts. But the baby cries. And the mother soothes it with "Hush, hush", bouncing it up and down on her hip, hoping to keep it still and silent.

Finally the train starts to move, our boxcar is yanked forward and we are jolted in the same direction. But we are so tightly compacted that no one falls – we just trample on each other. With the train in motion a bit of air sifts into the boxcar from the narrow shaft along the ceiling. Now the baby is bawling. But no one else is making any sound. We stand together like petrified beings bolstering each other up – the collective of old, young, women, men, children and a single baby. I no longer feel like I am being smothered. Somehow the motion of the train gives me comfort that soon this journey that began between dusk and dawn will end and I will be able to return to my own warm bed and fall into blissful dreams.

Someone in the deep interior of the boxcar asks, "Is there some water here?"

No one answers.

The same voice: "For the baby."

Another voice answers, "There is no water here. If the baby is thirsty, why can't the mother feed it?"

The train is turning a sharp corner, the boxcar tilts sideways, and we lean in the same direction. Again no one tumbles. An old man starts coughing. Someone says, "Asthma; he needs his medication."

Someone else answers, "There is no water. He will have to take it dry."

The train slows. Everyone breathes a sigh of relief. We have arrived, or are arriving, at our destination. Thank God it was a swift journey. Even the old man with the asthma wheezes less intensely. The wheels finally grind agonisingly to a stop. We wait. No voices outside the boxcar to open the door. Someone says, "The trains are backed up on the line, that's all it is. Don't get your hopes up."

"Well, I can't wait any longer." An agitated male voice to my right. The crowd around me shifts even more tightly, closing the tiny gaps between us as he moves through. I can hear the sound of water hitting the can. He is urinating. That's all we need on top of this, the stench of him relieving himself. The baby that was mewling up to now starts up again. If the doors don't open up very soon there will be a riot in here – we are all at the end of our tether.

The train trundles forward again. The jolt pulls us aft and then frontward. The man was right, this isn't a stop; the tracks are backed up. The mood inside the boxcar turns grim; the collective short-lived relief is sucked in and we become stalwart in our tolerance. No riot.

For several hours the train moves at a reasonable clip and by turns we tilt to the right and then the left. The shaft of sunlight emanating from the ceiling brings with it crisp, cold air that mixes with the stench inside the boxcar. Other people, men, women, children, have used the tin. The odour is so overpowering that it permeates our hair, our clothing; our breath is suffused with it.

"Is this the train to Munich? Are you sure?" I need an answer, a ray of hope to get me through this dreadful journey. Otherwise I won't be able to survive.

Alana Lipschutz looks down and smiles wanly. "I am not sure. But we will arrive soon and then you can go back."

Nothing makes sense: go and come back? Does this woman imagine this is some kind of carnival ride that one takes for pleasure? I am about to demand a more unequivocal answer, when a voice right next to where the wheezing asthmatic is located yells, "He is going into arrest, the colour is draining from his face!"

The collective takes comfort from his discomfort: at least *they* are not dying. No one says anything.

"Is there a doctor in here?"

Silence, just the monotonous grinding of the wheels and the creaking of the wooden boxcar.

"A nurse?" The single last hope fading from the voice.

The baby's mother pipes up, almost in a whisper, "I am a midwife and a trained nurse, but what can I do?"

We all silently agree. She can't even keep the baby comfortable; never mind a choking asthmatic.

"I can barely feel his pulse. He is dying. Anyone?"

The collective guilt of helplessness keeps us gravely silent. No one has anything to offer. Not even commiseration.

The train slows again; the wheels grind to a stop. Outside the boxcar, other than the sounds of nature mixed in with the creaking of cooling metal, it is still. We are in the countryside. It's not bustling Munich but we have reassuringly arrived at some bucolic destination. We can now disembark, drink some water, maybe eat, and most of all get away from the stench and the corpse.

There are footsteps approaching – boots on hard soil. A voice outside the door. A latch is pulled down and the door slides open, groaning on the rusted rut. Blinded by the glare of the midday sun, we can just make out the silhouettes of two armed soldiers standing outside with rifles pointed at us.

Our meagre hopes are dashed.

One soldier speaks harshly. "We have just crossed the border; you are now in Poland."

No one seems to be too bothered or alarmed by this piece of information. There are more immediate and relevant concerns.

"There is a dead person in here. And the bucket is nearly full." The disembodied voice that gave us the news on the asthmatic edges forward. He is a slight man, around thirty maybe, with a dash of dark hair and piercing blue eyes, dressed in a grey jacket, mauve sweater and black trousers. That took some moxie.

The youthful soldiers stare at each other. The one on the right looks up at the man and commands, "Wait!" He strides off nonchalantly to the front of the train. We all enjoy some respite from the darkness and despite still being tightly cooped up with the stench it gives us a minor sense of relief. One misery dispelled out of three is a gain under these circumstances.

The soldier returns with an older man, this one an officer judging by his epaulettes and his supercilious manner. He sniffs the air and mutters something under his breath. The two soldiers chuckle at the aside.

The slight man who earlier spoke to the soldiers leans out the door and addresses the officer. "A man with asthma has died in here because we couldn't get him his medication. And the waste bucket is full."

The officer looks at him contemptuously. "You can empty the bucket over there by the stream. The corpse stays on the train. Otherwise the body count will be short."

The man moves hastily through the crowd, who eagerly step aside to let him through. He gingerly picks up the sloshing bucket with both hands and takes it to the edge of the boxcar. Stepping down to the ground he reaches back and picks up the bucket, taking it down to the stream. Before he empties it out he leans into the stream and rinses his face and neck in the cool water and takes two gulps to quench his thirst. Reaching for the bucket, he drowns it to the rim in the stream and then raises it to rinse out the contents. He does this three times until the bucket is clean.

As he makes his way back to the boxcar he is blocked by the officer. "Did I say that you could drink from the stream?"

The man looks wide-eyed at the officer. He is

dumbstruck. "I am very sorry, sir, but you asked me to take the bucket to the stream. I didn't see any harm in refreshing my face and taking a drink of water while I was there." He sets the bucket down.

The officer signals with his chin to the two soldiers, and they grab the man on either side and drag him to the stream. The officer strolls casually behind. Once they reach the stream they force the man to kneel by the bank and dunk his head underwater. His pinioned arms are juddering wildly as he struggles desperately to rise above the water. The soldiers keep him submerged. Just as he is about to drown, his arms and body losing their fight, they raise him out of the water. He heaves desperately, spitting out gulps of water. His face is puffed red from the exertion and his eyes are bulging with terror.

"Was that refreshing enough? Do you need more drink?" The officer is leaning by his side.

The man fervently shakes his head from side to side.

"I am sorry; I didn't get your answer. Was that no, not refreshing enough?"

The man is unable to speak, overcome with fear and lack of breath. He nods yes, this time more eagerly.

The officer straightens out and signals to the soldiers. They dunk him again. The man struggles but this time with less energy, the fight wrung out of him; he may as well die.

They bring him up and drag his body back to the boxcar, heaving it in. It is limp, not showing any sign of life.

The three soldiers start sealing the door when a violent coughing spasm erupts. The man starts sputtering water and uncurls from clutching himself – he is still alive. They pull back and stare at him drawing deep gulps of breath. He leans forward, clutching at the side of the door.

The trio applaud him in unison.

Reaching outward, he grabs the bucket off the ground and points to it. "You are animals. You have no conscience. This is what I think of your Third Reich! Shit!" He spits violently on the ground.

We are all now gathered at the door. Maybe the riot that has been simmering is about to break out.

The officer is unperturbed by the insult and points instead to one of the two boys who are standing next to the woman with the baby. The soldiers reach in and grab him, flinging him to the ground by the officer's feet. With studied insouciance he unholsters his Walther PPK and shoots the boy in the head. He is dead instantly.

Despite being stricken with terror, we gasp in disbelief. This can't have happened. This whole scene was a hoax. It's a play. This can't all be over a drink of water?

Neither is the man daunted. He flings the bucket at the officer, who instinctively kicks it out of the way. Once more the officer signals to the soldiers. They lean over to the boxcar, grab the dead boy's brother and throw him to the ground by the officer's feet. Just as he points the Walther at the boy's head, the half-drowned man staggers out of the boxcar and grabs at his hand, pointing the gun at his own chest.

"Shoot me, you coward," he shouts at the officer. "Kill me!"

The officer shoves him aside, aims and shoots the brother. He too dies instantly. The officer holsters his pistol and smirks at the man. "You are too valuable to us. You have – what do you Jews call it? – 'chootzpah'? That is what we need where you are going; I will be sure to commend you."

The man crumples, deflated, to the ground, realising that the consequence of further remonstration will be the deaths of more vulnerable passengers: children, the mother with the baby, older men and women. He rises to his feet, picks up the first boy and heaves him into the boxcar. He removes his jacket and drapes it over his body. He does the same with the other boy, draping the jacket over the both of them. Looking back a final time at the armed trio, he picks up the bucket off the ground, flings it into the boxcar and clambers in.

The door is heaved shut, latched, and the train is signalled to continue with a sharp command from the officer.

We stand in stunned silence, our emotions collectively enmeshed with our relief at still being alive despite the hardship, the hunger, the thirst and abject discomfort. Perhaps of all of us, the mother with the baby is the most relieved. She was standing right next to the two brothers. The officer would have shot the baby first and then her. That would have elicited the most acute anguish.

We travel this way into the night, through the next day and then another night. By the third day the mother and the baby might as well have died two days ago, because they expire anyway due to the lack of food, water, proper hygiene and rest. Along with them, three other corpses are added to the body count: two elderly men and one woman. Altogether, eight are dead. But it might as well be all of us. We are wrung and numb, our ability to sense and feel progressively dissipated until by the second night we stand and breathe. That's it. Our eyes are shut; our hunger is forgotten; our thirst dissolved in dryness and our emotions depleted. Every so often a body tumbles. We immediately prop it up. There is no room for such luxury – not even for a corpse. We don't speak. The constant churning of metal on metal is the only sound that reminds us that when this train stops we might return to the land of the living. For now we are comatose.

The only thought, when I find a smidgen of strength to think, that runs through my head like the wheels beneath my feet is what the officer said: *What you Jews call it…* But I am *not* Jewish. My father served and died for Hitler. I was in the *Hitlerjugend* before I was sent to Berlin. What am I doing on this train?

When I do think it, I look up at Alana and Heinrich. But they are both insentient, so I can't ask them. If I am still alive when these wheels stop, I will ask the question.

We know the days and nights because of the light and dark that seep in from the narrow slit above our heads. On day three, it's light overhead; the constant churning of the wheels slows, then grinds, and finally the train shudders to a standstill. We dare not revive our spirits, so we all, to a person, wait in deep suspense, fearing to even hope.

After a moment, when our hearing has readjusted from the endless churning of the wheels, we hear voices outside. A multitude of voices, the neighing and snorting of horses, dogs barking. Our eyelids raise, little lights flickering in a dark room, and some of us even, foolishly, let a smile spread across our famished, weary faces. If we could raise our arms we would applaud.

BERLIN

Spring 1943

Kriminalkommissar Hans Oberschaltz sat erect in the chair opposite Professor Helmut Jodl, trying to give the impression that he was comfortable in the present surroundings and having an amiable afternoon chat. He was a tall man, with a head of very straight dark hair combed meticulously over his rigid skull. Not the weasel-faced type that the professor often presumed Gestapo officers to be. He imagined that, in another time, the *Kriminalkommissar* could have been either a banker or a fine jeweller. His hands, which he tended to use with great economy, coupled with his austere demeanour revealed him to be a careful man of closely guarded emotions, who listened attentively and moved with great expediency and a total lack of compassion for human emotion. In other words, in these times, a great asset to the Gestapo. No doubt, whether he had been recruited or had volunteered, his rise to the rank of *Kriminalkommissar* would have been rapid and smooth.

A number of times Helmut was tempted to break out of the boundaries of this formal, albeit friendly conversation and get onto a personal level with the *Kriminalkommissar*. But each time that temptation arose, he sensed it being discouraged through the hardness in his interlocutor's eyes. Nothing more. And just as clearly the boundaries were reinforced as a reminder to the professor to keep the conversation formal and above camaraderie.

"I hope you understand that in these times, full of danger," the last word spoken with deliberate omen, "it is important to remember that freedoms we have taken for granted can no longer be so, or even tolerated."

Here it was again: the rationale quickly followed by the threat. Helmut wondered if this manner of combining commonplace logic with an implied injunction was the result of Gestapo schooling, or rather an inherent trait Hans Oberschaltz brought naturally to the profession. He believed the latter to be more likely as he watched the man seated opposite him shift his hand ever so slightly to pick up the cup of coffee that he had reluctantly accepted, and which was the only concession to familiarity that he'd allowed that afternoon.

"Freedoms?" Helmut, refusing to concede to this intimidation, stroked his beard and slouched some more in his chair, in direct contrast to the rigidity of his visitor.

"I don't have to remind you that we are surrounded by enemies. Enemies that—"

The professor didn't let the *Kriminalkommissar* complete his sentence. The annoyance on the latter's face was marked by the slightest twitch of one eyebrow, just the one. It was obvious that his manner was such that, in whatever life he was in, military or civilian, he was not used to being interrupted. Yet Professor Jodl, accustomed to academic discourses, not only enjoyed interruptions but encouraged them. And anyway, the *Kriminalkommissar* had invited himself to the professor's house. And since it was his house, he felt that he could behave as he pleased.

"May I remind you that the reason we have enemies is because we started wars with everyone: the British, the French, the Russians. Not to mention the several countries that we have simply marched into without so much as a provocation."

"Herr Professor, I am not here to debate political policy with you. It is not my place or yours. The fact is that we are in a time of war, and while we are in a time of war we need to be extra vigilant, extra cautious about whom we associate with and what we say."

Yet again the mix of rationale and subtle threat. The *Kriminalkommissar* was, of course, referring to the questions that Helmut had raised specifically with regards to the evacuation of the Lipschutz family, and more generally the sudden deportation or incarceration of 'undesirables'.

Ever since the winter of 1938, two years almost to the day since Helmut had created a scene outside Herr Lipschutz's store, the Gestapo had had him under surveillance. He had obstinately stood outside the store and refused to be intimidated by the thugs that had come to smash the plate glass on Kristallnacht and pillage the merchandise. Oftentimes he wondered whether that act of defiance had hastened the deportation of the Lipschutzes. Fortuitously he was able to atone regardless of whether his actions had been the cause. But he had not merited a visit until he began to openly exercise his 'freedoms' by speaking his views publicly at the illustrious Humboldt University where he occupied the chair of professor in social sciences.

What brought this sudden outburst of views into the open was the gradual alienation of Jewish academics at the university. People that Helmut considered not only his equals, but also in many cases to be some of the brightest lights at the institution. Yet over the past two years, the university had been forced to liquidate the tenures of these academics by reducing them to ignominious duties. Professor Leiblinz, a veteran academic in the history department with many papers and books to his credit, was demoted to a lowly research position. Others less august were reassigned to home-tutoring children of the Third Reich. Doctors in physics and maths found themselves tutoring ten-year-old children for a pittance, barely able to sustain themselves, subsequently being evicted from their homes and reduced to living in shelters.

Helmut finally drafted a petition and, to his shame and dismay having managed to get it signed by only a handful of his colleagues, sent it to the Chancellor's office. He never got a reply. Instead he received a formal letter from the *Kriminalkommissar* suggesting a meeting at the professor's choice of time and place to discuss certain 'sensitive issues' that had arisen at his place of employment. Which had led to this meeting.

The professor chose to keep quiet, which took great reserve on his part following the last comment from the *Kriminalkommissar*.

"Sending petitions of protest to the Chancellor objecting to policy does not show support for the common cause of the Third Reich."

Helmut's reserve evaporated instantly. "Interfering with the practice of freedom in academic institutions hardly shows support for that most hallowed of all principles."

The *Kriminalkommissar* was undaunted; nary an eyebrow twitched. "Freedom? To some extent. We can't have enemies of the state wandering freely in the university to disseminate their poison."

At this Helmut straightened from his nonchalant slouch and leaned in closer to the *Kriminalkommissar*. "Professor Leiblinz an enemy? Disseminating poison? I am astonished that a man of your intellect should believe such drivel." *No harm*, Helmut thought to himself, *in mixing criticism and compliment in the same phrase. Use some of the same technique as the Gestapo.*

"Herr Professor, it is policy that citizens of Jewish birth are considered enemies of the Reich. Again, I am not here to debate policy with you; I am simply making sure that it is being carried out, and that others adhere to it. I have taken the time to come here, rather than invite you to the Plaza for this conversation, so I hope you take and appreciate the gesture for what it is."

Without any further discussion, Hans Oberschaltz stood up from his chair, ramrod straight, as if his back were propped up by a pole. Running his palm over his hair that had remained unruffled, in a gesture meant more to convey meticulousness, he reached for his cap, glided it smoothly onto his head and turned to walk out the door.

Helmut, unable to resist his curiosity, asked, "*Kriminalkommissar*, would you kindly indulge me in one personal question?"

Kriminalkommissar Oberschaltz paused as if to consider the propriety of the request within the context of his assignment, then grudgingly turned back to face the professor, standing fully erect in his uniform as if to intimidate his subject.

"Before this, before the war started and Germany went mad, what were you? I mean to say, what was your profession in civilian life?" Helmut smiled sheepishly at Oberschaltz as if to intimate that this was just idle curiosity, no more.

Without hesitation Oberschaltz clipped the edge of his cap's visor. "I was a banker." With that he turned again and walked briskly to the door. Opening it onto the street, he strode out in carefully measured steps and walked towards the open door of the waiting command car.

Helmut could not help noticing, even from the distance of the dining room, the three-pointed star emblem of the black Mercedes-Benz; a car normally reserved for the higher echelons of the Nazi Party. But even with his limited knowledge of protocol it was abundantly clear that Hans Oberschaltz was not a regular officer, or for that matter a man to be trifled with. If he had been granted this reprieve to banter with the *Kriminalkommissar* it was out of respect for his cousin, one of the elite commanders of the Third Reich. Certainly not in any deference to his brother-in-law Martin, who was an officer of little consequence holding down a mere desk job.

No doubt if Helmut continued on this path, the next visit would be in the company of Gestapo goons who would usher him unceremoniously to the headquarters at Prinz-Albrecht-Straße-8. There he would not be given the luxury of slouching comfortably to banter with senior officers.

Instead he would be shackled to a hard wooden chair and have questions barked at him by some lowly thug. He would be kept there for at least a week, and the routine of harsh interrogation, solitary incarceration, interrupted sleep and measly meals would be kept up until he recanted his views. He would then be escorted to the university and asked to vacate his office to be reassigned to some degrading role such as that of a library assistant.

If he still dared to persist in his activities, he would be picked up in the middle of the night and hauled into the Gestapo Headquarters, where this time there would be no interrogation. Instead it would be a period of relentless torture in which he would be subjected to beatings, freezing-cold baths, electric prods and worse. If he managed to survive, there would be no former life or job to go back to. He would be separated from his family and surroundings and sent to serve in a camp.

This he knew. One of the signatories on his petition, not fortunate enough to have Helmut's connections, lost his tenure, was forced out of his home, separated from his family and then, after enduring interrogation and torture at the infamous headquarters, was dispatched to a camp called Sachsenhausen. He managed to smuggle out the story of his ordeal, which surreptitiously reached Helmut's hands. Word had further reached Helmut that Professor Max Rosenberg, who had once occupied the prestigious chair of music at the university and who had dared to include Jewish composers such as Mahler, Schoenberg and Mendelssohn in his curriculum, had been subjected to the final ignominy following his incarceration. With no home or family to go back to, he was spotted, a broken and dispirited man, wandering the streets of Berlin begging, mumbling like an idiot to himself.

To watch this once very proud man reduced to such circumstances left previous colleagues wondering if death would have been a kinder indictment than this.

No doubt that was the message that the Gestapo was sending out in the most blatant fashion, and the reason their colleague had not been killed but allowed to return to Berlin: to wander the streets as a constant reminder to his erstwhile colleagues should they contemplate dissension.

Helmut remained seated patiently for almost five minutes after his guest left, then wandered unhurriedly over to the open door, pretended to look out and then finally shut it.

He then waited another five minutes before returning to the window and drawing the blinds back, and stood there pretending to stare out absently into the street. Much as he forced his demeanour to appear nonchalant, the truth was that the entire time that the *Kriminalkommissar* had been there, Helmut had had to strain to hear what he was saying over the constant pounding of blood in his ears, convinced that at any moment the *Kriminalkommissar* would jump out of his chair and demand to search the house. At which point Helmut's life would end, and those of his family and single fugitive. His certain ordeal and fate did not matter to him. But he did not wish for his daughter Anna and wife Magda to be subjected to the torture and eventual death that would surely follow as the punishment meted out to traitors of the Reich. As for the fugitive, well, she would be summarily executed on the spot. As he might be. And that would be the kindest punishment under the circumstances.

So he waited, making sure that the *Kriminalkommissar* had not found his attitude much too affronting, and on reflection decided to come back for another conversation. Maybe next time he would ask Helmut to accompany him to the infamous headquarters to deflate some of his hubris.

When he was absolutely certain that no one was coming, he climbed to the second-floor landing. Again, he waited, listening for any cars pulling up outside the house. Satisfied that he was being overly paranoid due to the recent visit, he walked to the middle of the landing and reached for an overhead tile, which he removed carefully and set on the floor. Above where the tile had been was a metal ring clamped to the ceiling. He pulled on the ring, which released a ladder that telescoped down to the landing. With the ladder in place he proceeded to climb each rung carefully until his head rose over the ceiling and into the roof of the house.

Peering through the dusty darkness of the attic, he could just make out his daughter Anna and her best friend Ruth Lipschutz crouched in the corner. Oblivious to the dangers that had been below them only minutes before, they were whispering and giggling to each other as though their camaraderie in the attic was as normal as a secret tree house they shared. Helmut could not help rejoicing at the sight, and at the minds of teens who so easily adapted to new circumstances.

Satisfied that all was well he descended back to the landing, pushed the ladder back in place, replaced the tile and wandered back down to the dining room. Inevitably, he thought to himself, this all-too-cosy set-up would have to come to an end. Either the Gestapo would figure out their mistake, which with each passing month became less likely, or more likely Magda would break down and blurt out some idiocy to one of her friends, despite her realisation that the consequence to Helmut and their daughter, not to mention her brother Martin, would be fatal, even though Martin was in no way directly implicated in this.

Far better, though hope dimmed with every failed attempt, would be if someone finally put the mad corporal out of his misery and Germany returned to some semblance of normalcy.

BELLEVUE HILL, EASTERN SUBURBS, SYDNEY

Autumn 1986

It now became awkwardly embarrassing. She would have to listen for his door opening and closing, wait a few minutes and then go out about her chores. Better than coming across Sam in the hallway and having to… what? She wasn't quite sure. She had suspicions, and in all probability good ones. And Sam, well, he was not quite candid about filling in the inexplicable gaps and anomalies. Instead he glossed over them with self-righteous indignation.

On the other hand, no hands that ever meddled in World War II, even peripherally, were clean. Ruth knew enough Jewish people, both Germans and non, who had actively cooperated with both the Gestapo and the SS. True enough that they did it in the interest of self-preservation.

But if one absolved their disgraceful collaboration on those grounds, why not the non-Jews?

Instead of looking from the perspective of Jewish and non-Jewish, the line had to be drawn along the act of murder: those that committed it and those that didn't. And it had to be active participation. It could not include those whose deeds led to the death of others, otherwise the net would spread far too wide and no one could ever be absolved.

In her view only the few, who were later bestowed the honour of being called heroes, could claim to have risen above self-interest and in the process saved the lives of others. The rest, and regrettably the majority, served only their immediate needs and those of their next of kin, at times even negating the latter. Such is the power of self-preservation over morality and decency.

Ruth was no hero. And, with bitter sadness, she hated to admit to herself in her darkest moments that neither were her parents. They just died because they were cruelly killed. But being killed doesn't turn one into a hero, no matter how cowardly the perpetrator. It just turns one into a victim.

She couldn't guess at Sam's role in the war. Before Ernie died she always believed that he was a fraud and that he was shielding his true identity behind that of a Jewish victim, to camouflage his involvement in war crimes.

But in deference to Ernie, who befriended Sam, she did not share her suspicions with anyone other than her husband, who dismissed her as being paranoid. Nonetheless, when Sam's wife, Emma, passed away and her single friends asked whether they could be introduced to Sam now that he was a widower, she declined by saying that he was not quite ready yet. He was still in mourning.

When Emma was alive they never went beyond the neighbourly courtesy of greeting each other in the hallway or chatting briefly outside the building when they happened to run into each other. Ruth had little doubt that Emma was Jewish by birth, but – of the one-parent only, or as she liked to jestingly call it – tangentially so. Which essentially meant that she was lapsed: neither attending *Schule* nor following the dietary rituals. In that regard Sam's subtle gaffes to a Jewish person would not have raised any suspicions with Emma. She wouldn't know any different.

One thing was certain: neither Sam nor Emma ever came to *Schule* during the high holidays, even when secular Jews attended. But then again, neither did Ernie, who couldn't be bothered sitting in a large hall reading from a dusty book, as he would disparagingly put it when she asked him to accompany her. If he was going to sit in a large hall with strangers he preferred to be entertained, in which case he went to a movie with Sam instead.

Last year when Emma had become gravely ill with emphysema, Ruth on a number of occasions stopped by with soups, pies, cakes and an offer to sit with her while Sam got some relief. While the offer was always gratefully acknowledged it was nonetheless politely declined. Ruth also doubted that the food she brought over was ever consumed. Whenever she returned to pick up the empty dishes and enquired about the contents, the reply was always the same: "It was very nice, thank you." Even the one time when she deliberately overloaded the soup with so much salt that it would have caused anyone to gag, the answer was the same. Ruth concluded that neither Sam nor Emma ate the food, and that they were masterful liars who chose to say nothing out of politeness. She would have preferred that they be less circumspect and more forthright by simply asking that she stop bringing food around. Throwing out good food or feeding it to the neighbourhood pets did not pay her cooking much of a compliment.

In retrospect as she considered these episodes she began to suspect that there might have been an even more sinister reason for Sam and Emma declining her offer to sit in on occasion, or accepting food that was never consumed. She was convinced now that by not encouraging her in either endeavour they had hoped that she would stop meddling in their affairs. Affairs that, in her heightened, paranoid state, she was certain did not bear scrutiny.

Her assumption gained momentum as she thought back to Ernie's friendship with Sam over the years. Despite their camaraderie it never followed its natural course into a couples' friendship: the four of them getting, or going out, together. Throughout the years she accepted that flaw by resigning herself to the notion that not every one of her married friends instantly translated into a couples' friendship; she had her own personal friends. However, given Sam and Emma's predisposition to keep her at arm's length she deduced that Emma either suspected or knew of Sam's secret, and hence once an opportunity afforded Ruth the chance to intrude in their lives, albeit with the best intentions, they blocked it off, politely but firmly.

Damn Ernie with his bonhomie and cavalier attitude in shrugging off her suspicions! May he rest in peace, but in such matters of judgement he was an idiot.

What could she do now, a lonely widow by herself? If she dared confront Sam directly, he would surely silence her.

Go to the police? What would they care about some old German masquerading as a Jew? They had enough crimes to solve without delving into what they considered ancient history.

Then an idea struck her. Why didn't she think of it before? Probably because she felt safe with Ernie around. But now that this ex-Nazi was hovering around trying to befriend her, she no longer felt that safe. She would befriend the cagey old impostor and get his prints, and maybe steal an old photo if she happened to be invited to his apartment. With those items in her possession she would send the photo and prints to the Simon Wiesenthal Centres in both Vienna and Los Angeles. If he was anybody of any significance he would certainly be in their archives.

What a coup that would be! That would make up for some of that other cowardly matter that cost that girl her life. At least it would give Ruth some peace of mind that she had brought one murderer to justice. Who knows, Sam might even be directly connected to her parents' deaths, and that of that unfortunate girl. Wouldn't that be a coincidence?

With a plan afoot, she waited anxiously for his door to open. She didn't have long to wait. As soon as she heard Sam push the latch into place and turn the lock she went to her door, armed with her shopping bag and purse, and opened it. Pretending not to know that he was in the hallway, she exited her home backwards and pulled the door to. She knew that he would not just ignore her and let her go downstairs without saying something.

"Ruth!" He almost shouted with glee.

Pretending to be startled, she jumped slightly and turned a half-circle to face him. "Sam. Going out shopping?"

"Yes. Well, no. I was going out for a walk. But if you don't mind, I will accompany you to the shop." Debonair as ever, as if the previous encounter had never happened.

"Why not?" Taking a firm hold of her purse and bag, she proceeded to walk down the hallway, letting Sam sidle up closely and follow her to the lift. He hastily pressed the button and they stood awkwardly, facing their reflections in the shiny steel door.

"Listen, Ruth, I did not mean to have an unpleasant encounter with you. I came because I was concerned. And, well, I don't have the best—"

The lift arrived, interrupting Sam, and they walked in. Mrs Beck, the obstreperous neighbour from Number 16 upstairs, was standing stoically in the car as if she had died and been transformed into a block of ice.

They both greeted her in unison with a cheerful "Good morning", to which she almost imperceptibly nudged the edges of her mouth into a rictus. Despite their warm greeting, she was not to be dissuaded from her cantankerousness.

"What animal is leaving these unpleasant deposits in front of the building?" Her voice, throaty and creaky at the same time, a combination of cigarettes and age, bellowed from behind them. "The other day I almost stepped into it on my way to the Opera House. I would have missed the first act on account of a turd."

The lift arrived on the ground floor almost at the same time as Mrs Beck finished her tirade. Eager to distance themselves quickly from her, in the event that there was more to say on the subject, Ruth and Sam walked briskly to the foyer door and emerged onto the steps leading to the pavement, both laughing quite audibly as the door shut behind them.

"I was dreading that she might ask me to clean up the mess," Sam uttered, still chuckling.

More laughter.

"I don't know what I would have said. Maybe, 'Mrs Beck, you will need to wait for Act II. There's quite a bit of mess.'"

They continued laughing as they made their way to the shop. Neither brought up the subject of their previous awkward conversation that had ended on a somewhat peevish note.

They were now standing in front of the delicatessen.

"Listen, I am going to walk down to the newsagent and get the paper. Perhaps you would like to join me for a bit of refreshment and maybe some patisserie at Marco's? When you are finished with your shopping, of course."

Ruth wasn't much surprised at the invitation. She knew that something along that line was coming; she just didn't know how soon. What did surprise and confuse her at the same time was her reaction to the casual invitation. She suddenly felt relaxed in Sam's company, and her previous convictions now appeared the product of a feverish brain beset by anxiety and abruptly relieved by the comedic encounter with Mrs Beck. She was almost ashamed of the thoughts that she had allowed to take root in her head, to the point of setting out a plan to act on them. Thank God she didn't, was all that she could think.

Maybe Ernie, God bless him, had been right after all. And maybe she needed to air out her suspicions to Sam's face, as she had yesterday – was it yesterday? – to get them out in the open and then just let them go.

Even if she was right, and she was beginning to doubt that she was, he was probably no more than a lowly bureaucrat gobbled up by the ruthless machinery of a mad dictator. And maybe her act of contrition, for that cowardly act all those years ago, was to reach out and befriend someone who perhaps had just as good a reason as she to lose sleep.

"Yes, why not? That would be very nice. I will see you at Marco's in half an hour."

Ever the gentleman, Sam bowed his pleasure at her acceptance and then, with a stiff and precise gait, made his way to the newsagent.

A lowly official, maybe, Ruth thought with some bemusement, *but an ex-Nazi just the same. And if not an ex-Nazi, then definitely an anti-Semite. They all walk like that.*

Well, maybe an ex-anti-Semite, she thought, less critically – *he was, after all, Ernie's friend.*

BERLIN

Summer 1943

Despite an ever-increasing sense of foreboding, the summer ended without any further incident. There were no more visits from the Gestapo, cordial or otherwise. Anna continued to attend school and bring back homework and books to keep Ruth up to date. Even Magda, who would normally be considered the weak link in this chain of secrecy, managed to keep her link unbroken. She kept hosting parties; going out on shopping sprees; often lunching with her friends. Maintaining an outward appearance of frivolity, despite the immense burden that Ruth's presence placed on her otherwise carefree personality, remaining steadfast in keeping the secret. Even if it was for the self-serving reason that revealing Ruth's presence would put everything Magda held dear at certain risk.

Neither did she convey her obvious annoyance at this unwanted imposition to Helmut, except on the one day when the milk had run low. They were having their regular family breakfast before Helmut walked Anna to school and Magda set about planning her mundane day of lunch, shopping and parties. Helmut was at the table with Anna, going over a classroom assignment that was due, when Magda turned angrily towards them.

"There is hardly any milk. Every few days we run out."

"Well, we all drink it, so it is going to run out. I can go out and get some if you need it right now." Helmut attempted to mollify her obvious frustration and head off any simmering confrontation.

"It would not be a problem if it was just the three of us." With that, Magda slammed the fridge door and sat down at the table in a huff.

"Magda, we all drink. All of us. And the share that you refer to is even smaller than ours."

"Yes, maybe, but it is a share still." With a flick of her hand she indicated her unwillingness to continue the discussion.

Helmut, however, sensed that this had more to do with the increasing sense of pressure that keeping Ruth hidden placed on the family and on Magda in particular. He started to wonder and worry whether this was the first crack in the hitherto impregnable facade; that with each passing year the chances of her being discovered lessened and, conversely, the chances of the Third Reich ending prematurely increased.

Yet, even though the length of time favoured them, keeping up the deception was inevitably taking its toll. Maybe more on Magda who, in addition to having to keep up false appearances, also had to lie to her parents and her brother Martin, an SS officer, albeit in a lowly position. Although

Helmut tried to keep his contact with Martin to a minimum, his distaste more for the uniform than for the man, running into him was inevitable when he came by to visit his sister and niece, or during the obligatory family gatherings. At one such occasion Helmut and Martin got into their usual squabble, with Helmut openly accusing Martin of mass murder.

"Otherwise, where are all these people disappearing to? Huh? Except for one colleague who has been reduced to a retard, I haven't seen anyone reappear. No postcards. No letters." Away from the peering eyes of the Gestapo that seemed constantly to be lurking in the shadows, here, sequestered among the family, Helmut felt emboldened and lashed out unreservedly with his accusations.

Magda could sense Martin's embarrassment. Sitting at the corner of the table next to their ageing and hard-of-hearing father, he reddened, the collar of his uniform tightening like a noose around his neck. With a quivering finger he reached into the collar and pulled at it to discharge some of the pressure from the mounting onslaught.

But that was not to be. Helmut, seeing Martin's silence as a vindication of his accusations, rose from his chair and turned to face their mother, Greta, a prim and proper elderly woman with permed blonde hair.

"Don't you wonder? I mean, you probably have neighbours that have suddenly vanished and nobody asks any questions?"

Stammering slightly, Greta turned to look up at Helmut. "These are difficult times. Things are not necessarily as we want them. But the situation is better for us than in 1929 when Gerhard lost his business and I had to take in ironing and washing just to survive."

"Better? How better?"

Gerhard, who everyone had assumed was unable to hear the conversation that had devolved into an open argument, interrupted in a thick, quavering voice. "I don't say it is better or worse. But the Jews, they don't believe in fair business. So what Herr Hitler is saying to some extent is true. They have bled Germany—"

Helmut was fully out of his chair now, ready to spring over to challenge the old man, who raised his hand, asking to be allowed to finish.

"I am not saying all Jews. But these," he waved his gnarled hand contemptuously, "these black-clad, bearded creatures; these are not Germans. They don't participate in German life or culture. They keep to themselves, conspiring – only God knows what they get up to."

Helmut laughed harshly. "I am sorry, I don't understand. Are you opposed to the Orthodox Jews, or to Jews in general because they are unscrupulous?"

But Gerhard became tight-lipped again. If Hitler's net caught some innocent along with what he considered guilty Jews, that was a price he was prepared to accept to restore Germany to prosperity. A hardened Teuton who had endured his share of hardships, he had come to accept life's rule that everything had its price.

Flustered, Helmut sat down and wiped his brow, perspiring even on this somewhat cooler and overcast day.

An awkward silence fell around the dining table, with only Anna whispering something to her grandmother with an impish smile on her tender face. Greta turned to Magda. "Anna tells me that she has made a new friend."

"What?" The unexpected turn in the conversation caught Magda by surprise. Helmut instantly blanched and looked hurriedly over in Martin's direction. "New friend? What new friend? Helmut and I don't know anything about this! Anna!" More than questioning, her tone was reprimanding.

But Anna wasn't saying any more. She looked over at her grandmother, who was now sharing her mischievous smirk.

Struck by the possibility that Anna might have revealed to her grandmother that she had befriended a Jewish girl, just when her grandfather was accusing the Jews of being un-German, Helmut was dumbstruck. Magda looked at him, her worried expression obvious.

"Anna can have a male friend at her age. That's not unusual," Martin piped up from his corner.

Both Helmut and Magda turned their attention to Martin, not quite taking in the lifeline he was throwing them. Once the initial panic settled, Magda turned back to Anna – "Is it a male friend, Liebchen?" – a warm and understanding smile evaporating the worry and panic from her face.

"I am not saying. But Oma knows."

Following the Sunday lunch, and back at their house, Magda turned to Helmut when Anna was out of earshot. "Do you think Martin knows and he was helping cover up the truth? I mean, my father is quite capable of saying something, not realising the consequence for us. He blames the Jews for his bankruptcy. He would think that he was doing the patriotic thing, you know."

Helmut, struck by what he considered the sincerest display of camaraderie from his wife in as long he could remember, paused to reflect on the likelihood. "It is possible that he knows. But I can't imagine how. So far as I know, other than the three of us, no one knows about Ruth."

Magda thought about it for a moment before replying. "What about her parents?"

"Surely you don't think that Heinrich and Alana would have said anything?"

"No, that wouldn't make a lot of sense. Did we ever find out what happened to them?"

Helmut merely shook his head.

"What about Helga, could she have mentioned something to my parents or Martin?" Magda asked, thinking back to her niece's stay with them.

"I don't see how, she went back to Munich with Uncle Wolfgang at the same time as Ruth came to stay. She never had a chance to talk to either your parents or Martin."

They pondered the situation for a moment before Magda appeared to reach a decision. "The truth is that none of us are safe as long as she is here. I think we should talk to Martin, who we can safely assume is in the dark about all this. Persuade him to take Ruth to your aunt in Zurich. He will help once he knows the danger to Anna and me."

Helmut was silent for a long time, then reached across, cupping her hand in his. "I think that of all the options, that's the best one at the moment. Unless Herr Hitler is kaput the next time they make an attempt on his life."

"Herr Professor, that's not something you can count on."

BREMEN

Autumn 1944

Despite the best attempts of the propagandists of the Third Reich – chiefly Goebbels, but also in no small part Streicher's *Der Stürmer* – the unfiltered news from the battlefront was that Nazi Germany was beginning to lose the war. On the Eastern Front, Operation Barbarossa ended with abysmal losses of a quarter of a million troops and half a million wounded after an initial onslaught which brought them to within twenty-four kilometres of Moscow by the middle of November.

But by December the first blizzards of winter had set in. The Wehrmacht was neither equipped for a prolonged war, nor for the severe winter conditions that engulfed the Soviet Union. By the first week in December the newly amassed Russian troops numbering nearly half a million were able to push back the ill-equipped, depleted and demoralised German troops by over two hundred miles.

The Wehrmacht had succeeded previously on the strength of short, intense battles or blitzkriegs, a lethal combination of air and infantry warfare that quickly overwhelmed the opponent and earned the Third Reich swift victories. But with Nazi Germany occupying ever larger parts of Europe, attempting to manage a war on two fronts and facing an increasing strain on its resources, the earlier successes, particularly on the Eastern Front, failed to materialise. The United States had also joined the war, squarely on the British side, following the Japanese attack on Pearl Harbor, and the pressure was beginning to mount on the Western Front as well.

Friedrich Becker was home on his first furlough since he'd enlisted in the SS. Seated in the back garden of the small cottage that was his parents' home, he tried to put forth the optimistic Nazi Party line to assure his parents and sister that all was well, and that despite the setbacks Germany would emerge victorious.

"It is only temporary, believe me. The Wehrmacht is a very well-oiled machine. Like any machine, sometimes it needs fine-tuning before it can resume operations." He was looking at his father, hoping that the analogy of machinery would explain and appeal to him at least, a veteran mechanical engineer working at the Benz factory.

The tall, slender man watched his son through his piercing blue eyes, a customary look of scepticism clouding his bony face. "Oh, I believe you. But you haven't told me what *you* think. You have told me what the party wants me to hear. I can almost tell you which Goebbels speech this analogy comes from."

"Herman! He is our son, and a staff sergeant. He is not going to tell you some made-up stories." Friedrich's mother, Marlis, ever espousing her belief in the military and its honour, would not surrender to the thought that her son could be delivering propaganda. A stout woman who until recently had worked at a garment factory, but due to a chronic arthritic condition gave up the job to work part time at a school, she looked upon her son with great admiration and respect, believing that he was serving Germany honourably despite her and her husband's distaste for Hitler and his party. In their minds, politics did not define the military.

"Don't be naive. The Wehrmacht of today is not like when Bismarck was around. Herr Hitler and his friends are of a different ilk. You know, the other day we received orders for bulletproof cars for all the elite. Can you believe it? When did people shoot at German generals and high-level politicians?" Herman chuckled disbelievingly.

"Now who is being naive?" Friedrich turned to face his father.

"Look, I am just asking whether all this expansion, conquering of other countries, wars with the Bolsheviks and the British is achieving anything, because if it's not, an awful lot of troops are dying for nothing. And don't tell me Germans aren't getting slaughtered in large numbers." He punctuated his sense of frustration at getting stock answers by jabbing a pointed finger directly at Friedrich.

There was a pause. An uncomfortable silence while Friedrich mulled over his answer as best he could under the circumstances, without revealing more than he should that would put both him and his parents at risk. The silence was briefly interrupted by his sister Brigitte, who brought out a tray of hot and cold drinks. Nobody spoke while she set the tray down and offered the drinks around. She put the tray aside by the door and returned to her seat next to her mother.

"Were you having a secret conversation about me?" Brigitte smiled at her mother. "Not about eligible bachelors again, I hope?" Five years younger than her sibling, Brigitte still lived at home, and at twenty-eight was considered at the upper end of the age scale in terms of eligibility. She wasn't quite being referred to as an old maid yet, but that description would draw nearer if she remained in her celibate state for much longer.

"No, dear. Your father, ever the great diplomat, was accusing your brother of lying to us about the war situation."

"I wasn't saying that he was lying. More like varnishing." Herman looked at his son again, this time with a kinder, more inviting expression.

Sighing with discomfort, Friedrich turned to his father. "What is it that you would like me to say?"

"Well, I would think that the truth would be a good start. We are all good Germans; we have a right to know what's going on. And right now I don't think that we are getting much of anything from our politicians, other than the Third Reich is going to last a thousand years. Yet, at the plant, more and more fathers are reporting deaths at the front or severely wounded soldiers." He spread his arms wide in a show of cloaking them in his secret.

"Well, wounded and dead men are part of the war," Friedrich blurted smugly, oblivious to his father's attempt to subtly trade one secret for another.

"Yes, I agree, but not when more of yours are dying and wounded than the enemy's. It should be the other way around if this Reich is going to last."

Once again the small gathering was left with an awkward silence.

Friedrich looked like he was juggling with several thoughts and emotions simultaneously. On the one hand he wanted to tell his family what he saw and knew. But on the other hand, if that knowledge somehow leaked from this household, it would put his parents and sister in peril and would almost certainly result in his being summarily dispatched to the Eastern Front, an almost certain death sentence; or even worse, internment at a concentration camp with the same final outcome.

Having made up his mind, he rose, picked up his drink, a cold Pilsner, and nodded towards his parents and sister. "Let's go inside." When they appeared to hesitate, he nodded towards the patio door. "Please."

A look of surprise and concern descended on them as they humbly followed Friedrich to the living room and proceeded to take their places around the comfortable fireplace, while he pulled the door shut and drew the heavy maroon drapes. Rather than sit down, he walked over to the fireplace and rested his drink on the mantelpiece. Brushing his hair back, he undid the top button of his SS uniform and unclasped the Iron Cross from his collar, setting it with a clink on the marble top.

"I am not going to varnish this for you. But I am also going to let you know that what I am about to tell you will put you all at risk. So if you want me to not continue, we can go back outside and resume our friendly conversation. Why don't you all tell me whether you want to hear what I have to say?"

In the small but comfortable room, normally resounding with lively conversation and dinner nearby, the words fell ominously, making the interior feel darker than it was with the drapes pulled.

Herman looked at his wife, then his daughter. Getting no protest from either, he nodded for Friedrich to continue.

"All right. In Germany, for the last couple of years there has been a process of evacuation of political opponents, mentally ill patients, homosexuals and anyone who is considered undesirable to the Third Reich, Jewish people in particular. At first the evacuation proceeded with small numbers, but lately the pace has increased to the point where we are running trains all day."

Herman put up his hand. "Trains to where?"

Friedrich shook his head sombrely. "I am not sure. But last month, they started a rotation of SS personnel and it turns out, according to those returning to home duty, that the destination is not Africa, nor Palestine for the Jews, but deportation to the east, and large concentration camps."

They sat stunned, looking at him, unable to grasp the import of what he was saying. The shock of the revelation was much too overwhelming to take in.

Herman started chuckling nervously. "What are you saying exactly?" he blurted. "That entire populations of Jews and non-Jews all over the Reich are being incarcerated en masse in large camps? How can that be possible? The logistics alone would be overwhelming – so much so that it couldn't be kept a secret." He turned to look at his wife, who sat dumbfounded, her head bowed, staring at the rug as if mesmerised by the pattern. Brigitte looked from her father to Friedrich and then back at her father, waiting for someone to say something that made sense, because this whole picture of mass incarceration was incomprehensible.

When the disbelieving laughter subsided, and Friedrich remained silent, his father faced him sternly. "Do you have any proof of this? I mean, I served in World War I and I can tell you that between truth and rumours there was a large gap of crazy stories, usually circulated by the enemy. Who told you this?" His tone was openly challenging.

"Do you remember Ulrich?"

"Which Ulrich? Ulrich Ebersbacher? The son of that idiot who has the hardware shop on Meinz Straße?" With that Herman jumped up, slapping his hands on his thighs as if that explained everything. "I mean, he didn't even finish high school. He left, when, almost five years ago?"

"That's right, he left at that time after he joined the SD," Friedrich continued for him, "but he also became an active party member – key role in Kristallnacht; then a senior assignment. And now he is a big shot. I don't think he was lying; all he said was that if we lost the war, there would be a massive mess on our hands."

"What mess?" Marlis asked a question for the first time.

"Resettling all those people, I assume all those hundreds of thousands of Jews, maybe millions. I don't exactly know." Friedrich's voice faded with the enormity of the sums.

His father, hearing the numbers, momentarily lost his balance and almost toppled into the couch. Once again a silence engulfed the room, although this time it was accompanied by a heavy sense of dread.

"Friedrich, you should have given us some warning of what you were going to say. I mean, if I knew what it was, or a hint of it, I would have objected. I am also speaking for Brigitte," Marlis uttered in a trembling voice laced with fear and grave concern. The information that Friedrich had imparted so brazenly clearly shook them, but at the same time, at least for Marlis, she was not sure that she should be privy to it regardless of whether it was true or false.

"Well, I am sorry if what I have said has disturbed you, but Father has been pressing me for information."

"Yes, but I thought that with all the drama that goes on, with Hitler and Goebbels making bombastic speeches, you would tell us there is some new plan of attack; you know, a military secret. An invasion plan." Marlis looked over to Herman, who seemed either lost in thought or still numbed by the shock of what he had just heard.

"How are they feeding and housing so many people?" Brigitte piped up from her corner, less concerned, but more curious.

"Brigitte, we don't need to know that," Marlis, said sternly, reprimanding her daughter for even raising the subject.

In a quavering tone, Herman asked his son, "What would they do to us? I mean, if they knew that you have told us?"

Friedrich looked around at his family with great concern. "I don't know. I really don't know. I mean, I told you because I think that I am going to end up at the Eastern Front, which means there is a good probability that I will either be seriously wounded or worse. I don't think that they are going to send me to serve in the camps. I am not considered elite enough for such duty."

"If you are not supposed to know, then why did Ulrich give you that information?" Herman, sitting close to the edge of the couch, holding his wife's hand, asked nervously.

"I think he made a mistake. He assumed all SS personnel were in the know, so to speak. But after he told me and a number of other personnel he was called into the station and I could see the *Standartenführer* reprimanding him."

"So you are in danger. More than we are," Brigitte offered openly. Seeing her parents' blank stares, she continued. "I mean, nobody knows that you've told us anything. But from what you say, they know that *you* know."

"That is correct. Which is why I am certain that I will be assigned to serve in Guderian's army in one of the Panzer divisions."

"What makes you think that you will be severely wounded or die?" Brigitte was now leading the conversation.

"Let's just say that the Eastern Front is not a good assignment with a safe chance of return. Given how the war on…" He stopped, considering the implication of what he was about to say. "It's just not a good assignment."

"Can you ask for a reassignment?"

"Not within the division that I am in."

"Why can't they just leave you where you are at present? What exactly do you know?" Marlis re-joined the conversation.

Friedrich thought for a minute before replying. "Well, the redeployment is going to happen. That's why Ulrich and others are in Berlin. They are rotating personnel. The assignment that I currently have, transport, is considered a rather cushy one compared to the combat units and Waffen SS that are deployed on the Eastern Front." Counting the points on his fingers, he proceeded to explain. "So I am going to be reassigned. The camps are out. I am not in that elite group, so to speak. That leaves a bureaucratic assignment or active duty. Given that my *Standartenführer* thinks that I am a lazy softie, and now he suspects that I know more than I should, I don't think he is going to think twice about sending me on an assignment where I have a less-than-thirty-per-cent chance of returning alive." With that he unfurled his middle and index fingers and raised them in a V-sign, having answered both questions.

"Can you go off to Holland?" Brigitte sniggered, remembering that at one time Friedrich had lived with a student from Utrecht.

"What do you mean, desert?"

"Sort of. Resign your commission and become a civilian."

"Sounds nice. If my chances of surviving the reassignment are thirty per cent, abandoning my unit and running off to Utrecht is desertion. The penalty is quick and simple: death by firing squad."

"Well, it was just an idea."

"Brigitte, maybe you should forget about your good ideas." Once again Marlis reprimanded her daughter.

With that the room fell into a heavy silence, each pondering their own fate, having become privy to information whose outward exposure jeopardised their relative safety. Moreover, the more immediate threat to their family unit – Friedrich's precarious fate in light of his imminent, and likely, redeployment to a dangerous duty – weighed on their minds.

Suddenly Herman perked up. "Assuming that what you are saying is true, and that Ulrich is now considered part of some inner circle, why can't we use that connection to help you?"

"And say what?"

"Well, that he should encourage them to either keep you in Berlin, where you are now, or reassign you to an office job."

Friedrich paused to ponder the possibility. "Well, rumour – everything is rumour – is that Ulrich somehow has a tenuous connection to Obergruppenführer Kaltenbrunner. I don't know what the connection is. But it would explain his rapid promotion."

"What is his rank?" Brigitte was curious, trying to recall the rather shy and plain-looking boy from down the road.

"*Sturmbannführer.*"

"Which is what?" Marlis shot back. "We don't know what these ranks mean."

"Well, he is just two ranks lower than my superior, who is in charge of the entire contingent of three hundred men at the train station."

"It sounds like he could be helpful," Herman proffered with dim hope in his voice.

"If he wants to be. But if the rumour about his connection to Kaltenbrunner is false, my superior could easily countermand any favour, and I'd end up, well, I'd end up where I'd probably end up, only quicker."

After some more discussion, they all agreed that it was the only viable option. It bore some risks, to be sure, but just the same, they outweighed the obvious dangers of doing nothing and facing the inevitable: Friedrich risking his life. With that resolution some of the earlier dread and doom lifted from the room and they all returned outside to continue their earlier convivial conversation.

Late in the evening, the family accompanied Friedrich to the train station, ending his brief furlough. They all hugged him warmly, each in turn looking at him intently as if trying to preserve his image in their mind, thinking privately that this might be the last time they would see him. Just as he was about to board the train, Brigitte came up close to him one final time and handed him a wallet-sized photograph that she had taken of them on his last visit when he received his SS commission at Grünewald. "Just in case… so you don't forget us."

At 7.42 precisely the train departed from Bremen Station back to its destination in Berlin. Friedrich leaned out through the carriage window and waved goodbye to his parents and sister, his face engulfed in the rising steam of the locomotive hurtling deep into the night.

A night that, in Berlin, was no longer quiet and dark as in the distance of Bremen. The nightly Allied bombing raids had begun and the city was aglow with fires from the many burning buildings. Air-raid sirens clamoured continually, accompanied by the sirens from ambulances and fire trucks.

Given this new reality, the prospect of staying in Berlin in a relatively safe bureaucratic position became, though still not as perilous as redeployment to the Eastern Front, a far less certain future than escaping to Utrecht. Added to the fact that Friedrich had neglected to tell his family that his redeployment papers had already been served; they were tucked firmly in his breast pocket next to the photo. Any discussion of countermanding that order was in effect for their benefit only, to allay their fears. The short furlough, with a week gone, had been granted on the premise that on his return he would be heading eastwards from Berlin, making the furlough his farewell.

BELLEVUE HILL, EASTERN SUBURBS, SYDNEY

Winter 1986

Ruth was back to setting the dinner table on Friday night. Since Ernie's death, she had abandoned the ritual, other than lighting the Friday-night candles. On the Friday following his death, she lit the candles absent the perfunctory blessings, and proceeded to dine on a meal prepared for two. Emotionally he was still there; his death had not quite escaped the confines of his life. But as the days passed and his ethereal presence evaporated, it was harder and harder to hold on to routines that had once served two people and now fitted poorly on one.

It was really just the mundane sort of things that annoyed and saddened her the most. Like walking into their favourite restaurant, a place they had frequented once a month, and where she was now welcomed with the greeting, "Eating by yourself?" It wasn't like they meant to rub it in. They were just making a polite enquiry so that they could direct her to the appropriate table. But that was just it; the appropriate table meant being shunted off to a desolate corner, wedged in between the toilet and the kitchen.

On her next visit she bluntly instructed the greeter to sit her at a more jovial table than the one reserved for singles ostracised by the death of their partner. When he stood confused, she bypassed him and walked straight up to the owner and asked for her and Ernie's table. Without hesitation he ushered her to their usual table with a warm smile, pulling out the chair and welcoming her back.

Then there were the movies. One ticket. Sitting solitarily with the other solos during the matinee sessions. Here no one said anything because they were all in the same boat. Rarely did she see any couples come in for the afternoon matinee session. She could easily invite one of her many female friends along. But it didn't feel the same. It was the earlier dilemma of giving in and giving up. Hard to do when you have spent every waking moment for the last forty years inseparable from someone who is no longer here.

Gradually she began to modify her routines. Instead of going to their favourite restaurant, she went to a café where she nearly always found someone she knew and joined their table. Instead of going to see movies, she joined a group of women her age that subscribed collectively to a season of plays and concerts. This way, she was no longer going out alone.

And now, well, she was beginning to think that maybe there was room in her home for someone else. A person who, only a week ago, she had contemplated turning in for crimes unknown. But perhaps, she reasoned, it was time to turn many pages at once. Let the past go. Otherwise it threatened to drag her into a well from which there was no egress; a life lived in darkness and alone.

As far as Sam was concerned, or whatever his real name and identity was, well, if he was an ex-Nazi, not all Nazis were bad; there were good Nazis, incongruous as that sounded. Germans who, due to fear, cooperated openly with the regime but secretly found ways to commit acts of bravery in spite of everything. Maybe Sam was one of those. Anyway, she was too old to engage in any witch-hunt. Ironically, for with time both Ernie and she had become inflexible and unforgiving in many ways, yet a change of circumstances such as she had been thrust into forced her to become more tolerant. Perhaps she could be the other side of the coin: the Jewish person to forgive the ex-Nazi who was looking for a way to rehabilitate and restore his life.

What was it that he said: *you are not the only one that cannot sleep?* Well, welcome to the club. A great many elderly Jewish people suffer from nightmares, more so later in life as they recall the horrors of the Holocaust.

Finally she settled on the comforting excuse that 'You only live once', and that if Ernie had befriended Sam, he couldn't be all that bad. This was reinforced by the fact that he had appeared at her doorstep at a crucial moment in time. So she decided to make room for Sam in her life and her home. Tonight she invited him to join her. She could be mischievous and ask him to recite the Friday-night prayers and follow with the blessing of the wine and the slicing of the bread. But that would be a cruel joke. Instead she would pray over the candles, the wine and the bread and then call him over. That way he need not be faced with the embarrassment of what to say and do.

No sooner had she rested the phone than he appeared at the door, propping it gently with a bottle of wine and a bouquet of flowers. An expensive spray of flowers, too. Yet, she thought with an inward smile, it is seldom that one brings flowers to a Friday-night dinner. He was treating this as a date. To her this was a customary meal on the eve of the Sabbath. Traditional, but not festive.

True, Sam's faux pas was not quite in as bad a form, she had to admit, as when two non-Jewish acquaintances from her bridge class that she invited years ago to a Passover dinner appeared with a plastic container from the local Greek takeout. Ruth graciously took the container, and once the guests were comfortably ensconced in the living room, adroitly placed it outside the door for next door's dog to feast on.

She and Ernie had often joked about the aftermath. Ruth had forgotten that she had placed the takeout outside the door, and one acquaintance noticed it on the way out and commented sourly to Ernie, who unhesitatingly explained that it wasn't for the dog, but Elijah: the mystery guest who is supposed to appear on this holiest of nights. Since then they had both referred to the dog as Elijah, much to the disdain of Mrs Fleischmann, the neighbour on the other side of Sam, who thought it in very poor taste to name a dog after a biblical figure.

Now as Ruth was preparing to bring the food out, Sam skilfully opened the wine and poured two full glasses. Ruth, spying him from through the serving hatch, thought, as she had the other afternoon, that he was behaving as a teenager might on his first date. She began to wonder whether he had always had a crush on her. Was he perhaps thinking that he would get her drunk and then make a move? Well, what if he did? Maybe a bit soon, she contemplated, but not an unpleasant thought. She tried to recall the last time she had felt physically attractive or attracted to anyone. Much as she loved Ernie, their life did not revolve around romance but had become a relationship of comfort. They were comfortable for each other. Like the slippers or the housecoat, or the very many routines they had become accustomed to.

This was something new, something fresh and perhaps a little exciting. How would it feel?

"Ruth?" Sam alerted her from the dining room. Forgetting the dinner and her guest, she had become lost in all the many ramifications that this date presented. He had just come for a Friday-night dinner and she was already entertaining a clear path all the way down to romance and the awkwardness that a new relationship entails, age notwithstanding. Maybe he was right to feel like a teenager on a first date. The heart is impervious to age.

"I am sorry; I was momentarily reminded… never mind." Carrying the first dish across, she set it down in the middle of the table and went back into the kitchen. Noticing her awkwardness, Sam got up and followed her.

"Listen. If this is too soon, I can always leave and come back at another time," he offered unconvincingly.

Seeing him standing in the kitchen doorway, apprehensive of her nervousness, she shrugged him off with,

"Don't be silly. I didn't go to all this trouble so that you could run off. Take this and go back to the table. While you are there, why don't you pick something you like to listen to?"

His face, which seconds earlier had sagged in the apprehension that she would respond in the affirmative and ask him to leave, now brightened and he eagerly grabbed the bowl and made his way back to the dining room.

Ruth waited a moment longer in the kitchen to see what music he would put on. Dave Brubeck. Of course. Soft and mellow jazz. Mood-setting. Sam was quite adept at this.

Finally they were both seated and starting to enjoy the meal.

"My compliments. When did you have the time to prepare all this?"

"That's all I have. Time. And plenty of it." Ruth set her fork down and looked across at Sam. "What do you do with your time?"

"Well, once I wake up, I prepare my own breakfast, then I go down to the shops, have my morning walk. I sit in the café, read the paper. Three days a week I play bridge. Two days I volunteer at the gallery. Time passes."

"Yes, it does. It's over two months since Ernie died. I can hardly believe it. I had these plans to box up all his clothing and give it to the local charity. Repaint the house..." She paused, feeling lost for a moment in recalling the minutiae involved in the aftermath of the death of someone close.

"So, what happened? It sounds like a good plan."

"What happened? What happened was I started to feel lonely. Which makes you depressed and not want to do anything. You just sit there watching the time pass, eventually wondering if there is any point to your life." She half expected Sam to lean over and place his hand over hers. Part of the plan, she thought cynically: the flowers, the wine, the soft jazz and now the comforting hand. To her surprise, he didn't.

"I had a different experience, you know, when Emma passed away. Being alone again, away from her love, allowed all the ghosts of the past to come back and haunt me; night after night." He looked directly at Ruth to see if she was comprehending his agony. "I no longer had her protection. Love, it protects you. I don't mean that first romance, but the bond between two people that care deeply for each other."

Ruth was surprised to see tears welling up in the corners of his eyes. Now she felt moved to reach across and put a comforting hand on his. The good Jew on the other side of the coin. Instinctively she did.

He momentarily broke from his anguish and pulled his hand away, resuming his meal in silence.

"What, Sam? What exactly are they haunting you about?" Her tone softer, seeking to break through gently, unlike the other time when she had probed for the sake of exposing him. This time she was looking to expunge the ghosts by exposing them.

"I don't wish to talk about it. Not now. It is a nice evening. Two friends having a wonderful meal together. I don't want to ruin the mood."

At least he left the door open, she thought to herself. "Would you like some more of the vegetables?" A mundane question to break the pall that had descended over the table.

"Oh, no. It's all wonderful. But I am getting very full and I would like to leave some room for dessert."

She laughed.

"Oh, I am sorry. I did not mean to suggest…" He reddened instantly. "There is no dessert. That's all right."

"Sam. There is plenty of dessert: strudel, chocolates, fruit. Whatever you like." With that she began to clear the table.

Looking fleetingly over at him, she noticed that he had half-turned to stare out the window at the settling dusk. A look of wistfulness descended over his face. Ruth set down the tray and waited for him to return to the moment.

"Oh, sorry. I was briefly reminded of another time in my life. All so long ago: the wonderful home-cooked meal; the essence of warmth; the dessert."

"Do you miss it?"

"Only little things. You know. I love Sydney, but occasionally I yearn for the snow-strewn streets. Christmas with my parents and sister."

Sam came back and started to help Ruth clear the table. The earlier sense of trepidation momentarily returned to the pit in her stomach. She resolved to allay it by rationalising that even though he was definitely a Gentile; even allowing that, in the extreme, he might have been a Nazi, he could in fact have been one of those that conspired against Hitler.

Still, the not knowing frightened her. Even if she knew the worst – precluding murder – she could resolve to deal with it in a rational way. They were both too old to mind the past, they had been neighbours for many years, Ernie had considered Sam a friend, and Ruth could even admit to herself that she found him attractive and sought his company.

But the fear of uncertainty unsettled her. She wanted to prod him regarding his family, to get a hinge on his past so that she could open the door to it. But all at once the not knowing made her feel more secure in the knowledge that it was better not to know. Her motivation was clearly selfish: she wanted him in her life and she wanted to know about his past, but she didn't want to lose him on account of it. Paradoxical thoughts swirled in her mind, bifurcating the evening: either she reverted to where she was a few days ago, with thoughts of loneliness and suicide; or she was on the cusp of a new life.

They washed up in silence: Ruth doing the dishes and Sam drying. After the dishes were done, they took out the dessert and cups of coffee, settling in the living room in front of the television. To her dismay the one channel that offered cultural fare had plenty of it, except it was documentaries on Hitler, followed by one on Goebbels. Not what she considered light-hearted entertainment for the start of the weekend.

"Would you like to watch a movie? Or continue to listen to music and talk?" she ventured.

"A movie? That would be nice."

She picked a light-hearted romantic comedy and they settled next to each other on the couch to enjoy it.

It was strange, she thought as she sat close by him; he almost felt like Ernie, except for the tension between them. Sexual tension? Or was it due to not knowing, and imagining that the aura of mystery surrounding him was sinister and exciting, like a character in some thriller? What if it turned out in the end that his story was quite conventional; death and destruction in World War II? Would the tension evaporate and he turn out to be another pair of comfortable slippers or a housecoat? Did she want a continuation of

Ernie? Or did she want the excitement of someone new and different; perhaps with a gaping flaw or secret that he had been struggling to cover up and keep at bay with his spouse's love, and now that that had receded, was drowning him?

Who is saving whom? she thought to herself. *Is he saving me or am I saving him? Or are we saving each other?* All of an instant she understood his anger the other day. He had come in the nick of time to save her, and he did. In return he wanted to be saved by her, and instead she started asking him intrusive questions before agreeing to toss him a lifeline.

Feeling guilty, she let her hand fall gently into his palm. This time he did not shrink away. Instead he cupped her hand, a sweet, warm sensation filling her.

I would never admit this to anyone, she thought to herself, *a Jew believing in God, but Ernie trusted him and subliminally drove him to be my companion after he died.*

She had let her superstition guide her this far. Now Ernie would have to trust her with the choices she made not to abandon his memory in creating new ones for herself with Sam, regardless of what his real identity was.

UTRECHT

Winter 1944

Much as Friedrich liked to think that he had become accustomed to the bone-aching winter chill, having grown up in Bremen, Utrecht was colder still. After leaving Bremen he disembarked the train at Hanover and, instead of heading east to Berlin, travelled south by bus, then west to Cologne. From there he continued travelling in the same direction, crossing the Dutch border at Veno, arriving first at Eindhoven and then finally north by train to reach his final destination: Utrecht. It was a circuitous route and added hours to his journey, but the further afield he travelled from his designated destination of Berlin, without being stopped, the more comfortable he became with his fledgling plan. Nonetheless, he reminded himself that he had not disposed of his uniform, which, along with his furlough papers, provided him with a safety net.

Neither in Germany proper, nor when he crossed over to Holland, did he have any problems in progressing from destination to destination. Despite his portent of danger at nearly every stop, he was only questioned once, at the border crossing in Veno. He had picked this remote and seldom-trafficked route in the belief that the personnel guarding it would be few and less wary. There was a single officer at the checkpoint and two *Gefreiters* – corporals, Hitler's rank, he chuckled inwardly to calm himself. The Wehrmacht *Leutnant* in command of the checkpoint wanted to know why an SS sergeant was entering Holland. Friedrich presented his furlough papers, which were still in effect, and explained that he was visiting a German relative residing in Eindhoven. The *Leutnant* examined the papers closely, matching Friedrich's card with his uniform, that of an *SS-Scharführer* – technically a rank lower than the *Leutnant*'s, but as a member of the Schutzstaffel it placed Friedrich in a higher echelon than a Wehrmacht officer – and then with "*Heil Hitler*", saluted Friedrich and let him go on his way.

As he was assisting Friedrich in re-shouldering his duffel, the *Leutnant* explained deferentially that the interrogation had been for his own protection: there were Dutch partisans who were inimical to the Third Reich and in particular to members of the Schutzstaffel, whom they would not hesitate to kill. Friedrich thanked him and made his way to the train station in Veno. It was now mid morning. He had been on the go for nearly twelve hours.

By his calculation it would take him just as long to arrive at Utrecht, barring any further delays. Despite the encounter with the *Leutnant*, which jarred him slightly, he still felt relatively safe. He was not a wanted man. Not as yet.

He had only received his orders the week before his furlough – his hunch had been right – and he wasn't expected for a further five days; with the chaos of the retreat, maybe six. But it wouldn't be long before his non-appearance at his assigned unit on the Eastern Front would be flagged as a desertion.

Shortly before midnight he emerged from Utrecht Centraal Train Station and headed out to Damstraat, walking in the general direction of Universiteit Utrecht. He had studied here pre-1940, completing three of the four years required to graduate as a doctor, and taking the final year at his premed alma mater of Leipzig. But that was before Germany decided to invade Holland, and before he donned the dreaded uniform of the Schutzstaffel. The *Universiteit* would offer him temporary accommodation in its dormitory for visiting graduates. But, as with all activities in wartime, his presence would be reported and, in this place, unwelcome.

The Wehrmacht was everywhere he looked: in train stations, on the street, in makeshift checkpoints, bars, restaurants, shops, mixing in with the locals, ostensibly integrating seamlessly with the population. But an occasional look at a local passer-by revealed the intense animosity underneath the false facade. He didn't doubt what the *Leutnant* had told him back at the checkpoint in Veno: they would murder him in a second if the chance presented itself.

He had to get out of his uniform quickly and inconspicuously before the *Leutnant*'s prediction came true. It would be sadly ironic if Dutch partisans killed him after having forestalled that fate by wearing the SS uniform. The time was now ticking from both ends: Germany and the hostile Utrecht populace.

Emma? Eventually, yes, if she or her parents still lived in the same place. She might have relocated from the two-storey house on Kromme Nieuwegracht that he had shared with her. But her parents, who were middle-aged when he met them, and whose house had been in the family for over a century, would surely still be living in theirs. Except…? He paused to consider the possibility. He looked around himself. There were a few people out at this time of night, mostly Wehrmacht personnel out drinking and consorting with the prostitutes; the occasional local making his or her way hurriedly, head bowed and their attention fixed on their feet.

Adding to his need to change for expediency's sake, he was also starting to feel the night-time cold seeping into his bones. So as not to attract any more attention than necessary he turned right off Damstraat and crossed over the bridge to Leidseweg, which ran along the canal. Few people milled about or walked along there this late. He found a damp bench and sat down to think. Emma van Bergen. Would she still want to see him, be with him? He had never returned after spending Christmas with his parents in Bremen as he promised. That was in 1937, nearly six years ago. What if she was no longer single?

She too had been a medical student, and would certainly be a graduate researcher by now, if not department head. When he came here in 1934 he hadn't planned on meeting and settling down with anyone; it was mainly a desire to complete his medical degree away from the virulent fanaticism that was sweeping across Germany.

Friedrich was immediately attracted to Emma's bubbly personality and what the French called joie de vivre that he so yearned for. She quenched his parched soul; he had always believed that his love for Emma was what solidified his rebellion against Germany. He no longer needed to carry that lugubrious yoke around his neck alone – she unburdened him.

But events in Germany conspired against them, added to which his inflexibility proved too much to overcome. Emma's mother was Jewish. Friedrich didn't even consider it a hurdle. But both her parents were resolute in that she ought not to give up her life in Utrecht and move to Bremen. They accepted him as a future son-in-law, welcoming him into their home, and without transgressing into rudeness questioned him on events in Germany to gauge his own beliefs. But he revealed nothing, not because he was prevaricating, but because he simply dismissed the National Socialists as an aberration not worth discussing. They were bound to crash and burn sooner rather than later.

But the Van Bergens saw his refusal to consider the new reality in Germany as delusional, with dire consequences for their daughter, and cautioned Emma in continuing the relationship, let alone making a life for herself in Germany. For her part, Emma pleaded with Friedrich to at least consider staying on in Utrecht until the upheavals simmered down and the political landscape became clear. But he refused, unwilling to accept that a party comprised of boorish thugs could rule Germany for too long. He had to witness and contribute to their demise first hand.

In the end they reached an impasse. Early one drizzly morning he collected a few of his belongings and headed solo to Utrecht Centraal, boarding a train that would eventually bring him back home to Bremen. It was intended to be his first Christmas at home in three years. He never intimated the depth of his relationship with Emma to his parents, other than to say that he had made a very close friend. Neither wrote to the other and, by the following year, what he thought impossible came to be: Hitler invaded Poland and Europe was at war again.

And now he was here, coming full circle to Utrecht after having been ensnared for six years in the bowels of the Third Reich in an ultimately futile attempt to forestall the inevitable. In a matter of days, or even hours, he would shed his abominable past and transgress to an irrevocable future that, should he be discovered, would cost him his life.

A gust of wind came up the frozen canal, adding to the bitter cold. His teeth chattered and his bones ached from the sub-zero wind chill. He needed to change, and soon, otherwise he would freeze to death. He hadn't brought along his SS overcoat – just warm civilian clothing; he hadn't expected that he would still be wearing his uniform by this point. But where could he change? An abandoned house? Too risky. A bordello? No one would question his changing clothes there. He knelt down and reached into his duffel, pulling out his fleece-lined jacket from the SS recruitment facility, sporting its medical insignia. Slipping on the jacket, his temperature warmed. He was about to pick up the duffel and continue on his way when a faint, childlike voice startled him.

"*Dokter?*"

Instinctively he reached for his Walther. A scrawny girl of about ten stood to his right with long, straggly hair, staring at him with docile, plaintive eyes in the moonlight. She was wearing what appeared to be grubby flannel pants and a tattered jumper. Her feet were clad in a pair of scuffed, torn, unlaced shoes. A waif. He pushed the Walther back into its holster and edged closer along the bench, his look quizzical.

She was pointing specifically to the symbol that identified him as a medic. "*Dokter?*"

Looking at where her finger was pointing, he smiled. Taking hold of her hand, he noticed that her nails were chipped and dirty and her fingers frostbitten. He thought immediately to hand over his jacket. But then he would be cold and in danger.

Instead he pointed. "Doctor, for you?"

Pulling back her hand, she shook her head and pointed to a location adjacent to the canal on Leidsekade.

Friedrich grabbed his duffel and bid the child forward to guide him.

Despite her impoverished and what he thought might be frail state she paced rapidly along the embankment and the street, gliding between the shadows thrown from the gabled houses across the way. Three quarters of the way up the empty street, she paused, crouched and looked in either direction. Friedrich immediately grew suspicious. Was she expecting someone? But she cocked her head for him to follow her across Leidsekade to a three-storey terrace that was engulfed in total darkness.

Rather than walking up the stoop to the main entrance, she beckoned him to follow her down a narrow staircase on the right side of the building. When they reached the basement she entered a doorway that creaked slightly as she pushed it ajar and disappeared into a room cast in darkness. Friedrich set his foot gingerly over the threshold and felt his way into the musty odour of the interior. He could hear a woman moaning somewhere in the gloom, but he couldn't tell where the sound was coming from.

He was about to enter fully into the room and call out when a hand rose up out of the darkness to his right. Instantly he felt the cold barrel of a pistol against his temple.

"You move, you die!"

BERLIN

Winter 1944

Despite the perceived danger that Ruth's presence posed, Helmut chose not to summon Martin to the house, but wait until he stopped by to visit his niece and sister. They happened to be out shopping or socialising, Helmut wasn't sure which, when Martin came by. He offered to leave and come back at another time, but Helmut insisted that he have a drink to take the chill off and wait. Martin, wary of Helmut's feigned camaraderie, tentatively stepped into the vestibule, hung up his thick overcoat and cap and waited to follow Helmut to the living room.

Helmut instead walked up the steps to the first floor and, when Martin hesitated, beckoned him to follow. As he reached the landing, Helmut pulled out a chair, climbed on it and reached up to the ceiling. He prodded a tile loose directly above his head, exposing the panel with a ring attached to it.

"May I ask what you are doing?"

"You will see in a moment."

Pulling on the ring, the hinged panel opened downwards, revealing the telescoped ladder. He dragged the ladder down until it was fully extended and then called out into the opening, "Ruth, can you come down for a moment?"

They both waited silently for what seemed like several minutes, but in reality was no longer than a minute, before they heard a scraping sound above their heads. The sound stopped.

"It's all right. You can come down." Helmut spoke up encouragingly into the recess.

Again they waited. Another minute later a small leg clad in dull grey woollen trouser and a brown shoe appeared in the opening and reached tentatively for the top rung. When the left foot was standing firmly on the rung, the right foot tentatively followed. And then slowly, gradually, a body started to appear as the feet stepped their way down the ladder, until a girl who looked no older than fourteen or fifteen, with fair hair, a pallid face, dainty features and green eyes, stood warily in front of Helmut. Seeing him staring directly over her, she turned and came face to face with a tall man attired in a black uniform with ribbons and an Iron Cross affixed to his collar. Two silver insignias that resembled thunderbolts were splayed across each collar. His face seemed fearsome; not angry, but decidedly hostile. He remained silent, his lips pursed in a disapproving scowl.

Ruth turned to look up at Helmut. "Is this the Gestapo? Do I have to go now?" Her voice was neither quavering nor frightened, simply accepting of an inevitable fate that had been long in coming.

"No. This is not the Gestapo. This is Anna's uncle, Martin. Magda's brother." Helmut pulled Ruth close against him, placing his hands protectively over her shoulders.

Martin turned angrily on his heels and literally marched across the landing and stomped down the stairs. For a split second Helmut feared that he would bolt out the front door and alert the Gestapo. But instead he barged into the living room. Helmut could hear bottles clanging and then the sound of liquor being poured into a glass.

The risk had paid off. He relaxed and told Ruth that she could go into Anna's room and wait. He was going to talk with Anna's uncle. At first she hesitated; she never went into Anna's room without Anna being there. But Helmut nudged her gently towards the door and nodded approvingly. Once she was inside he shut the door and went downstairs to join Martin.

He arrived in the living room to find Martin standing belligerently by the crackling fireplace, a glass of brandy in his hand. He had witnessed Martin angry before: his face ruddy, eyes squinting, his lips snarling over his teeth as if he was getting ready to bite. He had expected to find him in this state. But instead Martin bore an expression of fury held in check by terror. The glass in his hand was so firmly grasped that Helmut feared it might shatter at any moment.

At first Helmut thought that he might start off by describing the circumstances of how Ruth had come to be in the house, but seeing Martin in this state he was more inclined to wait and let him calm down, otherwise there was the very real danger that his brother-in-law would experience a cardiac arrest. No doubt his reaction was due to having been placed in an untenable situation.

Sensing perhaps that his grip on the glass was too firm, Martin set it on the mantelpiece and turned to look at Helmut. "I presume that Magda knows about this?" His tone was even, not accusing or reprimanding, but clearly demanding.

Helmut simply nodded.

"You realise what will happen if the Gestapo find out?"

Helmut nodded again.

Martin nodded with him. "I thought that you were foolhardy at times to say the things you did in public. But then, you felt protected."

Helmut was about to protest.

"No, please, let me finish. But this, this, this is not mere words. You have effectively harboured an enemy of the Reich."

Again Helmut was about to protest; Martin raised his hand firmly to stop him.

"This is treason. And the Gestapo are going to rightly assume that Magda and Anna are part of it. Which means that all of you will be shot. So I think maybe you don't care for yourself, or for Magda. But you must love and care for your daughter?"

Helmut remained silent.

"And now you have dragged me into this. So, Helmut, what is it you want? Papers?"

"We have papers."

"Then what?"

"Magda and I thought that maybe you can suggest a way to smuggle her to Zurich. I have a relative who has agreed to look after her."

"Smuggle?" Martin veritably hissed. "Smuggle?! Can you explain to me why I would want to smuggle a Jewish girl to Zurich?"

"All right, maybe 'smuggle' is not the right word. Escort. Escort the girl under your auspices to Zurich."

"Can I at least have a look at the papers?"

Helmut swiftly went over to the escritoire and retrieved a leather binder. Inside he located a neatly folded sheet of paper and a card with a photo, and took both over to Martin.

Examining the paper and the card for some moments, Martin appeared satisfied with their legitimacy. "So, Helmut. Why the sudden need to smuggle her to Zurich?" His tone was on edge now.

"Things being what they are now, Magda and I have become worried," Helmut replied quietly.

"Really. May I ask, how long has she been here?"

"Three years."

"Three years?!" Martin came forward, almost shouting.

"That's correct."

Martin sneered loudly. "And you expect me to believe that all of a sudden, out of the blue, you have become worried?" He paused to take another sip, enjoying ridiculing his brother-in-law. "Come, Helmut. What is it you are not telling me?"

Helmut swallowed hard, taking the ribbing that he normally dished out to Martin and his parents-in-law. "I missed something," he uttered under his breath.

Martin came up close to where Helmut was standing, his chest puffed up. "The great Professor Helmut Jodl, the huge genius, missed something." His mouth stretched into a contented jeer.

"Are you going to help me or not?" Helmut rebuffed him sullenly.

"Not until you tell me what you missed."

"Let's just say, if she is ever discovered her presence will raise more questions than the paperwork can support."

"What questions?"

"Like, why isn't she in school?"

"And, why isn't she?"

"Well, because she will be recognised."

"I see. Tell me something, Herr Professor; whose idea was it to involve me?" Martin stared apprehensively at his brother-in-law.

"Mine." Magda was standing in the doorway, clutching Anna's hand. They had come in quietly through the back entrance. "I asked him to ask you. It was my idea. Can you help or not?"

Martin nodded acquiescently. Tucking the paper and card inside his breast pocket, he rose, drained the last of his brandy and walked over to where Magda was standing. "Just so we are clear, I am doing this for you and Anna, not for him." He pointed dismissively at Helmut.

Helmut nodded silently.

"Tell her to pack a small suitcase. Never forget her new identity, no matter what happens. Give me the address in Zurich." He was back to his officious self, issuing orders.

Helmut was flooded with relief. He was almost tempted to hug his brother-in-law, except Martin's stern expression told him that that would not be appropriate at this moment. Instead he bounded up the steps and walked into Anna's room. A few moments later he re-emerged in the living room with Ruth in tow, holding a small suitcase and bundled up warmly in a thick overcoat and scarf.

"Ruth, this is Martin, as I explained before. Anna's uncle. He will escort you to my aunt in Zurich where you will be safe."

Ruth stared up at the SS officer looking down at her disapprovingly, yet his expression was no longer hostile, nor his demeanour threatening. She let go of Helmut's hand and walked over to Martin. "The professor told me to do everything you say and never forget my new name."

Despite his officious persona and the peril inherent in this undertaking, Martin couldn't help but let a fleeting smile cross his face. Gingerly he took Ruth's hand in his and together they headed into the vestibule.

Magda stood aside to let them through, while Anna and Ruth hugged each other, not saying anything.

As he was putting on his overcoat, Martin turned to face Helmut with a curious look on his face. "How do you know that halfway to Zurich I won't turn her over to the Gestapo? I could always say I discovered her hiding in an empty farmhouse. It happens all the time."

Helmut smirked. "It had occurred to me, except I never considered you an evil man, Martin. Just misguided." With that he leaned down to Ruth and gave her a warm embrace. "You will be safe with Martin. Once this is all over we will get together again: you, Anna, me."

Ruth held him tightly and then, prodded by Martin, shed his embrace.

Adjusting his collar against the icy wind, Martin took Ruth Lipschutz's, alias Helga Dreschler's, hand in his and together they walked out of the warm house into the freezing winter night. In the distance the sound of bombs could be heard clearly as they pounded the earth, wrecking the buildings and houses and killing their occupants indiscriminately. Ironically the person most in danger was the safest now as she followed her escort out of the fires and chaos of Berlin towards Zurich.

UTRECHT

Winter 1944

Friedrich froze in place. The command was in German, albeit accented, but if it had been in any language, reinforced with the pistol, he would have understood and obeyed.

With his visibility denied he kept a keen ear to the sounds around him so that he could gauge the size of the basement and who was in it. The moaning sound, coming from perhaps five to six feet to his left, was that of a female suffering from a serious injury or illness. He couldn't tell. The little waif that led him here had all but disappeared.

The person with the pistol to his right slowly reached over and felt for his holster. Friedrich moved his right hand in that direction to unbuckle it. A sudden blow to that hand made him recoil and yell out in pain.

"I told you not to move." The voice was harsh and cold.

Regaining his composure, Friedrich turned slightly to his right. "I was going to give it to you."

"What are you doing here?" It felt as though the voice was inches from his ear; he could almost sense the movement of the lips.

"The little girl. I thought she asked for a doctor."

"A doctor?" his interlocutor spat out in disgust.

Friedrich remained silent.

The moaning rose to an anguished plea, accompanied by some words mumbled in Dutch. Words that Friedrich thought he understood, but he remained quiet, refusing to divulge his past grasp of the language. His captors' ignorance could only serve to his advantage.

"I can help," he offered.

"Shut up." The person to his right then switched to Dutch and spoke rapidly to the inside of the basement. The only words Friedrich understood were 'Lotte' and '*kom hier*'.

A short silhouette materialised from out of the darkness and stood a couple of feet away. It was the waif that brought him here. Lotte.

The man resumed speaking quickly in Dutch. Friedrich grasped enough. They proposed to keep the wounded woman here until the dead of night and then transport her out. The speaker was instructing Lotte to deliver the message to someone on the outside.

"If you don't take her to a hospital or have a doctor look at her soon, she will die."

"I thought I told you to shut up."

Lotte spoke up. Friedrich listened keenly, trying to make out the exchange, simultaneously thinking that the uniform he clung to would either cost or spare his life.

"The girl says that you told her you are a doctor."

"Yes. That's right. I told you already, I am a doctor and I can help."

"I want you to listen really well to what I am going to say. Any mistakes and I will put a bullet in your filthy Nazi brain. Understood?"

"I am not a Nazi."

A snigger. "OK. I am going to move the gun from your head. You are going to put down the bag and walk away from it."

The woman on the floor nearby cried out in agony.

"I must help her."

"Don't worry about her. Listen to what I am saying to you." The barrel tightened against his temple. "I will turn on a lamp and you can then examine the woman. If you are not a doctor, we will know soon enough, in which case you will be shot. Is that clear?"

"Yes."

"OK." The gun's barrel moved away from Friedrich's temple and he felt a sharp jab in his lower back. "Go! Walk in a straight line."

To his left a kerosene lamp flickered on, lighting up the edges of the dingy basement. His guess had been right: five feet away to his left was a mattress on the floor. He could just make out the woman's head facing the wall, her hair matted to the side of her face. A greyish, frayed woollen blanket covered her body, which was curled over in agony. There were some implements next to the mattress and a jug of water.

"Go!" He was prodded again.

"What is wrong with her?"

"Never mind that. Just go over and help her."

"But I need to know what happened so that I can treat it." He instinctively turned to face the speaker, but his movement was halted by a fierce blow to his face. Friedrich stumbled sideways.

"Don't look at me again." The arm came forward with the pistol pointing at the mattress. "She was shot."

"When?"

Another voice from inside the basement spoke out in Dutch. Friedrich understood but waited for the translation. As long as they didn't know he spoke Dutch he could stay one step ahead of them in case they decided to harm him.

The man holding the gun replied, "We think an hour ago."

"You think?"

"Well, we don't know. She was brought here in this condition. We don't actually know when it happened."

"You need to get her to a hospital."

"No hospital."

Friedrich started to unbutton his tunic as he came closer to the body on the mattress.

"Don't look at her face."

Kneeling by the edge of the mattress, he peeled back the filthy blanket, peering at the body to determine the source of the wound. An oozing gauze covered the right side of her abdomen next to her kidney. Next to the wound were several wadded-up rags that they had used to stem the bleeding. She had lost a lot of blood and was still losing more.

Turning his head away from her face, he felt her forehead and then touched her wrist to feel her pulse: she had a high fever and her pulse was very faint. He doubted that he could save her; but he needed to save himself regardless.

"She is in a very poor condition. I will do everything I can. But if I treat her, I can't go back. You understand that?"

The person holding the gun spoke to the interlocutor deep inside the basement. Rapid Dutch. Friedrich's command of the language wasn't that fluent.

"So?"

Friedrich instinctively tried to look up, but immediately turned back. "I need to change out of the uniform. I have civilian clothes in my duffel. I will need a clean gauze, or cloth. Hot water. A knife and something to heat it up with."

Another exchange in Dutch between the two men, the speaker outside his view saying, "Koert?" – so presumably that was the name of the person holding the gun to Friedrich.

"OK," Koert agreed.

Friedrich rose up, facing the wall, unbuckled his belt, peeled off his trousers, removed his tunic and holster and tossed them in a bundle to the side. He then knelt down to reach for his duffel.

"Wait!" Koert prodded him in the side before he could reach for the bag. He picked up the duffel, loosening the drawstring and, holding it upside down, examined the contents as they tumbled to the floor. "OK, you can get dressed."

"Get rid of that." Friedrich pointed to his uniform bundled next to the bed.

By the time he was dressed in civilian clothes, a pan with hot water had been placed next to the mattress by Lotte; a lit candle was placed alongside it, and several more rags added to the bundle.

"I need a knife, or some sharp object."

This prompted another exchange between Koert and the speaker in the recess of the basement.

Koert leaned forward and handed Friedrich a pocket knife. "Don't get any ideas. We will not hesitate to shoot you."

Friedrich slowly peeled back the gauze that was now drenched in blood, at the same time turning up the flame on the lamp. The bullet had penetrated deeply, most likely buried either in heavy muscle in the back or near the kidney. Either way he would have to stem the bleeding fast if she were to have even a remote chance of surviving.

Taking one of the rags, he soaked it in the pan of hot water, rinsed it and began cleaning the wound. It was still oozing, but the bleeding had slowed. Either the pulse had weakened further, or she had lost so much blood that it was draining slowly.

Heating the blade on the candle, he brought the knife close to the wound and started scraping at the edge.

The woman screamed.

"You will need to put something in her mouth and hold her still."

Koert spoke to Lotte. The little girl came up, wadded one of the cloths and forced it into the woman's mouth. The woman shuddered. The man from the dark recess of the basement appeared in the gloom and held her down from behind by both shoulders.

Friedrich resumed scraping along the edge of the wound. At each movement of the knife the woman bucked and screamed into the rag stuffed in her mouth. The man holding her down had to lean forward and place his knees astride her head to gain purchase. Friedrich marvelled at her strength: her injury was grave; she had lost a great deal of blood; she was feverish, yet she was able to overcome the person holding her down. And he was no weakling; Friedrich sized him up in the glow cast by the lamp: broad shoulders, burly arms and thick hands. He could only see him from the neck down. He had a straggly beard and was wearing an army fatigue, like a jacket, either brown or green.

The cloth that Friedrich was using was soaked with blood. He set it aside, dipped a fresh one in the pan, cleared the skin and blood and gently pulled at the edges of the wound. He needed to reach inside with some implement and attempt to dislodge the bullet.

He looked at the bearded man assisting him. "I need a pair of tweezers, something to reach inside the wound."

"Tweezers?" The voice sounded confused.

Koert translated. No movement.

"Also, I will need something to anaesthetise the wound and calm her down. If she passes out, we may lose her."

He could hear footsteps moving behind him, a door opening, and then footsteps approaching the mattress. A bottle clinked to the floor and a thick, twisted steel wire was placed on the mattress. The bottle's contents were clear.

He dipped another cloth in the pan, rinsed it, then poured some of the liquid onto the cloth. It smelled of vodka. Picking up the makeshift tweezers, he cleaned them with the cloth.

"Pour some alcohol down her throat and then hold her down firmly."

Koert started to translate, and the bearded hulk nodded, picking up the bottle. He removed the wadded cloth stuffed in the woman's mouth, forced her lips open and poured two sips from the bottle into her mouth.

She convulsed, sputtering, and started coughing violently. Her head and torso came forward off the mattress. Her hair fell to the side of her face. Friedrich caught a quick glance. But that's all he needed.

"I know this woman." He spoke to no one in particular.

BERLIN

Winter 1944

The pounding had become incessant. Previously the bombings came mostly under the cover of darkness. Now they came like hornets in the twilight hours of the evening; other times, early in the morning. It was turning into a dull carnage exacted to inflict the greatest loss of human life and destruction of property. And it was indiscriminate. Those who had valiantly opposed the barbaric and inhumane dictatorship faced the same barrage from above as their tormentors.

Helmut would sometimes wait until mid morning before heading out to the university. The air bombardments would taper off till the early evening, giving him a window in which to venture out. It was safer, but not entirely so.

As he made his way through the ruins and the smouldering city he kept looking out for toppling walls and mortar battered by the nightly raids, cupping his nose and mouth intermittently to protect himself from the billowing acrid smoke: pyres of human and horse flesh set alight to stem the spread of disease. There was hardly enough time between raids to collect the dying, let alone the dead. No time to grieve. No time to dignify them by whispering a hurried prayer over their mangled corpses.

He wanted to pause and feel the intense pain that the annihilation of his beloved city wrought on him. But there was no time even for that.

He staggered over the rubble on what used to be pavements, watching the ambulances and the fire trucks lurch by, their sirens more mournful than urgent. Every so often they would stop momentarily and then continue on, overwhelmed.

Between the corpses and the walking dead, soldiers shuffled in an absent daze, wondering what happened to the Great Reich: the Thousand-Year Reich that had been cut short so abjectly and abruptly. Squeezed in a merciless vice by the Russians to the east, and the Allies pushing through the Ardennes to the west.

Helmut no longer allowed Anna to leave the house. He tutored her in the evenings. Magda still went out on occasion, beaming with feigned confidence that the Reich's armies would prevail. She had heard through friends that a General Wenck was retreating to retaliate. Hitler had ordered him to protect Berlin by any means.

Helmut did not bother arguing that Hitler and his delusional high command could issue whatever orders they wanted from the *Führerbunker*. The reality was that the momentum had irrevocably shifted: Germany was in retreat, and the Allies and Russians were on the offensive. It was only a matter of time before Germany would be forced to capitulate; the only question was, how long?

The longer it went on, the greater the carnage and the potential peril to Helmut's family.

He had not heard back from Martin, which in this climate could be construed either way – there was just no way of knowing. He could only hope that they both made it safely across the border to Zurich. Helmut wished that he had had the prescience to ask Martin to take Anna as well. At least she might survive and have a life after this madness ended. But he knew that even for an officer of Martin's rank, ferrying two girls across the border would have been too risky. He mightn't get either through, and the danger to Ruth was much greater. So Anna had to face the risk of Germany's destruction and inevitable capitulation.

Magda was just relieved that Ruth was gone. She didn't ask whether there was any word from Martin. Anna simply said that her friend had gone away to be safe. Magda frostily agreed; "Good – we can be safe now, as well."

While Helmut felt bolder in his defiance of the Nazi regime, now that it was on the retreat and facing a final and punishing defeat and demise, he also knew that should he vocalise his views openly, he would be placing himself in grave danger. Desperate people, such as those that still clung to the current regime, would act impetuously, figuring that they had nothing to lose.

Especially the SS troops, whose fate would be dire once the Nazi rule collapsed: patrolling the rubble-strewn streets, exhorting the weary and shell-shocked Wehrmacht soldiers back into battle and certain death. They would not hesitate to pull their pistols and shoot. Anybody. They wouldn't even ask for papers.

Life became cheap when there was so much death and destruction around.

So Helmut kept to himself, his anger smouldering inside of him, his rage directed at the lunatic corporal who kept on issuing orders to phantom armies instead of trying to save what was left from the onslaught that rained daily over Germany.

By the time he made it to the university grounds he was inclined to be grateful to some deity that had spared his life for another day, if for nothing else than to witness the abject capitulation of the Nazis.

At times Helmut was tempted to call his cousin again, who had since risen to the rank of *Oberkommando der Wehrmacht* in the Third Reich, but each time he refrained. He doubted Alfred could reveal anything substantive without imperilling them both, ultimately not shedding any new light. But even a tiny morsel would be more than the vacuous propaganda spewed by Goebbels' diatribes and Streicher's vituperative *Der Stürmer*.

Helmut remained reluctant: on the one hand he believed that Alfred – principled, ambitious, loyal, a man of honour – would not sit well with the excesses of the Third Reich. The favour that Alfred granted some years ago had proved Helmut right: family traits prevailed above all. Yet the halcyon days of the Thousand-Year Reich were pulverising to dust. Would Alfred be as magnanimous in this climate of defeat, treachery and desperation?

Added to this was the fear that the Gestapo would intensify their eavesdropping scope and efforts to include the Nazi elite in the aftermath of the *Schwarze Kapelle*; a plot in which a group of high-ranking German officers and commanders conspired to assassinate Hitler, resulting in the execution of some five thousand co-conspirators. A frank conversation between two cousins on the dire status of the Reich would mete out a similar fate to Alfred Jodl, regardless of his rank, and without a second thought to his cousin Helmut, given his penchant for being a burr in the side of the Third Reich.

It couldn't be denied that the smell of capitulation was in the air: the unopposed nightly raids, the exhortation to phantom armies, and the strident tenor of the propaganda that was beginning to sound more hysterical than lyrical. But even a regime on the brink could last a while by sacrificing every able-bodied and even infirm person in the Reich to rise to the defence of Hitler's ideals: young, old, even women.

Helmut needed to know how far from the edge; how imminent the demise: days, weeks, months – surely not years? He could ask Martin when he returned, but he was an official engulfed in the same fog of propaganda drivel that Helmut and the rest of the nation were subjected to.

But Alfred would know.

If the answer came back that the regime was tottering on the edge of collapse, maybe Helmut could be encouraged to shift his effort from passive to active. If, on the other hand, it was a matter of months, then maybe it was time to flee the Reich before the unrelenting onslaught killed them all.

He had to take the risk. He called his uncle. He would know how to reach his son Alfred without stirring the tentacles of the Gestapo.

MASCOT, SYDNEY

Winter 1986

The nondescript two-bedroom house lay two hundred metres from the street, bordered by a manicured hibiscus hedge, a small patch of lawn, and a petunia and bougainvillea flower bed flush against the small patio. In its heyday it was referred to as a small English cottage, but nowadays it was just a dilapidated small house, disadvantaged by bordering onto a busy street and without parking.

The owner, when she first came to Sydney from Germany more than half a century ago, had thought the suburb quaint and quiet. Particularly this street. Yet with the passage of time the street had turned into a busy byway from the airport to every other suburb. It had missed by little distance the middle-class suburban status accorded the nearby suburbs of Eastlakes, Kingswood and Pagewood. Mascot aged ungracefully into a lower middle class.

Most new tenants who came to live here bought into small plots and tore down the dilapidated cottages, replacing them with two-storey houses with the de rigueur parking taking over the small patches of front lawn and hedges. Helga Dreschler didn't drive, so the lack of parking did not figure in her decision. Back then it wasn't even a consideration. Few people in Sydney's inner suburbs owned vehicles – or if they did, parking on the street was plentiful.

Either way, by the time her place sold she would be dead and the proceeds would go to her chosen inheritor: the German Lutheran Church in Sydney. Until then she continued to live, driven not by the fear of death as some were at her age, or the love of close family – she had none – but vengeance. A single purpose driving her determination to seek out and have her revenge on the one person that she held responsible for destroying her life and cheating her out of her fate.

AUSCHWITZ

Winter

The doors on the boxcar slide open front and back and soldiers with bayonets prod us to the sodden ground from behind. We tumble like sacks of grain, no one has the strength to clamber down. We land in puddles of slush, breaking our fall, with Heinrich stumbling and falling and Alana helping him stand up. In front of us is a wide wrought-iron archway with the words *Arbeit Macht Frei* wrought over the massive gates. On either side of the gates are tall barbed-wire fences surrounding barrack-like buildings with watchtowers, guards, dogs, and armed German soldiers ordering us into a snaking queue parallel to the width of the boxcar, four deep.

Wizened though I am for my years, I come to the instinctive realisation that the nightmare that I thought had ended, has actually just begun.

A German officer on horseback trots to where we are standing and looks down at us with loathing as though we are a herd of diseased cattle. He yells a command to his left and three soldiers come running from inside the gates. He begins issuing directions to each of us individually.

I am close to the front of the queue. I steal a glance sideways, astonished at the number of people that have been compacted with me for three days. As the queue starts to move forward I quickly notice that the older members of the group are instructed to go straight ahead, the younger men to the left and the rest of us to the right. When it is our turn at the front of the queue I am directed to the right. No instruction has been given to the Lipschutzes – they are directly behind me.

I muster a reserve of strength that I didn't know I had, and in a voice hoarse from enduring three days without food or water I utter weakly up to the soldier monitoring the splitting of the queue, "I am not their daughter; they are not my parents." I point to the Lipschutzes directly behind me.

He doesn't respond. Instead he looks up at the officer mounted on the horse, who narrows his eyes quizzically. The soldier repeats what I said. The officer grins savagely at the soldier, who proceeds to approach me, reaching for the club holstered on his belt.

A large, burly man I haven't noticed before, not part of our contingent, races over from the sidelines and grabs me, apologising obsequiously to the soldier and the officer in turn. He pulls me over to the procession on the right, having already passed the selection. Once we are out of earshot he kneels close to my ear and whispers, "Do not ever speak to them – he was going to beat you to death."

I look back to see the Lipschutzes. They are not following me; instead they are trudging with the group going straight ahead. The showers, we are told. They look over at me, smile wanly, and that is the last I ever see of them. I know now that I am totally alone.

It is not that I felt a sense of attachment to Heinrich and Alana, despite having spent three days standing in their midst. But they were the last link I had to my old life that vanished in the demi-light of dawn. They were a crumb to help me find my way to Berlin, and from there trace my life back to Munich. I belong somewhere, even though my *Oma* let me go. There has to be a place left for me that will not disintegrate into nothingness once it becomes my home.

On this cold, overcast, blustery day we pass underneath the looming iron gate, abandoning a life that we once knew. Even though the last three days are hardly ones to yearn for wistfully, they were our last vestige of a time when we were theoretically free, before we were dragged from the warmth of our beds, before we were thrust into a cattle boxcar in numbers three to four times the ordained capacity, and before we were subjected to the cold terror presaging our eventual fate. With the first few tentative steps a life that once belonged to us as individuals is taken from us. We become a mass, a multitude, treated as such as the women in our group are herded into Barrack C. Despite the dismally dark, dank and stark circumstances that greet us as we walk in, I am not repulsed. The train journey experience was a preamble that emotionally inured me to this.

In here the women are arrayed on pallets four high, with a dozen bodies lying across each row head to toe. The occupants study us with the vacant, sunken eyes of doomed beings. They are dressed in threadbare, sack-like outfits that are meant to replace dresses, a further attempt to denude us of any trace of the individualism that marks us as people. I am directed to a pallet three high from the ground. I crawl in and try to squeeze in among the bodies there. I find a wedge and force myself in. Courtesy is not a useful attribute here.

Beyond the immediate stench there is a generalised burning smell that pervades the entire camp: acrid, dense and constant. Through the slats that look out onto the yard directly in front of me, I don't see a fire. But off in the distance there is a massive smokestack, and it is billowing; what are they burning? Our clothes, our luggage, our possessions, the dead who expired in transit, or some unknown thing that I am yet to discover? I mysteriously arrived carrying nothing.

I lie back on the wooden slat in the space that I claimed for myself and close my eyes. I try to wonder what will happen to me. Then I feel a tap on my shoulder. I jolt upright and look to my right. A shrivelled hand belonging to a woman who must still be young, but has aged through the experience of the inhuman conditions that pervade the camp: exhaustion, starvation, terror; the boxcar was a prelude to this. She is speaking to me in a language that I have never heard before. I shake my head. This time she speaks in accented German.

"Where are you from?"

"Munich," I reply, and fall back onto my wooden pillow. I am not feeling particularly chatty.

"I am from Budapest."

I say nothing.

"I didn't want you to fall asleep. There will be a roll call in a few hours."

I still do not reply. But I wonder about the roll call. It is probably another obsessive preoccupation with numbers: *The corpse stays on the train. Otherwise the body count will be short.* So what? I fail to understand this; it's not like they care if we live or die. So what if the count is short?

It must be that they keep a register of all people arriving at the camps and match it against the numbers deported. It is simply accounting for stock. We are herds of undesirable people. I recall again the reference to Jews. But is it just Jews in here, or are there others? Again I think of how I am going to speak out without getting clubbed to death.

"People who come from transport fall asleep and they miss roll call. If you are absent they will kill you."

No doubt, I think to myself. *And then you are transferred from the register of the imprisoned to the register of the dead. But the total count is correct.*

I might be able to learn something from this woman – at the very least I won't be beaten to death.

I open my eyes, rising up on my elbow. "Are you a Jew?"

She looks at me like I am an idiot. "Of course."

I fall back again. What if Oma lied? About everything – not just about my father being killed by communists or Jews, but the whole pretence about him being a Hitler supporter, a loyalist to the Nazi Party, letting me wear the *Hitlerjugend* uniform, the nightly broadcasts? I know Oma was displeased with the latter; her face always turned sour at the sound of Hitler's voice. Yet, she crossed herself twice a day, went to church, and there were crosses all over the house. I distinctly recall that she prayed with a Bible with the imprint of the cross on it.

Was that all a subterfuge as well, an attempt to cover up her Judaism, so that we wouldn't get deported? Yet my aunt in Berlin, Magda, she is definitely not a Jew. She didn't bother with any pretence.

Ultimately I ended up with the Lipschutzes. They are Jews. What if I am a half-caste; my father was non-Jewish and my mother Jewish? That might be a possibility, and would explain why Aunt Magda was so disapproving of my arrival. No, that does not make sense – my mother was her cousin; the other way around it might be plausible. But then Father died for Hitler; but what if he didn't die *for* Hitler, but *because of* Hitler?

I have to make some sense of this.

"You are not?" My pallet companion is interested in the same thing that I am puzzling over.

Without rising to face her, I pose the question, "What if my father was killed by Hitler, but my mother is not Jewish?"

"Then you are not Jewish." She sullenly leans back and loses interest in me.

That's it for our budding friendship. I wait for roll call.

I manage to doze off for a short while. No dreams. Just the portentous sense that the rest of my foreseeable life is cast in darkness, and that each passing day, if I survive, will be a struggle to keep doing so. What ominous events might befall me, I don't know, but with the abrogation of my freedom I have no choice but to face them. That is the horror of it – the inevitability of doom.

Roll call.

We are led outside by a group of burly women who are dressed akin to prisoners but carry a level of authority delegated by the uniformed Germans. I learn from one of the prisoners of the recent boxcar journey that they are called *Kapos*, and the one in charge *Blockälteste*, or block elder, who is in charge of our barrack. They are in effect prisoners presiding over other prisoners – namely us. I readily observe that their zealous level of cruelty exceeds that of their masters. You move too slow, you are clubbed; you move too fast, you are clubbed. You pause, you are kicked to the ground. Needless to say, if you fail to appear for roll call, as already advised, you are killed.

I stride per the convoy tempo.

We assemble in the yard abutting our barracks in quadrants. There, a total of about a thousand inmates are amassed in front of a dozen or so gallows arrayed with ropes hanging from their masts, a thick noose at the end of each one.

I stare, reflecting on my short life and wondering if, after all I have endured, I will be selected for one of these. I dare not ask the prisoner to my right. Her head and shoulder are swollen for providing me with the information about the *Kapos* and the *Blockälteste*.

Soldiers appear from one of the barracks, each leading a tightly bound prisoner on a leash. The prisoner is led up to the gallows, their neck is placed in the noose, their hands tied behind their back, and their bare feet are inspected to be securely bound. The soldiers accompanying the condemned then march down to the base of the platform and stand at attention in front of it.

An officer, the same one that welcomed us earlier, rides on horseback in front of the group and reads out the sentence. Fortunately I am German and understand what is being said. The condemned number fourteen: nine men and five women. They are sentenced to hang until they die. The reason for this verdict is that, while they were on duty outside the camp, they captured a wild pig, killed and ate it.

I am absently wondering if the lesson to all of us is that we are not supposed to eat without permission, or is it perhaps that they failed to share the feast with the camp commandant?

At the nod from the officer, who turns towards the condemned, each soldier pulls a lever and the body drops through the platform. The bodies fidget momentarily and then cease, lifeless.

If I ever wondered about the population of the camp, I don't think that these hapless collection were Jews. They didn't look German. But Jews wouldn't kill and eat a pig. This much even I know. But then again…?

Soon after we are commanded to disperse and are herded back to the barracks. Our entertainment for the evening is complete.

I am back on the wooden slat with a wedge of bread, a cup of coffee and a metal bowl of broth. I am starving, so I eat with relish. I dream of Oma's schnauzer, Arlo, and the delectable meals that it used to be served, that in this instance would qualify as a sumptuous repast.

This is the first chance I have had to reflect on all that's happened over the past few days; that's all it has been. Time-wise it was short, but emotionally it's been years of growth cultivated in a boxcar. I discovered my physical and emotional endurance deprived of food, water, space and hygiene, the presence of which I had hitherto taken for granted. Confronted with the barbaric and senseless murder of the two boys, my age or younger, I developed the innate ability to compartmentalise the incident and store it somewhere inside the insanity that is within all of us. The difference is that those killings were executed with icy indifference in the cold light of day. They could have been insects for all he cared. Pawns to make a point.

But insanity can also act as a cocoon to protect us from the normal horrors that surround us. If we are mad, we don't react. Only people possessed of normal faculties react to the conditions to which we are subjected; to witnessing the hanging of fourteen human beings for trying to relieve their grinding hunger by killing and eating a pig raw.

So I am now mad Helga. I think of the executions as the evening performance. I finish my meal and lie back. I am full, but I feel sick. I dare not think about the chewy stuff that was in the broth.

I try to fall asleep thinking about what it is that I will be doing every day for as long as I am imprisoned. Despite my pallet mate dismissing me with contempt because I am not Jewish, I am determined to elicit some information from her. This time I tap her on the shoulder.

She turns to me with a surly look. "What do you want?"

I attempt to put as much warmth into my voice as I can muster. "What happens here every day?"

"Don't worry, you will find out." With that she turns her back to me.

Roll call.

My first duty is with a group of other German women to sort out the clothing and luggage of those entering the showers. We march over to the gate and walk along the fence till we come to a huge hall. Outside are stationed several hulking men with wooden carts. They are waiting. The two large doors to the hall are open. We are told to wait by the fence opposite the men, leaving a clear path to the hall.

My rational thought is that our task is to match up the discarded clothing with the people that emerge from the shower. Alternatively, they are to be issued camp overalls and we are to load their clothing onto the barrows to be burned. Hence the billowing smokestack. I am sort of envious; I, and others in my bunk, were never given the opportunity to shower after being cooped up for three days in the boxcar, despite the filth that we were subjected to.

Aside from one other person the other women in the group are seasoned 'sorters'. But we dare not dialogue with them.

Minutes later a train arrives and the procession of the hordes begins: showers, barracks, hard labour. The queue that was directed to proceed straight through arrives at our location. They are commanded to discard their clothing, personal belongings and luggage. I watch them impassively, wondering what selection criterion is used to determine who goes where. I can only come up with one: they all appear either too frail or too old or too young to work. The odd mother with children is also escorted through with polite assurances from the German soldiers who stand at the doors to the hall: "No, the water is not too cold; your children will be fine" – that type of thing.

The hall fills up in a matter of minutes. The queue is empty. The few remaining stragglers are crammed into the hall by the hulking men who are minding the wooden carts. The doors are forced shut and a wooden beam is thrust across to seal them. I wonder at the efficiency of it. How did they know to cram just about the right number of people into the shower hall? The obsession with numbers again.

We wait. I am also wondering why, if the people emerging from the showers are to have their clothing returned to them, we were never instructed to mark them or their belongings. I come to the conclusion that they are never to be reunited with their clothing or belongings – they are to be issued with camp outfits. Hence the wooden carts are to ferry the mounds beside us to be burned. One lingering thought: these people are not selected for hard labour or menial tasks, such as I, so what do they do? I can't imagine that they are just allowed to lounge about all day and consume the splendid food. Remember the slogan on the gate, *Arbeit Macht Frei*; what work will these people be performing to make them free?

I soon find out the answers to all of my questions.

Instead of the sound of people happily bathing with soap and warm water, washing the filth and grime of their train journey from their bodies, ear-shattering screams emerge from the hall. The solid wooden doors are pounded on and tested by people frantically trying to get out, as if from the flames of a fire; they bulge, but ultimately withstand the pressure and remain sealed. Gradually the screaming subsides to a few whimpers and then the silence of the grave.

We wait.

The German soldiers, who greeted the now-dead arrivals with warm reassurances, smile contentedly at a job well done and nod to the hulking men with the wooden carts. They roll the carts up to the doors, remove the beam, unlock the wooden doors and step back for the gas to clear.

At a nod from one of the soldiers they begin the task of removing the hundreds of bodies inside. I dare not look. Once again I recede into the safety of madness that I have discovered within myself. There is no place other than that to compartmentalise this horror.

Simultaneously we are given the order to sort through the clothing and retrieve any valuables: gold, silver, money, jewellery. Naturally, should we find something of value and steal it we will be shot. That last superfluous injunction was for our benefit, the new recruits. I would have guessed it anyway.

I lean by the mound next to me. Prayer books, a silver wine goblet, money, photographs, a gold ring, a diamond bracelet, a pearl necklace; in essence, the precious mementos of a life. At first I sort slowly, hesitantly, treating each item as though it were a person. Letting the spirit imbued in the object infuse with my feelings to give it some meaning. Trying to imagine the person that used to wear or treasure this object. But looking to my right, I notice that the experienced sorters are working mechanically at a fast rate. If I am to survive this duty I'd best bury my thoughts and feelings in the madness locker. I attack the mounds with renewed vigour. Soon I am pulling out all the valuables with such efficiency that I rival my two nearest companions. A German soldier leans in and rewards me for my effort with a pat on the back.

I do this all day. By nightfall, either no more trains are due, or we are relieved to return to our barrack while another shift is assigned to take over. As I am walking back I look to the right and notice the billowing smokestack. Corpses and clothing reduced to ashes.

I am drained, emotionally and physically. I understand the moral contempt of the inscription above the gate, *Arbeit Macht Frei*, that greeted me when I arrived. *Work Makes Freedom*. Here it means that if you work, you are free to live.

A sumptuous meal awaits me. It is my first for the day. I finish it ravenously and then lie back to sleep. Tomorrow I need to recover more valuables, and faster. There will be the same number of trains. I don't even think about the people that were asphyxiated to death in the hall.

I sense a tap on my shoulder. My friendly pallet mate. I don't bother rising, I merely half-open my eyes and lean my head in her direction.

"You understand now what we do?"

The question does not elicit an answer from me, merely a shrug of my shoulders.

Roll call.

I have been on sorting duty for nearly a month. I have excelled at this. The *Blockälteste* pulls me out of the queue as we are headed for another day of sorting. I am being transferred from Barrack C to Barrack H. I will be assigned to sewing uniforms.

I should be relieved. But I don't function this efficiently, normally. I live in a constant state of insanity when I am awake and at work. So I am disappointed. I ask if there was anything wrong with my performance.

The *Blockälteste* gives me a strange look. "You are a very good worker. That's why you have been assigned to work in better conditions. You will have your own bunk and better food."

That sways me. Better living conditions appeal to my normal side. Otherwise my insane side would be demanding to continue sorting. I have been getting so good at it that I could do a train in under an hour. You learn a skill, you become proficient at it, you don't want to give it up. Plus, I don't like change.

I don't need to collect anything from the pallet that I sleep on including a small burlap sack that I used to store half of my evening bread ration; it became my breakfast. With the promise of better rations, I leave it behind for a new arrival. I am not that sentimentally attached to this barrack. There's no one to bid farewell to.

The first thing I notice when I enter Barrack H is that it is physically just as grim inside as Barrack C. But instead of pallets, there are bunks with mattresses and blankets. The mood here is also not that sombre. The labour is probably as hard and long; the meals just as sparse – albeit better quality – and the conditions as unforgiving. Any infraction that is deemed serious can lead to instant death. The discretion is at the hands of those that rule by whim.

I am assigned to a lady from Minsk. Her name is Hannah. No German, and I don't know any language she speaks. I don't even know where Minsk is located.

Roll call.

We are still required to muster in quadrants. I stand with a different group from my previous sorters' barracks, with Hannah and other ladies assigned to less soul-destroying duties. Thirty men and women are arrayed in front of us. No gallows. This group conspired to escape by digging a tunnel under one of the fences and a number of them made it all the way to the woods beyond. These thirty are the ones who were caught entering the tunnel. If they are not to be hanged or gassed to death, I can't imagine what punishment awaits them, other than that it will result in their deaths. That is a certainty.

The camp commandant has finished reading the sentence and is now elaborating the verdict. They are to be shot. Hanging is too slow for this many and gassing is too invisible. They need to make a spectacle of them to send a message. I think that by now we all get the message, but many of us figure that we will die here anyway, so the risk of escaping and getting caught rivals the certainty of staying and dying slowly.

A group of riflemen emerge from the barracks and line up in front of the group, who are not even tied to a post. At a nod from the commandant, shots ring out, breaking the morning stillness, and thirty bodies crumple to the ground. The smokestack, which hasn't ceased billowing for as long as I have been here, will soon be emitting the remnants of these thirty.

We are dispersed and I follow Hannah to the sewing workshop. No one says anything about the morning message.

Utilising abundant hand gestures, Hannah communicates the skill to me and I pick it up quickly. I start with sewing buttons on soldiers' uniforms for the first week, and by the second week I am assigned to sew hems, stitch collars, finish shirts and trousers, and even embroider ribbons for officers. If nothing else, if I survive this madness and am physically able, I will have learnt a trade. There – I have discovered a smidgen of optimism in this jungle of mass murder and mayhem.

Evening is less arduous when we return from our gruelling day of labour. We are not emotionally wrung out from fortifying ourselves in the face of the daily horrors of sorting, but physically we are crushed. We can barely manage to feed ourselves, despite the fact that the sustenance is better and the ration larger.

Months pass, and now with the onset of winter again, the harsh weather takes its toll on the ones that become sick or are physically debilitated. Corpses are wheeled out in the morning. The decision is simple; if you miss roll call, you must be dead. Alternatively, if you are alive and didn't make it to roll call, you will be clubbed to death. So the numbers deplete but are quickly replenished by eager new hands.

At times as I work mechanically I spare a thought for the Lipschutzes, who never made it past day one. I also wonder at how I ended up in their house in Ruth's stead. I struggle with that memory, but snippets surface from time to time. I have some recollection of Ruth, their daughter, appearing at my aunt's house and being sequestered in the attic. But memories like that in the circumstances under which I exist cannot be relied upon. So I dismiss them as nonsense. But nonetheless, the images nag at me to make sense of them, clues to how and why I ended up here with her name.

It is a mystery. As is my life in Munich that vanished with my past as if I never had one, an ordinary life that became less so with the early death of both my parents. Being taken in by Oma and then one day finding myself in the home of Aunt Magda. Did those circumstances somehow contribute to my ending up here? If so, why with the Lipschutzes? That's the part that doesn't make sense.

It is nigh impossible to think rationally when I am constantly exhausted, mentally drained and shivering night and day.

Hannah died last night. The part of me that can still retain some semblance of normalcy feels pain at her loss. I witnessed her gradual deterioration but there was nothing that I could do to alleviate it. You carry your own load here. If you straggle the *Kapos* cull you from the herd, club you to death and add you to the smokestack. So to forestall that fate Hannah remained strong for as long as she could, but in the end she succumbed to influenza, added to her physical and mental strain, and passed in the night. I stole a glance at roll call, watching as her body was wheeled to the crematorium to be incinerated. Another year here and it could be me.

The pain I carry for Hannah makes me angry. I have steeled myself against displaying any emotion that might make me stand out, until now. The people that I witnessed suffocating in the hall, and whose clothes were still warm from their bodies, were strangers after all. It was a horror to hear and needed to be instantly stored in the madness locker. The hangings, shootings, clubbings; they too were terrifying to watch, but still happened to strangers.

In Hannah I made a friend here. She taught me basic phrases in her native Russian and I was able to teach her enough German that she could comprehend the sentences and verdicts of the camp commandant. I thought of asking the *Blockälteste* for medicine, or at the very least to let Hannah rest. But I was afraid that that would call attention to her illness and weakness and she would be put to death instantly. Instead I left her half my broth every evening and, without the *Kapos* noticing, I relieved her of some of her sewing pile.

Despite it all she succumbed and now I am friendless. Yet her sister, who witnessed my care for Hannah, befriends me. When night comes, we talk about her.

"Your sister saved my life." Communicated in a combination of hand gestures and simple sounds and words.

Surprisingly, her sister, Sarah, speaks almost fluent German. "I was studying music in Vienna when the Gestapo arrested me. I learnt enough German to be able to follow the lectures."

"I am sorry about your sister."

"She was very fond of you, even though you are not Jewish."

I think about that for a second. I have no clear answer to that; it's all wound up in my father's cause of death.

"I don't think it matters much around here."

"I agree. I meant that as a compliment."

In the morning I am showering before roll call. Not that they mind our hygiene for our own sake, but they want us clean if we are to sew Wehrmacht uniforms. I was the last one in the shower stall and am just getting out when I slip on a bar of soap that someone carelessly left on the floor. I knock myself unconscious against the sharp edge of the wall separating the showers from the sleeping quarters. My last thought before my consciousness evaporates is that I will become a tendril of smoke this morning.

My vision is hazy. I am lying down. There are two people hovering above me. Doctors, nurses, I am not sure, but when they see my eyes open they smile. Were all my experiences horrific nightmares? Pleasant thought, but no such luck.

The man leans down and explains, "You suffered a mild concussion; you will be able to return to your barrack tomorrow and continue working."

Some concession. I shut my eyes again and think back to the train and the man who confronted the officer: *You are too valuable to us*. His life was spared. I am German, an efficient and reliable worker; they need me. As long as I don't become sick like Hannah I will be kept alive to work – grist to the mill. The insidious slogan is reinforced once again. Whoever came up with it was inflicted with an evil sense of humour.

A day later a *Kapo* escorts me back to my barrack. The *Blockälteste* greets me like a long-lost friend.

"How are you feeling?"

I nod my head and shrug.

"We know who carelessly dropped the bar of soap on the ground. It will never happen again."

I dare not wonder what hapless individual paid with her life for this casual accident. But I missed roll call twice. Whoever it was would have been the feature of the moment and either hung, shot or, if it was just the single culprit, clubbed to death for the benefit of all.

My silence is taken as approval for the punishment meted out to this individual. I feel sick; maybe *I* was careless for not seeing the bar on the ground? But when you are exhausted, freezing and rushing to appear at roll call to spare your life, a bar of soap on the ground can go unnoticed. I want to yell at this cretin and expunge all the anger, hatred and pent-up revulsion from within me. But I know that someone else will pay for my insurrection. I'm the same as the man on the train; too valuable. They will track down the person in front of me who failed to notice the bar of soap and feed them to the smokestack.

I am tempted to ask who it was, not out of any macabre interest, but in the ardent hope that it was not Sarah. But it is best for me not to know. Because if it was Sarah and she was executed I will lunge at this *Blockälteste* and gouge her eyes out. If I do, these sick lunatics will probably promote me to work directly under the camp commandant: *You are too valuable to us, plus you demonstrate willpower*, or whatever that silly Jewish word was.

So I maintain my stony silence and remain standing at attention.

"Anyway, you are not working at this camp any more. You are being transferred to a smaller camp nearby making munitions. Your rations will increase to two meals per day and you will work less hours." She nods at the *Kapo*, who leads me back to my bunk.

He looks curiously at me. "Don't you have anything to take?"

Imbeciles.

After I can't remember how many years at this camp, I am finally leaving, being driven by a motorcycle with a sidecar to the munitions factory housed within the satellite base. The man driving the motorcycle is a German soldier, perhaps just a little older than me. I must be just turning sixteen – if I can remember my age without celebrating my birthday. He looks over at me with a lascivious smile. Even though I am at the age where boys would ordinarily arouse interest in me, the feelings associated with that yearning are so remote now that they are lost and forgotten. If I ever outlive this nightmare I will have to excavate deep within my soul to rediscover them under the rubble.

As we pass under the infamous slogan I can't help but look back. I can still recall that fateful, overcast day when I was almost beaten to death for stating a harmless truth. I was trying to save myself, but in this world of perverted logic it would have cost me my young life. I should feel relief for having survived this place despite the daily threats and exposure to death. But I don't. I lost too much, and the shards of dignity and humanity that I have retained are so few that they don't give me a breath of freedom, just more incarceration, albeit with better conditions. Doubtless any serious infraction deemed by those in charge will end my life. That will never change.

We enter the woods. I like nature. But here is the place where fourteen human beings ultimately paid with their lives for capturing and eating a pig. Thirty others had their escape curtailed by being shot for attempting it. I can only wonder what other horrors happened here.

My escort brings the motorcycle to a halt. He clambers down from the seat and comes around to the sidecar. He leans in and starts kissing me. I would normally be shocked, but that sense has become jaded, so I am merely startled at the sudden turn of events. I instinctively repel the attack, but that only provokes him more. With one hand he holds the nape of my neck firmly so that I cannot escape the thrusting of his tongue, while with the other he is forcing his fingers into my private part.

Modesty is not an affectation that is maintained for long in the camp after being constantly asked to strip and searched by both women and men. But my virginity is a part of me that I have retained in the silent promise to myself that if I ever walk away from this horror physically unscathed, I will treasure it as the sole part of me that is unmolested. It appears that that promise is about to be violated.

I struggle valiantly but he is young, well fed, physically robust and in heat. He lifts me out of the sidecar with ease and flings me onto the soft ground. With two swift movements he rips the sheer underwear that I fashioned from loose cloth and lifts my dress over my waist. The thrust is deep and sharp, like a knife. My head falls back in surrender.

"I like girls that fight back," he boasts as he is thrusting.

For the first time I feel like crying. But instead I bury my shame and wretchedness in my madness locker and commit his face to memory. I am acquitted of this violation in the knowledge that I did not invite or permit it. Like my incarceration, it was involuntary.

He thrusts some more, jerks with relief and stands up.

"I am good. Huh? You Jewish bitch." He spits down at me.

I wipe my face and want to tell him that I am German just like him, with one key difference: I am a human being and he is a perverted, sick creature. He clambers back onto the motorcycle, kicks the engine to life and waits for me to re-enter the sidecar.

I rise, staggering, pull up the strips of fabric that are left of my knickers, straighten out my dress and get back into the sidecar. Our journey resumes. He no longer looks at me, leeringly or otherwise. I could delude myself into thinking that he is ashamed, but that would be a benevolent thought on my part. It is more likely that I have served his immediate urge and he is now eager to dispose of me. He would probably shoot me and leave me in the woods to die, except for the obsession with numbers. I am being transferred from one camp to another. If I don't arrive there will be a shortfall in the count. Sometimes the most infinitesimal, petty predilections spare your life.

The new camp does not have two barbed-wire fences, watchtowers or dogs guarding it. Not even a ditch to separate it from its surroundings. A mere chain-link fence, and a single soldier stands on guard at the gate. There is no slogan over the gate, just a cornerstone with the name of the munitions factory.

My rapist, Klaus (I find out his name from the guard that greets him), drives me to the quarters at the back of the factory. He kills the engine and comes around to the sidecar.

"Can I help you out?"

This person is utterly devoid of empathy and conscience. Fifteen minutes ago he raped me violently without the slightest remorse, called me a Jew bitch, spat on me, and now he wants to courteously help me out of the sidecar as though I am his date arriving at the ball.

His abrupt and obsequious turn of behaviour leads me to believe that this is another absurd example that exists in this benighted circle of hell, along with the obsession with numbers, the contempt for human life, the severe and harsh punishment for the slightest infractions: the code of conduct that prohibits the rape of munition workers. Not for any honourable reason other than we are valuable fodder for the Wehrmacht war machinery and raping transferees between camps is verboten.

I shake my head indignantly, climb out and stride in front of him. On some visceral level he has violated the last remaining vestige of personal dignity that I possessed, transgressing into the madness locker; that place where I compartmentalise the daily horrors and humiliations that I witness or endure so that I can paradoxically remain sane. My reaction transcends rationality, it is of a wounded animal, and as such I care not for the consequences.

I can't resist my impulse. "You called me a Jewish bitch, you raped me and injured me with your violence. You then spat on me."

He is turning red and beginning to lose his composure. "No one will believe you."

"I don't care if they don't believe me! I am German just like you. I am not Jewish; not that that makes any difference. But you make me ashamed, not just for what you did, but *because* I am German. You are a disgusting, vile savage."

"Please. No good will come of it. I have parents in—" He is snivelling in a bleating tone.

Without a thought I fill up my mouth with saliva and spit at his face so that the glob lands like a burst balloon. "Why don't you tell that pathetic story to your commanding officer, you sorry excuse for a soldier?"

With that I march off with more than a semblance of dignity and some of my honour, at least emotionally, restored. Physically I am violated; there is nothing I can do about that. I count myself fortunate that to this point I had not been molested, beaten or abused. It is ironic that, now that I have been elevated to work in a more skilled task with better conditions, this has happened to me.

In this dark and dismal world that I exist in, I count my blessings in small scraps that infrequently and sluggishly make my way. This was not one of them, but on the bright side, if one can see it that way, he didn't murder me in the woods to cover his rape. He could have easily done so and lied that I tried to escape. The lunatics that preside over him would have believed it. Naturally my corpse would have been splayed over his sidecar like a trophy, otherwise there would be a shortfall in the numbers.

I literally stomp into the barrack. There are single bunks here stretching twenty across on either side. A grey striped mattress lies bare on each frame and a dark woollen blanket is neatly folded at the foot of the bed. Each bed has a small locker with a mess kit: metal cup, cutlery and a bowl. It is more like a spartan army barrack than the cattle shed I left behind.

It is empty. The workers are at the factory. I don't have anything to unpack, so I walk back out and look around to see where I will be working. This camp is about a tenth of the size of the one I left. It doesn't take me long to find the plant. A soldier is standing guard outside the entrance.

"Why are you not at work inside?" He signals with his head.

"I was just transferred here. So I am reporting to work."

He nods and opens the door for me.

There are dozens of desks and tables scattered throughout the factory floor. Above each work area is a bright lamp. Each work station is surrounded mostly by women and the occasional male worker. They appear to be assembling units and then passing them down to a conveyor as it moves around the factory.

A female German officer approaches, striding in a military fashion to where I am standing. She looks me up and down. "You look rumpled and dishevelled. What happened to you?"

"I don't have good clothes."

"Follow me."

At the back of the factory are the toilets and changing rooms. I am instructed to discard my clothing and slip into an overall and underwear supplied by the factory. I reappear shortly after, having showered the blood and grime and changed into new clothes.

"You will work there, assembling bullets and guns." She points to a table three down from where we are standing.

The work is monotonous, the hours are long and, as in the other work barracks, there is no food or drink. Nor do we get any breaks. Ironically, the work that I found the most rewarding was being a sorter – I didn't have time to think. But by the time they moved me to sewing I was at my breaking point. There are only so many live bodies that can stream, naked, by you before it guts your soul. Particularly when they walk past willingly anticipating a refreshing shower after their train ordeal.

Back in the sleeping quarters, I am provided with a warm meal that is more varied and better quality than the dregs I am accustomed to. For the first time in years I see green vegetables in my ration. Even a piece of meat, although I dare not enquire as to its origin. There is tea and coffee, and while we eat hungrily, there is not that all-consuming voraciousness that was customary at the other camp. It is a full meal and there will be another one in the morning. I don't have to sequester a piece of bread for my breakfast.

The lady in the bunk next to me asks me the usual questions.

"I am from Munich. I am not sure if I am Jewish. I think my father may have been."

"How long have you been in the camps?"

I don't have a precise answer for that, so I leave the question unanswered.

I lie back on a mattress that smells musty, but just the same is more comfortable than the wooden pallet and slats. My body actually finds the contours and sinks in.

Roll call is at nine. Same routine. I am wondering what entertainment we will witness here.

The camp commandant does not ride on horseback. Instead he strides through the quadrants in a chivalrous manner. He is handsome in an older-person sort of way, clean-shaven, with a sculpted face, strong jaw and a full mane of sandy-blond hair. His eyes, which I can't fail to notice when he strides past, are deep blue. Away from here you could imagine him to be an actor.

"Our quota is enormous. We are at war with the world."

This is definitely news. I am reminded of Oma's refrain – *Do we need another war?* – in response to a Hitler diatribe.

"We are going to increase the shift time by two hours. But we will add a ten-minute break and some extra food and drink rations."

He is strutting along, whacking the back of his thigh with a razor-thin leather switch. I am curious – where is his horse? That must be standard issue to all camp commandants. Maybe the horse tried to escape or ate hay without permission and they hung or shot it the previous day. I am reflecting on last night's meal.

"You must meet your quota. If you don't, the German people will fall under the heel of the Bolsheviks. You must not let that happen." He accentuates each word, emphasising their significance and the unspoken consequence of failure.

I don't think that he is making points here. We are all probably thinking that if *Der Führer* is quashed we will all get to go home and resume our normal lives. Or whatever can be considered normal after experiencing camp life courtesy of the Third Reich.

A large man two quadrants away snorts. The camp commandant quickens his pace to where the man is standing and glowers at him.

"What did you find amusing?"

The man mutters something I can't make out. The commandant, apparently satisfied with the answer, turns to leave, but then with a swiftness that belies his suave demeanour swivels back and attacks the man with the switch, forcing him to the ground, his arms flailing over his head to shield himself from the incessant lashings. He repeatedly stomps on the man's head with his hobnailed boots, then steps back to hurl kicks at his groin, abdomen and face. Blood pours from the injuries and the man becomes senseless. Without much ado the commandant pulls out his pistol and fires two shots at the presumed offender.

And I thought we wouldn't be entertained here.

The commandant regains his pace as if that was a distraction of no significance and resumes his speech. "Work harder. Work faster. Do not make mistakes. We can't afford mistakes. A mistake here is a dead soldier in the field. And you *all* will be held to account." He is poised at the front of the muster. He salutes Hitler. We respond enthusiastically and march off to commence our extended shifts.

The body of the dead man is left to fester in a pool of blood.

In the evening my interlocutor from last night, Gertrud from Westphalia, tells me in a confidential whisper that the large man had a respiratory difficulty. He wasn't snorting mockingly, he was just clearing his nose so that he could breathe. He is not the first unwell person to die in my presence. There is no room for sickness in the Third Reich. I could have told him that.

With the extended shifts taking their toll, more bodies are left behind in the barrack each morning. There are no large, burly men to wheel out the corpses; we are forced to go back and collect our erstwhile colleagues, place them in a wheelbarrow – nothing quite so dignified as a wooden cart – and tip them unceremoniously into a mass grave nearby. We pour lime over the corpses to douse the stench of decomposition. Soon replacements arrive to replenish the denuded numbers. I assume I was one for just such an occasion.

We don't get any news in here other than exhortations to work harder and faster. But from the mood of the camp commandant I get the sense that the war effort is not going well. On a number of occasions the lights go out during the night shift and production is interrupted. We aren't relieved of our shift, just commanded to sit and wait.

Whoever the enemy is, they must be making inroads. The ground has been shaking and the walls trembling from the relentless shelling. Each day the pounding gets worse, and yesterday one of the barracks was destroyed. We came out to see it engulfed in flames.

Roll call.

The normally suave camp commandant is looking ruffled and less debonair. "Due to the need to provide more munitions at a faster pace, we will be relocating to another factory. It will happen this month. There will be no change in your work schedule until you are commanded to move."

No exhortations to work harder and faster, nor threats of death for each failed part that results in the demise of a Wehrmacht soldier. There must be a great many of those, too many to attribute to a single worker. The enemy must be exacting a significant toll. I have learnt to suppress any public display of emotion after my experience on the train all those years ago. Inwardly I am starting to hope again that my nightmare will end and I will survive my incarceration. But I don't gloat.

The shelling is now constant, with a number of bombs landing nearby or inside the compound. Several barracks have been destroyed. Their occupants are moved into our quarters, so that now we have three rows instead of two and thirty bunks to a row. The food rations have been reduced. We are told that this is due to the imminent relocation. The real reason is obvious to all of us: the shelling is disrupting the supply lines, depleting not just our food, but raw materials for our munitions.

Every day our work is stopped due to the shortages. But we are not relieved to go out and enjoy the shelling. Instead we are commanded to clean the floors, bathrooms, work areas, and tend to the compound to clear the rubble.

I return to my quarters totally exhausted and near to starving. I must be approaching womanhood by now and imagine that my normal weight ought to be twice what I am currently. In the shower my ribcage protrudes through my skin. My hipbones jut out to my sides and my legs resemble matchsticks. Skeletal is the term. Despite there being many more of us in the barrack, order is maintained and, after consuming our meagre rations, the lights are turned off. I now sequester half my bread. Breakfast may not be coming.

UTRECHT

Winter 1944

He had hardly finished saying the words when two sets of hands grabbed him from behind, thrusting him against the adjoining wall, knocking the wind out of him. One of the men forced his head backwards, exposing his neck, thrusting a knife under his larynx. A trickle of blood oozed from the pressure.

"Who are you?" It was Koert, holding his head in a vice-like grip.

"Friedrich Becker."

The two men pinning him against the wall exchanged rapid dialogue in Dutch. Friedrich, in his state of confusion and panic, didn't grasp any of the words.

"You better tell me that you had nothing to do with her shooting," the man holding the knife flush against his neck growled at him, edging the blade deeper.

"What? No. Of course not." Despite the chill, he was perspiring profusely. He could feel the cold sweat trickling under his arms and down his back. He heard his voice burbling from the pressure on his vocal cords. But more likely it was the fear pounding in his ears.

A weak voice interrupted their interrogation, coming from the floor behind them. It was the woman who had been shot. She spoke in Dutch.

The knife and vice-grip relaxed simultaneously. The other man, not the bearded hulk who had assisted Friedrich earlier, relaxed his grip, letting Friedrich's body come away from the wall. "Sorry." A crooked smile spread over his craggy face. He patted Friedrich's shirt, smoothing out the wrinkles, and stepped sideways to let him return to his patient.

Wobbling, Friedrich fumbled his way back to the mattress and knelt down. His hand shaking, he picked up the makeshift tweezers and set about dislodging the bullet.

"Friedrich. Fancy meeting you here, of all places." The irreverent sense of humour, even in her state; he welcomed its sound.

"Where else would I be, Emma?"

"Buying postcards from Hitler." She tried to laugh a little, but her voice shook and a tremor coursed through her body.

"Please don't speak. I need to do some more work here. Try and stay calm."

Emma took as deep a breath as she could, then let the tension seep from her body.

Friedrich pointed to the lamp and asked Lotte to bring it closer. He peered into the wound, which was now clean and free of gunshot residue. Nothing. He started to prod again. Emma lurched forward. The bearded man who had pinned her down earlier leaned forward again, holding her down by the shoulders.

"I will need to prise the wound open; you will need to get me more alcohol. Also more rags."

He could hear feet move around behind him, objects being moved. From the corner of his eye he could see rags and a bottle of what looked like spirits tossed onto the mattress.

He nodded toward the bearded man, who now didn't seem to mind being seen in the lamplight. Despite his shaggy, rugged appearance he had a kind pair of eyes and an avuncular face. In another time he could have been a strong but gentle family man.

The rugged man introduced himself as Theo. He picked up the bottle and leaned forward, pouring slowly into Emma's mouth. She spluttered but held most of it down, heaved, then lay back again.

"You trying to get me drunk, Fred? You know it won't work."

"It's working." He tried to smile again.

Friedrich resumed his prodding, prying, prising, and soaking up the blood. He stopped every few minutes to mop her forehead, check her pulse and temperature. She stabilised, but was a long way from recovery. It was going to be a long, dark night of morbid thoughts and a fight against the damage of the injury: without instruments, without anaesthetic and without medicine; in dim light and unhygienic conditions. The odds were terrible. Worse than terrible, hopeless, but he couldn't give up.

Emma had fainted. The pain would have been excruciating, beyond even her good humour and great strength to withstand. In a way he was glad. If she died, she would never know.

After what seemed like an eternity, while he was prodding, he sensed something solid stalling his progress. He leaned back, took off his shirt and ripped a sleeve. He tied it around his forehead to stop the perspiration dripping onto the wound. Behind him Theo and Koert stood guard, every so often checking the doorways. Neither of them enquired as to his progress.

Friedrich resumed his primitive surgery, using both the penknife and the makeshift tweezers. He was terrified of nicking an organ or cutting a blood vessel. Then it would be the end and he would be responsible. He had both his knees on the mattress for comfort and purchase and, leaning over the gaping wound, he delved again. Again, the clinking sound and feel. He found the bullet. Slowly, evenly, carefully, he clamped the tweezers around the base of the bullet and pulled. The tweezers slipped, and the bullet remained lodged, unmoving.

The metal casing was twisted and he couldn't get a firm hold on it. He tried again, putting more pressure on the tweezers. It started to move, but the tweezers folded back.

"*Scheiße, verdammt, Scheiße!*"

Koert and Theo came closer. "Can we help?"

"I need proper instruments," he shouted back at them. He looked at his watch hurriedly: 1.40am. He had been going at this for nearly an hour non-stop. *She won't last much longer.*

Koert and Theo exchanged urgent words. Theo left in a hurry. All that Koert said was, "Wait. Can you wait?"

As if he had a choice.

Half an hour later Theo burst in, sweating, with a gleam in his eyes and a hearty smile. He was holding a swaddled blanket. He set it on the floor beside Friedrich. He unfurled the blanket to reveal a set of instruments, gauze, a roll of bandages, and medicines.

"What did you do, rob a hospital?" Friedrich couldn't help but smile to himself.

"Never mind what we did, save Emma," Koert ordered him firmly.

Heartened, Friedrich reached for the forceps. He clamped them a few times, disbelieving their presence in his hand. He moistened one of the rags in antiseptic and once again leaned into the gaping wound. Following the same path as before he delved into the aperture between the renal artery and the kidney where the bullet was lodged. Clamping the forceps firmly, he pulled at the crumpled metal and pulled it outward. It came out with ease and he dropped it alongside the lamp. It landed with a clink.

Moistening another rag with antiseptic, he cleansed the wound and picked up the penknife, flicking it open. He warmed its edge over the flame and then cauterised the edges of the wound. Emma twitched, moaned and then returned to her unconscious state. He continued in this way until the wound ceased oozing and firmly pursed it together. He finished by placing an antiseptic gauze over it, holding it firmly in place with bandages.

The rest was in fate's hands. He had done his best. All they could do was wait. The time: 3.05am. Exhausted, they all sat back against the walls and attempted to catch some rest. Sometime during the early hours dawn crept through the transom windows, bathing the basement in a greyish light. Shapes and forms were beginning to coalesce into people and objects. He could almost see them clearly now: Theo, Koert, Lotte and the man who had forcibly held him against the wall.

It all seemed like a nightmarish tale that had unfolded and now, with the danger dissipated, he was once more in a dingy basement with the strangers who had crowded his brain in an effort to save the woman he loved, lost and hopefully regained.

The adrenaline seeped out of him, and he felt drained. He hadn't slept properly in days, always on the lookout for danger, wondering if at the next checkpoint, the next city, he would be stopped and questioned. Now, for the first time, he might be able to rest. They couldn't betray him without suffering the same fate, and neither could he.

"I am going to lie down for a little to regain my strength. If anything happens, wake me." He was speaking to Koert, who merely nodded.

He crawled over to the edge of the mattress and lay at Emma's feet. His brain was muddled with images: the train station at Grünewald, his parents, the SS, trains again, this time to Eindhoven and then to Utrecht. Trains and more trains, with tracks stretching out in front of him leading nowhere. Ultimately he was lost.

At some time in the day (he knew it was day, because the basement was bathed in natural light), a hand touched his, clasping it firmly. The feeling surged through him, taking him back to an earlier time, before this darkness and madness. A feeling that he never forgot, just shelved in the quest to survive.

He couldn't come awake.

The next time he became conscious it was dusk. A blanket had been spread over him. But he was no longer alone. Someone was lying next to him. He felt the shape: Emma.

He came fully awake. Theo was seated in the corner by the door.

"Is she all right?"

Theo held up his hand, rose, went to the back room and fetched Koert.

"You feeling better?"

"Yes. Is she all right?"

"Weak. But she woke hours ago and then fell asleep again."

"Thank God." He was momentarily relieved, but the anxiety returned. He had crossed over; there was no turning back. Any day now he would be reported as a deserter. If he were caught the penalty would be swift and certain. He had to escape the confines of the Third Reich.

He lay back next to Emma and starting planning the next part of his journey.

A soft voice woke him from his reverie. "Friedrich."

He looked up; Emma was looking at him from the pillow.

"How are you feeling?"

"Better than you look, I hope."

"Still the one with the funny lines."

"*Ja*. See where it got me."

"I am glad that I was here to help."

Her eyes brimmed momentarily, and she reached for his hand and held it close to her chest. "Thank you."

He couldn't think of what to say.

"What happened to you, Friedrich?"

"I don't know, Emma." He paused, trying to assimilate, with the benefit of distance and hindsight, the last six years. "I am not sure. I tried to be a hero. But the truth is, I was afraid to die, so I hid inside a uniform thinking it would protect me. In the end it didn't make any difference. I was going to die. So I deserted."

"We are all afraid to die, Friedrich. Me too. I got shot, not because I was a hero, but because we were ambushed; outnumbered."

He tightened his grip, affirming the love which he had lost and rediscovered.

"What now?"

"Well, I was making my escape when I was summoned here by a little girl. Lotte. But I am a wanted man now. So I can't stay. I need to leave as soon as possible."

"Don't think that I am not wanted either. They know about me now. So I am on the target list as well."

Friedrich paused to consider the new reality. "Can your friends, colleagues, help?"

"There is a way across via Belgium and then the Channel to England. But it is risky."

"No more than staying here."

Emma called out to Koert. He came in from the back room. She spoke with him briefly in Dutch and then reverted to German to address Friedrich. "The crossing is arranged for tomorrow; do you think I can make the journey?"

"If not, I will have to carry you."

Now it was her turn to smile. Only it still hurt.

They reminisced for many hours about the time lost. Emma had never married; had completed her study, and then the Germans invaded. Her parents, fearful that her mother would be arrested and deported, fled to England to live with her brother. She then led a double life: a doctor by day and helping the underground by night with medical assistance, money and safe houses. This was one of them.

"I often thought of writing but I was afraid that I would get you in trouble. I wasn't sure how or what you were doing. I knew that the Gestapo would be vigilant. If I had written to you, me being Jewish, that would have caused you problems. Was I right not to write?"

"In the end it didn't matter. Trying to stay my destiny became my destiny. Not staying here with you all those years ago, I ended up here anyway. It's like we can't cheat our fate. It finds us and makes us realise who we are."

He edged slowly up the mattress and came close up by the pillow. He found her lips and kissed her, gently at first, then when she didn't react with pain, more deeply. Together they lay on the mattress, hugging each other closely.

Friedrich fell asleep feeling secure in himself for the first time in his life, regardless of the physical danger that surrounded him. His love for Emma, the only other person he had ever truly loved, sustained him. Whatever happened tonight, tomorrow and the day after that, he would take one day at a time until he reached his destination, wherever that may be. *Love – it protects you*, was his last conscious thought before his eyes closed.

SURRENDER

May 1945

Roll call.

We step outside and mechanically line up in rows and columns in our designated quadrants. And wait. And wait.

After nearly an hour the realisation sinks in that the camp commandant and his officers have deserted the factory and left us to be shelled to smithereens. We start to disperse in a disorderly fashion. Each group walks up to their designated *Blockälteste*. They shrug at our questions; they know as much as we do, which is nothing other than that we have been abandoned.

It takes a while longer to sink in that we are, in essence, free. But free to do what? We have been incarcerated for so long, commanded to work at certain tasks, that our free will has been abolished. We can't function without commands, we can't be motivated without threats and we don't know where to go, where we are. Spiritually we are still imprisoned.

We walk to the gate and stop. This is the only home we know. The only refuge that we have in this world is this compound. We have no money, no belongings and no way to contact anyone in the world from which we were forcibly removed. So we loiter, wander over to the food supply shed and force open the doors. We find little inside. Certainly not enough to feed the thousand or so inmates incarcerated here.

We have to organise and leave, or stay and starve. A bleak choice under the circumstances, but that is the reality.

Suddenly we hear excited shouts from the direction of the gate. We dash out and join the small group gathered there. In the distance, almost a mirage it is that far away, we make out the shimmering image of an army approaching: tanks, armoured vehicles, jeeps, marching troops. At first we are apprehensive that our freedom has been short-lived and this is the replacement for the deserters.

But that fear is quickly dispelled when we recognise that the flag flying at the front of the contingent is a red star, not a swastika.

We are liberated; the Third Reich, which, from the vague memory of my early teens, was supposed to last a thousand years, has come to an abrupt and early end. The army advance until they are facing our group gathered at the gate. They stop and stare at us. We must be a sore sight: a ragged group of emaciated inmates on the verge of utter despair and death. An officer steps forward from the Soviet army and comes up to our group, studying us intently from left to right. He addresses us in Russian.

"Who is in charge here?"

No answer. I must be the only one that understands the question thanks to my years of sewing with Hannah and then Sarah: the sisters from Minsk. My first inclination is to point to the *Blockälteste*, but they are prisoners just like us and with the Germans gone, so is their authority.

I step out of the group and stand in front of him. I explain in halting Russian that there is no one in charge and the Germans have abandoned the camp.

He turns back and addresses the lieutenant colonel in charge of the battalion.

"Do you need medical help and food?"

I presume that the question is perfunctory. I merely nod and wave at the crowd amassed behind me.

He turns to the lieutenant. An order is issued and two large trucks rumble into the compound. Within minutes the tarp is rolled up and basic supplies are brought down: bread, potatoes, milk, rice, beans. We set out to get tables from the work factory and create a serving counter for the food. We are so used to order that those being served get in a queue and hold up their mess bowl, cup and cutlery. I assist with the serving.

My service at the food queue is interrupted and I am asked to help translate for the medical staff: malnutrition, too extreme to be relieved with a simple meal; sores; welts; blisters; dysentery; amputated gangrenous limbs; lice; dental caries. There is such a variety of ailments that only the most urgent, life-threatening cases can be tended to.

After a while I get to sit and have a small meal myself. I am starving too, though I neglected that in the exigency of tending to the others. I sit on a makeshift bench next to the barrack wall and cradle my bowl. The officer who addressed me at the gate approaches and sits next to me.

"I am sorry about what happened to you."

I shrug. Though many are weeping quietly, others are crying openly with relief and remembrance now that their harrowing ordeal has come to an end.

"How come you speak Russian?"

I explain about the Minsk sisters.

"Are they here?"

"No. At a huge camp." I point westwards. "One of them died from illness and starvation."

"Oświęcim?"

I look at him questioningly. He explains that it is a town some fifty kilometres west. There is a very large concentration camp next to it with tens of thousands of inmates. A lot of dead, a lot of dying; he knows little else. But he has heard reports. Bodies piled high. The Germans in charge were taken prisoner.

An idea sparks in me. I ask to borrow his combat knife. He hands it to me hesitantly. I pull up my dress to reveal my inner thigh, not feeling even slightly immodest. With the sharp edge of the knife I cut through a crude scar in the flesh. Immediately blood seeps out. I wipe it away with my hem, exposing the wound, and pull out a diamond ring with a gold band. I salvaged it in one of my first days at the camp.

I initially took it because the woman headed to the shower was so beautiful that I couldn't let her be destroyed without retaining something of her memory. When she tossed the ring onto the mound next to where I was standing, I grabbed it and slipped it between my toes. I was working so fast that the *Kapos* failed to notice the sleight of hand. That night, while relieving myself, I placed it inside my vagina. Later on, when I was transferred to sewing, I stitched it inside my thigh. It's been there ever since.

I hand the knife back.

My Russian officer is called Marat Fedchenkov. He is twenty-eight and from St Petersburg. He is staring at the ring, emitting a long, soft whistle. "Yours?" he enquires with a chuckle.

"Does it matter?"

"No. I am sure that you have earned it."

"I want something for it."

He nods.

I point to the pistol holstered at his side and make the universal sign for money.

"The gun is no problem. Money – how much?"

I am dumbstruck. There are multiple reasons I can't answer that question: I don't know the value of Russian money; and if I did, how much does one need out in the world? Can Russian money be spent in Germany? The only currency that I understand is my food and my health. The loss of either means the loss of my life.

I don't answer.

"What is your name?"

I am so used to answering to the name on the roll call that I am about to say 'Ruth'. But I am free; I no longer have to dissemble.

"Helga Dreschler. I am from Munich." That simple admission reinforces my sense of freedom.

He rises and walks away. After about ten minutes he returns and hands me a heavy object wrapped in a grey woollen cloth. The gun.

"There's six bullets. Be careful. There is also money. I don't know if that's enough, but that is all I have."

I stand up and hug him; not easy for me after all that I have experienced, culminating in the rape. We separate. I hand him the ring. He wishes me good luck and heads over to his men.

I follow to where Major Fedchenkov is issuing orders.

"How do I get to Oświęcim?"

He leans over and whispers, "You have more jewellery?"

I am about to shake my head when he breaks out in laughter. He points to a jeep with a Russian soldier seated behind the wheel. I eagerly head over, but then I recall my last trip with a soldier. But two others, one a woman officer, join us.

We travel for nearly an hour along a trail that is strewn with rubble, burnt-out tanks, armoured vehicles and charred bodies lying on the ground in abnormal shapes: hewn by the all-consuming fire.

As we approach Oświęcim, we avoid the actual town and first head west and then south to arrive at a large contingent surrounding the camp. At first I don't see it, but as we get closer I can't fail to notice the ominous slogan over the massive gates that greeted me on that overcast day all those years ago. I shiver, even though I am bundled in a warm overcoat. The jeep pulls up alongside a group of soldiers that are lounging by a truck.

The driver points casually at the gate. "Oświęcim."

I nod, and step out of the jeep firmly clutching my woollen parcel. I already have a story to get me into the camp. As expected, I am stopped at the gate.

"I am a nurse. Major Fedchenkov sent me."

"Papers."

"I don't have papers. But that jeep brought me, you can ask them."

He looks over at the driver, who is still seated firmly behind the wheel. The guard cocks his head at him. The driver nods. The guard steps aside to let me in.

I didn't know in what state I would find the camp. I look over to my right along the fence that leads to the killing hall. There are mounds of unsorted clothing and luggage lining the path. The massive doors to the hall are open, with three wooden carts standing empty and askew by the entrance. There are no bodies on the carts or in the hall that I can see from where I stand. I edge closer. The putrid odour of death still lingers in the air. I wonder how long ago the murders ceased. From the untended mounds on the ground, I presume not too long.

I walk further into the camp and look to my right at the barrack where I spent years sewing, first with Hannah and later with Sarah. I don't expect to find Sarah, but there are several piles of emaciated bodies lying dejectedly by the wall, discarded carcasses like washing ready to be hung. Every so often a gaunt, lifeless face peers at me from within dead, sunken eyes.

The corpses were stockpiled in transit to the crematorium. Deserting soldiers and *Kapos* fleeing the advancing Russian army have left their handiwork in full display. I have seen and not acknowledged this before when I worked as a sorter. Bodies pulled out from the hall, transfixed in masks of terror, sometimes clutching one another, other times a mother holding a baby or young children. Then I ignored it in my need to remain sane, banishing the images to my madness locker. I now absorb and reflect that I need to get on with the task I came to execute.

I want to believe that Sarah has survived, or at the least is in one of these piles and I can grant her some dignity by touching her body and saying a few words. I don't pray. But it is a hopeless thought; the bodies are too wasted to identify men from women. The only way to tell would be to examine genitalia, and even then I would never recognise a face.

I walk away, one hand clutching my mouth, the other my woollen parcel.

In the compound where we mustered every roll call to watch hangings, shootings and clubbings, and to be repeatedly threatened with death for every slight infraction, I see it. Hundreds of German soldiers seated on the ground with their hands resting on their heads. I am immediately disheartened. How am I going to find one lowly private in amongst these many prisoners?

The German prisoners are divided into similar groups as we were, several hundred in a loosely cordoned circle. Beside each group are two Russian soldiers noting the rank, name and number of each prisoner on a pad. I think of an excuse as I approach the first group.

"I am looking for a German soldier. His first name is Klaus. I don't have his last name. But he is either a private or a corporal."

The man closest to me doesn't look up for my paperwork. "Your interest?"

"I am a nurse sent over by Major Fedchenkov. This soldier has a very infectious disease. I need to take him out of the group and place him in quarantine."

"I don't know this Fedchenkov. I report to Colonel Volkov. He is over there. If he says it's OK, then it's OK."

I turn to look at where he is pointing. A stout man with a large handlebar moustache is barking out orders to a group of men hauling supplies. Judging from the medals and epaulettes adorning his torso and shoulders he appears to be a veteran officer who is not going to be easy to bluff.

I walk over and stand deferentially just to his right.

He is about to turn and stomp in my direction when he nearly bumps into me. "What are you doing here? What do you want?"

"I am sorry. Major Fedchenkov sent me. I am to pick up a German soldier who is carrying a highly infectious disease and place him in quarantine."

"Major who?" he shouts, impatient to get on with his task.

"Fedchenkov."

"Never heard of him. Why do you come to me? I am in charge of this whole division. I have two days to clear this mess and transport the Germans to an internment camp. I don't know anything about Fenenko or this sick German. They are all sick. Go and speak to the men over there. They have the lists."

"It's Major Fedchenkov. And do I have your permission to escort the man?"

Volkov has already stormed off to another part of the compound. He is waving his hand dismissively at me. I take that as a yes.

"Klaus is the first name. And Volkov said yes." I am back with the sergeant who told me to get permission from the colonel.

He is perusing the list. "No one here by that name. Try the next lot."

I search about six groups of prisoners numbering close to eight hundred men. A couple of them are named Klaus, but when I peer over the crowd I don't recognise anyone.

I cover several more groups of men. No luck. I am starting to think that maybe he deserted or was killed, when I notice a number of men hauling corpses away, commanded by Russian soldiers. The corpses are being placed on carts and wheeled to a large pit. I quickly walk towards them and study the desultory group of a dozen German prisoners loading up the carts. I see him.

"That man needs to come out of the group."

"Why?" A stocky, unshaven officer looks over at me sullenly. He is brandishing a pistol that he is using as an incentive to make the prisoners work faster. He is shouting at them in Russian to do so. I doubt that they understand what he is saying. But they get the message reinforced by the pistol.

"He is carrying an infectious disease."

"Who authorised this?"

"Volkov." It's an easy answer. He is never going to go and get confirmation from the irascible colonel.

"What is his name?"

"Klaus."

He picks up a list that is lying on the ground, checks the name, then walks over to Klaus. He slaps him hard on the back of the skull just as he is loading another corpse onto the cart. "You are sick. Get out of here."

Klaus cowers and stares up at the Russian soldier. But remains in place.

The Russian officer kicks him and points toward me, commanding in Russian, "Go! Go!"

Klaus peers at me, thinks he is saved from this abuse, then recognises me. He falters, then stops a few feet away. "What… what is he saying? Why is he hitting me? Are they going to kill me?"

I smile warmly at him. "No. They are going to give you a medal of honour."

He remains standing where he is.

"Come. You need to come with me."

"Why? Why?" He looks back at the Russian officer, who brushes him off. "Where are you taking me? Are you going to kill me because of… what happened?" He is limping by my side, nagging me with his questions.

"No. I am not going to kill you. But I had syphilis. So you need to be treated or you will go mad."

He clutches his face. "Oh my God! I have parents in Frankfurt. A brother. A sister. If I die… oh my God!"

On the way to the gate we pass a truck with medical supplies and nurses tending to a queue of camp inmates. I walk up to one of the nurses and ask for two masks. She reaches into a box next to her and hands them over.

I place one across my face and hand one to Klaus. "Put this on."

"Why?" He pinches the mask like it's a filthy rag.

"If you don't put this on," my voice through the mask is muffled, "they will take you into custody. If they find out you have a deadly, infectious disease they will put you to death. You will never see Frankfurt again."

"Oh my God!" He slips the mask on with shaking hands.

We proceed to the gate. I am stopped again.

"You can leave. But you can't take this man with you. He is a prisoner."

I stand my ground. "This man is sick. He has an infectious disease. If he remains here he will infect everyone else, including you. Do you want that?"

The guard hesitates briefly. "Where are your orders?"

"Volkov gave the order. He didn't have time to write it up. You want me to leave this man in your custody and get the order?"

He looks at Klaus anxiously. "What could happen to me?"

"You could lose your penis." I presume to threaten his masculinity.

The soldier steps aside and waves us through.

An unattended jeep is parked haphazardly nearby, one of many.

"We already know you can drive. Get in."

Klaus quickly climbs in and waits for me to do the same. I point him in the direction of the woods where he raped me. He nods, starts the engine and the jeep kicks up a cloud of dust behind us. I remove my mask and he follows suit.

We reach the outskirts of the woods and he drives along the same path as he did the last time. Once we are by the copse where he attacked me, I order him to stop the jeep. He continues driving. I jab the gun into his side.

"Stop the jeep and get out or I will shoot you."

He looks over, sees me brandishing the pistol and brakes hard. We both pitch forward. He lunges for the gun and attempts to wrestle it from me. But I have the upper hand. I shove him with my free arm and whack the side of his head with the butt. He falls sideways.

"Turn the engine off. Get up. Now, and get out of the jeep!" I am out of the vehicle, poised menacingly in front of the grille. Should he attempt to drive off I have the gun pointed directly at him and I won't hesitate to shoot.

His right hand trembles as he reaches for the key and the engine falls silent. Placing his left hand over his head, he clambers out of the jeep and comes to stand by its side. He places his other hand over his head.

"Are you going to kill me?" His voice is steady but frightened.

"I haven't decided." I direct him with the gun to walk over to the right and sit on a mound.

"It was a mistake."

"No! A mistake is when you buy the wrong size. What you did was rape me."

"I thought you were a Jew."

I am flabbergasted. "What does that even mean?"

He is smirking. "Well, they are killing them anyway, so I thought why not have some fun?"

"Some fun. So you are thinking, *This person is about to be killed, so I will rape them and spit on them*?"

He is shaking his head. "I should have killed you when I had the chance."

"Yes, you should have. On your knees."

"What, are you really going to shoot me?" His eyes fill with fear.

"No. We will pretend."

His mouth trembles and he starts sobbing. "I have a brother and sister—"

"I don't want to hear about your brother and sister, or your parents, or about damned Frankfurt. Shut up!" I am screaming at the top of my voice, unleashing my pent-up hatred and fury.

"You can't just shoot me and leave me here to die."

"Why not? You raped me here. So what's the difference?"

"I am only twenty-three. I didn't mean to do what I did. It was stupid, very stupid. I have a baby sister who doesn't even know me." He is bawling pathetically, glancing left and right in the hope that someone will save him.

"Say your prayer."

"What?"

"Say your final prayer."

"I don't know how to pray."

"Neither do I. So it's too bad for you."

He looks up at me, horrified, unable to believe that his life is about to end. I have seen that expression before, but carried with more dignity, in the eyes of those about to be hung or shot to death. And the two young boys on the train – their memory enrages me.

I pump two bullets into this coward's head. It explodes with shards of bone and gushes of blood. He wobbles for a second, then falls over.

I lower my gun hand and feel expiated. One single, solitary, miserable life to right all the wrongs that I have witnessed, all the injury and pain that I endured. Yet I feel relieved. I am just a single, small, broken person, and this is the best that I could do to even the score.

"Are you finished? Or are there more Germans you need to kill?"

I jump and spin around with the gun raised. It's Major Fedchenkov. He is standing next to the jeep, arms crossed over his chest, grinning smugly.

My heart is drumming in my ears. "What are you going to do?"

He cocks his head at Klaus's dead body. "I saw him try to escape."

"Why did you follow me?"

"To make sure that he didn't kill you."

"You knew about this?"

"No. But you gave me a very valuable ring for a handgun and some money. I figured that it must be worth a great deal to you. I wanted to see what you'd do with it."

I don't say anything.

"This is our job, to kill Germans. You want to come work with us?"

I shake my head.

"Then what?"

"There is something I don't understand. I must go back to Berlin."

"OK. I'll drive you to Oświęcim. From there you can get a train across the border and to Berlin."

I climb into the jeep and we drive off, leaving his motorcycle behind which I can see further afield. I am satisfied. For now. But there is still a great part of my life that I can't account for: the last horrible six years that will forever haunt me. I need to learn how I got here in the company of the Lipschutzes and ended up with their daughter's ID.

Marat Fedchenkov drops me off in Oświęcim; a picturesque little Polish town bordering hell nearby where countless people were gassed to death. No one heard a single scream. Like me, they chose to bury the horror to stay sane.

We hug again. I even venture a comradely kiss on his cheek. He holds his palm open. "You won't need this any more. You are free now."

I place the gun in his hand and walk away into the train station. No, I won't need the gun. But I won't be free, truly free, until I know what happened to me.

Getting from Oświęcim to Berlin is more complicated than Major Fedchenkov anticipated. The train from Oświęcim in Poland only travelled as far as the German border city of Dresden. I had to break my journey and stay in Dresden overnight. The city is a shambles: buildings and houses reduced to rubble, roads impassable, social services in disarray, the population that is still alive forced into makeshift shelters and churches, driven by days of relentless shelling and the fires in the aftermath. After being turned away from a number of shelters that were filled beyond capacity, I am directed to an agency assisting displaced and destitute Jewish people to be repatriated to the fledging state of Palestine or their pre-war home town.

Fortunately the shelter is located only a few streets away from Dresden Central Station on Leubnitzer Straße, which means I can resume my journey the next day with relative ease. The wooden board hanging askew on the wrought-iron fence reads: *Flüchtlings und Ausreisezentrum*, Refugee and Repatriation Centre, with the Star of David painted prominently below as opposed to the de rigueur Red Cross. I walk inside the two-storey building and find myself in a dingy, dimly lit hallway that smells dank and musty. At the centre stands a rickety desk manned by a gaunt man of indeterminate age – somewhere between thirty and fifty – wearing a peaked cap and hunched over a stack of papers. He resembles a dishevelled bank clerk. Without saying a word, I place my previously issued ID card on top of the stack.

He looks up, nods his head, writes down my ID number, which matches my tattoo, then adds my name, Ruth Lipschutz, and next to it, Berlin.

Standing up, he shakes my hand warmly and bids me to come in, belying his earlier impersonal attitude. As I follow him I can't help noticing his rumpled, oversized suit. He has either been starved or the suit has been procured from a charity bin.

We enter a large hall that must have served as a kindergarten or meeting hall at one time. Scattered haphazardly about the perimeter are mismatched chairs with men and women slouched on them, couples bunched together on ratty sofas and a few children roaming around unattended. No old people. Little wonder, I think to myself: they were sent to the showers on arrival. There is an air of despondency and aimlessness about the place, despite professing to be a gateway to repatriation.

A man comes out from one of the rooms adjoining the hall and introduces himself as Aaron. "Have you eaten? Would you like something?" His eyes betray a gentleness that I cannot assimilate, given the barbarity and horror that I have experienced up to now.

"No, I haven't eaten."

"Please come with me."

We go through a passageway that leads into an open area furnished with a long, scarred wooden table on which are laid out loaves of crusty bread, a tureen of stew or broth, a bowl of boiled potatoes, some mouldy pieces of cheese and bottles of water – no meat. There is a long bench on either side with a few people seated, helping themselves.

I stare at the food and drink. How often did I dream of this, lying on the hard, damp wooden bunk, shivering under the thin, tattered blanket? Picturing in my mind clean food, while clutching a dry slice of mildewed bread until the morning so that I could survive the day?

"Ruth? Efra tells me that is your name?"

"Sorry. I am not used to seeing food."

Aaron laughs drily. "Who is?"

When I still do not move, he steers me gently towards the bench and helps me sit down.

"Please, eat. You need to regain your strength." He places a plate and a bowl in front of me with cutlery. "I will come by a little later and we can talk about the future."

The future? What future? I don't have a future. I have a mission to understand my past.

I lean diffidently across the table and pick up two slices of bread, some mouldy cheese and a few potatoes. The instinctive fear of being shot or hung for this transgression makes me pause before putting the plate down in front of me. But then, watching the others, it passes, and I start to chew slowly, enjoying the meagre meal, keenly aware that I can replenish the plate again.

Aaron comes by afterwards with Ephraim – the man who greeted me at the entrance, whom they called Efra. They sit down opposite me and pour corked wine into smudged glasses, sliding one over to me.

"So, Ruth, you are from Berlin. Is there someone there that we can locate for you?" Efra looks hopefully at me.

I shake my head.

"Anywhere?" This time Aaron asks, hope fading from his voice.

"Munich. I am originally from Munich. But I was staying with my aunt in Berlin when I was arrested by the Gestapo."

"Oh, that's a good start. Better than most people here, who have lost everything and everyone. If you can give us the address we can make some enquiries and see if we can help reunite you." They sound elated and relieved at the same time.

I remain silent.

"Well," Efra looks across at Aaron, "why don't we let Ruth rest for the night and we can make the arrangements in the morning?" They both look at me. "Ruth?"

I nod my head acquiescently.

I follow Aaron back across the hall, then turn through a dark passageway to a room at the far side of the house. It is sparsely furnished with mattresses, blankets, pillows and scuffed, worn luggage; scattered throughout with men, women and children camped around their forlorn belongings. Aaron points me to a mattress, blanket and pillow that are unoccupied.

I stare around me: an encampment of abandoned souls, unwanted, not belonging anywhere; lost, forgotten people. Ironically, I have become one of them.

"Bathrooms are shared. Sorry. They are through there." He points to a narrow corridor nearby.

As I lean against the wall on the ratty mattress, I study the faces around me. Some appear to be in a protracted state of shock. To my immediate left, an older man – or maybe not so old, most likely aged by an experience similar to mine – coils a leather strap around his hand, up his forearm, past his elbow, tightening it around his upper arm, then proceeds to place a similar strap around his forehead, tightening it at the back of his head. Both straps have a little black cube, one that protrudes from the crook of his elbow and the other just above the bridge of his nose. He then places a little cap on his head and begins weeping and praying, bobbing as he murmurs.

I start to sense that in some small way the enormity of the destruction, death and misery that I have witnessed diminishes my quest – I ought to feel fortunate to be alive, forget the past and get on with the future. Although I suffered unjustly, I might have suffered a similar fate had I never left home – with the uncertainty about my past. Maybe even been killed, regardless, by the relentless shelling.

But ultimately there is no telling how things might have turned out if my life had taken a different path. It was wrested from me at a young age and thrust into a harrowing six years that I will never forget. And unless I am able to discover how I ended up on the train with the Lipschutzes, I might never be able to reconcile my past and move on. Presently, I am here: homeless and nearly destitute, waiting as a Jewish refugee seeking to gain passage to Berlin. And from there? It all depends what I find out when I get there.

The older man next to me stops praying, unravels the straps, removes the cap from his head and, with a deep, anguished sigh, sets the prayer book down. He looks over at me, his eyes straining in the dim light.

"You are by yourself?" He has a kind, gentle, wheezing voice, barely audible over the din of fire trucks and commotion outside.

"Yes. I think so."

"I lost my dear wife and young daughter. They were murdered the first day that we arrived at the camp." Once again he sighs deeply, tears filling his eyes.

"I am very sorry to hear that." It sounds cold and dispassionate, but under the circumstances I don't know what else to say – I have long since forgotten the common expression of decency and compassion. A stranger telling me that his wife and daughter were murdered. What does one say? I lower my eyes, looking over at his gnarled hands clutching the prayer book as though it is his lifeline to salvation.

"Can I ask you a question?" I look curiously at him.

"Of course," he replies eagerly.

"How come you still believe in God, after all that's happened to you?"

For a minute he looks down, rubbing his eyes vigorously as though the answer has to be coaxed from within. Then when he looks up his face transforms in defiance. No longer is he old, worn and haggard, but reignited with a sense of righteousness. "The faith in God is not only based on good happening, but also bad. God is not a shield against injustice or evil, but like insurance: if you or your loved ones are harmed or maligned, eventually he will do the right thing. I am here. You are here. Broken, certainly. Battered, definitely. But we are alive. And where is Hitler and his Thousand-Year Reich?" He stands up and spits on the ground. "That's where. You understand? Hitler is dead," he shouts out to the dozen people in the room. "Dead and finished. With the damn Gestapo and the SS. Kaput! But I am here. So God made sure that we win in the end."

Those in the room who understand what he said clap in approval. The others, not understanding German, simply nod, assuming that if some clapped it had to be good.

I refrain.

The man sits down on his mattress again and looks over at me. "You are coming to build *Eretz Yisrael*, the homeland for the Jews?"

I feel embarrassed enough taking food and shelter meant for Jewish people, although in some vicarious way I endured their fate. "Not right away. I have been displaced from my home in Berlin. I need to go back and see what's happened to my home, my family."

"If they are Jews then they were sent to the camps and the house seized by the SS, I am sorry to say. Hitler and his madmen spared no one and took everything."

"They may have come back."

He nods, betraying little confidence. "They may." He nonetheless appears satisfied with my answer and does not pursue the matter further. After a few moments he picks up his prayer book, cap and leather straps, nods in my direction and walks over to where a young woman is nursing a baby. (I presume that she and the baby were in hiding – otherwise they would not be here.) I wonder whether in some symbolic way he has rediscovered the family he lost.

I lie back down on the mattress, trying to get some rest before my journey to Berlin. The nationality on my ID card reads German, and the point of origin Berlin. I don't anticipate a problem getting into the city. But I am unclear as to how to locate the street, or even the suburb from where I was taken. I only have a small amount of money left. Aaron or Efra may be able to help me a bit more. But in a few days I will be penniless.

I become anxious thinking that I may never achieve my quest owing to something as trivial as money, but then I start to relax. I survived the concentration camp, the daily horrors, the killings, the nightmares, the piles of corpses, the rape, and the near-starvation rations. God did not want me dead. Because if he did, his angel of death was working overtime for six years alongside me. God – whichever god, Jewish or Christian – wanted me alive. To survive. With that thought I fall asleep.

BERLIN

Autumn and Winter 1945

Helga travelled north by train from Dresden to Berlin with the entire sector wholly under Russian control. The journey, which would under normal conditions take only a few hours, took the entire day from the time she left the Jewish shelter. Aaron and Efra had been able to locate the address for the Lipschutz family by searching through records of deported and displaced Jewish families. There was no record for a Dreschler family, though, and Helga couldn't remember offhand the surname of her aunt's family; to her they had always been Aunt Magda and Uncle Helmut. She distinctly recalled that her aunt had lived next door to the Lipschutzes, a fact that both beguiled and frustrated her in trying to understand how she had ended up with the Jewish family.

More fragments of memory started to surface, forming part of a large and intricate puzzle. At first there was nothing but scattered pieces and a generalised idea of how the fragments might belong together. Then a framework, and then gradually pieces falling into place where there had been nothing before but empty space. She remembered Oma telling her that she could no longer look after her and would be going away to be taken care of in a home for old people. She also recalled the trip from Munich to Berlin and arriving at her aunt's place. A small room upstairs; a girl her age, blonde, blue-eyed, living in the room alongside. Or was that the girl next door, Ruth?

Suddenly another piece fell neatly into place. Visiting the Lipschutzes. An eerie feeling; being uncomfortable in the presence of the rangy, matronly woman: Alana Lipschutz. And a small girl who looked like the girl whose room was alongside hers. Sisters? Couldn't be.

It was no good. No point in coaxing the pieces to rise out of the fog and then trying to force them into place. In time, maybe when she got to Nürnberger Straße, her memory would be jogged. She stared out the window of the slow, creaking train, forcibly suppressing the memory of another journey cooped up in a boxcar.

At nearly every station along the two hundred kilometres, she was forced to disembark and present her travelling papers. Aaron had attached a letter to her ID card documenting her point of origin, pre-deportation, as Nürnberger Straße, Berlin. Once she entered Berlin proper, the sector under British control, the disruption and interrogation became even more rigorous: with whom did she live at this address? When did her journey begin? Was she travelling alone? The questions came tumbling down like an avalanche designed to frustrate her journey. But she was determined to reach her destination and visit the street, the homes of the Lipschutzes and her aunt and uncle. She had lost nearly six years of her young life, had been subjected to horrors she could never forget; it was essential for her to learn the truth of just how and why she had accompanied Alana and Heinrich on that train journey.

While her papers were being examined she took the time to survey the skyline and the surrounding streets. She had seldom spent time visiting the city the first time around. But she recalled from the few occasions when she had accompanied her aunt and cousin shopping that the cityscape had been graced with magnificent museums, awe-inspiring cathedrals, grand buildings, stately concert halls; the pavements teeming with people looking at shop windows displaying beautiful clothes, and necklaces adorning the collars of mannequins. Like Oma promised she would have one day. Now Berlin looked like a sister city to Dresden. Tenement houses sheared in half, their residents exposed like wiggling insects to the world. The palatial buildings that she remembered reduced to smouldering piles of ash, the wide streets choked with rubble. The once elegant people who had strolled through the streets window-shopping, now wandering dazed, desperately seeking morsels of food or the most sought-after commodity: cigarettes. At every corner, she noticed British soldiers being pestered for a few cigarettes.

She remembered from both the camps where she had been incarcerated the never-ending pangs of hunger; the search for and hoarding of scraps; the infinite fatigue; the shivering cold. Nobody had thought about cigarettes there. This was new. About the only difference from Dresden was that in Berlin a few buildings did remain standing, albeit damaged. And there were no fires, though there must have once been; the air smelled of acrid smoke.

She had left the train at Meininger Berlin Central Station and was walking warily through the streets to her destination when a passing jeep slowed down and stopped next to her. She didn't think she stood out from anyone else, other than she was perhaps better clad in the thick Russian overcoat that the major gave her and clutching her belongings and little money tightly to her chest.

The British soldier who disembarked from the jeep started up with the usual drill of questions after he examined her papers. She felt like she had repeated the answers ad infinitum.

"As it says, Nürnberger Straße."

"What's in Numbarger Street?" His German was passable, but his pronunciation laughable.

"My aunt and uncle."

"Their names?"

"Helmut and Magda."

"Surname?"

"I don't remember."

"How come you don't remember the surname of your aunt and uncle?"

"Dreschler. I think."

Back to the jeep in a casual stride, nothing so urgent when she had wasted the entire day being forced to disembark from trains, interrogated at checkpoints and stations, delayed while the papers were examined. Her ID card and papers had been examined so many times that they were in danger of disintegrating.

"Are you Jewish?" He was back with the papers folded and ready to be handed back to her.

"I don't see that it matters. You are not the Gestapo."

"No, I am not." His manner was becoming less inquisitive and more churlish. "But I mean to be helpful."

"Thank you. You can be helpful by letting me continue to my destination." She eyed him defiantly.

"Well, you can continue. If you don't find anyone at Numbarger, there's a shelter for Jewish people not too far away." With that he gave her a limp salute and sauntered to the jeep, muttering something to his companions, who sniggered in reply.

She wasn't delayed again until she reached Lietzenburger Straße, which was one street away from Nürnberger. A jeep passed by with two British soldiers, slowed, but did not stop. Her pulse quickened as she reached the corner of Nürnberger. Where ought she go first? The Lipschutzes' home? Was it likely that anyone would be there? Alana and Heinrich had been in the same queue at the camp, but behind her. Could they have survived? She never saw them again past selection. Were they directed to the showers or hard labour? She seemed to recall the showers, in which case their house would be vacant. Had she been ordered to sorting on that day she would never have recognised their clothing. All she was able to remember was that Heinrich wore a delicate pair of gold-rimmed reading glasses and Alana a blood-red brooch. She didn't know much about gemstones, other than hearing Heinrich mention something about selling the ruby; it was very valuable.

She turned the corner. The houses were not nearly as damaged as in the other areas that she had walked through.

She looked up the numbers, then started to walk down the street, every so often looking up at a building. There were only a few people about, and no children. Quiet. She suddenly recalled angry voices and a struggle, followed by car doors opening and closing, trucks rumbling and the clanging of metal. Pounding on house doors, and being cold, almost shivering, and then warm and then cold again. She hastened her pace. The fragments were coalescing into place, guided by an invisible hand on a puzzle. What happened on that morning? Was it morning? No. She remembered dark. But if it was dark, why was she carried out in the open?

She halted in her tracks as if stuck by a bayonet. Carried. She was carried, but from where, to where, and why? Who was carrying her? Helmut and Heinrich? Voices. Quiet, but muttering with an urgent undertone. She was cold and then warm. Was that because she was taken out of and then put back into bed? Bitter. Swallowing something bitterly unpleasant. Then becoming sleepy, almost unconscious. Was she drugged and carried, and if so, why?

She needed answers to help her put the fragments together. Otherwise they were just bits floating disjointedly on the surface.

She halted in front of the Lipschutz house, then walked up the steps to the front door. It was barricaded, with an official notice affixed to the door. It was more of a decree, advising that the house had been commandeered by the SS with the date and time stamped below, and the commander's signature and insignia.

There was no point in knocking on this door. She walked back down to the street and approached her aunt's door. One of the windows to the left was shattered and had been boarded up with cardboard and newspaper. She knocked. No sound of approaching steps. She knocked more vigorously. Silence, other than the street noises behind her.

She was at a dead end. She roamed the street for a while, hoping to recognise something, anyone, anything, not sure of what her next step should be. She had no plan beyond coming here and finding out what happened to her. Having exhausted her only leads she was left rudderless, like the others drifting the streets in search of the pieces to rebuild their shattered lives.

"Now what?" she kept muttering to herself.

Dusk was beginning to settle on the torn city and she would need to leave and find a place for the night. She had started to walk away from her aunt's house when she noticed a slender, austere-looking woman with a supercilious manner and grey hair peeking from beneath her headscarf approaching on her side of the street carrying a bag. She watched her walk past, giving Helga no mind, and climb up the steps to Aunt Magda's house.

Aunt Magda?

"Excuse me."

Startled, the woman turned slowly to face her, annoyed by the distraction.

"You may be able to help me."

"I doubt it. I don't have any food or money. There is a shelter around the next corner." With that she turned and continued up the steps.

"Pardon me. I didn't mean like that."

The woman stopped again and set her bag down, studying her interlocutor more carefully.

"I am Helga Dreschler."

The woman nearly fell back, seizing the banister at the last moment to steady herself. "Helga?!" Her voice quivered with surprise and excitement.

Helga kept staring at her aunt disbelievingly, relieved that at last she had found a home. She belonged somewhere.

Magda set her bag down. "What happened to you? If you hadn't told me who you were I wouldn't have guessed. Where is Wolfgang?" Her tone was warm and friendly, but her reserve held her back from hugging her niece.

"I haven't seen Wolfgang since he dropped me off at the train station in Munich."

"You mean since he picked you up to take you back to Munich?"

"No. He never took me back to Munich. I haven't seen either Wolfgang or Munich since Oma sent me here to live with you."

This was distressing news to Magda's ears. Helmut had lied. But she wasn't going to reveal her dismay to Helga until she had spoken with him and determined why he had done so.

She regained some of her composure. "Anyway, I am glad that you are well and have come back from Munich." Glossing over the fact that Helga had just told her that she had not been back to Munich. If she was curious about where her niece had been, she chose to keep that door firmly shut rather than peek behind it.

Helga decided to strike back and slash any veil of etiquette. "I wasn't in Munich. I was in a concentration camp."

Fortunately Magda had not surrendered her grip on the banister. Had she done so, this revelation would have caused her to lose her balance and tumble down the steps. She instinctively tightened her grip and let her features betray her shock. So many questions crowded her mind at once that she couldn't even begin to articulate one.

They stood there in silence, staring at each other, engulfed by the single thought that a terrible miscarriage of justice had transpired, and from Magda's perspective only one person remained alive who could explain it: her husband.

She regained her balance, nodded quietly to her niece, picked up the bag and set about unlocking the front door. She stood aside to let her niece in and, once inside, pushed the door closed. She bade Helga to follow her to the kitchen so that she could unpack the meagre groceries. She placed each item carefully in its designated cupboard, folded the bag away and, with a trembling hand, picked up the kettle, filled it up with water and set it to boil on the stove.

Helga, not knowing whether she was meant to stand or invite herself to sit at the small dining table, decided not to trespass too eagerly on her aunt's hospitality, and remained standing.

"I will prepare some hot drinks for us. I am afraid there is no coffee anywhere to be found. Oh, that I wish Herr Lipschutz was back. He always had everything that I liked." Magda turned away from the counter, seeing Helga standing obediently by the table.

Magda pointed her to a chair, poured two cups of hot tea, added a plate with two slices of buttered bread and joined Helga. She shrugged unapologetically at the modest repast. "There isn't much around at the moment."

Helga picked up a slice of bread and eagerly drank the hot tea. She was hungry, made more so by being in a home that was meant to be her own.

Magda refrained from opening the topic that she knew Helga was eager to bring up. For Magda it breached conventions. There were topics that one just didn't converse openly about. It was the painful intimacy that made her uncomfortable. Like when her closest friend told her in confidence that her husband had lost his virility: a war injury, a grenade. It crossed the boundary from juicy gossip to intimate detail, giving Magda a window into their private lives she would have rather remained shut. She would have been satisfied to just be told that he was experiencing some difficulty in bed. That couched the impotence in a clean, soluble dose of conversation. Magda couldn't mentally digest the picture of the man with his penis flaccid or even deformed.

A girl she had never set eyes on had appeared on her doorstep at the tender age of twelve with a worn suitcase, a note and some money. But the dire consequences of World War I had placed burdens on distant relatives who had fared better. Magda accepted that responsibility grudgingly even though technically she was not the girl's aunt but her mother's cousin. In six years Helga would be gone and so would the money for her upkeep. But then unexpectedly, Helga's Uncle Wolfgang fetched her back. Biologically he had a stronger claim on Helga, and besides, it was secretly a small relief to discharge that responsibility early, what with all the accruing hardships.

It was strange, though, that Wolfgang never asked for the upkeep money that Helga's grandmother allocated to be sent back. Magda didn't imagine him to be a man of means. Then again, he was another conundrum; Magda knew of him, but not *him*.

So she asked Helmut to place the funds in a savings account for Helga in the anticipation that Wolfgang – or even Helga herself, when she came of age – would come asking for it. A princely sum it wasn't, but it was enough to get Helga on her way, an orphan without access to any other means.

Now it turned out that Helmut had lied. What else did he lie about? Helga's money? Did he lie about that too? He had told Magda that it was in an account under her name.

Added to the tremors shaking Magda's fragile world, the erstwhile girl, once plump, with a cheeky smile and a mischievous disposition, was sitting in front of her a ravaged woman with sunken cheeks, haunted eyes, unkempt hair and bundled in a Russian greatcoat, telling her that she had been in a concentration camp. It was another window that Magda wanted to keep firmly shut and bolted. It would have sufficed had Helga told her that she didn't spend the war years in Munich, and now that the dreadful war was over, she had returned to her surrogate home.

Where she had been was of no consequence just now. Ironically, given Helmut's prevarication, Helga now had a stronger claim to staying in this household than when she first crossed the threshold with a note, some money and a prayer. They had a moral responsibility considering the tragic fate that had befallen her. She was placed in their care, they were given the money to support her, and somehow they failed abysmally in that responsibility and she ended up in a concentration camp. While at the same time, a girl that Magda had no moral responsibility towards, Ruth

Lipschutz, spent the better part of the war years cooped up in their attic, sharing their meagre supplies, placing them at great risk and finally, to remove that guillotine hanging over their heads, was escorted to Switzerland at a mitigated risk to Magda's brother, Martin. What a cruel twist of fate.

Helga stared at Magda as she processed all this quietly in her head, nibbling on the bread, sipping the tea, and avoiding her gaze.

"Don't you want to know what happened to me?" Helga prodded in a firm tone.

Shaken out of her thoughts, Magda picked up the empty plate to make some more buttered slices.

"Aunt Magda, I asked you a question."

Magda mulled the question for a moment, then replied, "Helga, you may not believe this, but I don't know how that happened, other than through some terrible misunderstanding."

That coward Klaus called Helga's rape a mistake; now this one was calling her deliverance to hell a misunderstanding. "No! I don't believe it was a misunderstanding. I believe it was deliberate."

"Deliberate? I am sure it wasn't deliberate. Who would do such a thing?"

"I don't know who or why, but I do know that I ended up in a boxcar, transported over three awful days without eating or drinking, then shovelled out like garbage at Auschwitz, a death camp. I watched and experienced horrors that I will never forget. So, no, it was not a misunderstanding."

"I don't know what to say, Helga. I don't know what you want me to say. I always believed that you were back in Munich with Wolfgang."

"Really? Did you ever bother to check?"

"No. No. I must admit that I failed in that. But you must remember that the only link to your family was your grandmother. I never had any contact with you, your mother or Wolfgang. So once you left, and with your *Oma* dead, that connection was broken."

Silence returned to the room. Magda removed the loaf from the cabinet in which it was stored, cut two more slices, buttered them evenly, and returned the plate to the table.

"Did you want some more tea?"

"Aren't you the least bit curious as to what happened to me?"

"You just told me."

"No. I mean at the camp. On the train with the Lipschutzes."

Magda staggered, grabbed hold of the back of the chair and toppled into it. Helga leaped up and took hold of her aunt, helping her straighten out in the chair. Magda was mouthing words and pointing to the sink. Helga, confident that she was propped up in the seat, walked over to the sink, filled up a glass of water and held it to her aunt's mouth.

Magda thanked her by merely nodding her head. Her face was ashen. She tried to reach for the remaining water that was resting on the table, but her hand was trembling too violently to be able to firmly grasp it. She dropped her hands into her lap in resignation, shaking her head in disbelief. It was all starting to make sense, even if she didn't know all the machinations behind the scenes.

The sound of the front door interrupted the mood of gloom in the kitchen. It was Helmut, with Anna in tow.

They both appeared in the kitchen doorway, Helmut smiling cheerfully and holding Anna's hand, when he stopped abruptly in his tracks, alarmed.

"What happened to my wife? Who are you?" Staring aghast, first at Magda and then at Helga.

"Helmut, Liebchen," Magda attempted weakly without looking in his direction, "this is Helga."

It was Helmut's turn to be stunned. He studied Helga's face closely but couldn't find the girl he knew in the features that he saw.

Anna stepped forward. "Helga, are you back from Munich? Will you be staying for good?"

"No, and I don't think so." Helga stared coldly at Helmut, whose expression remained frozen in a mixture of disbelief and dread.

"Anna, why don't you go upstairs and let your father and me talk with Helga?" Magda turned to her daughter.

"Yes, Anna. Please let us have a word with Helga in private."

"No, Anna, please stay. There is nothing private or confidential in what we are going to talk about, is there, Herr Professor?" Helga glared disdainfully at Helmut.

Anna looked from one parent to the other and, seeing as neither objected, took a seat at the table. There was one left. Helmut, forced by the circumstances, slumped into it and sat staring down at the surface of the table.

"So, here we all are. No point in wasting time with small talk, is there, Professor? Why don't we get right down to how I ended up in a boxcar with Alana and Heinrich Lipschutz and then got stuck with their daughter's ID as an inmate in Auschwitz?"

The stinging salvo from Helga was met with a gasp from Anna, then followed with deathly silence.

"Well, as no one is volunteering any ideas, why don't I start by repeating what Magda told me? She says that you told her that I was fetched by my Uncle Wolfgang and taken back to Munich." Helga stopped and glowered directly at the professor. "But that can't be true because Auschwitz doesn't look like Munich." Magda hadn't actually said that, but Helga surmised it from her insinuation.

It was a shot in the dark, but had clearly hit its target. Helmut turned shamefacedly red, and looked over at Magda, who averted her eyes and didn't bother correcting Helga.

He was left hanging alone by his own lie. Clearing his throat, he looked both at Magda and at Helga. "That, regrettably, was not the case."

"You know, these euphemisms are beginning to tire me. A German soldier raped me and called that a mistake; Magda, upon hearing what really happened to me, called it a misunderstanding; and now you, Herr Professor, are wrapping it all up in a neat bow and calling it regrettable. The tragic truth is that I can't change what happened to me, but I would at least like to know why it happened." She once again gazed sternly at the professor.

Silence.

"Papa?" Anna looked over at her father.

Instinctively Helmut reached across the table and attempted to place his hand over Helga's. But she drew it back as if stung. Nobody spoke.

Helmut rose up and poured himself a cup of the now-tepid water from the kettle, mixed in some tea and sat back down again. In a low, laboured voice, he began to unburden himself. "Well, what happened was that the Lipschutzes received word that they were due to be deported. Heinrich came over and asked if we could look after Ruth at least until they were resettled. I agreed."

Everyone remained silent, letting Helmut continue uninterrupted.

"About a week later, while it was still dark outside, there was a knock on the back door. Heinrich was standing there with Ruth. She had a small case with her belongings. I led them upstairs and we settled her in the attic." Helmut sighed deeply before continuing. "When we came down, you were standing there." He paused to look at Helga. "You pointed at Heinrich and me and said you would tell the Gestapo where Ruth was hidden. The rest I am certain you can work out."

"Actually, I can't. If Ruth was sleeping comfortably in the attic, who were the Gestapo supposed to take in her stead?"

"I am not sure about that detail, but I presume that Heinrich had a story worked out."

"I am sure that he did not. Either way I have some experience with the SS and Gestapo. Trust me, they would not have believed him. But let's leave that minor detail aside for the moment. Please go on."

"Both of us panicked. There was not a moment to lose. The Gestapo and SS were rounding up people around the corner and were already knocking on doors in our street. Heinrich immediately climbed back up to the attic to take Ruth back. But you said that you would tell anyway." Helmut stopped, shrugging helplessly, the choice inevitable.

Helga remained steadfast in her gaze, but her mind was preoccupied with the memories rushing back. The fragments were coagulating like magnets forced together: the struggle, the bitter potion to knock her out, the rush through the street. Feeling cold, then warm, then cold again. Being cradled in someone's lap, dozing off to the movement of the truck. Waking up groggy in the train station.

"I have heard enough. I can't think of how to describe your actions other than disgraceful and cowardly. You chose a grocer's daughter over me, your relative."

"I don't think that *we* made that choice, Helga; you gave us no choice. It wasn't just the Lipschutzes that you condemned to death, but also us, your relations, for helping them. If I had not acted to save my family, you would be the only one sitting at this table today."

Silence hung over the room as each one considered the choice and the consequences. Finally Helga spoke up.

"I can in some perverted way understand you doing what you did, Helmut. But I can't believe that Ruth never stepped up to save me. I could have died so many times in her stead. I don't say that the fate that I endured was just for anyone. But it wasn't *my* fate."

"How was she to do that, Helga? She was in the attic all those years." Anna spoke up for her friend.

"But she isn't there now, is she? The war has been over for some time. Yet she never came forward, never came to look for me. I was her scapegoat, wasn't I?"

"To a point. But we felt unsafe with our decision anyway, and Martin, my brother, escorted her to Switzerland a year ago. I know that it's no consolation to you—" Magda offered.

"Wait!" Helga interrupted. "You mean to tell me that she has been gone for nearly two years?"

No one dared answer that question.

Helga grew visibly agitated and stood up. "I will spend the night here because I have no other choice. In the morning, please accompany me to the bank to retrieve my money. I presume that that is where you put it?" She directed her question to Helmut. He nodded quietly. With that, she turned to leave.

"Helga, your grandmother meant for this to be your home. So far as I am concerned, I am happy to respect that wish." Magda attempted to offer some consolation in retrospect.

Helga turned back, softening some in her stance. "Aunt Magda, this is not my home. It never really was. I wouldn't feel safe here. The last time you sacrificed me to save your grocer's daughter. This time around you might sell me into prostitution to obtain groceries. Ten years from now, you will say that it was an unavoidable necessity. The truth is that I don't want what is left of my life to be a litany of euphemisms."

"But what are you going to do? Where are you going to go?"

"Wherever it will be, it will be as far from here as possible, and to forget that I was ever here."

They could hear her steps as she ascended the staircase and walked across the landing to the very room from which she had been abducted all those years ago. The three of them sat in their pain and humiliation. Helmut sipped his cold tea and then stood up to rinse his cup.

"Helmut, why don't you sleep down here, at least until I can work all this out in my head?" Magda turned to her husband.

He turned back swiftly. "What? You are blaming me for all this? It is very well for her to come back here all high and mighty and blame us. She put herself in this mess when she threatened to betray us to the Gestapo."

"A mess that you put us in in the first place."

"Maybe so. But Heinrich was a dear friend, I wasn't about to turn him away."

"I agree with Papa. I am sorry about what happened to Helga, but I never liked her from the start. She was mean. Ruth was my best friend." Anna reiterated her father's sentiment.

Helmut waited for Magda to recant her request, supported by his daughter's backing. But it didn't come. Shortly after, Anna and Magda went upstairs to bed while Helmut stayed downstairs.

In the morning he accompanied Helga to the bank, gave her the money in full, and parted company from her at the same train station where she had disembarked a day ago. No more was said of the discussion of the night before.

He bade her goodbye and good luck. And that was the last they saw or heard of Helga Dreschler.

BELLEVUE HILL, EASTERN SUBURBS, SYDNEY

Winter 1986

They had progressed to dating: going out to the movies, restaurants, a few plays; and trips on the ferry to Manly for lunch, the Blue Mountains for the day, Bondi Junction for an afternoon of shopping. Activities that Ruth, in the final months of Ernie's life, had deferred from engaging in. Her life had been restricted to visiting him first in the nursing home, then at War Memorial Hospital while he was recuperating, and then back at the hospital as his condition inexplicably deteriorated, where he finally died.

If she had to admit it to herself, the restrictions on her life, in those long months before Ernie died, had caused her depression which, in the aftermath, had brought her to contemplate suicide, rather than, as she initially thought, his death itself. It was a selfish thought, to be sure. But realistically we all are, with some heroic exceptions, selfish when it comes to our needs. And though she was deeply saddened to lose her partner of many decades, it could have just as easily been her that passed on first, in which case she wouldn't have wanted him to mourn her unnecessarily. Life, after all, is lived once, and there is little point in spending your remaining years grieving over someone whose fate you couldn't alter.

And there was also the other thing that, with the passing of the years, had diminished in prominence. She never spoke of it to anyone. Not even Ernie. In the early years she wondered why. She was, to an extent, troubled by her indifference towards the sacrifice made by someone else in her stead. But as with all things, she reasoned, it was her good fortune and she had thrived on it. Had she been apprehended with her parents then she would have calmly accepted it as her fate, suffered the horrible consequences; may or may not have survived. And in the end, if she had ended up surviving, she would have endured a life shadowed by nightmares, as did those people she knew who were euphemistically referred to as Holocaust survivors.

Like the Miskys from Warsaw – survivors? She wondered if they really survived, or just lived through the horrors to emerge emotionally gutted. Physically scathed, gradually healed, other than the tattoos on their forearms, but emotionally destroyed. If she imagined the horrors that she had seen in the film archives as her experience, she couldn't see a way to reconcile that with her ordinary life after the war. How do you conduct a normal life with an abnormal experience? You walk into a grocery store, do your shopping and then reflect that five, ten years ago you shovelled thousands of bodies from the showers into the crematorium to burn. Imagining it could never be the same as experiencing it in your own flesh and blood.

As with the people who inanely blather, "I can imagine", or "I know how you feel", or "I know how you must feel." No, you don't. Because it is not an experience that you underwent with your own flesh. You are only imagining it vicariously. But your flesh and blood were not infused with the experience. It is just an ephemeral thought. Like a movie; a good movie. You sit there, savour the experience, emerge from the dark cinema, make some inane comments and then forget about it as you devour another piece of strudel and sip your cappuccino.

Admittedly she couldn't upbraid those she ungraciously referred to as the ministering tittle-tattles who superficially engaged in any experience as long as it made for good conversation – conveying their grief here, their compassion there – without holding herself in opprobrium for discarding her parents so swiftly and adopting the Jodls as a matter of convenience and safety. What did that meddlesome Jewish troublemaker from Nazareth say? *Judge not and ye shall not be judged*. Well, on this count, he was right.

Did she dwell on her parents' fate? Not for long and not too deeply. Did she seek out any survivors, once the camps were liberated, for any morsels of information on what might have happened to them? Had they been killed instantly? Together? Separately? Or were they systematically ground down until they died as a result of starvation, deprivation and harsh labour? She never did, not even once. It wasn't that she didn't care, but she reasoned, always with self-preservation in mind, that it was best to let sleeping dogs lie, or in this particular case, let sleeping dogs die. Because... well, because there might be one dog that was not quite dead. And it was this dog that she feared alerting to her whereabouts.

Her trail from Zurich, after Martin had left her with Helmut's acquaintance, disappeared into a maze of bureaucratic subterfuge. First she was Swiss; then she was German again. Then she was an Austrian Jewish refugee in need of assistance making her way to England, and from there to Australia. She could have easily stayed in England. There were enough sympathetic people ready to assist, particularly when they heard that she was an orphan, and about her wondrous tale of survival. (Naturally, with a few modifications and embellishments. The last thing she wanted to do was leave a very clear anecdotal trail that would bring her to the attention of the press and of that sleeping dog who might be lying in wait with one eye open.)

It didn't take long to arrange, via the Australian High Commission in London, papers to travel to Sydney. She was even able to secure free passage. Australia was eager to attract young people to its distant shores. And she was young. She was also fleeing, trying to put as much distance between herself and what she feared, through her sense of guilt, would be a very vengeful person. She may not have needed to flee, but there was no way to enquire as to that person's fate without alerting her to her whereabouts.

So on a blustery day in 1947 she set out from Portsmouth to Sydney on a voyage that took the better part of a month. When the ship docked she was pleased to have arrived safely, but wistful at having to reorient herself within a culture that was very foreign to her. A society preoccupied with bonhomie, excessive drinking and sport, none of which suited her temperament.

At first she figured that with time she might be able to make her way back to Europe. Yet, with the passage of time she discovered enclaves in amongst the alien culture that imported and preserved a European way of life: the Eastern Suburbs of Sydney. She settled there, finding work as a dressmaker, and by night taking accounting courses. And that's how she met Ernie. A former doctor and a refugee like many others, forever scarred by the experience that had brought him to these shores by way of Africa and a desire to put up a wall between the past and the present: he gave up medicine and took up the sterile world of numbers in its stead.

She liked him instantly. He had an easy-going manner, not the usual lugubrious demeanour that European men seemed to carry about them like a shroud. A wry sense of humour that made her laugh, and a none-too-inquisitive manner that left her to her secrets. Her parents had died in the Holocaust. She had no other relatives that she knew of. That was that. He didn't dwell too long on her lack of interest in trying to locate any. She just told him that she preferred to sail adrift from all of that past and start a new present. He accepted that without too much curiosity; after all, he understood walls – he had erected one to protect his sanity.

It wasn't long before he was offering to help her with her lessons, which led to him appearing more and more often in the tiny flat that she was sharing with another lady. When things got more serious, he suggested that she move in with him rather than upset her flatmate, who appeared to frown more often now when he appeared on the doorstep.

At first she was reluctant, thinking that her reputation, little known as it was, would be tarnished; a single woman moving in with a single man. But she trusted Ernie enough to know that, as the saying went, he would make an honest woman out of her.

And true to his intentions, and to her relief, he proposed two months after they moved in together. From that point on she started to breathe easier. Her name was now Weissman. Not that it was Lipschutz before – she had travelled under an assumed surname from London. But taking on a married name created a colder trail for anyone that may be seeking her under her birth surname.

Nearly five decades later, Ernie was dead. Decades that passed in silent contentment as her life progressed uneventfully from wedlock to parenting (the one child only), to receiving her accounting degree and setting up a practice with Ernie (Weissman & Associates), and to retirement. A retirement that only lasted a brief nine years before Ernie fell ill, recuperated and then relapsed and died.

In the obituary notice Ruth announced the passing of a loving father, husband and grandfather. She also felt comfortable enough to mention that the surviving spouse, Ruth Weissman, was née Lipschutz. A casual reference, if any, to another time and another life. And nearly six decades on, it was nothing if not a small tribute to her parents' memory that she had immortalised them somewhere in this new land where she had built her life. A trivial gesture at best, given that in all likelihood both Lipschutzes were dead, due either to old age or having perished in the Holocaust.

If anything it was done more to appease her conscience in having ignored their memory hitherto.

But a gesture that, alas, had the unfortunate ramification of awakening the sleeping dog who had been scouring the papers avidly, week in and week out. Asking about her in centres where Jewish people might congregate. Reading through obituaries. Following the personals in the papers. There were vague references; none that proved fruitful. But this was the first real clue that led her right to her quarry. And none too soon. At the age of seventy-eight the clock was winding down on this promise of vengeance. And if revenge is a meal best served cold then this one would prove to be delectable, for if anything it was frozen.

It didn't take Helga long to trace the obituary notice to the cemetery, and from there to the funeral parlour. From the funeral director it was an easy leap to Ruth Weissman's address in the Eastern Suburbs. By comparison, a walk in the park versus the search she had conducted in Zurich to unearth the whereabouts of her namesake. Locating her. Following her to London, only to lose the trail there in the boatload of émigrés that made their way to the US, Canada and Australia.

She settled on Australia after deciding on a hunch, that in later years she came to doubt many a time, that if she were Ruth she would travel as far away from Europe as she could. And like Ruth, she decided that no place was further than Australia.

And now she was watching and learning the movements of her quarry. From across the street she noticed her arm in arm with a tall Aryan-looking gentleman, both appearing very happy as they emerged from the building in Bellevue Hill and walked amiably to Bondi Junction, no doubt for an afternoon matinee and early dinner.

"Well, well, well, it didn't take long for dear old Ruth to find a replacement for the recently departed Ernie; always the pragmatist. No time to waste. Except this replacement gentleman doesn't look that Jewish. But what do I know? What does a Jewish person look like? That collection of Nazi elite – Goering, Goebbels, Himmler and even Hitler – hardly resembled anything like model Aryans: tall, blond, blue-eyed, with broad shoulders and rugged muscles. Alter egos of what they wished to be." Helga was anxiously muttering under her breath from the coffee house across the street as she studied Sam Steimatzky and Ruth disappearing around the bend towards Bondi Junction.

As she sat there over a cup of coffee and a muffin, running her hand through her scraggly grey hair, mumbling nervously, her eccentric behaviour perturbed the waiting staff. After one hour of watching her they decided that she was an elderly person suffering from dementia, but not necessarily dangerous.

As soon as Ruth and Sam were out of sight, Helga wrote down the time on the pad in front of her: 3.34pm. Figuring that it would take them twenty minutes to get to the mall, and that they would then watch the four o'clock matinee, stop for a light meal and then head back, by her reckoning they ought to reappear around that corner no later than 7.15pm. She raised her hand to alert the waiter.

A courteous, Italian-looking waiter appeared at her side instantly, hoping that she would ask for the bill, pay and leave.

"What time do you close?"

"We stay open till eight for takeout. We only serve coffee and pastries after 6.30pm. Will Madame be wanting the bill?" he asked, ever so solicitously, hoping that the reminder would nudge her to leave.

Ignoring the waiter's question, Helga went back to studying her pad, on which were listed various times of arrivals and departures, broken up by days. So far, three, starting with the early-morning constitutional for Ruth's beau, right to the lunchtime appearance of Ruth as she emerged to catch the 326 bus to Double Bay, joining the other ladies for the afternoon coffee klatch. On other days the schedule varied for Ruth, but never for her date. He was as precise as a Swiss watch. Which confirmed Helga's suspicion that he was either the eponymous nationality or German. Her instinct told her the latter.

Her first objective was to compile a weekly schedule for the two and then plot how she would take her revenge. At first she thought the optimum time would be when he was out. But on reconsideration she decided that having him in the apartment at the same time would serve her purpose admirably. She would set it up in such a way that he would be culpable if he so much as uttered her name, and would therefore be forced into eternal silence regarding her crime. In effect, he would be her silent alibi.

Serendipitously, the plot that she devised in her cold rage played better than she had imagined once she inadvertently stumbled upon his secret. A secret that would bind them both to their graves.

BELLEVUE HILL, EASTERN SUBURBS, SYDNEY

Winter 1986

Outside it was drizzling, the rain beating a steady tempo as it fell on the rooftops, then cascaded down the gutters to the street below. He looked up at the sky: dark and cloudy. It didn't really matter; he wasn't going anywhere. He heard the lift door open below and the detective's footsteps as he exited the car and made his way to the gate.

Instinctively he looked at his watch: 3.45. They had been talking for almost two hours. He had told him everything he knew; as a neighbour and acquaintance and, in the short time since Ernie passed away, as a friend. That's all he could ever say. Yes, they had developed a closer friendship once Ernie had died. But that was normal: both their partners were dead and all they had was each other. What did they do? What retired seniors usually do: movies, theatre, galleries, trips, restaurants.

Did he hear anything unusual next door? Not that he could recall. If he had, he would have awakened and checked on Ruth – "I mean Mrs Weissman," he hastily corrected himself. The interrogation, if that's what it is when a detective has a conversation with you, amiable though it might have been, enquired as to whether Mrs Weissman had expressed any concern or worry to him regarding a threat to her life. No, of course not. What threat would a seventy-six-year-old woman be facing, other than the random, unpremeditated acts of violence perpetrated against older and younger citizens alike?

Unexpectedly, the conversation turned to himself. The detective wanted to know when he had arrived in Australia. Sam was deliberately vague; he replied that he had arrived just before the end of the war. Where did he come from? Sam hesitated momentarily, wondering whether he should make reference to his original country of birth, or the fake identification that he had used to get into Australia. He decided not to risk it. What would be the point in lying? He wasn't responsible for Ruth's murder. He replied that he came from Germany.

At this point the conversation, and now he was sure it was more of an interrogation, turned ominous: the detective asked him whether he could have a set of his fingerprints.

For a split second Sam's demeanour of bereavement dropped and he became tense and perturbed. He wanted to know whether it was common practice. Did all the tenants have to provide a set of their fingerprints? The detective was deliberately oblique: no. Then why was he being targeted?

At the detective's answer, Sam relaxed and resumed his bereaved countenance. No, he was not being targeted, but most likely his fingerprints were in Ruth's apartment. If they could eliminate his fingerprints and hers, then what was left would belong to either Ernie, whom they could disregard, or more likely the intruder who caused her death.

After some more rather inane questions, the detective departed. Any longer and Sam felt that he would start to suffocate under the pressure. And once that happened he would need to reveal what he knew in order to be able to breathe again. Except that he doubted that the detective would believe a word he said. He would either be sent off for a psychiatric evaluation or written off as a crazy old coot. There was absolutely no evidence to back up his story. Not a shred. Throughout the whole time the killer was in the apartment she wore a pair of surgical gloves. The one item that was broken was cleaned up and everything that had been disturbed was set right. He made sure of it. Ultimately the body was disposed of in a manner that made lividity impossible to determine, which is what the forensic team would use to pinpoint the time of death.

He shut the door quietly and went back inside the apartment. He looked around the room: the table, the couch, the rug, the cushions. Pieces of a surreal event that took place no more than twenty-four hours ago. As he tried to conjure the images they seemed to be enshrouded in a white light, disjointed and soundless. The pall of madness, he imagined. What else? He slowly wandered over to the bedroom. It was immaculately neat and tidy, as he had left it. The bed made. The wardrobe doors closed. The few personal items neatly arrayed over the night table: clock, his allergy medication, a glass of water, a pair of cufflinks. No items of clothing discarded anywhere. The hardwood floor polished to a sheen. The louvre blinds pulled down and the slats slightly ajar, letting in a pall of grey light.

He sat down on the corner of the bed, clasped his head in his hands and muttered to himself in German: "*Was nun? Wie kann ich leben?*"

Now what? How do I live with this?

For the first time in more years than he could remember, he heard his voice in his native tongue. In all the years since he deserted he had stopped speaking it. He always spoke in English, even when prompted to speak German by people that suspected it was his native language. In time he started to think and dream in English. It was easy to fall into the habit, living as he did in Australia. Everything was conducted in English: conversations, radio, TV, movies, social events, living with Emma, newspapers. Once, when he was in a bookstore he picked up a copy of *Der Spiegel*. The featured article was about Hitler's diaries. He was tempted to buy it. Perhaps it would help him reconcile his desertion with his guilt over his abandonment of his family. But when the owner of the shop said something in German, Sam immediately set down the magazine and walked out.

He wasn't Friedrich Becker. That was another identity, moulded in a time and place that he had no control over. A time of madness. And he escaped. And now it was madness again, resurrected from that period, only this time, where was he going to escape to? He had escaped into a Jewish identity and made a life for himself in that persona. Perhaps not convincingly so, but a life just the same. As the years wore on he stopped feeling that he was escaping. He began to relax into his adopted skin. He even tried to mimic Jewish hand and speech mannerisms, with comical results. Once when he was practising in front of the mirror, Emma looked curiously from the doorway and laughed at him. At first he was ashamed to be caught in the lie. But then as he watched himself in the mirror he laughed too. He could work it, but unconvincingly. These were traits that just didn't belong with his physical appearance and demeanour.

And anyway, he was much too self-conscious to be able to act the part. So he maintained the lie and let people accept him or not. Ernie and he became close friends. Played bowls, sat in the café regularly, on occasion even went to the movies without their wives. Ernie was Jewish. He didn't question Sam's Jewishness. Most likely because he was avowedly secular and couldn't care less about the not-so-subtle distinctions. To Ernie, Sam was just another German. Whether he was inherently Jewish never entered the equation. He liked him and that was enough for Ernie. Besides, Emma was unquestionably Jewish and she married him – as Ernie sternly pointed out to Ruth during one of her paranoid suspicions. "Have you considered that he might be a convert, after all? We do have those in the Jewish sect."

For an unfathomable reason Sam suddenly remembered another time, long ago, when he was sitting on another bed in a small apartment in Utrecht. And here he was again. But instead of being full of hope, he was filled with dread and sorrow. And there was no door out. He was caught in his own misery. The escape caught up with the escapee. And he was now totally alone. There was no country to return to. There was no family to reach out to. There were no friends to befriend. The only life left for him had been wrenched away by some demonic lunatic possessed with the idea that her life had to be vindicated.

She should have killed him too. What point was there in leaving him behind? *And maybe that was the point.* Mad people have an uncanny ability to think at an ingenious and devious level. She wanted him left behind to suffer.

"How could this happen?" he kept repeating to himself. It was as if a masterful player had tricked him into this position from which he could not extricate himself. He had been controlled like a marionette, the strings pulled from somewhere above him as he was twisted one way and then another, all the while made to believe that his life was going somewhere. It was going nowhere except the inevitable denouement; he had cheated fate in Germany only to be revisited by that same inevitability a half-century later.

He started to look around the room as if expecting a secret panel to open up offering a chance to escape into another life. His eye caught a dark, glistening object by the glass of water. He leaned over to the nightstand and picked it up, studying it curiously. It was a hairpin. He brought it close to his nose and sniffed it. The fresh scent of spring rose up into his nostrils and warmed his interior. It was Ruth's. The smell of her hair.

He collapsed onto the bed, clutching the hairpin as the only remaining memento from their short time together, and started sobbing uncontrollably. "I have failed you. Oh, how I have failed you. I thought that I was protecting my life. But I have no life to protect." He cried for the first time in his life. For all the suppressed memories that rendered him impassive: his sister and parents – did they pay for his desertion? Emma, whose love he abandoned and then redeemed; the Dutch partisans who, at her behest, put themselves at risk to help him escape; Ernie, who loved him like a dear friend but never truly knew who he was; and now Ruth. The guilt of accumulated lies heaved up from within and the load lightened. The more he cried, the better he started to feel. He felt relieved to be finally letting all the guilt out and facing up to the reality of who he was.

Slowly he stopped shuddering and lay quietly on the bed as he had lain with Ruth the previous afternoon. That dreadful moment when the knocking on the door roused them both from their light sleep as they lay in bed, holding each other. It was Sam's apartment; so he untangled himself gently from Ruth, went over to the closet and took out his robe, shut the bedroom door and walked into the living room. Waited for the knocking to repeat itself. Maybe it was a mistake. Maybe he could return to lying in bliss in a warm bed with Ruth while it rained outside.

It was no mistake. The knocking repeated itself.

He walked softly over to the door and peered through the peephole. An elderly woman with scraggly grey hair bundled into a kerchief stood staring intently at the door. She had on a thick overcoat that looked tattered and dirty. A friend of Emma's? He couldn't remember anyone who looked like that. A friend of Ruth's? She wouldn't be knocking at his door.

"Yes?" He could hear his voice, reedy and uncertain. He tried again, this time more boldly. "Yes? Can I help you?"

"I am sorry to disturb you, sir. I am from the Jewish Agency. We have some forms that I need you to fill out."

He was surprised at the tone. He didn't expect a woman who looked so scruffy to sound like that. She had a distinct Germanic accent, officious and hurried.

"Just a moment." He quickly looked around the apartment. They had left their clothes scattered on the couch and the dining-room table. He smiled inwardly. Like a pair of lustful teenagers. He quickly bundled up the clothes, opened the door to the bedroom and dropped them just inside.

"Who is it?" Ruth's sleepy voice enquired from the bed.

"Sorry to wake you. It's a woman from the Jewish Agency. Some forms that I need to sign. I suppose it is to do with Emma."

"Jewish Agency? Are you sure? What forms? What's her name?" Ruth, who was acquainted with the agency, thought it rather bizarre that they were calling this late and this long after Emma's death.

"I didn't ask." Sam smiled inanely.

"Ask before you let her in."

"OK." He closed the bedroom door and returned to the front door. The woman was still standing there with the same intensity, staring at the door.

"Can I ask, what forms are these?"

"They are to do with your late wife. She left a bequest and we need you to sign the release form."

It made sense to him, although he couldn't remember what particular bequest this could be. But Emma, who was Jewish on her mother's side, might have signed some bequest that was not part of her will.

He unlatched the chain, unlocked the door and opened it.

As soon as the door was open a .45 appeared from under her overcoat. "Step inside. Don't make a single sound. Understood?" The woman who at first had appeared elderly and scruffy took on an air of menace and resolve that made Sam unhesitatingly obey her orders.

Still facing him head on, she stepped inside, then pushed the door closed with her back, locked it and then pointed the barrel of the gun at the table. "Sit down."

"Listen, if you want money, you don't need to threaten me with a gun."

"Shut. Up. Just. Shut. Up. And don't say anything unless I ask you a question. Now, sit down!"

With the last command it suddenly occurred to Sam that the conversation had reverted to German. She was giving him orders in German and he was responding in kind. Without any further conversation Sam walked, crab-like, all the time keeping his eyes on the barrel, over to the lounge and sat down.

"That's better. Now, where is your lovely friend Ruth Lipschutz?" As she uttered the unfamiliar surname she bared her teeth with menacing delight.

"Who?" His first instinct was to assume that it was another lady in the neighbourhood and that all this was a misunderstanding.

"I asked you once. I am going to ask you again in case you didn't hear me the first time: where is your lady friend? The one you came back from the movies with?" Her wild eyes averted to the kitchen, the closed bedroom door, the hallway leading to the bathroom and the second bedroom.

"She went back to her apartment," Sam replied firmly, to leave no doubt in her mind that it was the truth.

"Really? I saw you two come in here about an hour ago. Then the lights went out. But the front door never opened again. So how did she end up in her apartment?"

"What is it that you want?" Sam raised his voice in the hope that Ruth would hear the conversation and exit out the window to the deck below and flee.

"Stay where you are and don't move. Don't even flinch." She moved with surprising agility over to the kitchen and peered quickly inside. Focused her eyes down the hallway. Came back into the living room. "Is she in the bedroom?"

Sam remained quiet.

"What is your name?"

Sam was momentarily relieved that the focus had shifted from Ruth. If she realised what was going on she might already be making her escape. This change in attention would buy her more time.

"Sam," he replied offhandedly, eager not to betray his anxiety.

"Sam what?"

"Sam Steimatzky. What do you care?"

"I don't know. You look familiar. Older. But definitely familiar. Now, why don't you knock on the bedroom door and invite your friend to join our little party?" Once again she was pointing to the hallway leading from the back of the living room.

"It's not a bedroom. It's a study. And there is nobody in there."

"I don't care if it's a horse barn. Get up. Go over to the door and knock on it." Suddenly her eyes flashed with anger and her voice adopted a shrieking tone.

Sam, jarred by the change, stood and walked shakily over to the 'study' door. He knocked.

"Knock louder."

He did as she commanded.

Ruth's sleepy voice resounded from behind the closed door. "What is it, Sam?"

"Tell her that an old friend from Berlin can't wait to see her." The woman sniggered.

Again Sam did as she ordered him to.

"Which old friend? What's her name?"

Sam turned away from the door. "She wants to know your name."

"I heard. I am not deaf. Tell her it's a surprise."

Ruth did not wait to hear the answer. The door opened and she appeared, wary, in the doorway. Her eyes hadn't adjusted to the darkness in the living room. She strained to see who the person was that was claiming to be her friend.

"Well hello, Ruthy darling. Isn't this a cosy set-up? Meeting up at the butt end of the world after all these years," she berated Ruth caustically.

Ruth came further into the room, squinted at the speaker, looked puzzled at Sam by her side. Then saw the gun. "What's going on? Sam? Helga? My God! Helga? Is that you?" Recognising Helga her surprise moved from the gun. Despite all the intervening years Ruth did not fail to recognise the menacing voice instantly, even though the face and hair had altered considerably. She had lived constantly with the fear that one day there would be a price to atone for her omission. The older she got, the more she felt that she had cheated that fate. But now it was here to exact its price.

"I am so glad you remembered; I would have been really angry, *really* angry, if you hadn't."

Hugging her housecoat tighter around herself, Ruth came further into the room so that she could see Helga clearly. "What are you doing here? When did you get to Sydney? How did you find me?"

"Shut up, you witch. This is not a social call. I didn't come here to catch up with you. You and that man, Sam or whoever he is, go sit over on the couch." Helga raised the gun higher and pointed it directly at Ruth, then at the couch.

Both Ruth and Sam moved meekly over to the couch and sat down on the edge of the seats. As soon as they were seated, Helga dragged out a chair from the dining table, pulled it over to the other side of the coffee table and sat facing them.

"Now, Mr Sam, you are going to be the jury. I will be the prosecutor and the judge. On trial is a Jew called Ruth Lipschutz, who let me take her place in Berlin – oh, what, Ruth dear? Fifty years ago. Left me to die in her place. I spent over six years in a concentration camp. I was raped. Starved. Frozen. Had to endure horrors I will never forget. All because this bitch sitting next to you wouldn't come forward and tell the SS that I am not her." Helga glowered at Ruth, all the time keeping an eye on Sam to make sure that he wasn't going to try and make a move for the gun.

"It's not her fault." Sam intervened without being asked.

"OK, Mr Jury. You can also be the defence counsel. If I am going to play two roles, you can also have two roles. You will be the defence counsel and the jury.

"Now, Ruth, your defence counsel says it was not your fault. I say that it is. You knew exactly what happened and hid in the Jodls' attic for God knows how long, and let me take your place. What do you say to that?"

Ruth remained stone-cold silent, stunned by the surreal developments. Despite the heater being on and being bundled in a warm housecoat, she started shivering.

"It was a terrifying time for all of us. She did what she could to survive," Sam offered.

"Very good. Now, as judge I can ask the defence counsel a question: where were you during the war?"

Sam hesitated for a moment, then looked directly at Helga. "Same. Concentration camp."

"Really?" Helga jumped off her seat and came over to him. "Pull up your left sleeve."

"Why?"

Helga lurched forward and struck Sam across the shoulder with the barrel of the gun. Wincing with pain, he unbuttoned his cuff and folded his sleeve upwards.

"Turn your arm so that I can see your wrist. Now!"

Sam obeyed instantly, fearful that she would strike him again.

"Where is the number tattoo, Mr Sammy? Huh? Lying scoundrel." She looked over at Ruth, who was trembling uncontrollably. "What's the matter? You are afraid that I am going to hurt your friend? Don't worry about him." She turned back to Sam. "Let me see your wallet."

"It's in the bedroom," Sam replied weakly.

"So it is. Go in there. Keep the door open, so that I can see what you are doing. I am going to point the gun directly at dear Ruth here. If you try anything I will kill her." Helga backed away from the coffee table to give him room to make his way to the bedroom.

The women watched him enter the bedroom and fumble about in the pile of clothing until he found his trousers, pulled out his wallet from the back pocket and came back into the living room.

"Put the wallet on the table."

Sam set the wallet down and went back to sit next to Ruth.

"Uh-uh. Not so close. I need to see your hands." Helga reached down and picked up the wallet. Peering inside, she pulled out a number of bills and threw them on the floor. Same with the credit cards and driver's licence. "How interesting. No family pictures. The mysterious Mr Sam Schmaltzy. Oh wait, what do we have here?" Helga was folding the wallet in two now that it was empty, but the middle part felt hard, like a piece of paper or a card was wedged in there. Her fingers reached into the crevice and dug out a worn sepia photo that was so frayed it looked like it might disintegrate in her hand. "This is a nice photo. Mummy, Daddy, and in the middle, Mr Schmaltzy, except – well, well – you are wearing an SS uniform, I believe. Friedrich Becker, according to the writing on the back. That would be you, would it not, Mr Lying Shit-matzky?" She glared at him, flinging the wallet with such force that it made a slapping sound when it hit his face.

Ruth stopped shivering and cringed backwards with revulsion. "You are SS, Sam?"

"Yes, Sammy. Are you SS? Wait. Wait. I remember now where I recognise you from." Helga flew out of her chair and raced over to the mantelpiece, grabbing the first object that came to her hand. It turned out to be a souvenir snow globe from the Opera House. Raising her arm, she flung it at Friedrich. The globe connected just below his right ear, leaving a thin gash that immediately started to bleed.

"You were the bastard at the train station on that day when I travelled with her parents. Matter of fact, you welcomed her father with a nice round of kicking."

Ruth, at her end of the couch, started to convulse, and at the last revelation belched and then threw up.

Helga's gun hand was trembling violently. It looked to Friedrich as if she would fire accidentally at any moment.

"Why don't you kill me, if that's what you want? Let Ruth go. She has done you no intentional harm."

"Shut your stupid mouth!" Helga screamed. "I don't need advice from you on what I should or shouldn't do. I have earned, you hear me, *earned* this moment. I waited for over fifty years not knowing if I would ever get my revenge. The last five years I began to doubt myself, thinking that maybe she went to the US or Canada. But no, I stuck with this backwater. Lived in a small house in a smelly suburb. Waited patiently. And then there it was, a small notice. Ruth Lipschutz. My heart swelled. My joy abounded. It was like my life suddenly had meaning. Do you understand, Mr SS Shit-matzky? Huh, do you understand?" With that she grabbed a small potted plant off the mantelpiece and hurled it violently at Friedrich, this time hitting him squarely in the chest. The impact knocked the wind out of him. He buckled over and gasped desperately to regain his breath.

"You are insane," Ruth uttered, quavering, hunched deep inside her housecoat, fearing an equal reprisal.

"What did you say?" Helga lurched over to where Ruth had slumped, the colour drained from her face replaced by a sickly yellow pallor.

"Nothing." She dared not raise her eyes to confront Helga, speaking unevenly. "I am feeling sick. I can barely breathe."

"Oh, you poor thing. What you need is a few days in a concentration camp. The conditions are excellent: room and board, free meals. Every day some new adventure: hangings, killings, gassings, beatings. Ask your dear friend here. He can tell you all about it." Helga walked over to where Friedrich was slumped over. With the toe of her boot, she kicked him in the groin. He let out a sharp cry, then rolled to the floor clutching his crotch in agony, lying in a foetal position.

Ruth's colour was starting to turn from yellow to blue. Her shallow breathing reduced to wheezing and she started to hack and sputter sporadically. But she couldn't take in enough air to relieve the strain. Her chest tightened and started to feel heavy as though someone had placed a large load over it.

Despite his own condition, Friedrich could see that Ruth's was critical. "Help her, you idiot. She is going to die if you don't. She is going into shock," he blurted from his position on the floor.

"You must be deaf, or maybe you don't understand German as well after all these years. I told you from the beginning to not speak to me—"

Before Helga could finish, Ruth let out a sharp heave as though her chest had collapsed inwardly, and she fell to the floor, landing in her own vomit.

"Ruth!" Friedrich yelled, rising to his knees. Helga strode over the low coffee table and struck him with the butt of the gun over his right ear, just over the gash oozing blood. He heard a sharp whistling sound, then fell unconscious.

Friedrich didn't know how much time had passed. All he could remember was that Ruth had been going into either cardiac arrest or shock. He tried to rise to his feet, but the pounding of blood in his ears kept him off balance. He opened his eyes to try and look around the room, but it was spinning so rapidly that he quickly shut them again so as not to get sick.

"You are with us again, Friedrich?" A wicked snarl reverberated somewhere in the room. He couldn't quite tell where in the darkness.

"What's happened?"

"I am afraid your dear friend didn't make it. She had a heart attack. Not shock. Your diagnostic skills are as bad as your acting."

"Oh God. Ruth." He clasped his hands over his face and started to sob. "Dear God. What for? After all this time? What is the point? What is the point?"

"Your sentiments are wasted on me. Now get up!" Helga snapped from somewhere in front of where Friedrich was lying.

He tried to rise again, but the pounding in his ears increased. He reached out his hand to the edge of the coffee table to steady himself and then fell back awkwardly on the floor.

"Now listen, Mr SS Shit-matzky. I don't give a damn about your SS past and all that. That's your problem. But if you so much as mention my presence here I will be calling every newspaper and sending them a copy of your lovely photo. I am sure that they will be very interested in how an SS man masqueraded as a Jewish Holocaust survivor."

She waited for him to acquiesce. Friedrich remained mute.

"It is now just before midnight. So you have had a nice little nap. At two o'clock you will help me carry Ruth down to the dumpster and place her body inside. You can then come up here and clean up the mess. I will be gone and you will never hear from me again. Understood?" Helga's voice was ice cold. There was no emotion in anything she said. It was as though she was reciting directions to a destination, not instructions on how to dispose of a body.

Again Friedrich remained silent.

"What, have you gone deaf?"

Friedrich could see her shadow in the corner, seated at the dining table, drinking impassively from a glass.

"I heard you," he replied meekly. "Why do you want to put her in the dumpster? Isn't it enough that you have killed her? Do you need to humiliate her too?"

"What do you suggest? That we leave the body outside her apartment? Or even *in* her apartment? That's not very smart. This way there is a good chance that the garbage truck will collect her and dump her body somewhere far away. By that time all evidence will be lost."

"Dump her?! Ruth is not garbage, you vile old wretch," Friedrich hurled back at the impassive shadow.

"If I didn't need your help I would get rid of you too, so I would suggest that you keep your mouth shut and leave the planning to me." Helga's voice cut like a razor blade, making Friedrich flinch at her words even though she hadn't moved from her position.

While they waited, the silence of the night gradually engulfed the room, leaving the ticking of the kitchen clock to fill the void. It ticked precisely in second increments, and at every minute interval they could hear the hand move. Once Friedrich heard Helga lift the glass up to her lips and take a sip. Then the ticking sound returned to fill the silence. Friedrich fidgeted on the hard wooden floor, a hundred questions burning in his mind, but he daren't ask them for fear that she would kill him too. Twice he looked over to where Ruth lay bundled in her housecoat, immobile, the life gone out of her. When did she die? How soon after he passed out? Did she say anything? Did she forgive his deception? Did it contribute to her shock, regardless of what Helga claimed, which brought on the cardiac arrest?

He was a coward. That much was clear in his mind. If he had to trace a thread through his life, the one prominent attribute that he could point to throughout would be cowardice. Fear of not belonging; fear of belonging; fear of being captured; hiding shamelessly in the skin of the very people that he committed to persecute at the start of his career. Then the tide turned. He hadn't sensed it so much as refused to be its vanguard. But then he got lucky when his fear parlayed into an escape from judgement, and once again when it provided him with the opportunity to shield himself behind a mask, that had now fallen, killing the very person that he thought he would spend the rest of his life with.

And now again. Instead of getting up and strangling this insane person, he sat calmly on his haunches, waiting to carry Ruth down to the dumpster from where her body would eventually end up in a massive trash heap and be picked clean by scavengers. And afterwards? He would keep quiet. Go on about his life, carrying his awful secrets with him to his grave.

How could he die like this? How could he die? Alone. There was no one left. The thought of dying with these awful secrets haunted him. Maybe that was hell. Dying with horrible secrets and having to be buried underground in a box and have your secrets as your constant companions for infinity.

"I can't die like this."

"What are you mumbling over there?" Helga was alerted to his distinct muttering.

Realising that in his feverish state he had spoken out loud, he quickly corrected himself. "I was asking what time it is?"

"Time to go. Get up and tie the belt around the housecoat so that the body doesn't fall out."

Helga stood at a distance without moving, probably expecting him to heave the body over his shoulder and carry it out. *She is not only crazy, but impractical*, he thought to himself; *there is no way that I can carry the body out on my own.*

Without asking, Friedrich fetched a hand truck that he had kept in a storage locker which the movers left behind. He wheeled it out to the hallway, laid it on the floor and rolled Ruth's body onto it, making sure that her back lay flat against the curved support brackets, and rested her legs over the lip. Holding her firmly by the shoulder with one hand he tilted the hand truck upwards, keeping it at an angle, making sure that she did not tumble head forward, and started wheeling the body out. Helga opened the door, took a look out at the hallway and signalled him to go, keeping a close watch from behind as she followed him. They had to stop twice: once when the lift rose from the ground floor to the top floor, and another time when Helga thought she heard a door opening – it was a false alarm, someone had just secured the lock before turning in. They took the lift down to the basement level. As soon as the door slid open,

Helga peered out again, making sure that the coast was clear, and they proceeded to make their way to the rubbish room. A single weak light illuminated the immediate area. Helga went through the red-lidded wheelie bins – reserved for common garbage, not recyclables – until she found one that was nearly empty. This time they lifted the body together off the hand truck and heaved it over the edge. At first it plummeted in with the legs sticking out, so they had to drag it out, fold it in half and wedge it in. It still stuck out a little, so Helga gathered a discarded quilt from a nearby yellow bin and spread it over the top, shutting the lid.

It was done.

Helga straightened and brushed herself down. Adjusting the kerchief over her head, she looked up at Friedrich with contempt. "You are a disgrace. A shameless coward. I am counting on that, plus the photo that is in my possession." With that she walked out of the rubbish room, over to the nearby hedge bordering the building, crawled through a hole in the shrubbery and disappeared into the cold and wet night.

Friedrich looked up at the building to see if any lights were on. All the windows except his were dark. He wheeled the hand truck out of the basement, back over to the lift, and pushed it inside and up. By the time he returned to his apartment it had started to rain again. He went about methodically sweeping up the broken pieces of the snow globe, cleaning the vomit and straightening up the dishevelled room. By 3am it was as neat as it had been before the madness erupted.

He looked over the room carefully, picked up Helga's glass off the table, emptied it over the sink and then went to the bedroom. He lay down on the bed that was still unmade and smelt of Ruth.

I am what I am. If I had courage I wouldn't be here. I would have died years ago. So many times I could have died. But I didn't. So maybe it is my fate to be a coward and stay alive after all the heroes have died.

With that silent pronouncement he reached for the lamp and clicked the switch, plunging the room into darkness. He soon fell asleep.

BERLIN

Winter 1945

In May 1945 Germany surrendered. The defeated Third Reich rose from the ashes of World War I promising a thousand years of prosperity, might and glory. But it soon became all too clear that the vehicle on which it had risen was Icarus. A regime built on hate, murder and oppression. Hitler's promise fell short by 987 years, and he committed suicide in his bunker rather than face the disgrace of defeat.

In the new reality, the victors of World War II, the US, the Soviet Union, Britain and, by special dispensation, the French, divided Germany into four zones of occupation and its capital, Berlin, into four sectors. Those who had remained steadfast in their defiance of and opposition to Hitler and his murderous henchmen, if they were fortunate to still be alive, were vindicated by the defeat of the Nazi regime; whereas its fervent supporters hastily severed their affiliation to avoid the hand of justice that went scouring for the perpetrators.

In the aftermath, those on the home front disbelieved the eyewitness accounts of concentration camps and factories of death. It sounded positively medieval, something that could not happen in twentieth-century Germany. Yet the picturesque cities and towns all throughout Germany from which Jewish inhabitants had been wrested bore testimony to the obliteration of the erstwhile vibrant communities. In a spate of blind madness, few in Nazi Germany had the prescience to grasp that annihilating Jewish existence was tantamount to eliminating the progenitors of the New Testament, the spiritual backbone of German and European thought and culture. And in so doing, ultimately cheating believers out of the Second Coming: indeed, had the Messiah and saviour Jesus Christ had the misfortune to return during the reign of the Third Reich he too would have been rounded up and exterminated.

There were exceptions, though few they were, like Helmut. As he sat huddled with his wife Magda and daughter Anna in the darkness, waiting for the light to return, strangely, despite the misery of destruction and death, an inner peace and contentment filled him. Hitler was gone. Too late, perhaps, to save the Lipschutzes, but not too late to set about the work of rebuilding Germany, which Hitler had brutally mangled and destroyed with his sick madness. Helmut had heard the stories like everyone else and disbelieved them. It was not possible.

There was little point in discussing it with Magda. She would say something infuriating like "Jewish lies; they are segregated in East Germany or somewhere else, where the

Nazis put them for their own protection." And Anna? Well, he did not want Anna to know of such horrors so soon. There would be time enough for that one day, but not now.

The power had been out for a week. Running water was intermittent at best. Social services were at a standstill, other than the constant wail of ambulances and fire trucks. Above the din, Helmut thought he could hear knocking at the front door.

He was weighing up whether to get up and open it. They had meagre amounts of food and almost none left to share. But there was shelter over their heads, clean water and some clothing. He could spare that.

He got up warily, taking his torch, and followed its beam to the door. He waited. The soft knocking sound repeated. He stood still, hoping that the stranger would give up and leave. But the knocking intensified; the caller uncertain if the occupants had heard them.

He unlatched the chain, turned the key and pulled back the heavy door. A man in dishevelled civilian clothes stood looking at him in the darkness. Helmut couldn't make out his face clearly, but he could tell the man was gaunt and leaning wearily against the doorpost.

"We can't offer you much in the way of food; just some drink, clothing and shelter."

"It's me, Helmut. I need somewhere to hide."

He recognised the voice immediately. "Martin?"

"Yes, can I come in?" He was already resigned to being told no.

Helmut extended his hand eagerly to the broken man across the threshold. As they moved into the vestibule, Helmut grabbed his brother-in-law around the shoulders and hugged him warmly. "It's good to see you, Martin. I was not sure where you were, or even whether you were still alive. Come in. Magda will be thrilled to see you."

As soon as Martin stepped into the dark living room, Magda leaped out of her chair and came over to hug him tightly. "I was so worried. I did not know who or where to contact. I wasn't able to contact anyone. There is no one anywhere to speak to. I am so very happy to see you."

"Believe me, I am happy to be here." The worry started to lift from his expression as he took in the warm faces of his remaining family. He nodded towards Anna. "Your friend made it safely to Switzerland."

"Thank you," she mouthed quietly.

Magda looked over at her brother. "I will make you some tea and give you some bread and cheese and maybe a potato or two. That's all we have at the moment."

Martin nodded gratefully. "That's all I want for now. And to sleep a little."

Magda took the torch from her husband and followed its beam into the darkness of the kitchen. With her out of earshot, Helmut turned to Martin and asked the grave question that hitherto was just rumours. "Is it true?" He spoke ambiguously for Anna's sake.

"Is what true? That we surrendered?" Martin looked confused.

"No. About the Jews. What I have been hearing. Cousin Alfred would not return my message, so I am totally in the dark."

Martin swallowed nervously, then nodded towards Helmut. "I don't know what you heard, but whatever you heard, it's worse, much, much worse."

Helmut couldn't be sure, but he thought he could see tears welling up in Martin's eyes. Through the sadness in his voice, all he could think to say was what had previously come most unnaturally to him. "*Gott im Himmel rette uns.* Now that we are no longer consumed by madness, how are we ever going to explain this?"